Praise for Margaret Moore

"Entertaining! Excellent! Exciting!
Margaret Moore has penned a five-star keeper!"
—BJ Deese, *CataRomance Reviews*
on *Bride of Lochbarr*

"Margaret Moore's characters step off the pages
into your heart."
—*Romantic Times*

"Ms. Moore…will make your mind dream
of knights in shining armor."
—*Rendezvous*

"…an author who consistently knows how to mix
just the right amount of passion and pageantry."
—*Old Book Barn Gazette*

"When it comes to excellence in historical romance
books, no one provides the audience with more than
the award-winning Ms. Moore."
—Harriet Klausner, *Under the Covers*

"Her writing is full of humor and wit,
sass and sexual tension."
—Elena Channing, *Heart Rate Reviews*

"Margaret Moore has a captivating writing style…
that lends itself to pure, fluid prose
and vivid characterizations."
—C. L. Jeffries, *Heartstrings Reviews*

"Fans of the genre will enjoy another journey into the
past with Margaret Moore."
—*Romantic Times*

MARGARET MOORE

LORD of DUNKEATHE

HQN™

ISBN 0-373-77040-5

LORD OF DUNKEATHE

This edition published by arrangement with Harlequin Books S.A.

® and TM are trademarks of the publisher. Trademarks indicated with ® are registered in the United States Patent and Trademark Office, the Canadian Trade Marks Office and in other countries.

www.HQNBooks.com

Printed in U.S.A.

With special thanks to my family
for their encouragement and support.

CHAPTER ONE

Glencleith, Scotland, 1240

"PLEASE TALK TO HIM, RIONA," eighteen-year-old Kenneth Mac Gordon pleaded as he walked beside his older cousin in the small yard of the fortress of Glencleith. "He willna listen to me, but he might to you. Thane or no, we're poor and he's got to quit offering food and shelter to every sod who shows up at the gate, or we'll no' have two coins to rub together."

"Aye," Riona Mac Gordon reluctantly agreed, "but it'll break his heart if he canna offer the hospitality of his hall."

The red-haired Kenneth pounded his fist into his palm for emphasis. "Father must face facts. We're poor and getting poorer. He's *got* to stop inviting every stranger he meets for a meal and a night's lodging."

"I'll have a word wi' him and see if I canna make him understand we need to be more careful," Riona acquiesced as they reached the gate. Nearby, chickens scratched and pecked in the hard-packed earth near the stables. The wooden stakes that made up the outer wall were falling down in more than one place, and the gate couldn't have kept out a determined child. "Maybe if I tell him you'll have naught but some rocky ground and a run-down fortress to inherit, he might listen."

"You should tell him that there's nothing left for your dowry, either."

"I don't care about a dowry," Riona answered. "Your father did enough taking me in when I was a wee bairn and treating me like a daughter e'er since. Besides, I'm too old to think about marrying now. I'm long past the first blush of youth, and none have offered that I cared to wed."

"You're not too old. That fellow from Arlee didn't care about your age."

"That's because he was fifty if he was a day—and nearly toothless to boot. If that's the sort I'll have to choose from, I'll gladly die a maid."

"After rising from your sick bed to make sure all's in hand before you go," Kenneth noted.

"Somebody has to look after you and your father."

"Aye, and the rest of the folk in Glencleith. Tell me, how many cottages have you visited in the past fortnight? How many complaints have you heard and dealt with on your own without troubling Father?"

Riona smiled. "I dinna mind. And the women feel better bringing their troubles to me."

"That's as may be, but it's a fine job you do, sparing Father worry—although a little worry might do him some good. Maybe if we told him I'll have no money and you'll have no dowry, that'll finally make him see the light."

Riona sighed and leaned back against the wooden palisade. It creaked so precariously, she immediately straightened. "How I wish Uncle had plenty of money and a fine estate, that he could live as he would, without a care in the world. It's no more than he deserves, for a kinder, more generous man doesn't live. He'd teach these Norman lords about hospitality."

"Aye, that he would." Kenneth brushed a lock of his curly hair out of his eyes, then kicked at a stone near his toe. "Some day, Riona, things will be better. I promise."

"At least our people can be happy knowing you'll be just as fine a lord as your father, although perhaps a little more practical."

That brought a smile to Kenneth's freckled face that still had more lad than man in it. "I hope so. Tell me, do ye think Old Man Mac Dougan's really as sick as he claims? He's been dying—or claiming to be—since I can remember."

"Aye, I do," Riona replied. "He was that pale, I'm sure he isna well. I tried to get him to leave that drafty cottage of his, but he wouldn't hear of it."

"Just took the food and fuel you brought him, is that it?"

"Aye, but I worry about him, there by himself. Maybe I can persuade—"

"Ooooh, there was a fine lass from Killamagroooooo!" a male voice bellowed in song beyond the gates.

They both stiffened, like a hound on the scent.

"There's Father now," Kenneth unnecessarily said, for there was only one man in Glencleith who sang so loudly and lustily. "He sounds happy. *Very* happy."

Riona didn't point out that Uncle Fergus usually sounded happy. If he sounded *unhappy,* that would be cause for surprise.

"Here's hoping he got a good price for the wool, then," she said as she opened the gate.

"Here's hoping he hasn't brought back half a dozen tinkers or paupers he met along the way," Kenneth added as he hurried to help her. "I should have gone with him. I would have, if he hadn't left before I got back from hunting. I half think he did that on purpose."

In the interest of family harmony, Riona didn't tell Kenneth he was right. She'd tried to talk Uncle Fergus into waiting for his son's return, only to have him wave her off and say he'd been dealing in wool since before she was born. That was true, but Riona also suspected he'd been getting cheated since before she was born, too.

"If he's in a good mood," Kenneth proposed, "now might be the best time to suggest he be more...or less—"

"I'll speak to him right away," Riona replied. Delaying wasn't going to make her task any easier.

Through their unguarded gate came their ancient

nag pulling a cart with tufts of wool clinging to the rickety sides. Uncle Fergus was perched on the seat, his *feileadh* belted low beneath his ample stomach, his linen shirt half-untucked. Wisps of his shoulder-length iron-gray hair had escaped from the leather thong he used to tie it back. He looked disheveled enough that Riona might have suspected he'd been drinking, except that Uncle Fergus rarely imbibed to excess, and never in the village.

"And I brought her hooooome from Killama-groooo!" he finished with a flourish before beaming down on his son and niece like a triumphant general home from a long and tough campaign.

"Ah, here you are and both together!" he cried, tossing aside the reins and rising. He spread his arms as if he wanted to embrace the whole of the small fortress, walls, stone buildings and all. "Riona, my beauty, I have such news for you!"

In spite of what she had to tell him and her fear about the price he'd gotten for the wool, Riona couldn't help smiling. She was beautiful only in her uncle's loving eyes, but his epithet always made her feel as if she might be a *little* beautiful.

"*Such* news—and I might have missed it if I'd waited," he said with a wry look at his son. He turned and started to climb down, almost catching the fabric of his *feileadh* on the edge of the seat.

With a soft and mild curse, he tugged the fabric down so that it again covered his bare knee.

"Is your back troubling you?" Riona asked anxiously, as both she and Kenneth hurried forward to lend him a hand. "You didn't help unload the wool, did you?"

"No, no, my beauty," he assured her. "I let those young lads of Mac Heath do all the work."

Kenneth shot Riona a disgruntled look. Mac Heath was not known for honest dealings and Riona didn't doubt that if Kenneth had his way, they'd never speak to Mac Heath, let alone sell any wool to him.

"Why Mac Heath?" Kenneth asked.

"Because he gave me the best price."

Riona and Kenneth exchanged another glance, only this time, Uncle Fergus intercepted it.

"Now, children," he chided, although even his criticism was jovial, too. "There's no need for such looks. I did as you suggested, Kenneth, and asked more than one how much he'd pay. Mac Heath gave the most."

Riona guessed Mac Heath had done that because his scales were weighted. Before they could say anything more about that, though, Uncle Fergus threw his arms about their shoulders and gave them another expansive smile as he steered them toward the hall.

"Now let me tell you what I heard. It's *wonderful*, something that's going to make all the difference in the world to you, Riona," he finished with a nod in her direction.

She had no idea what that could possibly be, unless he'd heard of a way to feed a small household for free.

Uncle Fergus dropped his arms as they reached the hall, a low rectangular stone building ten feet by twenty.

"You know of Sir Nicholas of Dunkeathe? The Norman fellow King Alexander gave that huge estate to, the one south of here, as a reward for his service?" Uncle Fergus asked as he led the way over the rush-covered floor to the central hearth where a peat fire burned, even on this relatively mild June day.

"Yes, I've heard of him," Riona replied warily, wondering what on earth that Norman mercenary could have to do with her.

"So have I," Kenneth said. "He's as arrogant as they come—which is saying a lot, since he's a Norman."

"He's got some right to be arrogant, if what they say about him is true," Uncle Fergus replied. "It's not every man who can start with almost nothing and make his way so far in the world. Aye, and he's handsome as well as rich, and a friend of the king to boot."

"So what has he to do with Riona, or she with him?" his son asked with a puzzlement that matched Riona's.

"She's going to have a lot to do with him," Uncle Fergus replied as he threw himself into the one and only chair to grace the interior of the hall. "Word's gone out that he's looking for a wife. Any and all who meet the requirements are welcome to attend him at his castle and he's going to pick a bride from among them. We're to be there by noon on the day of the feast of St. John the Baptist—Midsummer's Day. Sir Nicholas wants to make his choice by Lammas."

"From the twenty-third of June to the first day of August isn't very long," Kenneth noted. "Why is Sir Nicholas in such a hurry?"

"Anxious to have a wife to help him run his castle, I don't doubt. And who better to be his bride than our Riona, eh?"

Riona stared at him, completely dumbfounded. Uncle Fergus thought she ought to marry a Norman? He thought a Norman nobleman would want to marry her? Maybe he *had* been drinking.

Kenneth looked just as shocked. "You think Riona should marry a Norman?"

"That one, aye, if she can. A woman could do a lot worse."

Riona found that hard to believe, and so, obviously, did Kenneth. "Even if Riona wanted him," he said, darting her a look that showed how unlikely that would be, "what about these *requirements* you mentioned?"

"Oh, they're not important," Uncle Fergus declared, waving his hand dismissively. "What's important is that this rich fellow needs a wife, and Riona deserves a fine husband."

"Surely he won't want me," Riona protested.

Uncle Fergus looked at her as if she'd uttered blasphemy. "Why not?"

She picked the reason that would hurt him, and herself, the least. "He'll want a Norman bride."

"Well, he was born a Norman, I grant you," Uncle Fergus reflected as he rubbed his bearded chin. "But he's a Scots lord now. Dunkeathe was his reward from Alexander—our king, not the English one. King Alexander's taken two Norman wives, too, so why shouldn't a Norman wed a Scot? And didn't Sir Nicholas change the name of his estate back to Dunkeathe from that ridiculous Norman name, Beauxville or Beauxview or whatever it was?"

"But he was a mercenary, a hardened killer for hire."

"Aye, he was a fighter, and poor, as well," Uncle Fergus said. "I can respect a man like that, who's made something of himself."

"He'll no doubt want a wealthy bride."

"Aye, and we've no money for a dowry," Kenneth added.

Although it was true that they had almost nothing in the way of gold or silver, Riona cringed when she saw the stunned disbelief in her uncle's blue eyes. "What, there's *nothing?*"

"Not much," Kenneth replied, his resolve slipping into prevarication. "I've been trying to warn you—"

"Aye, aye, so you have," Uncle Fergus said, his brow furrowing. "I didn't think it was as bad as all that."

Riona had rarely seen her uncle look so worried, and she hated being a cause of distress to him now. "It doesn't matter. I don't—"

"Aye, what does the money or lack of it matter in the end?" Uncle Fergus declared, smiling once again as he interrupted her. "If it was some other woman, it might, but you're the prize, my beauty, not a bag of coins."

She tried another reason. "Uncle, I don't know anything about running a Norman's household."

"What's to know? You've been running mine since you were twelve. Besides, from what I hear about Norman women, they're a poor lot. Spend all their time at embroidery and gossip."

Not wanting to remind him that the Mac Gordon's shining glory had dulled in the past one hundred years, Riona refrained from noting that running the household of a minor Scots thane with a small holding was very different from managing that of a Norman overlord with a vast castle and estate. "Most of them must be more industrious. It surely takes a great deal of time and effort to run the household of a lord."

"They can't be any better at it than you'll be," Uncle Fergus replied confidently. "You're the most clever girl in Glencleith. Look how fast you learned the Normans' language."

"Who'll look after things here if I'm gone?"

That gave Uncle Fergus a moment's pause—but only a moment. "The smith's daughter, Aigneas, will do for a while, until Kenneth finds himself a wife. She's a bright lass." His father winked at Kenneth. "I don't think you'll mind that, eh, my son?"

As Kenneth blushed, his father addressed Riona. "We'll have to suffer a bit, it's true—you've spoiled us something fierce, Riona. But that's a sacrifice we'll have to make. It's time we thought of your happiness, not our own. The rest of our people might better appreciate how good you've been to them over the years, too."

In spite of her uncle's kind and flattering words, Riona had another reason not to go. "Sir Nicholas will want a young bride. I'm too old."

"You're no flighty, giggling girl, I'll grant you—but that's a point in your favor," Uncle Fergus replied.

He hoisted himself to his feet. Giving her a woeful half smile, he gently took hold of her shoulders. "Riona, my beauty, it's past time I quit being so selfish and keeping you here with me. I should have been more encouraging, maybe, to some of those young lads who started to come 'round when you were younger, except there wasn't a one I thought deserved you. But you should have your own home, with a husband who loves you and children to honor you."

When she started to protest, Uncle Fergus interrupted her. "There aren't many I'd consider for you, but this one I would. He's not a spoiled gentleman who's never done so much as a hard day's riding. He's worked for what he's got and your sweetness and wisdom will make things smooth between you.

"As for the dowry, or lack of it, it's love that matters, not money. Once he meets you, he'll surely fall in love with you. And while we're poor, our family name is an old and respected one.

"What harm can it do to go meet the man? If you don't like him, we'll come straight home again."

Uncle Fergus spoke so kindly and looked at her with

such love, she felt like a brute for not instantly agreeing that she should try to marry Sir Nicholas of Dunkeathe, or do anything else Uncle Fergus asked of her.

Her uncle slid a glance to her cousin. "While we're at Dunkeathe, you'll be in charge of Glencleith, Kenneth. It's about time you had some practice."

Kenneth's face lit up with excitement, and Riona realized that between the coming of Aigneas and this chance to lead, all of his former objections were done away with.

She couldn't fault Kenneth for that. He was young and keen to find his way, and this would indeed be good practice for him. As for Aigneas, Riona wasn't sure of the depth of Kenneth's feelings for her, or hers for Kenneth. This might be a way for them to find out how deep their affection went.

His father gave Kenneth a little frown. "Aigneas'll stay with her father and just come to the hall in the day," he warned.

Abashed, Kenneth didn't meet his father's gaze. "I expected as much," he mumbled.

"Good. And there'll be no sweet-talking her into giving you more salt for your dinner. You'd think we were as rich as the king, the way you sprinkle that about."

As Kenneth frowned, Riona thought of something else. If she went to Dunkeathe with Uncle Fergus, that would mean several days they wouldn't be in Glencleith, eating their own stores. Her uncle would be

someone else's guest rather than an overly generous host.

"All right, Uncle," she said. "You've convinced me
I should at least go and see this paragon of a Norman."

Uncle Fergus hugged her, fairly beaming. "That's
my beauty! And if he doesn't pick you, he's a fool and
not worthy of you anyway."

Riona wasn't nearly so sure of that, and it might be
a little embarrassing for her to find herself being compared to other women and no doubt found lacking, but
if going to Dunkeathe made Kenneth and Uncle Fergus
happy, and saved them some money, surely she could
endure a bit of discomfort.

"WHAT DID I TELL YOU, Riona, eh?" Uncle Fergus cried
as their cart came over the ridge of a hill a few days
later.

Beyond lay a river valley, and standing to the east of
the river was Castle Dunkeathe, a massive feat of ma-
sonry and engineering that had to impress anyone who
saw it.

Around it, other, much smaller buildings comprised
a sizable village, and there were farmsteads along the
road leading to it, as well as fields of barley and oats,
and meadows for grazing sheep and cows. The hills
around the valley were wooded and Riona supposed the
overlord and his friends hunted there with their hounds
and hawks.

It made quite a contrast to Glencleith, which had

some of the poorest, most rock-strewn land in the country.

"Did I no' say it was quite a fortress?"

"Aye, you did, and aye, it is," Riona murmured as she studied the huge edifice that had been years in the making.

Two thick stone walls and a dry moat comprised the outer defenses. Towers had been constructed along the walls to watch the road and the river and the hills beyond. The gatehouse was like a small castle itself and dwarfed the wagons passing under the wooden portcullis.

She couldn't begin to fathom how much stone and mortar it had taken to construct it, or how many men, or the cost. Sir Nicholas must have been paid very well by King Alexander, and with more than the ground this castle stood upon.

He must have an army of servants as well as soldiers and archers, too. There were times it was difficult to keep things running smoothly on her uncle's small estate, so she could only imagine some of the difficulties the lord of Dunkeathe must encounter. But then, he would have a steward and others to help him.

Perhaps the rumors of Sir Nicholas's prowess in battle and tournaments weren't exaggerations, after all. If he came from the humble beginnings her uncle claimed he did, he certainly had achieved a great deal, if one measured success by wealth and this fortress alone.

"We're not the only ones who came in answer to the

news of his search for a bride," Uncle Fergus noted, nodding at the other carts and wagons already on the road ahead of them.

Several of these vehicles were richly decorated and accompanied by guards. Other men, cloaked and riding beautiful horses decked in colorful accoutrements, rode with them, and Riona assumed these were noblemen. More wagons held casks of what was likely wine or ale, and baskets or sacks of foodstuffs—enough to feed a multitude by the looks of it.

Just how many women was Sir Nicholas expecting?

Riona tried not to think about that, or compare those people and their wagons to her uncle's rickety cart and their old gray horse. She wouldn't worry about her dress, or her uncle's Scots attire.

"King Alexander must have been very pleased with Sir Nicholas's service," she said as they approached the mighty gatehouse.

"Aye, I heard he was vital in putting down the last rebellion," Uncle Fergus replied. "And he's bonny to look at, so they say," he reminded her with a wink. "*Braw* and rich *and* handsome—that's rare."

At the gatehouse, two armed soldiers stepped into the road, blocking the way. Both wore chain mail with black tunics over top, and carried spears as well as swords sheathed at their waist. Several soldiers patrolled the wall walk above, as if Sir Nicholas was expecting to be under siege at any moment.

Yet the times were peaceful enough, and it would

take a large army, much determination and a lot of effort to capture this castle. Riona couldn't think of any Scot who had such a force at his disposal, or who'd willingly rebel against Alexander now, for to move against the Norman would be a move against the man who'd rewarded him, too. Perhaps this show of force was just that—a show, intended to illustrate to all and sundry the might and power of the lord of Dunkeathe.

"'Ere now, what's this?" one of the soldiers asked, his accent revealing his Saxon heritage as he eyed them suspiciously. "Wot's in the wagon?"

Riona wasn't impressed by the man's insolence. They should be addressed with more respect, no matter how they were dressed, or the state of their cart and horse.

"Our baggage," she answered shortly. "Now if you'll be so good as to move out of the way—"

"I don't take orders from the likes o' you," the soldier retorted. He ran another scornful gaze over them, his sandy brows furrowing. "Who do ya think you're foolin'?" He turned to his fellow soldier. "'Ere, Rafe, they must think we're bumpkins or sommat."

Uncle Fergus's hand went to the dirk in his belt. "What are these louts saying, Riona?" he asked.

While he'd learned Norman French, Uncle Fergus had never troubled himself to learn the language of the *Sassenach*. He'd always left it to Riona to deal with merchants or traders from the south.

The last thing Riona wanted was a confrontation between her uncle and these likely well-trained and probably vicious soldiers. Uncle Fergus had been a fine fighter in his day, but that was long ago.

"Leave this to me, Uncle," she said as she climbed down from the cart. "I'll speak to them and make sure they understand who they're talking to."

The thin guard gestured at the cart with his spear. "You've come wi' somethin' to sell, I'll wager, and likely aiming to cheat. Well, whatever it is, his lordship ain't buying." Still using his spear as if it were an extension of his hand, he pointed down the road. "Turn around and go back to the bog you come from."

Riona tried to keep a rein on her temper as she marched up to them. "This is Fergus Mac Gordon Mac Darbudh, Thane of Glencleith," she declared as she stopped in front of the soldier and shoved his spear aside.

"Oh, this man in the skirt's a thane, is he?" the guard replied with a smirk. "Thane of the Bog of Bogworth, I think. And who're you? His daughter? Or his…something else?"

Riona's lip curled with disgust and she drew herself up to her full height. "He's my uncle. *I* am Lady Riona of Glencleith, and you will let us pass, or I'll tell your overlord of your insolence."

The stocky man's eyes widened. "You're a lady, are you?"

A look of sudden comprehension came to his beady black eyes and he grinned as he nudged his companion.

"Look 'ere, Harry. She says she's a lady—come to marry Sir Nicholas, no doubt." He tilted back his head and called up to the soldiers on the wall walk. "Did ya hear that? She thinks she's got a chance for Sir Nicholas!"

As they burst out laughing, Riona turned on her heel—and discovered Uncle Fergus right behind her.

"That's it," he declared, reaching for his dirk. "I don't know what they're saying, but I'm sure it's rude. I'm going to teach these *Sassenach* some manners."

She put her hand on his arm to prevent him from drawing his weapon. "Don't bother, Uncle. They're not worth the trouble. Come on, let's go meet their master."

Uncle Fergus hesitated and for a moment she feared he would indeed try to fight the more heavily armed and younger soldiers. But then, to her relief, he nodded. "All right," he grudgingly agreed. "He's more important than these worthless louts."

Wondering how they were going to get inside the castle, Riona walked back to the wagon and climbed onto the seat. As Uncle Fergus joined her, she looked at the two soldiers, who were still standing at the gates, smirking and laughing, and got an idea.

She raised the reins and briskly slapped the horse's back, not hard enough to hurt, but sharp enough to startle. With an indignant whinny, the mare broke into a run. Just as startled, Uncle Fergus gave a yelp and grabbed on to the seat.

"Out of the way!" she shouted to the soldiers.

One shoved the other into the moat, then fell after him, their mail jingling as they rolled down to the bottom.

Serves you right, she thought as their horse slowed to an anxious trot once they were through the gatehouse and into the open space of the inner ward. She glanced back, fearing the men at the gates or on the walk would give chase. She heard someone shout to let them go and leave them for Sir Nicholas to deal with.

Not the most comforting of thoughts, but at least she hadn't let the soldiers send them away like unwelcome beggars.

"Oh, my beauty, they'll be remembering you!" Uncle Fergus exclaimed as he started to laugh.

She wasn't sure that was a good thing. "I shouldn't have lost my temper. Charging them like a warrior queen wasn't very ladylike."

Uncle Fergus patted her on the knee. "They were rude and insolent, and it's not as if you hurt them. When you're Sir Nicholas's wife, you can have them sent away."

If this was the sort of fellow the lord of Dunkeathe commanded, she certainly didn't want to be the lady of Dunkeathe. Indeed, it was all she could do not to ask to go home right now. This fortress was too enormous, too intimidating, too Norman by far.

They reached the second imposing gate. Through it she could see the courtyard—and a mass of wagons, servants, horses and soldiers. The noise they made was like waves on the shore, rising and falling, punctuated by the occasional neigh or a brusque order.

Riona steeled herself for another confrontation with insolent *Sassenach*, but this time there was just a single man standing beside the entrance. He was of middle years, Riona guessed, and definitely not a Scot, for he wore the dress of a Norman and had his light brown hair cut in that peculiar style they favored, as if someone had set a bowl on their head. He was holding a wax tablet and a stylus, so she assumed he must be some kind of clerk.

"The kitchen's to the left of the hall," the man said when Uncle Fergus pulled the horse to a halt.

Maybe he wasn't a Norman, after all, for he spoke Gaelic very well.

"That's good to know if I get hungry," Uncle Fergus replied, clearly trying to control his temper. "I'm Fergus Mac Gordon Mac Darbudh, thane of Glencleith, and this is Lady Riona, my niece. We've heard about Sir Nicholas's quest for a bride."

The man's eyes betrayed his surprise, but he quickly recovered. "I see. Have you some proof of your title?"

This was something Riona hadn't foreseen. She was envisioning an ignominious retreat past those Saxon guards when Uncle Fergus said, "If it's proof you need, I have the king's charter. I'm guessing a royal document with the king's seal will be good enough for you?"

Riona stared at him with surprise. He hadn't said

anything to her about bringing the charter; nevertheless, she was relieved to be spared any more embarrassment.

"Aye, it will be," the man said as Uncle Fergus climbed down from the cart.

He rummaged through the worn leather pouch that held his clothes. "Ah, here it is," he said as he pulled out a parchment scroll and unrolled it. "Sealed and signed by Alexander himself."

The man examined it a moment, and Riona realized she was holding her breath.

"Everything seems to be in order," the man said. He handed back the parchment to Uncle Fergus, who rolled it up again, and wrote their names on his tablet. "Welcome to Castle Dunkeathe, my lord, my lady. I am Robert Martleby, Sir Nicholas's steward."

"Delighted to meet you, Martleby," Uncle Fergus replied in his usual jovial manner.

"I'm pleased to meet you, too, my lord. Now, if you'll be so good as to carry on into the yard, the head groom will tell you where you may stable your horse and put your, um, conveyance."

"What about our quarters?" Uncle Fergus asked.

"There'll be someone in the ward to direct you," Martleby replied.

"Excellent!" Uncle Fergus exclaimed as he got back on the cart.

He lifted the reins and clucked his tongue, and the cart rumbled over the cobblestones into the inner yard. Once inside, the noise was overwhelming, worse than the celebrations of May Day and a market combined. There had to be a hundred people there, some still in their wagons, others mounted and more already on the ground. Servants dashed between the people and vehicles, and various soldiers milled about in small groups. Drivers shouted at each other as they tried to maneuver the wagons that held not just guests, but their considerable baggage, too.

Thank heavens trying to organize this crowd wasn't her responsibility, Riona thought. For once, she could just sit and wait to be told what to do, instead of having to figure out how to do it.

On the other hand, it was frustrating, too. Forming a line to speak to the man in charge would be one solution to some of the confusion. Setting servants to direct the drivers toward the stables would have been another. Assigning one servant to each guest, to see to their baggage and accommodation, would have lessened the chaos, too.

It took Uncle Fergus a while, but eventually he managed to get their horse and cart off to one side, away from the more crowded center. The odors coming out of the building closest to them told Riona they must be beside the kitchen.

"Now, Riona, which one of these fine gentlemen do you suppose is Sir Nicholas?" Uncle Fergus asked, scratching his beard as he surveyed the yard.

"I have no idea," she answered, her gaze going from one richly attired man to another. None of them looked like her idea of a hardened mercenary.

Uncle Fergus nodded at a haughty man of mature years, mounted on a gray horse. "What about him?"

"How old is Sir Nicholas?"

"Aye, you're right. That fellow's not young enough. Maybe that one there?" Uncle Fergus gestured at a man who was certainly young, dressed in bright yellow damask and mounted upon a white horse with very elaborate accoutrements of silver, like his master's spurs.

"He doesn't look the sort to have ever been a soldier," Riona warily replied.

Frowning with concentration, Uncle Fergus nodded. "Aye. That one wouldn't want to muss his clothes and fighting's a bloody, sweaty, messy business. Maybe him?"

Riona followed his pointing finger to a man standing in the middle of the yard surrounded by several well-dressed men and a few soldiers who all seemed to be asking questions at the same time. He was dark haired, but not exactly young, and he appeared distinctly harried as he gestured at the stables as if in answer to their queries. "I think he must be the head groom," she said.

"I think you're right," Uncle Fergus agreed as he started to get down off their wagon. "And since he's the fellow I'm supposed to see about stabling our horse and putting our cart somewhere, I'd best go speak to him. I'll try to find out about our quarters, too, while I'm at it. Stay here, Riona, till I get back. And keep an eye out for our host. I'm sure he's here somewhere, greeting his guests."

Riona wasn't so sure about that, although Sir Nicholas would be guilty of a breach of good manners if he wasn't. But since she had nothing else to do anyway, she nodded and waved a little farewell as Uncle Fergus set off through the crowd.

Wondering how long he was likely to be, and what Sir Nicholas was really like—for she didn't doubt Uncle Fergus's description was overly favorable—she turned her attention back to the people in the courtyard.

Several servants were unloading the wagons and taking chests and bundles into a large building on the other side of the yard that looked like a barracks, save for the narrow arched windows. Perhaps they were family apartments and servants' chambers.

Beside that was another long building, which she guessed was the hall.

In addition to the kitchen, there were stables and other buildings that were probably storehouses of some sort, and an armory. She suspected there were more buildings that she couldn't see to accommodate the garrison.

Maybe Sir Nicholas was looking out of one of the windows in the second floor of the apartments, watching them, smugly pleased to see all the people who'd come, and exulting in their urge to have one of their family meet his approval.

Maybe he was in his solar, trying to figure out how he was going to pay for the food necessary to feed this multitude, and where they were going to stay. Imagining a brawny, not overly intelligent ex-soldier worriedly scratching his head and puzzling over food was amusing, but not very likely. Sir Nicholas was obviously rich, as this castle attested, so he would surely not be concerned with such mundane matters.

Perhaps he'd gone out hunting, getting away from the hustle and bustle until all was settled. Then he could return in a flurry of hoofbeats, weapons, hawks and a swirling cloak, like a great hero coming home.

Well, there'd be at least one person in Castle Dunkeathe who wouldn't react with awe and delight, she thought, even if she did have to admit to a certain curiosity to see the man who could create all this fuss and bother over a potential marriage. Maybe he *was* quite a prize, given the number of people here.

She wondered which lady might win him. That one, just disembarking from her blue wagon? If she proved to be younger than she was, she'd be surprised. The brown-haired one walking into the hall? She, too, was finely attired, but she certainly couldn't be called graceful. And Riona could hear her giggling all the way across the yard.

Perhaps that very young, very pretty, dark-haired young woman wearing a lovely blue velvet cloak trimmed with red fox fur seated on a palfrey. Although she was as expensively attired as any and mounted on a very fine horse, she looked lost and lonely and more than a little frightened. She also didn't look much more than sixteen.

The poor thing probably didn't want to be here, either. Feeling sympathetic, Riona gave the girl a friendly smile when she looked Riona's way.

The girl's eyes widened with surprise. Still smiling, Riona shrugged her shoulders, as if to say, "I don't know what I'm doing here, either."

The girl returned her smile, until the young man in yellow damask approached her and commanded her attention. He helped her dismount and then they went into the hall.

When they were gone, Riona idly surveyed the wagons and people left in the yard. She noticed a man she hadn't seen before leaning against the stable wall, watching the activity in the courtyard, just as she was.

He couldn't be a nobleman, for he wore only a leather jerkin without a shirt beneath, exposing his broad chest and arms. The rest of his clothing was likewise simple and nondescript—brown woolen breeches, a wide belt with bronze buckle, scuffed leather boots. It was obvious from the way his breeches clung to his thighs that more than his arms were muscular, and his lean, dark features proclaimed him a mature man in his most powerful prime.

He must be a soldier off duty waiting for an order, or the person issuing them. He might even be a Scot, for although he wore the dress of men from the south, his dark brown hair hung to his shoulders—a far cry from the style favored by the Normans.

In his watchful stillness, he reminded her of a cat.

She'd known a feline to sit outside a mouse hole, un-moving, unflinching, for an entire morning waiting for the mouse to show itself. She didn't doubt this man could wait with the same sort of patience for his prey. Sir Nicholas must pay his soldiers well, for surely a warrior of that sort didn't come cheaply.

One of the maidservants, a pretty woman with a mole on her breast, hurried past. The man glanced her way, which wasn't surprising. What was surprising was the way the pretty servant reacted. Instead of smiling flirtatiously, as she had with several other men, both noble and servants, she became wary, perhaps even frightened. She quickened her already brisk pace and hurried past Riona.

The man's gaze followed the servant—until it met Riona's.

It was like being pinned to the ground and studied at leisure. Never had she been subjected to such intense scrutiny, from anyone. Never had she been so taken aback and flustered by a man's look.

She immediately averted her eyes. Yet in the next instant, she regretted her trepidation and commanded herself not to be so silly. Why shouldn't she meet his gaze squarely? It wasn't as if *she* were a servant or hireling that he had any power over.

So she boldly raised her eyes to return his steadfast gaze, determined to keep looking at him until *he* looked away. Their gazes met, and held.

He slowly raised one dark brow.

Did he think he was going to make her look away with that unspoken interrogation? Did he think she would give him the victory in this strange little game? Never!

She leisurely arched her own brow.

His other dark brow rose.

Once more, she mirrored his action.

He slowly started to smile.

So did she.

Still keeping his gaze upon her, the man lowered his arms. Then he pushed himself off the wall and sauntered toward her.

CHAPTER TWO

HE WAS COMING TOWARD HER? By the saints, what was he going to say, or do? Maybe he was going to suggest…improprieties.

Riona's breathing quickened as she told herself she'd ensure he understood that she was a lady of virtue and honor. She wasn't a servant to whom he could make insolent suggestions.

And she shouldn't be blushing like an addlepated girl as he continued to stroll toward her with that leisurely yet purposeful stride.

If she quit staring at him, perhaps he'd be satisfied and leave her alone.

"You there!" a woman called out imperiously.

The soldier halted and they both turned toward the wagon from whence the voice came.

It sported a painted canvas covering that had an opening at the back like the flaps of a tent, now held apart by an apple-cheeked, middle-aged maidservant, her hair covered by a white scarf, her dress one of dark brown wool. Seated beside the maidservant was a pale young woman with blond hair wearing a gossamer veil of white silk kept in place by a thin gold coronet. Her neck was long and slender, and the square bodice of her dark green silk gown was embroidered with golden thread. As for her features, she would have been very beautiful, had her ruby-red lips not been drawn up into a disdainful sneer.

"Yes, you," she said in a haughty drawl as she addressed the solider. "Come here."

He did as he was ordered.

The rich beauty raised a bejeweled hand. "Unload that," she commanded, gesturing at a nearby wagon containing several wooden chests and boxes. "Ask my father, Lord Chesleigh, where they should go. And see that you don't break anything, or I'll have you whipped."

"As you wish, my lady," the soldier replied, his voice low and deep and as powerful as the rest of him.

By his accent, he was not, and never had been, a peasant.

Perhaps he was in charge of the garrison here, although why he'd stoop to such manual labor was a mystery.

Riona continued to watch as he undid the rope across the back of the wagon that prevented the boxes and chests from falling out. One by one, he lifted the pieces of baggage and set them neatly on the cobblestones, his muscles bulging and his jerkin stretching across his broad back. Even when he was nearly finished, he'd barely broken a sweat.

The older nobleman Uncle Fergus had suggested might be Sir Nicholas joined the young lady at the wagon.

"Be careful with those," he unnecessarily ordered the soldier before he addressed the lady. "I must say I'm most disappointed with our host. He should be here to greet us."

"It's just as well he's not, Father," she replied. "I'd like to change my gown before I meet him."

"We've only been allotted two small chambers," the nobleman grumbled.

"I'm sure that once you explain what we require, he'll gladly provide it. You *are* Lord Chesleigh, after all."

With that, the young woman put out her slender hand for him to help her, the golden rings on her fingers flashing in the sunlight. Rising with regal dignity, half crouching because of the canvas covering, she had to bend over before setting foot on the stool another servant hastened to set in place.

To give the beauty her due, she managed to invest even that activity with grace and dignity. As she straightened, her gown fell into smooth, fluid folds below her slender waist and the golden embroidery of her gown twinkled in the sunlight, while the gilded girdle about her slender hips shone. With her other hand, she held up her dress, exposing one delicate leather slipper before she stepped onto the ground.

It seemed almost a wonder she would deign to walk on anything so ordinary as cobblestones.

Lord Chesleigh glanced at the soldier. "Ask Martleby where the baggage of Lord Chesleigh and his daughter should go, and see that it's taken there."

"Yes, my lord."

Lord Chesleigh ran an imperious gaze over the man. "And be quick about it."

The Norman lord then swept past the soldier as if getting within three feet of him might stain his garments. His daughter followed at a more graceful pace.

Instead of tending to their baggage, however, or calling for assistance, the soldier turned and started toward Riona.

She tried not to squirm or give any sign of dismay, even if she was dismayed. And excited. Which she shouldn't be. She should try to be dignified when she explained that she wasn't a servant or merchant come to trade.

He stopped about a foot from her wagon and regarded her steadily with dark, inscrutable eyes whose gaze never wavered. Again, she felt entrapped by it, and him. Although the sensation should have been unpleasant, it wasn't. It was…thrilling.

"Would you like me to help you with your baggage, too?" he asked in that deep, slightly husky voice that seemed to offer its own temptations, and convey more than a simple question.

What, in the name of the saints and Scotland, had come over her?

Before she could give an answer—any answer—a

movement on the wall walk above made them both glance up at the guard there. With a look akin to panic directed toward the man on the ground, the guard immediately snapped to attention, and Riona realized this fellow facing her was most definitely not a common foot soldier.

A relatively young and handsome man who looked like he'd been trained in arms and combat, and one of whom all the hirelings seemed afraid….

Of course.

"No, thank you, Sir Nicholas," she replied, giving him no sign that she was puzzled and curious. "I'm sure you've got plenty of other things to do."

His brows lowered. "As a matter of fact, I do."

"Then please, don't linger here chatting with me. My uncle and I can manage our baggage quite well."

The man she was now quite sure was Sir Nicholas of Dunkeathe bowed stiffly, then turned on his heel and strode away, leaving Riona to ponder why a Norman nobleman would pretend he was not.

A SHORT TIME LATER, the lord of Dunkeathe stood looking out the narrow arched window of his solar surveying the yard below, which was now almost clear of wagons, horses and guests.

The room was as austere as the man himself. No tapestries graced the smooth stone walls. An unpainted wooden chest with leather hinges and bronze lock that held the tithe rolls and accounts of the estate stood against the wall. The rest of the furnishings were like-wise simple and plain, and the floor was bare. On a table near the door stood the only articles of any beauty—a silver carafe and two finely worked silver goblets.

His hands clasped behind his back, Nicholas watched the young woman who had guessed who he was, or perhaps found out some other way. Since he'd left the courtyard she'd gotten down off the rickety cart, but she hadn't ventured from its side. She must still be waiting for her mistress or master to tell her where to go.

"Ten ladies, with their noble relatives, twenty-six servants, and one hundred and ten soldiers have arrived," his steward noted behind him. "That's two more ladies and their entourages than we'd expected."

Which one of the nobles did that bright-eyed, brown-haired young woman belong to? Nicholas wondered. She wasn't a servant of the complaining Lord Chesleigh and his beautiful daughter, or they would have chastised her for speaking to an unknown man.

She'd been amazingly and boldly impertinent to him in a way few women, and no servants, ever were. Indeed, she'd been so bold and intriguing, he'd been very tempted to suggest she join him in his bed. Her bright sparkling eyes seemed to promise passion and desire and excitement.

He wouldn't have, of course. He'd never in his life seduced a servant. And he certainly shouldn't now, when he was supposed to be wooing a wife.

Robert Martleby delicately cleared his throat, reminding Nicholas that he was still there.

Nicholas forced his mind to the issue at hand and turned to face his steward. "In spite of the unexpected arrivals, you've seen to it that all the guests and their servants have been accommodated?"

"Yes, my lord. We've had to pitch tents in the outer ward for several of the soldiers. I had some of ours join them, so there would be no accusations of poor treatment, and to keep an eye on them, as well."

Nicholas nodded his approval. "You'll have to find larger quarters for Lord Chesleigh and his daughter. He wasn't pleased with those you assigned him. He thought they were too small."

Robert frowned and studied the list in his hand.

"Does that present a problem?"

"Perhaps I can switch his chamber with that of Sir Percival de Surlepont."

"That would put Sir Percival's chamber next to mine?"

"Yes, my lord."

"Very well. See that the change is made—and make it sound as if that was a mistake that had to be corrected, and that this is some sort of honor to Percival instead of an inconvenience, or being done in response to a complaint."

"Yes, my lord."

"Who did Percival bring?"

Robert's gaze returned to the tablet. "His cousin,

Lady Eleanor." He raised his eyes to regard Nicholas. "Apparently he is her nearest male relation."

"What's she like?"

"Pretty and modest."

Nicholas recalled the young women in the courtyard, but no one in particular came to mind. The only two women he could remember with any clarity were that bold maidservant and the haughty daughter of Lord Chesleigh. "How old is Lady Eleanor?"

"Seventeen."

He didn't want a girl for a wife, but a woman capable of taking responsibility and leadership of the household. He had no desire to have to deal with a shy, fearful bride on his wedding night, either.

That impertinent, brown-eyed maidservant with the thick braids down her back, and the little wisps of hair that escaped to dance upon her intelligent brow, wouldn't be shy. His blood warmed as he imagined how she might react if he took her in his arms and captured her mouth with his.

"Sir Percival assured me her dowry would be substantial, my lord."

Once again Nicholas commanded himself to stop thinking about that servant. "I've heard the family is quite rich."

"Yes, my lord, they are, and a sizeable dowry will go a long way toward solving any difficulties…" Robert flushed and let the words trail off when he saw Nicholas's disgruntled expression.

"We've enough ready coin to get us to Lammas and through a wedding, don't we?" Nicholas asked. "The wool must have brought in something."

"Yes, it did, my lord, but I must point out that the expense of this…this…"

"I have to entertain my guests in the style they expect," Nicholas replied as Robert floundered for the word to describe his overlord's method of finding a bride. "I won't have them thinking I'm desperate— which I'm not." *Not yet, anyway.* "It's your responsibility to see that no one suspects I'm running short of funds."

"You're not yet in dire straits, my lord," Robert assured him.

"Good. By Lammas I should have a bride in hand, or at least a betrothal agreement and promise of a dowry. Who else has come?"

"Lady Mary, the daughter of the Earl of Eglinburg, Lady Elizabeth, sister of the Duke of Ansley, Lady Catherine, daughter of the Comte D'Ortelieu, Lady Isabelle, ward of Sir James of Keswick, Lady Eloise, daughter of Sir George de Chillery, Lady Lavinia, second cousin to the Duc D'Anglevoix, Lady Priscilla, niece of the Abbot of St. Swithins-by-the-Sea who came with her brother Audric, and Lady Joscelind, daughter of Lord Chesleigh of Kent."

Ah yes, the beautiful—and proud—Lady Joscelind and her equally proud and arrogant father. He wondered what they'd do when they discovered they'd been ordering their host about as if he were their lackey. That should prove interesting—although, given their natures, they might take offense that he hadn't identified himself. He'd have to ensure that he gave them a believable explanation.

Nicholas strolled back to the window and saw that the maidservant was still standing by the cart. She shifted her feet, as if her patience was wearing thin. "That's only nine," he noted, glancing over his shoulder. "Who's the tenth?"

"Nobody of any consequence, my lord. In fact, I probably should have denied them admittance to the courtyard, but the fellow did have a charter and you had said that all women of noble birth were to be considered. His niece meets that qualification."

Nicholas raised an inquisitive brow, just as he had in the courtyard. That serving wench had then done the same, surprising and secretly amusing him more than he'd been amused in…well, a long time. "Who is this nobleman with a charter you don't think should be here?"

"A Scot, my lord, the Thane of Glencleith. I asked those of our men who are Scots, and it seems he's the holder of a small estate to the north. Politically, he's completely unimportant, and I understand he's quite poor."

"Only one Scots noble came?"

"Yes, my lord."

Only one—and he was a lord in this country. Clearly it didn't matter to the Scots that he'd changed the name of his estate back to the original one, or that his sister had married into one of their clans. He was still, first and foremost, a representative of the Normans and their unwelcome intrusion into Scotland.

Yet whatever they thought, he'd earned Dunkeathe and recalcitrant Scots or no, he'd keep it. If he had to marry for money and influence to ensure that, he would.

A fist pounded on the door. Nicholas wheeled around just as the door flew open and a short, brawny, gray-haired, bearded, potbellied Scot wearing one of their skirted garments bustled into the room.

Before Nicholas could demand an explanation, the intruder came to a halt, put his hands on his hips, and smiled at them both. "Here you are!" he cried in heavily accented French. "Delighted to make your acquaintance, my lord. I thought you'd be in the courtyard greeting your guests, but obviously Normans have a different idea of politeness."

He looked around the room before his gaze settled again on Nicholas. "Wonderful castle you've got here. This chamber's a bit bare, but when you're married, your wife will change that."

Nicholas's first thought was that the man was half-mad, while Robert looked like he was going to faint.

"My lord, I—I—" the steward stammered, clearly aghast and at a loss to explain what was happening.

The fellow seemed harmless, if audacious. "Welcome to Dunkeathe," Nicholas replied, giving Robert a look to assure him he wasn't angry.

Robert recovered the powers of speech. "My lord, this is Fergus Mac Gordon Mac Darbudh, the Thane of Glencleith."

The poor, politically unimportant Scottish noble.

Whatever Nicholas thought of the man personally, and no matter how poor and seemingly unimportant he might be, Nicholas knew he had to be diplomatic. He'd lived in Scotland for a decade, and he still couldn't fathom the complicated relationships between the clans. It could be that this man had relatives who were far more politically important than he himself.

Therefore, he put a smile on his face and calmly inquired, "Is there something I can do for you, my lord?"

"It's not what you can do for me," the boisterous Scot replied. "It's what *I* can do for *you*. I've brought you the perfect bride." He smiled with immense, and quite sincere, satisfaction. "My niece, Riona. She's a very fine girl, my lord—no man could do better when it comes to marriage. She's a sweet lass, and she's been the joy of my life since she came to me when she was two years old and her sainted parents died.

"She's run my household since she was twelve, too," he continued before Nicholas or Robert could get a word in. "The servants follow her orders without question and while she keeps them in good order, they love her. I'll wager there aren't many Norman ladies so beloved by their servants as my Riona is.

"And she's clever, too. She keeps all the accounts and knows where every penny's spent. She's saved me many a penny, too, I can tell you—although that won't mean much to you, for there's plenty in your purse, I know. But still, no man wants a wasteful wife. Granted she's not got a large dowry, but what's that to a man of your wealth, eh? What are a few more coins in the purse if your wife's making your life a misery? Riona could never do that. She'll be a bride any man could be proud of and I wouldn't offer her up to just any man, either."

With that, he folded his arms over his chest and beamed as if he'd just saved Nicholas from a fate worse than death.

Unfortunately for Fergus Mac Gordon, his niece could be the most wonderful of women, but if she was poor, she had no chance of becoming Nicholas's bride. The personal attributes of his wife were considerably less important to him than the dowry she would bring.

Nevertheless, the man was probably as proud as all the Scots were, and he'd likely be insulted if Nicholas refused to consider his niece from the start, so he had best not be too quick to dismiss her.

"I thank you for bringing your niece to Dunkeathe," he said politely, "and I'm sure she's a very fine young woman. I assure you, I'll take all the qualities of every lady into account before I make my choice. Now if you'll excuse me, my steward and I have other matters to discuss."

"Of course you do!" the Scot cried. To Nicholas's relief, he didn't seem a whit dismayed by this polite dismissal as he backed toward the door. "You're a very busy fellow, I'm sure, with this great pile of a castle to tend to. So many soldiers, too—an army you've got, although who'd dare to attack you here? The man would have to be mad."

Then, just as abruptly as he'd entered, he was gone.

It was like the calm after a maelstrom. Or before a storm.

"My lord, I do beg your pardon," Robert said, clearly horrified by what had just happened. "I had no idea he'd do that, none whatsoever!"

At the sight of Robert's red, indignant face Nicholas had to turn away and look out the window again, for he felt the most unusual urge to laugh.

He noticed the maidservant was still standing by the cart. "I take it you personally didn't invite him to join us here?"

"Absolutely not, my lord!"

"Then it's not your fault."

"I'll inform him at once that he cannot remain here, my lord."

"I didn't say he had to leave. He's still the only noble Scot to come, and I don't think it would be wise to do anything that might cause him to depart before I make my final choice. The ties of blood and family go deep in this country. He may be of little importance, but he might have relatives who are, and they could stand against me if he feels insulted."

"I haven't heard that he has any relatives who might cause us trouble, my lord."

"The ties between clans are complicated. I can't remember half the clans my sister's related to now. It would be better to take no chances, so I should at least make it appear that I'm considering his niece."

Suddenly, the stocky Scot came rushing into the courtyard and headed straight for the maidservant.

"Riona!" he called out, waving. She waved back and hurried toward him eagerly.

God's rood, was *that* young woman the thane's niece? That woman he'd been trying not to imagine in his bed?

"So, here you are, brother. I should have guessed you'd be holed up here instead of talking to the bevy of beauties who've come to vie for your hand."

Nicholas briefly closed his eyes and prayed for patience before he turned around.

His younger brother strolled into the room and threw himself into Nicholas's chair and put his feet on the table. Like his brother, Henry was strong and well-muscled, a warrior in his prime, and now he sat smiling smugly as if he had not a care in the world.

Which was quite probably true.

"You may leave us, Robert," Nicholas said, subduing his envy of the brother who'd never shared his struggles.

"Yes, you may leave me to bid farewell to my brother," Henry said with a wave of his hand, "although I must say, Nicholas, I'm rather tempted to stay a few more days. I had no idea your net would gather such a fine catch. Mind you, that one with the giggle..." He shuddered and shook his head. "Not quite what I'd want to wake up to every morning."

"I didn't think you cared who you woke up with as long as you'd enjoyed yourself the night before."

Henry laughed. "Well, I'd care if she was my wife, which is why you won't find me sending out word that I'm in the market for a bride, with all and sundry welcome to come and vie for my hand. Really, brother, you make it sound like you're nothing more than a stallion ready for breeding."

Nicholas took two long paces and swiped his brother's feet from the table. "Keep your muddy boots on the floor."

Henry regarded him with annoyance. "Pardon me for not realizing you were getting so fastidious in your old age."

"That table cost more than I made the first six months of my service with the Duc D'Aubreay. You may be able to forget when we were poor, but I don't."

"I don't forget."

"Good."

Henry got to his feet. "So I do understand why you want a rich wife from a well-connected family." His temper, so easily roused, was dying down, as it always did. Eventually. "God's blood, so do I. It's the method I question, Nicholas."

Nicholas poured himself some wine from the silver carafe. "I see nothing wrong with having women come to me, instead of running all over the countryside trying to find a bride."

"I suppose it does make it easier—but wouldn't it be cheaper to go to them?"

It certainly would, but Nicholas didn't want anyone to realize he had financial troubles, not even Henry. "It's not the expense." He poured wine in another goblet and handed it to his brother. "I don't want to be long from my estate."

Henry took a drink and looked over the rim of the goblet at Nicholas. "If this were my estate, I'd get away as often as I could. The weather alone—"

"I don't mind the rain, especially when I have a castle in which to dry off," Nicholas replied as he sat in his chair.

"That does make a difference, I suppose," Henry said, leaning back against the table. "But there's the Scots to deal with. They're stubborn and coarse, the lot of them."

"That's what Marianne said before she married one of them," Nicholas noted. "Our sister seems quite happy now."

Henry sniffed and took another drink of Nicholas's fine wine. "She's a woman, and we both know women are slaves to their hearts. Would *you* marry a Scot?"

"I'd certainly consider a Scot if she had a large dowry and was from an important family."

"I really think you would at that."

Nicholas's temper flared. "I do live in their country, and it was a Scot who gave me this estate."

Henry put the goblet down on the large table. "You'd better be careful, or you might wind up more Scots than Norman, like Marianne. You've already let your hair grow long, the way they do."

"It saves time," Nicholas replied. "However, I doubt I'll ever be mistaken for a Scot, whoever I marry, and as for our sister, she seems content, and I'm happy to have her husband for an ally. I need all the allies I can get in this country."

Henry, who wore his hair in the Norman fashion, took a long drink, then wiped his lips. "Surely the woman herself should count for something."

"Naturally," Nicholas said as he set down his goblet. "She'll have to be able to run a household without pestering me about expenses or petty squabbles among the servants."

"You must want her to be pretty," Henry said. "Or do you intend never to see her by daylight? Or candlelight? Or torchlight?"

"Of course I don't want to marry some old hag. But as long as she's not repulsive, her looks are immaterial to me."

Henry didn't hide his skepticism. "You used to be more discerning. In fact, you used to be quite fussy in that regard. Considering this is a woman you'll have to make love to several times if you're to have heirs, I'm surprised to hear you claim otherwise."

"All I wanted from a whore was to slake my lust. This is different."

"Exactly," Henry cried triumphantly, "because presumably, she'll also be the mother of your children. You don't want a bunch of ugly brats, do you?"

"I want my sons to be courageous, honorable men, and my daughters honorable, demure women—as their mother should be. What they look like is less important."

"We'll see how serious you are about your future wife's appearance when you make your choice," Henry said as he pushed himself away from the table. "Now give me your hand. It's time I was on my way if I'm to reach Dunbardee before nightfall."

Nicholas rose and clasped his brother by the forearm. "Safe journey, Henry."

"If I hear anything of significance at court, I'll send word," Henry replied. "I do know what you did for me, Nicholas, and I won't forget. Anything I can do to help you, I will."

Nicholas regarded him with surprise, taken aback by this unexpected expression of sincere gratitude.

Henry sauntered to the door. "Farewell, brother." He paused on the threshold and gave Nicholas a sarcastic smirk. "Whatever you do, don't sell yourself short."

The warmth engendered by Henry's words of appreciation fled.

"I'm not selling myself."

Henry replied with aggravating condescension. "Of course you are, just as the women will be. But there's no need to lose your temper, brother. That's the way of the world. Goodbye, and good luck."

AFTER HENRY had left him, Nicholas again went to the window, hands clasped behind his back. The sun was past midday. Henry would have to ride swiftly if he was to reach Dunbardee. He'd enjoy that. Henry was young and he'd always been reckless—because he could afford to be. *He* hadn't had to pay for their sister's time in the convent. *He* hadn't had to ensure that his brother had the best training and arms, while he managed with whatever he could afford after their needs were met. Henry had never slept in stables to save the cost of a night's lodging at an inn, or gone without food.

Henry hadn't been the one to promise their dying mother he would always look after his brother and sister, a vow he'd willingly made and done his best to keep.

Henry didn't know that as the years of struggle had passed, Nicholas had vowed to do everything he could to rise in the world, to a place where he'd be rich and respected, safe and secure, where no one could take anything away from him, or threaten him or his family.

With that in mind, he'd trained and fought and won this estate by dint of his skill at arms alone, without the benefit of noble patronage or connections.

Yet even so, that wasn't enough to rest and be content, not in this world. To hold it, he needed a rich wife from a powerful family.

And, by God, he'd get one.

CHAPTER THREE

JOINING HER UNCLE, Riona came out of the chamber made over to her use while they were in Dunkeathe. Together they were going to the hall to enjoy the special feast in celebration of St. John the Baptist's Day and, so Uncle Fergus said, to welcome all the guests in fine Norman style.

Since their two small rooms were farthest from the hall, it made more sense to leave the building by the guarded outer door than go along the upper corridor. Riona suspected their rooms were really intended for the body servants of the household or the guests and had been pressed into service because so many had come to Dunkeathe.

The size and location didn't trouble her a bit. The chambers were more than large enough for herself and Uncle Fergus, and they had the additional virtue of privacy. At home, she shared a *teach* with several other women of the household; here, since she had no maid, she had the chamber to herself. Tonight, she wouldn't have to listen to Maeve snore, or hear Aelean get up to use the chamber pot. She wouldn't be bothered by Seas and Sile whispering for what seemed an age before they fell asleep. Tonight, she would be blissfully alone, in welcome silence.

"I wonder what they'll feed us," Uncle Fergus mused as they strolled through the courtyard. "I've heard the Normans drown everything in spicy sauces."

"I'm sure there'll be something we'll like," Riona assured him as she linked her arm though his.

The air carried a whiff of smoke from the bonfires being kindled in the village to celebrate Midsummer's Day.

"Aye, I suppose," her uncle replied. He slid her a wry glance. "I'm also wondering what you'll think of Sir Nicholas."

Riona tried not to betray any reaction at all, but she couldn't subdue a blush. "He's probably a very impressive soldier."

"Oh, aye, he's *very* impressive. A fine fellow."

Uncle Fergus looked particularly pleased, as if he were contemplating a great secret. Her suspicions aroused, she immediately asked, "Did you meet him?"

And if so, what did Sir Nicholas say to you?

Instead of answering her question, Uncle Fergus ran a studious gaze over her simple dark green woolen dress. "I should have bought you a new gown."

"This is more than good enough," she said, smoothing down the gown with her hand. "I'd feel uncomfortable in silk or damask or brocade. Did you meet Sir Nicholas earlier?"

"Something smells good," Uncle Fergus noted as he pushed open the doors of the hall and ushered her inside, still not answering her question.

Which was momentarily forgotten when Riona entered the magnificent, and crowded, hall. It was easily sixty feet long and thirty feet wide, with a raised dais at the farthest end and pillars down its length to support the high roof. Wide beams rested on corbels carved to resemble the heads of various animals. A long table covered in white linen stood on the dais, along with carved chairs. A colorful tapestry hung behind it, and more decorated the walls. The rushes beneath her feet released the odor of rosemary and fleabane.

More than finely dressed nobles filled the room and created the noise. Here, as in the courtyard, what seemed a bevy of servants hurried through the hall, some still setting up tables and covering them with linen, others lighting torches. Hounds wandered about, snuffling at the rushes and looking around expectantly, often in the direction of a door that led to the kitchen, for wonderful odors wafted to her from that direction.

More than once the servants collided, argued and cast annoyed looks at their fellows. A few of the younger servants appeared utterly confused, and had to be pointedly reminded about what they were to do.

There was no woman who seemed to be in any position of authority here, only the steward they'd met at the gate. Standing in the corner near the dais, he looked harried and rather lost. Obviously he wasn't prepared for this responsibility, or maybe he was overwhelmed by the number of guests.

She could have told him that the tables should have been set up much earlier, with the linens to come shortly before the meal was served. More specific directions would help bring better order to the rest of the activity, and the younger servants should only be entrusted with the most basic of duties.

She wondered how well the kitchen servants were organized, until it occurred to her that none of this was her concern. She was a guest here, like all the other nobles.

Suddenly, everyone simultaneously stopped talking and moving, and turned to look at her and Uncle Fergus. Disappointment flickered across their faces and was soon replaced by scorn and derision.

"I suppose they were expecting Sir Nicholas," Uncle Fergus remarked. He didn't seem to notice that people were looking at them as if they were spattered with mud. Or dung. "I don't see him here, but there's Fredella."

He smiled at a woman dressed in a plain gown of dark blue wool, with a simple leather girdle about her ample waist, and a square of linen on her head. Her garments, as well as her friendly face, suggested to Riona that she wasn't a lady, but perhaps a servant of one of them. Either that, or they weren't the only poor nobles who'd come to Dunkeathe.

Whoever she was, it was like Uncle Fergus to make

friends with anyone and everyone, rich or poor, peasant or noble—another reason she loved him.

"She's the servant of Lady Eleanor, the cousin of Sir Percival de Surlepont," Uncle Fergus explained, nodding at a man on the other side of the hall. "He's that overdressed puppy we saw in the courtyard and that's Lady Eleanor beside him."

Riona instantly recognized the young man who'd been wearing yellow damask. Lady Eleanor was the pretty girl who'd seemed so unhappy. She didn't look any happier standing beside her cousin in the hall, attired in a gown of deep red cendal trimmed with gold, like the circlet on her dark brown hair. Sir Percival had changed into a tunic of peacock blue, trimmed with brilliant green, and he had a large gold chain around his neck. His boots alone—leather dyed scarlet and embossed with gold and silver—would likely pay for her uncle's wine for a year.

All the nobles were similarly dressed in sumptuous, colorful and expensive garments, embroidered with lovely threads of bright colors. The quality and number of materials was mind-boggling, and as for the cost, Riona could probably feed their entire household for half a year on what it cost for a single gown one of these ladies wore, not to mention the gold and silver and costly gems they wore on their fingers or around their necks.

"If you'll excuse me, Riona, I'll go say hello to Fredella. She was very helpful to me when I was looking for the fellow in charge of the quarters."

Uncle Fergus didn't wait for Riona to agree, but bustled off toward the older woman. Since she couldn't call him back without attracting more unwelcome attention, Riona moved to the side of the hall and surveyed the gathered nobles.

Across the chamber, Lord Chesleigh, in a long black tunic, held forth about the rising cost of wine to a small group of noblemen. One of his listeners had a very bulbous red nose and he swayed so much that Riona suspected he'd been into the wine already. A younger man, not so brilliantly attired, hovered on the edge of another group as if he were too shy to join it, yet didn't want to leave. A lady in that small gathering kept glancing at him as if she wasn't sure if he should go or stay, either.

"What can Sir Nicholas be thinking, letting that fat little Scot stay?" a haughty and unfortunately familiar female voice drawled nearby, so loud and imperious, Riona couldn't ignore it. "I wouldn't believe it, except that his steward told me it's true."

Lady Joscelind, in gold brocade, with her blond hair covered in a shimmering veil, stood with a small circle of young women several feet closer to the dais, her back to Riona. The one who giggled was among them, and another who looked rather sickly. A third wasn't exactly slender. The last wasn't particular attractive, but she seemed less impressed with the beautiful Lady Joscelind than the others.

"If *that's* a Scots noble, we'd be doing their peasants a favor ruling their country," Lord Chesleigh's daughter continued, raising her slender hand in a languid, yet graceful, gesture before she let it drop. "And who'd want to stay here anyway? The people are such savages, and the weather! My father tells me it rains nineteen days out of twenty."

It was bad enough the vain creature had disparaged Uncle Fergus. Now she was disparaging Riona's country, too?

Glaring at the beauty, Riona marched toward the little circle.

"But if Sir Nicholas chooses you, you'll have to live in Scotland," the sickly looking young woman simpered, likewise not seeing Riona bear down upon them.

The other women did, and if Lady Joscelind had been less determined to express her opinions, she might have realized something was amiss.

"Only a part of the year," she smugly and obliviously replied. "We'll be spending a great deal of time at court."

"England is welcome to you," Riona snapped as she came to a halt behind her. "We don't want you here."

"Of all the impudence!" Lady Joscelind exclaimed, whirling around in a blaze of silk and thick perfume to meet Riona's glare with one of her own. "How dare you interrupt our conversation?" She waved her away. "Be about your business, wench, and be glad I don't have you punished for your insolence."

"Oh, aye?" Riona replied, raising her brow as she crossed her arms, ignoring the other women who exchanged shocked or wary glances. "You think you wield such power over me?"

"If I don't, somebody here must, impudent wench."

"I answer to no one here, except Fergus Mac Gordon Mac Darbudh, Thane of Glencleith."

Lady Joscelind smirked. "So you belong to that comical fellow, do you? Well, go tend to him, then."

"My lady, do you not know who I am?" Riona asked, her voice low and firm and full of contempt.

Lady Joscelind's smooth white brow furrowed with annoyance. "I neither know, nor care."

"You should."

Lady Joscelind's cheeks turned pink, but her haughty demeanor didn't alter. "Whoever you are, you hussy, I am Lady Joscelind, the daughter of Lord Chesleigh, and you had best remember that."

"I am Lady Riona of Glencleith."

"*Lady* Riona?" the beauty scoffed, running a scornful gaze over Riona's garments. "I don't believe it. You're nothing but a servant."

"Whether you believe it or not," Riona replied, "Sir Nicholas and his steward know that it's true."

Lady Joscelind's eyes narrowed with suspicion, yet when she spoke, she was still scornful and dismissive. "If you are who you claim to be, I assume you've come here to meet Sir Nicholas. You think *you* stand a chance of impressing him?"

"As it happens, my lady, I've already met him. And so have you, although you didn't know it." Riona letely unaware that anything untoward had happened, e pulled Fredella forward. "Riona, my beauty, this is redella."

Fredella's smile was nearly as jovial as Uncle Fergus's. "I'm delighted to meet you, my lady, and I'm sure Eleanor will be, too," she said. "My mistress is a shy girl, but she'll want to be introduced to you."

"We'd be delighted to meet her, too, wouldn't we, Riona?" Uncle Fergus answered for her.

Remembering the smiles she'd exchanged with the younger woman, Riona had hope Lady Eleanor wouldn't prove to be another Lady Joscelind. "Aye, I'd be happy to meet her."

"Not now, though," Fredella whispered with a worried frown as she drew them both away to the side of the hall.

"Why wait? She's here and so are we," Uncle Fergus said, not bothering to lower his voice.

"Because Sir Percival's with her. He, um, doesn't think much of the Scots, I'm afraid," Fredella replied, her plump cheeks coloring.

Uncle Fergus glowered at Sir Percival. "Doesn't like Scots, eh? Because we don't fuss with our hair and spend more on a tunic than many a poor family earns in a year?"

"Neither Eleanor nor I share his prejudice," Fredella hastily assured him. "My own mother was a Scot, you ee."

Uncle Fergus stopped glaring at the Norman and ve her a smile. "Was she now?"

smiled without mirth. "I don't think you ma
favorable impression."

Lady Joscelind's jaw dropped, then ind.
snapped shut. "I should think I'd remember bein
duced to Sir Nicholas."

"I didn't say you'd been introduced. I said
met him."

Riona spotted Uncle Fergus coming toward her
Fredella in tow. "Now if you'll excuse me, I should
my uncle, whose family have been thanes and ch
tains here since before the Normans existed."

She started to leave, then turned back. "Oh, and I
remind you that Sir Nicholas holds this land by the
grace of Alexander of Scotland, not Henry of England,
so if there's a court he and his wife should attend, it's
that of Scotland. That's provided he even picks you, of
course," she finished with another smile that suggested
she found that highly doubtful.

Then, she swept away from the Norman ladies, leaving Lady Joscelind to wonder how and where she'd
met the lord of Dunkeathe.

Riona wished they hadn't come here. She wish
Uncle Fergus had never heard of Sir Nicholas's plan
find himself a wife. Most of all, she wished the kin
never invited the Normans to Scotland at all, or pai
cenaries to serve him, even if rebellion and rival
to the throne were part and parcel of the histor
land.

When she reached Uncle Fergus, who see

smiled without mirth. "I don't think you made a very favorable impression."

Lady Joscelind's jaw dropped, then indignantly snapped shut. "I should think I'd remember being introduced to Sir Nicholas."

"I didn't say you'd been introduced. I said you'd met him."

Riona spotted Uncle Fergus coming toward her with Fredella in tow. "Now if you'll excuse me, I should join my uncle, whose family have been thanes and chieftains here since before the Normans existed."

She started to leave, then turned back. "Oh, and I'll remind you that Sir Nicholas holds this land by the grace of Alexander of Scotland, not Henry of England, so if there's a court he and his wife should attend, it's that of Scotland. That's provided he even picks you, of course," she finished with another smile that suggested she found that highly doubtful.

Then, she swept away from the Norman ladies, leaving Lady Joscelind to wonder how and where she'd met the lord of Dunkeathe.

Riona wished they hadn't come here. She wished Uncle Fergus had never heard of Sir Nicholas's plans to find himself a wife. Most of all, she wished the king had never invited the Normans to Scotland at all, or paid mercenaries to serve him, even if rebellion and rival claims to the throne were part and parcel of the history of her land.

When she reached Uncle Fergus, who seemed completely unaware that anything untoward had happened, he pulled Fredella forward. "Riona, my beauty, this is Fredella."

Fredella's smile was nearly as jovial as Uncle Fergus's. "I'm delighted to meet you, my lady, and I'm sure Eleanor will be, too," she said. "My mistress is a shy girl, but she'll want to be introduced to you."

"We'd be delighted to meet her, too, wouldn't we, Riona?" Uncle Fergus answered for her.

Remembering the smiles she'd exchanged with the younger woman, Riona had hope Lady Eleanor wouldn't prove to be another Lady Joscelind. "Aye, I'd be happy to meet her."

"Not now, though," Fredella whispered with a worried frown as she drew them both away to the side of the hall.

"Why wait? She's here and so are we," Uncle Fergus said, not bothering to lower his voice.

"Because Sir Percival's with her. He, um, doesn't think much of the Scots, I'm afraid," Fredella replied, her plump cheeks coloring.

Uncle Fergus glowered at Sir Percival. "Doesn't like Scots, eh? Because we don't fuss with our hair and spend more on a tunic than many a poor family earns in a year?"

"Neither Eleanor nor I share his prejudice," Fredella hastily assured him. "My own mother was a Scot, you see."

Uncle Fergus stopped glaring at the Norman and gave her a smile. "Was she now?"

"Yes, from Lochbarr."

"A fine place, that," Uncle Fergus said, his anger lessening. "And the Mac Tarans are a fine clan." He gave Riona a significant look. "That's the clan Sir Nicholas's sister married into."

"Oh, you've heard of them, have you?" Fredella asked.

"I don't think there are many Scots who haven't," Uncle Fergus replied. "A fine group of fighters always come out of Lochbarr."

"Eleanor's often longed to go there, to see the things I've talked about," Fredella said, "but that Percival wouldn't let her. She's hardly been able to see anyone, either. To keep her pure, he says, as if she had no virtue or modesty to speak of. She's been raised better than that, I can tell you, by me and her dear sainted mother."

"She's an orphan?" Riona asked.

"Since she was ten. That's when that Percival got the charge of her. If you ask me, he's got more love for those ridiculous boots of his than he does for his cousin. He's just waiting for somebody rich to offer to take her off his hands. He makes me want to spit!"

"Poor bairn," Uncle Fergus murmured.

Riona shared his sympathy. She could imagine how her life might have been had her kindly uncle not taken her in. Yet in a way, she also envied Lady Eleanor, who had at least known her mother. Riona had no memory of hers, who had died in childbirth, or her father, who had died of a fever a short time later.

A sudden stir near the steps leading from the hall to the apartments made Riona turn. The mighty lord of Dunkeathe strode toward the dais. Now he was finely dressed in a black, thigh-length tunic and breeches and polished boots. His hair was still the same, though— long and waving to his shoulders, like her country-men—and he still had the same angular handsome features, and those eyes that seemed more hawk than human. Yet in those clothes, with the attention of every-one in the hall upon him, he looked more like a prince than a soldier. How could she ever have assumed he was anything but a noble lord? The only common thing about him was the sword hilt sticking out of the scab-bard attached to his belt. It was exceptionally plain, just a bronze crossbar wrapped with leather, as any foot soldier might possess.

She looked to Lord Chesleigh and his daughter, to see if they recognized him. The Norman nobleman was staring at Sir Nicholas as if he was seeing an appari-tion; his daughter's face was bright red, and although she lowered her head, Riona saw enough to know that she was flushed not from shame, but with indignant anger.

That didn't bode well for a match between the lady and the lord of Dunkeathe, unless Lord Chesleigh and his daughter thought him worthy enough to overlook what had happened in the courtyard.

Sir Nicholas came to a halt in the center of the raised platform, in front of the high table. "My lords and ladies, knights and gentlemen, welcome to Dunkeathe. I am both flattered and delighted to see so many of you here." He made what was, she assumed, supposed to be a smile. "I especially welcome the young ladies, although there are so many of such beauty, grace and accomplishments, I am overwhelmed."

Riona didn't believe that for a moment.

Sir Nicholas turned to his steward, who was standing at the left side of the dais, a wax tablet in his hands. "If you would begin, Robert."

The man consulted what was obviously a list. "My lord, may I present the Duke of Ansley and his sister, Lady Elizabeth."

A man of middle years, with a sizable belly and attired in a long blue robe, hurried forward, leading a lady likewise plump, wearing a gown in an unflattering shade of burgundy. Sir Nicholas bowed, as did the nobleman, while the lady made her obeisance.

There were no smiles exchanged, and the lady was clearly nervous.

The steward proceeded to introduce all the ladies and their relatives one by one. The woman who'd been less impressed with Lady Joscelind was Lady Lavinia, the second cousin of the Duc D'Anglevoix, who had the longest, most arched nose Riona had ever seen. He also seemed a bit put out, darting annoyed glances at the steward and the man who'd just been introduced. Clearly D'Anglevoix felt he should have been called first.

The round-eyed Lady Priscilla, who came next, giggled the entire time she stood before Sir Nicholas, and the young man beside her looked as if he'd gladly gag her as he led her away. The Earl of Eglinburg, who likewise hadn't missed many meals, strode forward so quickly, his daughter, Lady Mary, had to run to keep up with him, for she was short while he was tall.

Sir George, he of the bulbous red nose and swaying gait, slurred a greeting and nearly fell over when he bowed. His daughter, Lady Eloise, who was neither pretty nor plain, looked understandably and completely mortified, while Sir Nicholas's expression didn't change a bit.

Lady Isabelle blushed bright red when she was introduced, no doubt not just because of the inscrutable visage of their host, but also because her guardian, Sir James, tripped on her silk gown as he led her forward. Next to be called, the Comte D'Ortelieu looked as if he considered this whole exercise rather beneath him, while his daughter, Lady Catherine, turned as white as her gown and seemed about to swoon at any moment.

None of them, it seemed, recognized Sir Nicholas from the courtyard.

Then Robert Martleby summoned Lord Chesleigh and his beautiful daughter. His expression haughty, Lord Chesleigh strode forth, escorting Lady Joscelind. For a moment, Riona thought he might chastise his host. Instead, the man bowed and said in a hearty voice that was only slightly condemning, "My lord, this is a very great pleasure, but you should have declared your-self in the courtyard."

That caused a bit of a flutter among the other guests.

"He was in the courtyard?" Uncle Fergus loudly whispered. "Where? I didn't see him."

Maybe her uncle hadn't met Sir Nicholas after all. "By the stable. He wasn't dressed like that."

Uncle Fergus chuckled. "Clever man, to watch the ladies before they knew who he was, to see how they really are."

Riona's gaze darted back to the man on the dais. Was that why he'd done that?

"I should have enlightened you, but I was not prop-erly attired to receive my noble guests," Sir Nicholas replied, "and I couldn't refuse the request of so grace-ful and beautiful a lady."

Riona was somewhat amazed Lady Joscelind didn't clutch her father's arm to steady herself when the lord of Dunkeathe addressed her in that deep, seductive voice.

As for Sir Nicholas's excuse, Riona could more eas-ily believe Uncle Fergus's explanation. She suspected there were very few things that could embarrass a man like Sir Nicholas, and she was sure his clothing wouldn't be one of them.

Any offense clearly forgiven, Lord Chesleigh smiled with genial bonhomie. "Nonetheless, my lord, you must accept my apologies for any inadvertent offense."

Sir Nicholas's next words, spoken with no real contrition, convinced Riona there was indeed another motive for his behavior. "As you must accept mine for not introducing myself."

Lord Chesleigh fairly beamed as he reached for his daughter's hand and drew her forward. "May I present my daughter, Joscelind."

She made a deep obeisance and when she rose, presented a charmingly flustered countenance. "I also beg your pardon, my lord."

"Think no more about it, I beg you, and please, consider Dunkeathe your home while you're here."

If ever a man could make a woman swoon with his voice alone…

"And a very fine fortress it is," Lord Chesleigh said. "I commend you, my lord."

Sir Nicholas gave him another very small smile, and a brief bow. "Thank you." Then he glanced at his steward.

Lord Chesleigh and Lady Joscelind took the hint and moved away.

After a quick look around the hall to see if there were any other ladies waiting to be introduced, Uncle Fergus started forward. "Come on, Riona, our turn next."

She had no desire to parade in front of all these people and be presented to a Norman lord like a fish on a platter. Unfortunately, Uncle Fergus was already hurrying forward, so unless she wanted him to call out for her to hurry up, she had no choice but to follow. As she did, she reminded herself that if she had no wealth, fine clothes or beauty, she still had much to be proud of. Her uncle and cousin loved her, she was as noble as anyone here and she had one considerable advantage they lacked.

She was a Scot.

"Fergus Mac Gordon, Thane of Glencleith," the steward announced. "And his niece, the Lady Riona."

"Ach, we've already met!" Uncle Fergus cried, grinning at the lord of Dunkeathe as if they were boon companions.

They *had* met! When? Where? Why hadn't he told her?

As her uncle looked at her and gave her a wink, she had her answer. He thought he'd been helping and kept this for a surprise.

In spite of his kindhearted motive, she wanted to groan with dismay, especially when Sir Nicholas's expression didn't alter, and snickers and disapproving murmurs reached her ears.

"As if anybody would want to marry *her*," Lord Chesleigh said behind her.

His scornful words lit her pride and roused her anger. Who was this Lord Chesleigh to speak so arrogantly? These men and their mute relatives were all here like beggars at this man's whim.

She would show them what Scots were made of, and that they were the equal of any here, including their host. She didn't care what any of them thought of her, even Sir Nicholas, with his grim face and arrogant method of finding a wife.

So she gave Sir Nicholas a bright smile and said, in Gaelic and in a voice loud enough to carry to the far reaches of the hall, "Good evening, my lord. Don't you look different in your fine clothes. I might never have recognized you, except for the hair."

Surprise flared in Sir Nicholas's dark eyes and there were more incredulous whispers behind her. They were all surely wondering what she was saying.

Let them wonder.

"My uncle didn't tell me you'd met, but I should have expected it. He's a very friendly fellow."

"Yes, he is," the nobleman replied, clearly recovered from his surprise—and in unexpectedly good Gaelic.

That took her aback, but she tried not to show it. He was the one who was supposed to be thrown off guard. "I didn't realize you spoke our language so well, my lord," she lied, for she hadn't expected him to speak it at all. "I'm most impressed."

"I suspect there's a great deal about me you don't know."

God help her, that voice of his was like temptation incarnate, and his gaze was so steady, she felt as if he was staring into her very soul, looking for the truth.

But she wasn't about to let him intimidate her here anymore than she had in the courtyard when she thought he was just a soldier. "I daresay you're right. I can only guess why you were skulking about the courtyard this morning instead of greeting your arriving guests."

His eyes narrowed very slightly. "I wasn't skulking."

"Whatever you were doing, I'm sure you had your reasons," she replied, telling him with her tone and eyes that she didn't believe his reasons would be sufficient for her.

His steward coughed.

She knew an attempt to interrupt when she heard it, and she'd said enough to show them all that she was proud of her heritage and the country that bred her. "Come, Uncle," she said, slipping her arm through his. "Let's leave Sir Nicholas to his other noble guests."

As they walked away through the crowd of muttering Normans, Uncle Fergus laughed softly. "He fooled everyone except my clever girl. You showed him some Scots spirit, too. He's got to be impressed."

Riona didn't care if Sir Nicholas was impressed or not, or what he thought about her. She couldn't imagine living in this place among the Normans and their Saxon soldiers, and certainly not with him.

CHAPTER FOUR

AS THE SERVANTS carried away the remains of the baked apples, Nicholas turned to Robert, seated to his left at the high table. To his right was the elderly priest who had taken residence in the castle after the chapel had been completed. Father Damon greatly appreciated the ease of his duties ministering to Sir Nicholas, as well as the household and garrison. The lord of Dunkeathe was certainly no stickler on religious matters.

Robert stopped looking at the table where the beautiful Lady Joscelind and several of the other guests were sitting. Nicholas couldn't blame the man for being distracted; so might he have been, if he hadn't encountered Lady Joscelind in the courtyard.

"I'm going to give the garrison commander the watchword for tonight," he said, rising. "If my guests require more wine or food, or music, it should be provided."

"As you wish, my lord. And the watchword is…?"

Nicholas gave his steward a small smile. "Restraint."

Robert's eyes widened, then he flushed. "Forgive

my lack of attention, my lord. I'm not used to being among so many nobles and several of the young ladies—"

"Are quite attractive," Nicholas replied evenly. "I might be worried your eyesight was going if you *weren't* distracted. I should return shortly."

He begged Father Damon to excuse him, and then left the dais. In truth, he was happy to get away from his guests for a little while. He, too, wasn't used to being around so many nobles who weren't also trained fighters waiting for a battle or a tournament. These high-ranking men were the same sort who'd treated him with scornful disdain before he'd earned his castle, with the possible exception of young Audric, who seemed a quiet, modest fellow.

As Nicholas made his way through the tables and the cloying odor of perfume, he nodded greetings to his guests. Whatever he thought of them personally, they were all powerful and important in their way, and he wouldn't offend them if he could help it. He'd come perilously close with Lord Chesleigh. He should have had the good sense to stay by the stable wall and not let himself be intrigued by a bright-eyed woman sitting on a ramshackle cart.

The boisterous Scots thane was seated toward the back of the hall, in a place that should have told the man, if he had any perception at all, that his niece was unlikely to be the object of Nicholas's favor.

Where was *she?*

Perhaps she was tired from her journey, or from up-braiding him in front of his guests.

He should be angry about that. He'd certainly *been* angry when she'd first spoken, but he'd found it diffi-cult to stay angry when she faced him with that vivid, defiant fire in her eyes and spoke to him not with coy-ness or even deference, but as if she were his equal in pride, if nothing else. He'd noted the regal carriage of her head that would befit a queen, and that she looked more noble in her simple gown than any of the ladies in their fine clothes and costly jewels.

It was a pity her family was poor and unimportant, for she would likely prove worth the wooing.

Once outside, he drew in deep breaths of the fresh air slightly tainted by the smell of smoke from the Mid-summer bonfires. The courtyard was too far from the village for noise to reach him from the celebrations, yet he didn't doubt there was much merrymaking and many games being played, with far more good humor and joy than that shared by those feasting in his hall. His guests, though, weren't friends or well known to each other, so what else could he expect?

He passed by the kitchen and glanced over the fence into the garden. It was a fairly large one, and normally provided enough for the needs of his household. An apple tree, now finished blooming, stood in the center like a guardian, as he was guardian of the people on his estate, watching over them as he'd watched over his brother and sister.

Someone was beneath the apple tree—a woman, seated on what looked like an overturned bucket.

It was the Lady Riona, gazing up at the sky through the leafy branches as if seeking heavenly portents. Or perhaps she was unwell.

Determined to find out why she was alone in the garden, he opened the gate and stepped inside. She quickly turned to look at him, then simultaneously jumped up and cried a warning.

Sucking in his breath, he instinctively and immediately drew his sword from his scabbard and crouched into a defensive position, ready to strike his attackers.

Who weren't there, he realized as he swiveled on his heel, looking first one way, then the other.

His ire roused like his blood, he glared at the lady as he lowered his weapon and demanded, "Why did you cry out?"

She met his gaze squarely. "You were going to crush the rosemary."

The rosemary?

He looked down at the row of plants at his feet, then brought his stern gaze to bear on her. "I'm used to warnings in battle or tournaments to save me from bodily harm or even death, not the potential squashing of a plant. In future, a simple word of warning would do, not a cry as if there are assassins on the walls."

"If there had been an assassin, I assure you, my lord, I would have shouted louder. Forgive me for alarming you."

She made him sound like some timid girl who saw a mouse. "I reacted as I was trained to do," he said as he sheathed his sword.

"So did I," she replied, calm and cool and apparently not a whit embarrassed or ashamed that she'd made him think he was being attacked. "At home, the garden is one of my responsibilities."

"And do you stand guard over it like an anxious mother hen? Are you handy with a slingshot?"

"I was speaking in general terms, my lord. I take care of my uncle's household, and that means I have to prevent waste and loss wherever possible."

She was still remarkably calm in spite of his obvious anger, and he suddenly felt like he was tilting at a wooden dummy who neither feared nor favored him.

"Your uncle informed me that you run his household," he said, walking toward her, this time mindful of the rows of plants. "He also claims you've done so since you were twelve years old."

"That's quite true," she answered.

"My steward says yours is not a rich estate, so I presume you haven't many servants to supervise."

"No, we don't," she confessed without rancor or embarrassment, "so I do a good deal of the work myself and have little time for leisure. As I was sitting in your garden, I was enjoying having nothing to do."

He thought of his early years as a soldier for hire. How he'd cherished every peaceful moment, every hour he had free to do with as he pleased. Then he recalled how he'd wasted some of those hours in brothels and taverns, and the memories soured. "I feared you might be sick and wanting some fresh air, although the night air may be doing you more harm than good."

"I'm not used to such a crowd and the noise they make. I wanted to have some peace and quiet, that's all."

From the direction of the barracks, the soldiers who'd finished their meal started singing a bawdy ballad, loudly. The shouts of a very angry and frustrated cook chastising the spit boy, the scullery maid and incompetent servants in general filled the air. At the same time, the door at the entrance to the hall opened, and Sir James and Sir George came stumbling out, obviously drunk and laughing uproariously at some shared jest.

Nicholas raised a brow, just as he had that morning when he'd wanted to see what that boldly staring maidservant—who was no maidservant—would do. "This is your notion of peace and quiet?"

She laughed softly, a gentle rising sound of mirth that he found most pleasant. "It *was* quieter here than your hall, my lord."

Sir James and Sir George staggered toward the well near the kitchen. Not wanting to have to talk to them, hoping they'd go back to the hall or retire for the night, he moved closer to the apple tree and its shadows, and her. "I should go and give the guards the watchword for tonight."

"Ah yes, the very many guards."

What did she mean by that? "I worked and strived

for many years for what I possess, my lady, and I intend to keep it."

"Obviously."

He didn't appreciate her tone. "The Scots king himself gave me this estate. If you aren't pleased by that, you should complain to him."

"Somehow, I don't think he'd much care what Riona of Glencleith has to say about it."

She stayed where she was when he joined her beneath the trees. The movement of the leaves made the moonlight shadows dance across her face.

Wanting to see her more clearly, he inched closer. "Your family has no influence with the king?"

"My family has no influence with anybody," she freely admitted.

The only other woman who'd ever been so frankly honest with him was his sister—yet the thoughts he was having about Lady Riona were far from fraternal.

"How exactly did you guess who I was this morning?" he asked, no longer able to contain his curiosity. "Or did someone tell you when you arrived?"

Again, she answered without hesitation, as boldly as he'd come to expect. "You weren't doing any work, although there was plenty for the servants to do, and I saw how the other servants and guards responded when they saw you. I realized you must in a position of some power or command, and I remembered what my uncle said about you."

Which was? Nicholas wondered, even as he told

himself the opinion of an impoverished Scots thane was completely unimportant.

"Your uncle claims you're very clever," he noted, "and given that you were the only person to realize who I was this morning, I'm inclined to agree."

That brought a smile to her face.

She wasn't a beauty, like Lady Joscelind, or even what he'd call pretty, but there was a vibrancy to her features, a liveliness and spirit, that fascinated him, especially when she smiled. Her bold responses were far more interesting than any coy answers from Lady Joscelind and her kind, too.

"They also weren't expecting you to be dressed like a soldier and unloading baggage carts," she continued. "Neither was I. I'm curious, my lord, as to what prompted that act of subterfuge?"

He suddenly wasn't so proud of what he'd done, or why. "You heard me give my reason to Lady Joscelind. I wasn't properly attired."

She regarded him with such outright and unabashed skepticism, he blushed.

It had been many years since he'd felt his face warm like that, and he was glad they were in the shade of a tree at night. "You could say I was getting the lay of the land," he admitted.

Her eyes narrowed. "I thought you were looking for a wife, not a fight."

"I was sizing up the players before the game commences."

She frowned even more. "It may be a game or amusement to you, my lord, but it certainly isn't to these nobles and the women."

Her words startled him. He hadn't given a moment's thought to what the women involved would think of his plan—until now. Yet he wasn't about to confess that to this slip of a Scot, no matter how she looked at him. "I'm not doing this for my amusement. I require a wife, and I see nothing wrong with inviting suitable women to Dunkeathe and choosing the best among them."

"And you will decide who is 'best'?"

"Who better? She will become *my* bride, after all."

"Yes, she will."

He could decipher nothing in her eyes or voice to tell him whether she thought that a worthy goal. Yet after what had passed between them in the courtyard, he was sure she found him attractive.

Determined to prove that to himself at least, he sidled closer and dropped his voice to a lower, more intimate tone. "So, what exactly did your uncle say about me?"

"Clearly he told me enough to guess who you were."

"So now you will prevaricate, my lady?" he replied, inching closer, willing her to be attracted to him, to feel the same sort of desire that was waxing in him. "After the boldness you've displayed, I'm disappointed."

She straightened her shoulders and that bold fire once more kindled in her eyes. "Very well, my lord. Uncle Fergus said you were young, skilled at arms and handsome."

He'd have to thank the man. "And you, my lady? Now that you've met me, what do *you* think of me?"

"That you're one of the most arrogant men I've ever encountered."

It was like falling into a freezing stream.

Before he could think of a suitable response, the door to the kitchen banged open, and a shaft of light nearly caught them. With a gasp, Riona ran farther back into the garden, to a place by the inner curtain wall deep in shadows.

Not willing to let this conversation end with her condemnation, Nicholas followed her to her hiding place, standing directly in front of her so that she was blocked from sight by his body. She was breathing rapidly, her rising and falling breasts pressing against her gown.

Her hair smelled of spring blossoms, natural and wholesome.

His annoyance lessened.

A servant hurried past without seeing them, yet when he was gone, neither of them moved.

"You don't find me the least bit attractive or intriguing?" he whispered.

"No."

"I think you do."

She looked to either side, then tilted her head to regard him with unwavering steadiness. "I have no particular interest in you at all. We're here because my uncle was convinced we should come, and I didn't have the heart to refuse."

"I don't believe you."

"Which would be further proof of your arrogance, if I needed it."

"Then why have you stayed in the garden?"

"Because I saw no reason to flee. Should I be afraid of you, my lord?"

God's rood, she had an aggravating way of accusing him. "Of course you needn't fear me. I'm a knight sworn to protect women, not harm them."

"Perhaps you should remind some of your fellow Normans of that part of their oath."

He didn't want to discuss the vows of Norman knights. Despite her words, he wanted to take her in his arms and kiss her until she was dizzy. Or begged him to take her to his bed.

"What of your potential brides, my lord?" she continued. "What if you're seen here in the garden with me?' *I* don't care what your Norman friends think, but shouldn't you? They probably already question your judgment for allowing my uncle and me to stay. What will they conclude if they hear we've been together, and so intimately, too? And what of the ladies? They may think twice about offering themselves to you."

His annoyance kindled into anger. "This is my castle, and I will do what I will."

"Not if you're to get yourself the sort of bride you're after," she replied, apparently not a whit disturbed by his tone. "I can hear them now." She continued in a slow, haughty drawl, in an amazingly accurate imitation of Lady Joscelind. "And the fellow had the effrontery, the *audacity,* the sheer *bad taste,* to actually talk to that poor Scot and his niece—and be alone with her, too. Really, what *can* he be thinking, consorting with those outrageous barbarians?"

"My guests are well aware they're in Scotland when they're in Dunkeathe," he retorted.

"They may be able to tolerate staying in your fortress, but they have no respect for the Scots."

"*I* have," he replied, not willing to be lumped in with the other Norman noblemen. "My sister married one."

"I had heard, my lord, that you didn't approve of her marriage."

His jaw clenched before he answered. "In the beginning, I didn't. But I've come to admire and respect my brother-in-law and his people. I'm also grateful to your king, who gave me this estate. The woman I marry will come to respect the Scots, too," he finished firmly.

She still seemed unimpressed. "Yet I can't help noticing, for all this supposed respect you feel for the Scots, that you neither said nor did anything to demonstrate that respect to your Norman guests when my uncle and I were in your hall."

"Because I saw no need," Nicholas countered. "You were managing quite well on your own. As for your uncle, I treated him with no disrespect, even when he barged into my solar while I was discussing business with my steward."

Her gaze faltered at last. "You must forgive my uncle his enthusiasm. He means well and—"

"And I mean what I say," Nicholas interrupted. "I think the Scots are a fine people—for the most part. I don't forget that my sister's own brother-in-law betrayed her and her husband, and that there were many in their clan who sided with the traitor.

"I also don't forget all the years that I was poor and treated just as you have been, by Normans like my guests. Never think that because I say nothing, I do not see. That because I don't chastise my guests, I condone what they do.

"But God's blood, Riona, I've served and fought and struggled for too long to give a damn about gossip. If I want to linger in my garden on a moonlit night, I shall."

He took hold of her shoulders and pulled her close. "If I want to be alone with you and talk to you, I will. And if I want to kiss you…"

He captured her mouth with his. His lips moved over hers with torrid heat as the desire he'd been trying to contain burst free.

For a moment, she was stiff and unyielding.

For a moment, until she began to return his kiss with equal fervor. Her arms went around his waist, pulling him closer, enflaming his passion further.

She was bold in this, too, just as he'd imagined. Daring and more stimulating than any woman he'd ever kissed, her lips and body filled with the same fire as her eyes. He could feel the need coursing through her, as it was through him.

His tongue pressed her lips to open, then smoothly glided inside. Her embrace tightened.

Drunk with desire, aware only of his need to feel her warmth around him, and the throbbing surge of completion, he moved his hand to seek her breast.

The instant he touched her there, she broke the kiss and pushed him away. Her eyes wide with dismay, her lips swollen from their passion, she stared at him as if he were a loathsome thing.

Without a word, not even another condemnation, she shoved her way past him and marched out of the garden.

While Nicholas stood where he was, panting and frustrated. God's blood, he never should have entered the garden.

Restraint, indeed!

THE FIRST RAYS of the morning sun were lighting Riona's chamber when she heard a soft tapping at her door.

"Riona, my dear, are you still asleep?" Uncle Fergus called quietly as she shook her head as if to rid it of the remnants of her dreams.

What little sleep she'd had after fleeing the lord of Dunkeathe and his kiss had been restless and disturbed. First, she'd dreamt of a great black crow with beady eyes carrying her off in his clawed foot. Then a sleek black cat had stalked her through the hall and corridors and apartments of Dunkeathe. Then, finally, she'd dreamt of Sir Nicholas himself, tall and dark and inscrutable. He'd swept her up in his arms and carried her to his bed covered in a thick black fur. He'd laid her upon it and then...

"I'm awake," she said, opening the door to her uncle. She'd been awake and fully dressed since dawn.

He bounded into the room like an eager puppy and seemed to fairly bounce as he went to the window and threw open the wooden shutter to look out into the courtyard below.

"A fine morning, my dear," he declared, gesturing at the window. "That's a good sign, eh? Three days without rain, and warm to boot!"

How was she going to tell him that they had to leave? She couldn't reveal exactly why she wanted to leave so urgently. It was too humiliating. She should have had more restraint, more self-control, more pride.

Or maybe she'd been *too* proud. Otherwise, she wouldn't have lingered in the garden, thinking she could hold her own against the lord of Dunkeathe. She wouldn't have been so sure that her scorn for his Norman arrogance would protect her against the other feelings he aroused.

Because it hadn't.

And there was more to fear than losing her uncle's respect if she told him what had happened in the garden. Uncle Fergus might accuse Sir Nicholas of dishonorable conduct and challenge him to combat.

If Sir Nicholas accepted that challenge, her uncle would probably die.

"It's a fine day for a journey, too," she began.

"Journey? Oh, aye," Uncle Fergus answered absently, still looking out the window. "But all the women who want a chance for Sir Nicholas had to be here by St. John's Day."

"I was thinking, Uncle, that it would be a good day to go home."

When he didn't answer, she realized he hadn't heard her because his attention was focused on something outside. Wondering what it could be, she went to the window and followed his gaze to see Fredella bustling toward the apartments, and carrying a bucket.

Clasping her hands nervously, she tried again. "Uncle, I don't think we should stay in Dunkeathe after the way we've been treated."

Uncle Fergus stopped looking out the window to regard her with surprise. "Sir Nicholas has treated us very well," he said, nodding at the chamber, which was indeed quite comfortable, as was the bed.

If she hadn't had that disturbing encounter to relive over and over, if that same excited, yet shameful, heat hadn't coursed through her body every time she remembered that kiss, if she hadn't had those disturbing dreams, she would have slept very well indeed on the soft featherbed.

"I wasn't speaking of Sir Nicholas," she clarified. "His other guests have been very rude to us."

Uncle Fergus took her gently by the shoulders and gave her a kindly smile. "They're just jealous."

Shaking her head, Riona moved away. "They don't respect us, or our country. I don't want to stay here to be the object of their scorn."

Following her, Uncle Fergus gave her an incredulous look. "Who cares what those ignorant Normans think? We know better, and so does Sir Nicholas. He's been respectful, and he's related to the Mac Tarans."

He sat on her bed and patted a place beside him. "Come here, my girl, and listen to me," he said gravely.

When she joined him, he put his arm around her. She laid her head on his shoulder, as she'd done many times before when she was troubled or upset.

"Riona, the Normans are generally a sad lot," he said. "Conceited and arrogant and rude. Yet whether we like it or not, because of our king and the rebellions he's had to deal with, they're here to stay. That doesn't mean we have to like them, of course, and who could? But there are a few worth getting to know, ones worth respecting, ones who could help Scotland. Sir Nicholas is one such Norman. As for the rest…" He blew out his breath as if snuffing a candle and waved his hand. "Ignore them, as I do. Why give them the satisfaction of having even that little bit of power over you?"

"So you *have* noticed what they were doing?"

Uncle Fergus laughed. "How could I not? I'm not blind or deaf."

"Doesn't that make you want to go back to Glencleith?"

"Not a bit of it. Just the opposite. I'll not let a Norman think he can sneer me out of a place. Besides, they only make themselves look foolish and petty with those antics, and I'm sure a man like Sir Nicholas isn't impressed."

"No, he—" She fell silent, lest she have to explain how she happened to know how Sir Nicholas felt about scornful, derisive Norman nobles.

"Now cheer up, Riona," Uncle Fergus said with a merry grin as he lowered his fatherly arm and got to his feet. "Don't fuss about the Normans and their haughty ways. Any Scot's worth a hundred of them any day, as Sir Nicholas has to know. I'll wager he's sorry he wasn't born a Scot himself."

Riona wondered if Sir Nicholas was *ever* sorry, about anything.

"Now come along, my beauty. We mustn't be late for mass. Then we'll see what sort of things these Normans eat to break the fast."

Although she wasn't in any great hurry to be anywhere near the dark, devilishly attractive and seductive lord of Dunkeathe, Riona could think of no reason she couldn't go to mass, short of feigning illness, and it was too late for that.

AT NEARLY the same time, Lord Chesleigh's daughter sat in front of her dressing table, finishing her toilette in no calm and placid frame of mind.

"I don't know why we bothered to come here," she declared to her father, her voice crisp and shrill.

Lord Chesleigh frowned as he came farther into the large chamber full of chests and opened boxes, their contents spilling onto the floor. "What's the matter now?"

"Don't you know? We've been made to look like fools!"

"When have I ever looked like a fool?"

"When we arrived!" she cried, smacking her palm down on her dressing table, rattling and shaking the small jars of costly perfumes and unguents and secret little concoctions to add whatever bloom might be missing from her cheeks and lips. "When our host tricked us into thinking he was nothing but a servant. When he didn't immediately reveal himself, and apologize."

Her father regarded her coldly. "There's no need for this display of temper, Joscelind, and certainly not to me. Sir Nicholas is well aware of who we are and that we're not fools. Why else do you think he did as you asked? Why else do you think he apologized? We are most certainly going to stay here and you're going to marry Sir Nicholas."

"He's just a minor knight in Scotland," she protested, rising to face her father. "You always promised me I would marry a courtier."

"Use the mind God gave you, Joscelind," her father replied with a hint of pique as he crossed his arms over his long moss-green tunic and the thick gold chain that dangled around his neck. "Sir Nicholas will never be a minor *anything* for long. He proved himself far more than a *minor* mercenary. Are you blind to this fortress and the men he commands? With his experience in battle and his wealth, Sir Nicholas is going to be important wherever he happens to live."

"Surely there has to be somebody in London I could marry instead, in Henry's court."

"I don't know what cause you have to complain. Isn't he young and handsome? I saw the way you looked at him."

"But what about that Scot?" Joscelind flung the last word at him like a curse. "I think he actually *preferred* her to me. *Me!*" She stamped her delicate foot. "I won't stay here to be humiliated!"

Her father shrugged. "You could find them in bed together, and it wouldn't mean a thing except that he's a man and she's a whore—which wouldn't surprise me in the least, considering the breed she comes from."

Joscelind raised her chin. "If she's the sort of woman to appeal to Sir Nicholas, I don't want *him*. I do have my pride, Father."

Anger flaring on his face, Lord Chesleigh covered the distance between them in two long strides. He grabbed her arms and held her in a viselike grip. "Listen to me, girl. You're going to stay here and you're going to do everything you can to get that man to marry you. I haven't hired the finest teachers, and given you all these clothes and jewels for *your* pleasure. You were raised to marry the man I choose, and by God, so you shall!"

Joscelind's eyes filled with tears from the pain. "I want my husband to be of use to you," she whimpered as he released her. "How can he be if he lives in this wilderness?"

"Because a man who can lead an army out of Scotland may one day have the chance to seize the kingdom. Henry's angering the English nobles by favoring his wife's French relatives, and one day, he'll go too far. There'll be a rebellion."

Joscelind regarded her father with a mixture of hope, greed and awe. "You think Nicholas may become the king of England?"

"Not Nicholas," her father declared, annoyed. "*Me.* Nicholas can provide men and arms, and he knows how to lead men into battle, so he'll be a very useful ally. If he's my son-in-law, so much the better, for his fate will be tied to mine whether he wills it or no, and he'll have to do his best to see that I prevail.

"So, while he may seek to sport with that Scotswoman, it's not who the man beds that's important. It's who he weds. He'll marry you, Joscelind, if you make an effort and don't act like a shrew in front of him. You're the most beautiful woman here, and I'm willing to pay a considerable dowry. Sir Nicholas must also be aware of my influence at court."

"But if he prefers Lady Riona—"

"I have ways to deal with anyone who gets in the way of my plans. Your part is to do all you can to win him, or I'll marry you to some rich old man and be done with you."

Joscelind blinked back tears. "Yes, Father," she whispered. "I will."

CHAPTER FIVE

RIONA STOOD BESIDE her uncle at the back of the small chapel. It wasn't a large building, yet it had a very beautiful and surely expensive window of colored glass depicting St. Michael, the warrior angel, winged and carrying a sword. In a niche at the right side stood a lovely statue of the Madonna cradling her infant son. The altar cloth was silk, and the candlesticks silver.

Riona suspected some of those attending mass were there because it was expected or they felt the need to impress their host. Sir George stood as close to the door as possible, as if he wanted to make a speedy exit, and Sir Percival yawned prodigiously throughout the service.

Some of the ladies were probably making petitions to Heaven and whatever saints might be listening to be selected as Sir Nicholas's bride. Riona, however, prayed for an end to the lust Sir Nicholas inspired within her, and the strength to keep her distance, as she should have done last night.

Her gaze strayed to their host, who was wearing a different black tunic of coarser wool. He was at the front of the chapel, beside Lady Joscelind and her father.

No wonder she'd dreamed of a black cat, for once again, he stood nearly motionless, watchful and attentive as the elderly priest led them through the service.

Uncle Fergus nudged her. "There's Fredella," he whispered.

Startled, and yet happy to have her wayward thoughts interrupted, she followed his gaze. Fredella was standing to the left of Lady Eleanor, who looked as fresh as a spring blossom in a gown of bright blue samite. Her cousin was with them.

Fredella looked over her shoulder, smiled and blushed when she saw Uncle Fergus, who lifted his hand and waggled his fingers in a shy sort of wave, as if they were two youngsters instead of a mature man and woman.

Riona looked down to hide her smile as the holy service came to an end. It had been over ten years since Uncle Fergus's wife had died. He had grieved a long time, as had all who'd known the kind, gentle Muireall, and she wouldn't begrudge him another chance for happiness. Neither, she was sure, would Kenneth, especially if he thought his father's new wife would curb his overly generous hospitality.

"Thank God that's over," Sir George muttered in a voice loud enough for everyone around him to hear. "I'm parched."

Lady Eloise, who stood beside him, gave him a warning look.

"Last night Fredella said to wait for her after the mass this morning," Uncle Fergus whispered to Riona. "She'll bring Eleanor to meet us, if she can get her away from that Percival. Let's go over by this pillar, so the vain puppy doesn't see us."

As they moved, the lord of Dunkeathe started down the aisle toward the door, the sister of the Duke of Ansley on one arm and Lady Joscelind on the other, followed by their male relatives, and Sir Nicholas's steward. It was quite clear neither lady was precisely pleased with this arrangement, and yet each was too outwardly polite and inwardly intent on keeping his favor to show it.

Then, suddenly, he looked at Riona.

Holy Mary, Mother of God, it was as if no time at all had passed since last night. As if he was still alone with her in the garden, seducing her with his voice and his eyes and his incredibly passionate kiss.

To her chagrin, he strolled closer, albeit still with the other two ladies on his arm. "Good morning, my lady, Mac Gordon," he said to them. "I hope you slept well."

Did he think she was going to blush and stammer and look away?

The blushing she couldn't help, but it signified the heat of anger, not embarrassment, as she faced the man who'd kissed her in the garden. "I did," she lied. "And you, my lord?"

"Not very well," he said. "There are too many distractions in Dunkeathe these days."

He smiled at both women before looking back at her.

"Perhaps an apothecary can suggest a potion," Riona replied.

"Aye, that's the trick!" Uncle Fergus cried. "I know one." He rubbed his beard and ruminated. "Well, I used to." He grinned and shrugged his shoulders. "But now that I think of it, it tasted like old boots."

Sir Nicholas smiled, although there was no warmth or pleasure in his eyes. "Then I shall forego it."

The ladies at his sides shifted impatiently.

Sir Nicholas inclined his head in farewell and escorted the ladies from the chapel.

"Now isn't he a fine fellow?" Uncle Fergus jovially declared as they watched them go. "Fine manners, too. And he likes you, Riona. That's obvious."

But why? Riona thought with displeasure. Why did Sir Nicholas pay her any attention? If it was only to bed, that was hardly a compliment.

"Here comes Sir Percival," she murmured, nodding as that nobleman, who was deep in discussion with the Comte D'Ortelieu, sauntered down the aisle. Lady Eleanor and Fredella moved toward the statue of the Holy Mother.

Sir Percival caught her eye. Before she could move away, he came to a halt and smiled with such smug satisfaction, it was all she could do not to curl her lip. "Good morning, my lady. Don't you look fetching today."

Clearly he seemed to think she would be pleased by

his flattery. No doubt he was the sort of man who believed any woman should be delighted by his notice.

"Thank you," she replied without an ounce of enthusiasm.

He waited expectantly, until he finally seemed to comprehend that she didn't intend to say anything more.

With a slight scowl, he turned away from Riona and started walking toward the door again. "Anyway, D'Ortelieu, as I was saying, I told that cobbler I was never going to pay for such shoddy work and he should thank God I didn't have him arrested."

"Wheest, what a *gomeral,*" Uncle Fergus muttered as Percival and the comte went out the door. "Looking at him, it's hard to believe the Normans ever conquered England." He shook his head, then grinned at Riona. "Now that he's gone, let's go meet Lady Eleanor."

Riona gladly joined him as he headed for the two women.

She expected Lady Eleanor to smile shyly and blush and not meet her gaze, like the timid girl she seemed in the yard and in the hall last night. Instead, Lady Eleanor turned to them with a friendly smile and listened with pleasure in her bright green eyes as Fredella made the introductions.

"I'm so pleased to meet you," Eleanor said to them both. She turned to Riona. "I've wanted to meet you since I saw you in the courtyard. You looked as if you felt as out of place as I did."

"Out of place? Nonsense!" Uncle Fergus cried as he slipped his arm through Fredella's. "You both belong here, although only one of you can have Sir Nicholas. I hope you're not going to get to fighting over him, because he's bound to choose my niece if he's got an ounce of sense. But cheer up, Lady Eleanor. He's got a brother, I hear, just as handsome if not so rich. Henry, I think his name is."

When Eleanor blushed and stared at her feet, Riona decided it might be better to leave her boisterous uncle with Fredella and speak to Eleanor alone.

"I've never seen a stained-glass window before," she remarked, nodding at it. "I'd very much like to see it up close."

"Yes, so would I," Eleanor swiftly agreed. "What about you, Fredella?"

"Oh, I've admired it already," she said, casting a coy glance at Uncle Fergus, who spoke without taking his eyes from her face. "You two go along and admire it all you like. We'll wait here."

Riona didn't hesitate to head for the altar, and the window behind it.

"Your uncle is a very friendly fellow," Eleanor noted as they regarded the depiction of the archangel in a flowing blue robe. "Fredella had nothing but good things to say about him, and I confess I thought she must be exaggerating. Now I see she spoke the truth."

"He can be a bit overwhelming at times," Riona replied. "But he's the kindest, sweetest, most generous man I know."

"I can easily believe it. He's like Fredella, who's been a mother to me since my own died." She gave Riona a sheepish smile. "Although I must confess, I wish Fredella would stop treating me as if I were six years old. No doubt she told you I was too shy to make your acquaintance myself?"

"Aye."

Eleanor wryly shook her head. "I was very shy when I was little. I used to hide whenever we had visitors. She still thinks I'm going to conceal myself in a cupboard when I see anyone new or unfamiliar."

"I suppose we must accept the fancies of those who've raised us. Uncle Fergus thinks I'm the most wonderful girl in the world and can't understand that everyone may not share that opinion."

"I wish my guardian was like your uncle," Eleanor said wistfully. "All Percival cares about is that I marry someone who's rich, or popular at court—somebody he can boast about being related to—and the sooner, the better."

"He could certainly brag about being related to Sir Nicholas."

"That he could, and he would. I forget how many tournaments Sir Nicholas has won and all the prizes he's earned, but Percival could tell you. You should have heard him on the journey here. I thought I'd scream or go mad."

She blushed and looked away "I fear I've said too much. I suppose I should be grateful to Percival."

"I don't know about that, if he thinks of you as merely something to be rid of, and a way to add to his own reputation," Riona replied. Once again she was grateful for her relative's kindness and sent up a silent prayer of thanks.

Eleanor sighed with relief. "I thought you'd understand, although I probably shouldn't be so outspoken to someone I've just met."

"I probably shouldn't have spoken to Sir Nicholas in the hall the way I did last night, either," Riona confessed.

"Oh, I admired you for that!" Eleanor exclaimed. "I wouldn't have been able to open my mouth in front of all those people, especially with Sir Nicholas looking at me."

"I don't think anyone else shared your admiration."

"Fredella did."

"Well, that makes two—three, if we count my uncle."

"Four. Sir Nicholas didn't seem upset with you."

Perhaps he'd had notions of seduction even then.

"I had no idea he spoke anything other than French. That was one thing Percival *didn't* tell me."

"Perhaps he didn't know." Not particularly keen to talk about their host, Riona glanced back at Uncle Fergus and Fredella. They were laughing and whispering, their heads very close together. "I hate to part them, but if you don't get to the hall, your cousin might start to wonder where you are."

"You're right. I do hope we can spend some more time together, though, in spite of Percival."

"I'd like that, too," Riona answered, meaning it. She hadn't expected to find a friend in Dunkeathe, but she liked Eleanor.

And perhaps having a friend would keep Sir Nicholas away.

"JOSCELIND'S paternal grandmother was the eldest daughter of the Earl of Millborough," Lord Chesleigh said, continuing his long recitation of the ancestry of his family as he rode beside Nicholas several days later.

They, and the rest of the hunting party, were riding through a grassy meadow on the northernmost hill around Dunkeathe. Nicholas and Lord Chesleigh were trailed by Sir Percival and a somewhat sober Sir George. The rest of the noble gentlemen, save for the two who had already departed with their female relatives and various retainers, came after, along with servants to carry the animals they killed. Ahead were beaters, sent to rouse the game, whether pheasants, or grouse or, if they were fortunate, a stag.

Unfortunately, it seemed as if every bird or animal had somehow gotten word of their approach and fled.

Perhaps it was the noise from the back of the group. Mounted on one of Dunkeathe's mares, Fergus Mac Gordon was regaling the servants with the tale of a hunting mishap involving a dog, a dirk and a boot. Say what one would about the boisterous Scot, he was entertaining, and he'd been entertaining the men at the back of their party ever since they'd left the castle.

"Joscelind's maternal grandmother was the daughter of the Duke of Bridgewater," Lord Chesleigh droned on, "and therefore related by blood to the king himself."

"On the wrong side of the blanket," Sir Percival interjected, apparently as tired of Lord Chesleigh's recitation as Nicholas.

They'd been cooped up inside Dunkeathe by rain and fog for the past three days. When this day dawned clear, Nicholas had immediately proposed a hunt. That wasn't his favorite pastime—his youth having given him little time to indulge in sport and he still couldn't quite shake the notion that he had more important things to do—yet he was as eager to ride out of Dunkeathe as the rest of the men who had quickly accepted his invitation. His female guests, led by Lady Joscelind, declined because the ground was too muddy.

He wasn't sorry. It was wearying trying to be pleasant to all the ladies without making any one of them think they were too far in his favor.

Lady Riona had already left the hall when he'd proposed the hunt, and he could guess why. She didn't want to be anywhere near him—which was just as well, because he couldn't afford to be anywhere near her, either. Bedding a thane's niece, no matter how tempting, and with no promise of marriage, would surely cause a great deal of animosity among the Scots. Therefore, he intended to avoid her as much as possible. He would have sent her home the day after that memorable kiss, except that it might cause grumbling among the Scots, too.

"Wasn't Lady Joscelind's grandmother the duke's dairymaid, Lord Chesleigh?" Sir Percival inquired.

Lord Chesleigh frowned and twisted in his saddle to regard Sir Percival with a cold and angry eye. "William the Conqueror was a bastard, which proves that blood will show itself."

"Oh, indeed, it will," Percival said with a mocking smile. "Fortunately, my family carries no such taint."

"Would you insult my family?" demanded Lord Chesleigh.

"Not your entire family," Percival retorted as his steed pranced nervously. "Just your wife's mother."

Nicholas nudged his gelding between them before challenges could be issued. "Gentlemen, please. I'll make my choice, as difficult as it's going to be, based on the lady's own merits."

"Here, here!" Sir George piped up, wiping his lips with the back of his gloved hand, having just taken another gulp from the wineskin he'd brought. "If it's merit you want, my lord, you couldn't do better than Eloise. She's a good girl, she is. Not the most lively you'll ever meet, but who'd want a lively wife? That way leads to trouble." He made a sodden wink. "Take it from me. A lively woman may be entertaining at night, but in the day, it's quarrel, quarrel, quarrel."

Thinking of one bold, lively woman, Nicholas was inclined to think that the nights might provide ample compensation. That kiss—

He commanded himself not to think about that kiss.

"Yes, the apple rarely falls far from the tree," Lord Chesleigh remarked, speaking quietly so that Sir George wouldn't hear. "I understand Sir George's arguments with his wife were legendary."

"I certainly wouldn't want an argumentative wife," Nicholas agreed. "I require peace in my household."

"Of course you do," Lord Chesleigh said. "After your years of combat, you wish to enjoy your well-earned prosperity. And I'm sure you won't want to be troubled by any domestic strife. Joscelind is well able to run a household, my lord. She'll keep a tight rein on your servants, and your purse strings, too."

"He makes it sound like a man wants a second steward for a wife," Percival declared behind them. "Can you see Sir Nicholas asking his wife for money?" He changed to a mocking, high-pitched tone. "Please, my dear, may I have a few pennies for a drink with my friends?"

"He doesn't want a girl barely out of the nursery, either," Lord Chesleigh said through clenched teeth. "He surely requires a woman who can manage the household without having to ask about every little thing."

"I suppose that would be the one advantage to marrying an *older* woman," Percival said, his voice full of venom, and as if Lady Joscelind was a crone instead of a woman who, granted, was somewhat older than most when they wed.

Lady Riona was even older than Joscelind, Nicholas guessed, yet he couldn't think of her as "old." As for being competent, everything he'd seen in Dunkeathe since her arrival told him she surely would be. The servants were always pleasant, yet deferential, when they served her, and hurried to do anything she asked of them. He'd overheard that maidservant with the mole on her breast whose name he could never remember tell another about some suggestions Lady Riona made regarding the storing of the linens, and it was clear both maidservants were impressed. Even some of the Saxon guards, not normally the most mannerly of men, bowed and touched their spears to their helmets in salute when she passed by.

"Speaking as a man, I prefer youth and beauty in a bride," Sir Percival declared. "Wisdom will come soon enough."

"Some never achieve that state," Lord Chesleigh growled, staring straight ahead.

"Is that comment a reference to me?" Percival demanded.

Maybe suggesting this hunt had been a bad idea. At least in the hall, the men could amuse themselves with chess or games of chance, and there were the ladies to keep them on their best behavior.

A horn sounded.

Twice.

"A stag!" Percival cried, digging his spurred heels into his horse's sides.

Whether he enjoyed hunting or not, the prospect of a chase set Nicholas's blood pumping furiously and as Percival's horse leapt into a gallop, Nicholas spurred his own.

When they reached the beaters, the men excitedly pointed toward a dip in the ground of a bracken-filled meadow. "That way, my lord!" they shouted over the barking and baying of the hounds who were charging toward the edge of the depression. "He's in the gully! He's a big 'un!"

The stag leaped into view. It fairly flew over the open and rocky ground, the hounds blurs of brown and black as they gave chase toward a rocky valley.

The valley narrowed and ended in a sheer rock wall, where a little fall fed a spring. The stag, cornered, turned to face the hounds and the men who came after, led by Nicholas and Percival.

The well-trained dogs didn't attack, but stopped where they were, growling and crouching, some crawling on their bellies in excited anticipation while they awaited another whistle from the huntsmen.

Majestic, powerful and trapped, the stag stood motionless save for the quivering of its flanks. Nicholas knew it would fight to the death, using its great antlers as weapons, yet death would be its ultimate end. The dogs and men were too many, and the stag had no escape.

What sport was there in this? It was like slaughtering unarmed men, something he had always refused to do, no matter who commanded him.

What did any of these noblemen know of being cornered, trapped by circumstances so that all you could do was stand and fight, or die? Had any of them ever known true fear? Had any of them ever smelled the stench of terror that fills a man's nostrils as he waits upon a battlefield?

Had any one of them ever known hunger or thirst, or deprivation? He doubted it, and he doubted their female relatives had, either.

Not that he wanted to think of women suffering, but how could such women ever understand him and the fears that haunted him in the small hours of the night, when he awoke from dreams of battle, and sleep was lost to him? They wouldn't be able to comprehend the dread that what he had achieved could be taken away, and not just by death. It could be revoked with the stroke of one man's quill—the king's signature on a piece of parchment. And then he'd be as he was before: a penniless soldier with only a noble name and his father's sword to call his own.

As the huntsman gave the signal for the dogs to attack, Nicholas turned his mount away. He would go back to Dunkeathe and leave the others to deal with their prize.

Riding back through the excited mob, he didn't see Fergus Mac Gordon among the men or servants.

Perhaps the fellow had decided to return to Dunkeathe. Maybe he was already safely in the hall, drinking his host's wine and loudly praising his brown-haired niece, whom Percival would no doubt consider too old to be a bride.

The Scot hadn't seemed all that competent on his borrowed horse. Maybe when the call had sounded and the chase had begun, he'd been unable to keep up with rest.

Or perhaps something worse had happened. It could be that he'd fallen from his horse and was lying injured on the ground.

Or dead upon the bracken.

CHAPTER SIX

NICHOLAS IMMEDIATELY kicked his horse into a trot and rode back toward Dunkeathe. He dreaded finding a horse limping, its reins dangling, near a broken, bloody body.

He was about halfway home when he heard a familiar voice call out, "My lord!"

Relieved, he pulled his horse to a halt, to see Fergus Mac Gordon quite well and waving at him, standing in a farmer's yard beside a stone enclosure. Beside him, a peasant shifted his feet uneasily. The mare from Dunkeathe, tied to a tree beside the stone cottage, contentedly munched grass as if it had been there for some time.

Nicholas rode toward them, scattering several flapping, clucking chickens and one very indignant goose as he entered the yard.

"You've got to look at this lamb!" Mac Gordon cried when Nicholas dismounted. "I've never seen such fine fleece!"

It was only then that Nicholas realized the man was cradling a lamb as another might a child. Penned nearby, an ewe watched and bleated.

The peasant, a young man with messy brown hair and wearing simple homespuns, quickly tugged his forelock and stepped out of the way when Nicholas reached them.

"Feel that," Mac Gordon said, holding out the little white animal which didn't struggle at all, as if it felt quite safe where it was.

Nicholas dutifully ran his hand over the lamb's back.

"Nay, not like that," Mac Gordon laughingly chided. With his free hand, and not pulling on it hard enough to cause any pain, the Scot took a handful of the fleece. "Grab it."

Nicholas did as he was told. The fleece was soft, which wasn't unexpected, but otherwise, he didn't notice anything remarkable.

Mac Gordon gave him a beaming smile and fondled the head of the lamb as if it was a puppy. "Have you ever felt anything like that, eh?"

Nicholas still wasn't sure why the man was so excited. But then, what did he know of sheep? What did he care, except that his share of the sale of the wool brought him income, and their meat fed him and his household? "It's fleece," he said with a shrug.

"Wheest, man!" Mac Gordon cried, turning and letting the lamb loose in the pen. The little animal trotted over to its mother and immediately began to drink.

"That lamb's fleece is thicker than any fleece *I've* ever felt, and hardly a bristle in it," Mac Gordon declared. He grinned at the peasant. "Thomas here knows what he's got, if his master doesn't. That fleece'll make some fine wool. And it's not just the fleece—look at the haunches on him, too! Now that's what I call mutton!"

The Scot clapped his hand on the peasant's shoulders, as if they were the best of friends. "Sheep like this don't come by accident. This clever fellow's been doing some breeding, haven't you, Thomas?"

Thomas's face reddened, and reddened more when Nicholas addressed him in the tone he usually used with foot soldiers. "Is this true, Thomas?"

"Come, man, admit your genius!" the Scot exclaimed. "For genius it is and no mistake."

"Aye, my lord, I've been trying," Thomas said quietly, not looking Nicholas in the eye. "I let the sheep loose on the hills, like always, but I was careful to keep the ewes and rams I thought had better fleece and more meat."

"And there's more like it, he says," Fergus Mac Gordon said. "If that's so, you've got something more precious than gold or silver, my lord, for once metal's out of the ground, it's gone. Sheep like this will keep you rich for years."

Nicholas looked at the lamb again. Could it really be so important? And if it was, could that be the answer to his financial woes?

Perhaps eventually, but not this year. Lambs weren't shorn.

"What would you say to letting me bring some of my ewes here for breeding, eh?" Mac Gordon asked.

Nicholas thought of his nearly empty coffers. "You would have to pay for that."

And so might others—a source of income he'd never anticipated.

The little man's face fell. "How much?"

"My steward and I will have to discuss that." Nicholas glanced at Thomas, who nervously shifted his feet. "Thomas would levy it, and a portion would come to me as a tithe."

Thomas looked as if he'd just won a tournament.

"I'm sure Thomas will be reasonable," he added.

"Oh, yes, my lord, yes!" the young man cried. "Very reasonable."

Mac Gordon's face lit up again. "Then it's a bargain, and I'll tell my son when I go back home. He'll be keen to come when he hears about these animals. A fine eye for wool, he has, like his father," the Scot finished with a laugh.

"Perhaps on our way back to Dunkeathe, we can talk more about sheep," Nicholas said to the smiling Mac Gordon.

"I'd be delighted, my lord. Anything you want to know about fleece and wool—" He smacked himself on the chest. "I'm your man."

"Obviously you know a good deal more about them than I do," Nicholas admitted.

"Well, I'd wager you could teach me a thing or two about defending a castle," Mac Gordon answered as they strolled back to their horses.

Nicholas nodded as he looked around the farmyard. It was neat and well tended. This Thomas was clearly a conscientious fellow, as well as clever. Yet no woman or children had appeared in the door of the cottage, and he saw no sign of their presence.

After swinging into the saddle, he rode over to Thomas, who was still standing by the fence. "Do you live here alone, Thomas?"

"Aye, my lord, since my father died in January."

Nicholas had a vague memory of Robert mentioning taking a ram as a heriot from a shepherd. "Was a ram the heriot?"

"Aye, my lord. The sire of some of these lambs, he was."

"I shall see that it's returned to you, so that you can breed more of these excellent sheep."

"Thank you, my lord," the young man said, bowing.

"You can expect a visit from Robert Martleby in the next few days."

"Yes, my lord."

"You'll also go to all the other farms on my estate and select the sheep that you think are particularly fine. These will be added to your flock, as well, and I shall make you the head shepherd of Dunkeathe."

Thomas looked as if he might swoon, but gladly so. "Th-thank you, my lord," he stammered. "Thank you very much!"

"I believe in rewarding those who serve me well, Thomas. Remember that," he said as he turned his horse toward the gate.

Fergus Mac Gordon was just getting settled in his

saddle. It was quite clear the man rarely rode a horse, or hadn't in some time—another sign of his poverty, if Nicholas needed it.

"Farewell, Thomas."

The farmer bowed so low, his forehead nearly touched the ground. "Farewell, my lord."

After the Scot managed to get his horse under control, he came alongside Nicholas.

"So, my lord," Fergus said, beaming, "what else do you want to know about sheep?"

"OH, ISN'T THAT PRETTY!" Eleanor cried as she caught sight of some fabric in a tradesman's stall.

Riona smiled, as pleased as Eleanor to be out of the castle on this fine day after being forced to keep to the hall and her chamber by the rain and fog, as well as the dread of encountering Sir Nicholas. She had no idea what he might do or say if she did, and she didn't want to find out.

Fortunately, he'd kept his distance since that morning in the chapel. Even more fortunately, Eleanor never wanted to talk about their host, probably because both of them were ostensibly here for the same reason—to try to become his bride.

She joined Eleanor in examining the lovely, soft dark green wool interwoven with a bright red. At home she rarely had time for such activity. Most of her dealings with merchants were for practical necessities, like food or drink. "Nobody weaves as well as a Scot," she said proudly.

"If this is an example of Scots craftsmanship, I agree," Eleanor replied. "I hope Percival will let me buy it."

"Is your mistress going to purchase anything today?" the merchant asked Riona in Gaelic, smiling but uncertain.

Since she and Eleanor had been speaking French, it was no wonder he was confused, and if he thought she was Eleanor's maidservant, what else could she expect, given the difference in their clothing?

Riona genially replied in Gaelic. "We think your fabric is wonderful. The lady hopes her cousin will purchase it for her."

The tradesman's face fell slightly, but he kept smiling. "Oh, aye? And who might her cousin be?"

"Sir Percival de Surlepont. If an extremely well-dressed young nobleman comes to you looking for this plaid, that will be Sir Percival."

"He's the bonny fellow in bright green sarcenet who went hunting this morning?"

"Aye, that's him."

"Oh, Riona, look at this, too!" Eleanor exclaimed. "I've never seen such a lovely deep blue. How does he do it?"

Riona turned again to the merchant. "She likes the blue fabric, too. She wants to know how you get such a fine color."

The merchant's smile became genuine, and his eyes sparkled with a craftsman's pride. "Ach, you'll have me tell all my secrets?"

"Only if you care to share."

"Well, for the sake of your bright eyes and the lady's beauty," he said, giving her a wink. "Welsh blackberries."

"Ah, *Welsh* blackberries?"

He nodded. "They're the best for that dark blue."

"I'll remember that."

A group of children ran past. They halted near the stocks, where a man sat on a stool, his head and wrists held fast in the wooden slats. A boy about ten, with brown hair and freckles, cried out, "Murderer!" and pelted him with an apple core. Others followed suit, with mud.

Their victim raised his head and snarled at them, until they ran away.

"Is he really a murderer?" Riona asked the merchant, wondering if that was so, why he was only in the stocks.

"He killed the lad's dog a fortnight ago. It got to barking one night and that drunken lout beat it to death. Sir Nicholas ordered him to be in the stocks for two months, then to leave Dunkeathe and never come back."

Riona tried not to betray any overt interest in the lord of Dunkeathe or his justice. "That seems harsh."

"Sir Nicholas is a hard man, but he keeps the peace," the tradesman replied with approval.

She was quite sure Sir Nicholas and his soldiers were capable of maintaining order, which probably explained the merchant's admiration.

"Most noblemen wouldn't care two straws for a peasant boy's dog, but he did," the merchant continued. "He treated the boy as serious as if he was a grown man when the lad spoke up at the hall-moot. Still, nobody really thought Sir Nicholas would punish one of his own men over it."

In spite of her previous thoughts, Riona couldn't help being impressed, too. "That's one of his men?"

"Aye, an archer from the castle."

Riona recalled what she'd seen of Sir Nicholas when he was with his soldiers. He was generally grim, unsmiling, fully the commander. He seemed so with the servants, too, so she'd been dismissing him as simply a harsh, unyielding tyrant. Clearly, he did have some sympathy for those beneath him.

It was a pity he didn't show that side of himself more often. It would hardly cost him any respect, for she doubted there was a person who met the lord of Dunkeathe who wasn't in awe of his power and accomplishments. Even she—

She realized Eleanor was waiting and didn't understand what they were saying. She briefly recounted what the merchant had told her.

"His own soldier—and over a dog?" Eleanor said, her eyes wide.

"I was surprised, too," Riona confessed.

She wondered if Eleanor would reveal what she thought of Sir Nicholas now, but instead her friend gave a longing look at the lovely wool, sighed and said, "I suppose we should be getting back to the castle. The men may already be finished with the hunt and I don't think Percival will be pleased if he finds out I was in the village."

"I daresay Uncle Fergus and Fredella will be curious about where we went," Riona remarked as they started toward the castle. "That's if they've even noticed we're gone."

Eleanor smiled as they walked across the green, veering well away from the stocks. "I doubt they've noticed anything much at all, except each other."

"Uncle Fergus seems very taken with her."

"And she with him. Nothing would make me happier than to see Fredella happily married," Eleanor replied. She flushed and slid a wary glance at her companion. "Although your uncle is a nobleman and she's only a servant."

Riona hastened to relieve her of any worries on that score. "I'm sure his intentions are honorable. Uncle Fergus would no more be dishonorable than the sun would cease to rise. It simply isn't in his nature."

"Yet marriage between a thane and a servant? Is that not frowned on in Scotland?"

"Uncle Fergus says it's love that matters. He grieved deeply for my aunt when she died, but that was many years ago. If Fredella makes him happy, I wouldn't raise any objections. Neither will his son, I'm sure," she added sincerely.

Indeed, she was sure Kenneth wouldn't complain

any more than she would. They both loved Uncle Fergus too much to protest his choice of bride, whether she was highborn or low, rich or poor. "You won't mind losing your servant?"

"Not if her new circumstances are her choice and make her happy."

"What about Percival?"

"I don't think he even realizes Fredella's alive, most of the time. I doubt he'll notice if she leaves. I wouldn't ask him to find me another maidservant, though. I'd find one myself. I wouldn't trust his judgment."

Neither would Riona. "Then it's settled between us," she said, smiling at her young friend. "If they want to get married, we won't stand in their way."

Eleanor laughed merrily and so did Riona. She'd never expected to be friends with a Norman, but Eleanor was a kind, sweet girl who already seemed like the younger sister she'd never had.

"Riona!"

They both looked over their shoulders, to see Uncle Fergus and Sir Nicholas riding toward them. She would have feared Uncle Fergus had fallen and been hurt, except that he was smiling and seemed very happy.

Seated on his great black gelding, his back straight as a spear, the lord of Dunkeathe looked every inch the overlord he was, even though he was wearing a plain brown leather tunic, dark woolen breeches and scuffed boots. Nobody who saw him could doubt that he was a formidable man, and that the sword at his side had been used many times.

Nobody who saw him now would probably guess he could sound so seductive, or kiss with such—

"The hunt must be over," Eleanor said, a hint of panic in her voice.

"Maybe," Riona said uncertainly. "I wonder where the others are?"

"I don't know, but Percival's probably not far behind," Eleanor said as she gathered up her skirts.

That was likely true; Percival stuck to Sir Nicholas like a burr, as did most of the other noblemen, except Audric.

"I'd best return to the castle," Eleanor said anxiously. "Percival might be angry if he knows I came to the village."

"You go on," Riona said. "I'll wait for my uncle."

If she went back to the castle now, Uncle Fergus would surely wonder why she hadn't waited for them.

As Eleanor walked swiftly away, Riona inwardly girded her loins and prepared to ignore the dark lord of Dunkeathe as much as possible.

It soon became apparent that no one else was with them or coming close behind. The other noblemen and the servants accompanying them must still be at the hunt.

When they reached Riona, Sir Nicholas swung easily down from his saddle. She supposed he was used to doing that wearing chain mail and armor; his tunic and breeches must seem like a mere second skin to him. They fit him like a second skin.

Uncle Fergus had a bit more of a struggle to dismount, but soon enough, both were on the ground, holding the reins of their horses.

"Greetings, my lady," Sir Nicholas said evenly. "I see the sun has lured you from my castle."

"Good day, Sir Nicholas," she replied just as politely.

"Riona, my beauty, how good to meet you here!" Uncle Fergus cried, and oh, how she wanted to cringe when he used those words to describe her in front of their host.

"Hello, Uncle. Was the hunt not successful? Where are the others?"

"Hunt?" Uncle Fergus said, as if he'd forgotten about it completely.

"It went well. I left the rest of them to it after they cornered a stag," Sir Nicholas replied. "I found your uncle talking to one of my tenants."

Riona was burning with curiosity to know what Sir Nicholas thought of that, and why he'd returned with Uncle Fergus instead of staying with the other nobles, but she tried not to show any particular interest in anything his lordship said.

"You ought to see the lambs Sir Nicholas has on this estate," Uncle Fergus cried, throwing his arm about her shoulders and heading for the castle gates. "Fleece soft and thick, and a good leg for meat, too. Like nothing I've ever seen!"

"Your uncle assures me I've got something very valuable," Sir Nicholas agreed, his voice betraying only mild interest.

"*Very* valuable? Why, I don't think the man half knows what he's got! Worth a fortune, those animals. And he's going to let me bring some of our sheep to breed with theirs—for a fee, of course."

That sounded like a Norman's miserly way. "Of course," she said with a hint of disgust.

"Why shouldn't I make money, if I own the animals?" Sir Nicholas inquired.

"Aye, why shouldn't he?" Uncle Fergus asked. "They're on his estate and the shepherd's his tenant—a very clever tenant, too, that Thomas is."

"Thomas?" Riona repeated, recognizing the name. "That must be the young man Polly wants to marry."

Uncle Fergus laughed. "Ah, then she's a lucky woman, for he's a very fine fellow." He grinned at Sir Nicholas. "You ought to listen to what Riona has to say about *her,* my lord."

"I don't care to listen to gossip about the servants," Sir Nicholas said with stiff hauteur as they walked through the outer gatehouse.

Riona didn't want to talk to him about anything, either.

"It's not gossip, exactly," Uncle Fergus returned, "and if you want your household to run smooth, you ought to pay attention to what's going on among the servants, as Riona does. I've been spared some trouble that way, I can tell you."

"Never mind, Uncle," Riona said. "I'm sure Sir Nicholas doesn't require any assistance from me."

Sir Nicholas looked at her with his piercing dark eyes and his gaze felt like a flame on her skin. "Given that I'm used to commanding soldiers, not servants, especially female ones, perhaps I should hear what you have to say on the subject."

"My lord, I really don't think…" she began, desperately trying to think of a good reason to refuse.

"He needs your help, Riona," Uncle Fergus exclaimed. "Now be a good girl—"

He made her sound like a child!

"And tell him about Polly. Since I've heard all about it, you won't mind if I go on ahead, I hope?" Uncle Fergus asked with an eager look in his eyes that, Riona suspected, had a great deal to do with Fredella.

"I have no wish to detain you," Sir Nicholas said.

"Until later, then, my lord," Uncle Fergus cried cheerfully as, with a wave of his hand, he abandoned her.

"He seems in a great hurry," Sir Nicholas noted as Riona continued to walk beside him, silently commanding herself not to fall behind. She didn't want to look like a dog trotting after its master.

She wasn't about to tell him why she thought her uncle was in a rush to get to the castle, either. He'd surely disapprove of any nobleman preferring to be with a servant. "I don't think my uncle likes hunting, particularly."

"Neither do I."

She slid the Norman a skeptical glance as they reached the inner gate. "Then why did you suggest it?"

"Because it's a fine day, and I thought the other gentlemen would enjoy it."

That seemed to be the end of that subject. "About Polly, my lord—"

"I'd prefer to have this discussion in my solar."

"I'd prefer not to be alone with you, my lord."

He regarded her with a stony expression. "If you'd rather have this discussion about my servant in the hall or yard, that is, of course, up to you. However, I don't consider it wise to discuss one's underlings where anyone may overhear."

Unfortunately, he had a point, made even stronger when a stableboy, his expression inquisitive, ran up to take charge of Sir Nicholas's horse.

"Very well, my lord," she conceded.

Without another word, Sir Nicholas turned on his heel and started toward the solar, leaving her to follow.

CHAPTER SEVEN

ONCE IN HIS SOLAR, Sir Nicholas walked toward a small table bearing an ornate silver carafe and two finely wrought goblets. "Wine, my lady?"

"No, thank you."

He raised a quizzical brow as he poured the rich, red beverage into one of the goblets. "Are you intending to stand on the threshold for the duration of this conversation? That rather defeats the purpose of coming to my solar."

She swept past him to the center of the room. It was smaller than she'd expected, given the size of his castle, and very plain. The only ornamentation was the intricate patterns on the silver goblets and carafe. There were no tapestries, or anything else to provide a hint of warmth. The room was as cold and austere as the man himself.

As he closed the door, she gave him a calmly inquiring look. She wasn't going to let him think he could intimidate her—not if she could help it, anyway.

Yet being here with him, alone, seemed to set her body on fire, and the memory of that kiss....

"Please, sit down," he said, nodding at the one and only chair.

She went around the heavy trestle table and sank onto the seat. Holding his goblet lightly in his strong fingers, he, too, came around the table and leaned back against it only a foot or so away from her.

Why did he have to be so close? If he was trying to seduce her again, he had to realize it was hopeless. This time, she was ready for him—and his eyes and his voice.

"You must feel very secure here, to leave such fine pieces of silver in an unlocked room," she noted, determined to prove she wasn't rendered incapable of conversation in his virile presence.

"I have no fear of thieves. They know that my retribution will be swift, and severe."

"I saw your archer in the stocks in the village."

"Exactly so," he replied before he took a sip of wine.

"I didn't think Norman knights set such store on dogs."

"The lad did, and I won't have a soldier in my employ who would brutalize a creature so much weaker than himself."

She raised a brow as she folded her hands in her lap. "Interesting sentiment, coming from a mercenary."

"I fought men as well trained as I, not foot soldiers."

"And for that, you were duly paid."

"Yes, I was." He raised the goblet. "This was one such payment, and the three that went with it, as well as the carafe. I'm not ashamed of how I earned my living, my lady. I had little enough choice. It was fighting, or the church, and I would not have made a good priest."

No, he would not. The vow of chastity alone…

She forced herself to concentrate on other matters. "You said there were four goblets. What happened to the others?"

"They paid for my chapel."

His brow furrowed when he saw her expression. "It shocks you that I wish to show my gratitude to God by having a beautiful chapel? As it happens, I *am* grateful, both for my life and the rewards I've earned. Yet I'm not an expert at the running of a household." He set down the goblet and crossed his arms. "Which brings us to that girl your uncle spoke of."

"Polly, my lord," she replied. "And she's not a girl, she's a young woman."

He inclined his head in acknowledgment of her correction. "Which one of my maidservants is she?"

"You don't know who I mean?" she asked skeptically. The friendly, flirtatious Polly was hard to overlook.

He frowned. "Is it a sin that I don't know the names of all my servants?"

"I'm surprised that you don't know *her* name, my lord. She's the sort of vivacious, pretty young woman men remember."

His expression grew disdainful. "If you think I ought

to know her because I've bedded her, you're wrong. I don't dally with my servants."

"Then you would be a rare Norman lord in that respect."

"By that form of measure, I *am* a rare Norman lord."

The firmness of his answer, and the look on his face, gave credence to his words. Yet he was so handsome and well formed, she wouldn't be surprised to learn that he could have scores of women wherever he went—although, she had to admit, she'd heard no such tales.

"I don't dally with *anyone* in my household."

She glanced at him sharply.

"Usually," he added, his gaze seeming to grow more intense and inscrutable.

She couldn't prevent the blush that heated her face. But she wasn't going to act the shy maiden and be silent.

She got to her feet, so that she was face-to-face with him. "But not always. Not when you feel you can do so with impunity, I suppose."

"Not when the lady is willing," he replied. "Not when I'm willing, too. But when the lady later clearly wishes nothing more to happen between us, I respect her decision."

His gaze was so steady and unwavering, his voice so sincere, she believed him. Relaxing for what seemed like the first time since they'd kissed in the garden, Riona slowly let out her breath.

And realized they still had more to discuss. "While

you may not be a lascivious scoundrel, I fear the same couldn't be said of some of your guests."

Sir Nicholas's dark brows lowered, and it was like seeing a thunderhead forming in the distance. "Is there any particular man who presents such a danger to the women of my household?"

Before she could answer, he made an impatient gesture. "Don't tell me. I'm sure Percival's quite capable of saying just about anything to get a woman into his bed. Has he?"

"Not yet," she replied, "but Polly's a friendly young woman, and I don't think she realizes how easy it can be to succumb to temptation."

When Nicholas slowly raised a brow, Riona had to fight not to look away.

"Since those men are my guests," he said evenly, "it might be better if you spoke to her, woman to woman, and warned her of the danger."

Riona steeled herself against the power of his deep, seductive voice and his dark, penetrating gaze. "I did, and she assures me she's well aware of 'snares,' as she calls them. I gather your sister spoke to her of the dangers before she…" It probably wasn't wise to allude to his sister's elopement with Adair Mac Taran. "Before your sister married. Nevertheless, I still fear Polly might succumb. For her sake, as well as yours, you should encourage her to marry. I understand the young shepherd, Thomas, has expressed such wishes, and Polly's very agreeable, too. Unfortunately, she feels they're too poor at present and must wait until they have more money to wed."

Sir Nicholas strode to the arched window and spoke without looking at her. "It seems a bit hard on Thomas, encouraging him to marry a woman who can be tempted to stray. Maybe one day she'll be brought before me charged with adultery."

Riona rose and went toward him. "Perhaps, but I doubt it. Polly seems a good soul, and once she's married and settled down, I'd be very surprised indeed if she didn't prove to be a most excellent wife and mother. I would hate to see that chance destroyed because of some silver-tongued Norman who thinks maidservants are no more than whores without a brothel."

The lord of Dunkeathe turned and folded his arms over his broad chest. "Harsh words, my lady."

"Harsh truth, my lord," she said, "but one I think you'd find hard to deny."

"If Polly is willing to part with her virtue, why should I guard it for her?"

If he wanted a self-serving reason, she'd give him one. "Because, my lord, such a woman can also cause great dissension in a household. She will have those who envy her and despise her, and some who'll try to follow her example. You may find yourself with a few noblemen's bastards on your hands."

"You seem to care a great deal about people you barely know."

"At home, it's my business to be aware of what's

happening with the servants. Perhaps I shouldn't have interfered or listened to her troubles, but it's a difficult habit to break."

He moved toward the table. She backed away, until she realized what she was doing and how that might look to him.

He, too, came to a halt, lightly resting his hand on the back of the chair. She tried not to stare at his strong fingers, the knuckles, the sun-browned skin….

"I shall take what you've said into consideration," he said. "It seems my method of choosing a wife is yielding some unexpected benefits."

She tore her gaze from his powerful hand and regarded him steadily. "That may be, but I still don't approve of your means of finding a bride, my lord."

"Neither does my brother," he admitted, his revelation surprising her. "Unfortunately, I don't have the time to search the country for a suitable wife. It was easier to invite those who wanted to be considered to Dunkeathe."

"Like sending sheep to market," she charged, struggling to ignore the desire awakening within her.

His brows rose. "If these women are treated like so much livestock, that is the way of the world, my lady. I can't be held responsible for that. And if I hadn't let it be known I sought a wife, your uncle wouldn't have come to Dunkeathe. He's proving to be a very interesting man with very interesting ideas."

She didn't care to discuss her uncle with Sir Nicholas of Dunkeathe, so she started for the door.

"Is he really that knowledgable about sheep?"

Annoyed by Sir Nicholas's skeptical tone, she turned back. "Aye, he is."

"Then why are you so poor?"

She straightened her shoulders and prepared to defend her beloved uncle. "Because of his kindness. He never refuses to aid those who need help, or feed those who are hungry."

"So you're proud of him, despite his faults?"

"I *love* him, despite his faults—and because of them. We are none of us perfect."

Sir Nicholas's answer was so softly, gruffly spoken, she had to strain to hear it. "No, we are not. *I* am not." He started toward her.

Suddenly, all her brave defiance seemed to have deserted her. She swallowed hard and sidled backward. "I'm surprised to hear you admit it," she said, fighting to keep her voice steady.

"I know my faults, but I also know my strengths. Yet it seems you, my lady, are capable of arousing such desire in me, I become as weak as a lad."

He halted in front of her and a troubled look darkened his face. "God help me, how I wish you did not!" he whispered hoarsely as he pulled her close and his lips took hers with sure and certain purpose. His arms encircled her and held her tight against him.

Need, yearning, lust leaped into burning, vibrant life within her.

She couldn't help herself. She didn't want to help

herself as she leaned into him with her warm, yielding body.

Yet even as she returned his kiss with ardent passion, she knew this was wrong. They should not be here, together, alone and kissing. She should stop him. Make him let her go. Walk out of this chamber and never, ever come near him again.

But the desire kindling within her swiftly overwhelmed the voice of her reason. Her objections fell away, destroyed by the sensation of his mouth against hers, and that of his body, virile and powerful, hard against her own.

He tasted of fine wine, intoxicating and full-bodied. Rich and warm, like grapes in the sun.

And like the sun, she was hot. No breeze could chill the welcome warmth engendered by his touch as his hands slid up her back, clasping her even more tightly to him. No blast of winter could cool her ardor as she leaned into him, her breasts crushed against his chest.

Her hands glided around his waist, over his rough leather belt. How good this felt, how right. How perfect. More thrilling than anything in her life. When his tongue pushed against her lips, she didn't hesitate to part them, and welcome him inside.

His hand moved slowly down her back to cup her buttocks and press her against the evidence of his arousal. Her legs slightly parted to steady herself, she moaned softly, aware of his need, and her own. The moistness between her legs, the gentle throbbing that had an urgency she had never felt before.

She held him closer still, and her kisses became more urgent. More fervent. More demanding. This was what she'd longed to feel, on those long, lonely nights at home. How she'd dreamed of being held and kissed and touched, by a man who passionately desired her.

She'd feared this was impossible, forever denied, because she was not pretty and no longer young, and no man she could love had ever wanted to marry her.

This man didn't want to marry her. He might lust after her, but he would never marry her. There was nothing good or lasting or pure between them, but only unbridled, uncontrolled desire.

She broke away from him. "Stop!"

For a brief instant, she saw his shock. And then it was as if shutters had closed over his face, rendering it a wooden mask no more revealing than a plank. "If you wish, my lady."

"I do wish it!"

"And so I have stopped," he said, his tone reasonable, as he spread his arms wide.

"I have no desire to be the object of your lust. I refuse to be just a body in your bed, a means to sate and satisfy your lust while you woo another for your wife," she declared as she marched to the door.

She looked back at Nicholas of Dunkeathe over her shoulder. "Have no fear, my lord, that I will speak of what's happened between us," she said, while he stood as still as a marble statue, "I won't, because it's to my shame, as it *should* be to yours."

With that, she threw open the door and strode out of the room. They couldn't stay here another hour, not after what Sir Nicholas had done.

And what she'd done, too, the small voice of her conscience prompted.

She ignored it, just as she ignored Lady Joscelind and the other ladies by the hearth who stopped talking to stare at her as she stalked past, determined to find Uncle Fergus and leave this place without delay.

Some of the ladies were sewing, while Lady Joscelind idly strummed a harp. Lady Catherine and Lady Elizabeth weren't there, of course. They'd already had the great good sense to go. As for the rest, let Sir Nicholas have one of them and be damned.

Then she spotted Eleanor, seated at the edge of the group, looking at her in amazement. She couldn't stop to explain—not yet—and she was sorry they would have to say goodbye to her. She'd miss Eleanor and she was certain Uncle Fergus would regret bidding farewell to Fredella, yet they simply couldn't stay.

She reached the courtyard and there was still no sign of Uncle Fergus. Perhaps he'd gone to the village, or out to the farms, looking for more marvelous sheep.

She continued to the gate and spoke to the two Saxons on guard, the same ones who'd been so insolent that first day.

The stocky one ran his gauntleted hand nervously up and down the shaft of his spear, and his cheeks colored. "My lady, thank you for not saying nothing to Sir Nicholas about…about what happened there at the gate Midsummer's Day. We're right grateful."

The other one eagerly added, "If we'd a-known who you was—"

She was in no humor to forgive insolent Saxons, any more than she was willing to consider their overlord an honorable knight. "I haven't told Sir Nicholas *yet*."

The big one's eyes widened in his plump face, while the thin one blanched.

"I—it was a mistake and we won't make it again," the first guard stammered.

"So perhaps next time you'll think twice before treating visitors to Dunkeathe in that impudent manner. If I hear of such behavior again, I will most certainly inform Sir Nicholas."

She wouldn't, of course, because she wouldn't be here. Later, when she was gone, they'd probably curse her for scaring them, but she didn't care. "Have you seen my uncle?"

"Yes, my lady. He went to the village."

She nodded her thanks, then hurried through the inner ward, past the tents and small groups of men huddled together playing drafts and gambling. Others were polishing armor or mail. A few were singing, a rollicking song about a bed and several wenches.

They clearly had as little respect for women as Sir Nicholas, and were likely just as full of base animal desire.

She kept walking until she got to the market square. She scanned the people milling about and looking at the items for sale.

She couldn't see Uncle Fergus anywhere. She walked a little way through the market, avoiding going near the archer who was still in the stocks. She passed the tavern—full of happy revelers, it seemed—as well as the chandler's stall, the baker's, the wool merchant's and several other stalls, all before she decided it would be better for her to await Uncle Fergus back at the castle. As she waited, she could pack their things ready to leave at dawn tomorrow.

As she returned the way she'd come, she glanced down the alley between the butcher and the baker. Two people were standing close together, whispering and gently kissing like two young lovers.

It was her uncle and Fredella.

Feeling as if she'd been caught eavesdropping, Riona stumbled back and immediately hurried away.

Losh, she knew Uncle Fergus liked Fredella, and while she'd discussed their marriage that very morning with Eleanor, seeing them together forced her to realize just how much Uncle Fergus cared for Fredella. He might very well want to stay until they were wed.

Perhaps Uncle Fergus could stay while she returned to Glencleith. The sheep could be his excuse. Yes, surely, somehow, Uncle Fergus could remain and she could think of an excuse for leaving on her own. Something about the household, maybe. Something she'd forgotten to tell Kenneth…

The tavern door opened, nearly hitting her. As she came to a gasping halt, Sir Percival came staggering into her path.

Grinning like a death's head, the drunken nobleman straightened. Given his disheveled hair and clothing, she suspected he'd been doing more than drinking.

Before she could go on her way, he stepped in front of her and blocked her path. "Well, well, well, what have we here?"

She went to go around him. "Pardon me, my lord, but I have things to do."

He grabbed her arm to halt her. "Important things, are they?"

"Yes. Now you'd better let me go or—"

"Or what?" he said with a leering smile as he pulled her closer. "You'll scream?"

Did this skinny, overdressed dandy think he could intimidate her? What a fool! "Or you'll regret it."

"You're fortunate I find women who present a challenge so exciting, else I could get angry. I've heard the Scots are a proud and feisty people. I admire spirit," he said as he started to pull her into a narrow alley that reeked of piss and dung between the tavern and the chandler's stall next to it.

"We're a good deal more than that," she said, making no effort to halt their progress. Although he had a sword and probably a dagger, she wasn't the least bit afraid. She'd been taught to defend herself and was quite ready to do so, and he was so drunk, he could hardly stand.

"You're damned fetching, too," he said, pushing her back against the wall.

His stinking breath hot on her face, he leaned forward to kiss her.

"And we're not afraid to hurt blackguards like you," she retorted as she grabbed his shoulders and swiftly raised her knee, hitting him hard.

He groaned and, clutching at his crotch, staggered backward. "I'm going to tell Sir Nicholas about you, you…!"

"Please do," she replied, keeping her eyes on him as she backed toward the entrance to the alley. "Tell him all about it. How you were drinking and wenching in the village after the hunt and then lustfully pulled me into an alley and tried to kiss me.

"Or are you going to say I set upon you with no provocation?" she inquired as Percival's face reddened. "That I just went wild and attacked you for no reason? I'd take care what you say to Sir Nicholas about me, for if you imply that I behaved wantonly, I'll tell him exactly what happened. Who do you think he'll believe?"

"He doesn't like the Scots any more than I do, you stupid whore!" Percival cried, lunging for her.

She was sober and he was drunk, so it was easy to neatly sidestep him. He went sprawling in the mud and whatever else was on the ground.

"I'm willing to say nothing of this disgusting incident, but if you ever come near me again, I'll go to Sir

Nicholas and tell him everything," she said, mindful of Uncle Fergus, and what he might do if he heard of Sir Percival's unwelcome advances.

Percival was a fool and easily defeated when he was drunk, but he had surely been trained to use his weapons, and in a fight, sober, against her uncle, he might be able to do serious harm.

"You'd better keep away from the servants, too. Sir Nicholas takes a very dim view of men who try to seduce them."

As Percival struggled to his feet, she hurried off, back to the castle to pack her things.

Tomorrow, she would gladly leave this place and not look back.

KEEPING A WARY EYE on her cousin, Eleanor watched as he staggered about her well-appointed chamber like an enraged and caged beast. In one hand, he held a wineskin that he'd nearly emptied. His wet hair hung limply around his face and she'd heard him drunkenly shouting at one of the servants to take away his clothes and burn them. He had washed after his fall in the village and was once again well-dressed in costly attire. Unfortunately, the wine and his fetid breath overpowered the perfume he'd liberally sprinkled on himself.

"You'll not speak t' her or that uncle of hers, and neither 'ill Fredella, d'you hear me?" Percival charged, slurring his words and sending spittle flying as he paused to glare at Eleanor. "You stay away from 'em!

I only tola…tollerrr…tolerated 'em 'cause Nicholas seems t' like that oaf."

He wiped his chin, then took another gulp of wine.

Eleanor clasped her hands and pleaded, "Surely there's no harm—"

"Are you *deaf?*" Percival shouted, waving the wineskin at her, his face reddening. "I said you can't speak to 'em and you'd better bloody well do as I say!"

He took another drink from the wineskin, his fifth since coming to her chamber, and he stumbled into her small table, rocking it and sending a clay vessel of soap crashing to the floor. Eleanor stood still, too terrified of her enraged cousin to even try to pick up the pieces.

"She's prob'ly not even a lady—they prob'ly forged that parchment her uncle showed Sir Nicholas's steward, and that Robert's too stupid to see it."

He sat heavily on the end of Eleanor's bed, and his head fell forward, his shoulders slumped.

"But if Sir Nicholas likes them…" Eleanor ventured, daring to hope his tirade was over.

Percival raised his head and glared at her with his bleary, bloodshot eyes. "I still don' want you talking to those two. You should be talking t' Nicholas and doing everything you can to get him. That's why we came, not so you could be friendly to savages who wear skirts and have ugly nieces."

"But Percival," Eleanor implored, "I can't force Sir Nicholas to like me. If he doesn't want me, what can I do?"

Percival rose unsteadily. "You can *make* him like you."

"I'm trying but—"

"The hell y'are!" he retorted, shaking the wineskin at her.

"Percival, please." She spread her hands in supplication. "I'm doing all I can—"

"Do more!" her cousin roared before he drained the wineskin and tossed it aside.

"I don't think I could ever be happy with such a man."

"Happy?" her cousin screeched.

With a snarl, he grabbed her by the throat and shoved her backward onto the bed. "Happy?" he shouted. "Did anybody ask me if I'd be *happy* you were left on my hands?"

He shoved once more, then pushed himself away. "If you weren't pretty, I'd've packed you off to a convent by now. Maybe I should. Maybe I will."

Coughing, she stared up at him. His expression was as fiendish as a gargoyle.

"If you don' do as I say, Eleanor, I'm goin' send you t'a convent—in the most remote place I can find. I'll tell the nuns you're a lewd, wanton wench and ought t' be kept under strict watch. By God, I'll tell them to wall you up in a cell to keep you away from men—don't think I won't!"

Holding her throat, sure he meant it, sure he could and would do what he said, Eleanor envisioned spending the rest of her life in such imprisonment and started to cry.

"I'll try to do better," she sobbed, her breath coming in great gasps, unable to look at her cousin's cruel face. "I'll try to talk to him. I'll try to persuade him to marry me. But if I can't…if he chooses another…" She slid down onto the floor, kneeling at Percival's feet, her hands clasped as she pleaded. "Please don't send me to such a place, Percival. Please! I'll die!"

He only scowled at her the more. "Then see that he picks you, you useless cow."

He staggered out of her chamber, slamming the door behind him and leaving Eleanor weeping on the floor.

CHAPTER EIGHT

As THE SERVANTS began to clear away the remains of the evening meal, Lord Chesleigh turned to Nicholas with a smile that reminded Nicholas of a toad.

He was regretting inviting the remaining nobles to take their turn seated at the high table. Before, he could enjoy his meals in relative peace, perusing the occupants of the hall as he wished. Now, he had the talkative, boastful Lord Chesleigh on his left, and his daughter, who at least wasn't so inclined to talk, to the more honored right-hand side.

"After that fine meal, what say you to some dancing, my lord?" Lord Chesleigh suggested.

Before he replied, Nicholas subdued the urge to survey those in his hall once more to see if Lady Riona had come after all. He could guess why she hadn't, especially since her uncle wasn't there, either. They were probably packing their things, determined to leave in the morning. Later, they'd probably tell every Scot they knew about the lascivious, sinful Sir Nicholas who'd set out to sully a virtuous lass's honor.

So much for any hope that he'd ever be accepted in

this country. It had been a faint one, but he had harbored it, especially since he'd come to accept his sister's marriage to Adair Mac Taran.

"An excellent proposal," he replied to the nobleman, hoping he didn't make a fool of himself. "And you, Lady Joscelind?" he politely inquired of the beauty beside him. "Would you care to dance?"

"I would enjoy it very much, my lord," she answered, her voice so soft he could hardly hear it, and her eyes demurely lowered.

Did she really think he could forget the forcefulness of her voice in the courtyard when she'd ordered him to unload her baggage? Maybe she thought her beauty and her father's wealth and power would be sufficient to make him forget.

Perhaps he'd have to overlook that behavior because of the rewards such a bride would bring.

"I'd like to refresh myself first," she said. "If I may."

"Of course. I shall eagerly await your return."

Lady Joscelind gracefully rose. She looked down the hall, silently signaling her maidservant to attend her.

Nicholas followed her gaze, then once more scanned the hall. His noble guests appeared well fed and generally happy, several of the men still excited by the hunt. Robert sat between Lady Priscilla and Audric, across from Sir George and a very annoyed looking Lady Eloise.

The Scots thane and Lady Eleanor's maidservant weren't there, either, although Eleanor was, looking rather pale. Perhaps she was a sickly sort—one reason he could give Percival not to wed her, should that prove necessary.

Nicholas gestured for the maidservant nearest to come closer. It was Polly, the one who was going to marry Thomas and had been so grateful for the small dowry he'd given her to allow that to happen soon, he feared she'd swoon when he told her. "Tell Robert I wish to speak to him, and I want the tables taken down."

She nodded and hurried off to do as she was bid.

"Very pretty wench," Lord Chesleigh remarked.

"She's betrothed to my head shepherd," Nicholas replied, his tone containing a mild warning.

"So I heard. My daughter told me something of that, and I understand you gave her a dowry?"

Nicholas regarded the nobleman with an inquiring look, although he probably shouldn't be so surprised that such news had traveled so quickly. He wondered if Lady Riona had heard it, and if that mollified her anger any.

"Not that I blame you, my lord," Lord Chesleigh continued with a sly and knowing smile. "She seems quite…entertaining."

"I don't sport with my maidservants."

Lord Chesleigh colored at Nicholas's brusquely spoken words. "So I was given to understand. But you must admit the dowry suggests—"

"The dowry was a gift to encourage her to marry and get out of my castle, lest she be seduced by men who ought to know better."

Lord Chesleigh's brow lowered. "And just what are you implying?"

Nicholas clenched his jaw and reminded himself of this man's influence and wealth. "That she is a pretty, weak and foolish girl whose head could be easily turned. I have no desire to have such a potentially troublesome maidservant in my household."

Lord Chesleigh relaxed. "Ah, I see. Very wise, my lord, very wise."

Nicholas didn't think the man meant that for a moment. He was probably the sort of nobleman who'd been brought up to believe that maidservants were his by right, there to satisfy him whenever and however he required.

Robert hurried up to the high table. "My lord?"

"We wish to have dancing, Robert. Inform the musicians."

"At once, my lord."

He turned to go, but Nicholas couldn't resist the urge to call him back. "I see the Scots thane isn't in the hall."

"No, my lord. It's my understanding he went to the village and hasn't yet returned."

Lord Chesleigh gave a sly chuckle. "No doubt to partake of the twin temptations of the tavern."

At that very moment, Sir George drunkenly raised his goblet and called out for more wine. Robert gave a barely perceptible shrug, then hurried off to fetch the musicians they'd hired until Lammas.

"It would seem, my lord," Nicholas remarked, "that the same temptations are shared by many men, wherever they are born and bred."

"Lady Eloise's poor mother was forever at her prayers," Lord Chesleigh replied, nodding at Sir George. "Married to such a sot, she must have had plenty of cause to pray for patience, help and guidance."

"All of us should pray for those things."

Lord Chesleigh clearly hadn't expected that answer. "Yes, well, naturally...although it's obvious God has other rewards to bestow," he finished with a gesture that encompassed the hall.

Still mindful of the man's place at court, Nicholas didn't tell him that if God saw fit to reward him, it wasn't simply because he prayed. He'd earned it, through hard work and sacrifice and in the spilling of blood, both his and other men's.

Fortunately, before he said something he'd regret, Lady Joscelind returned. She'd dabbed a bit more perfume on herself, and taken off the silver circlet and pale blue scarf she'd worn at dinner. Her shining blond braids hung down past her waist and were bound with silver casings.

"I wanted to be cooler for the dancing," she explained in answer to his unspoken question, and with a charming smile as he dutifully led her out to join the other nobles forming a circle for a round dance.

Sir George was barely able to stop swaying as he

waited beside his daughter. The Earl of Eglinburg looked as if he had indigestion, while his daughter seemed dwarfed by Sir James of Keswick. Quite unnoticed by her kinsman D'Anglevoix, Lady Lavinia smiled coyly at Audric.

That was an interesting development, Nicholas thought as the tabor player began a jaunty rhythm. Maybe he wouldn't have to worry about finding a diplomatic way to tell Lady Lavinia and D'Anglevoix that she wouldn't be his choice.

"I'm so delighted you agreed to the dancing, my lord," Lady Joscelind said softly as she stepped from left to right in front of him.

As she moved, Nicholas could appreciate why Lord Chesleigh had suggested this activity. His daughter was an accomplished dancer, it seemed, both elegant and graceful.

"Anything I can do to accommodate you, my lady, is my pleasure," he replied.

She raised her eyes for an instant, then lowered them again as if looking at him directly was both a bold and irresistible impulse, and one of which she was ashamed.

He was sure that was very effective on green lads and young knights, but he was neither, and he'd seen such a coy gesture many times before, from all sorts of women, so it had little effect on him.

They turned, raised the hands that were closest to one another and, their palms together, walked down the hall in time to the music before turning and making a few more steps in place.

Lady Riona wasn't coy, nor did she pretend to be, and he'd always preferred bold women. Still, as he'd said to Henry before his brother left, these were different circumstances, and in spite of the desire Riona aroused in him, he should never have suggested going to his solar. He still couldn't understand how he'd been so weak and foolish as to give in to the temptation to kiss her.

Yes, he could. Only she, of all the other women he'd ever met, made him forget everything else when he was with her. Only she inspired that incredible, undeniable passion that made him put the need to kiss her above anything else. Unfortunately, only she, of all the women who'd come here to try to become his bride, was completely unsuitable.

"Have I offended you, my lord?" Lady Joscelind asked, her alabaster brow furrowed with worry.

"No."

"Then you are preoccupied with serious matters?"

Nicholas cursed himself for being so obviously distracted. This woman was the sort he'd most hoped would come to Dunkeathe, and he was ignoring her. "Forgive me," he said with a little bow as they turned again. "I fear I've spent too much time among soldiers to be pleasant company for ladies."

"Some men prattle on with nothing at all to say, while a wise man has little need to speak," she replied. "Your accomplishments speak for you."

"As do yours, my lady."

She blushed and lowered her eyelids again, her lashes fanning on her soft cheeks. Her lips were full and ruby-red, her body shapely, her features lovely—and yet she stirred him not at all.

Nevertheless, mindful of his need to marry well, he commenced uttering flattering nothings as they danced. He was no smooth-tongued courtier, but he'd known a few knights who were notable for their abilities to woo women, and he'd learned a thing or two along the way.

Whether Lady Joscelind found him sincere or not, he couldn't tell, but she didn't give any sign that she suspected he wasn't, and when the dance ended, she gave him a glorious smile that he should have been thrilled to see.

As she eagerly slipped her arm through his to allow him to lead her back to her father, he reminded himself again how much he needed to marry a woman of her family's wealth and status.

They were not yet to the dais when Sir Percival hurried up to them, followed by his cousin. Lady Eleanor's eyes held the sort of grimly determined expression Nicholas had seen on the face of men encountering a much better armed opponent in battle.

"Dancing, eh, my lord?" Percival said cheerily. "Wonderful. Eleanor's an excellent dancer."

Lord Chesleigh frowned at Percival, who blatantly ignored him, while Lady Joscelind held Nicholas's arm a little tighter.

Lord Chesleigh might not be pleased but, Nicholas thought, he could hardly be faulted for dancing with the other ladies until his choice was made. "I shall be delighted if she will dance the next with me."

After Lady Joscelind reluctantly released her hold, Lady Eleanor put her trembling hand in his to be led into the square of couples forming for the dance.

Her trembling was nothing like the way Riona trembled when he touched her. This was fear, not desire.

"I'm not going to bite you, my lady," he said, attempting to put the girl at ease. She only flushed and still didn't meet his gaze.

The dance began, and as he circled her, he contemplated what it would be like to wed her. According to Robert, her family's wealth was at least as great as Lord Chesleigh's, and there were relatives besides the vain Percival who were not without influence at court.

Lady Eleanor wasn't as beautiful as Joscelind, but she was pretty. And she'd probably never dare to complain, or contradict him. She'd surely never refuse to do her duty in his bed. She'd be a very meek, dutiful and submissive wife.

He didn't want a wife who was dutifully submissive. He wanted a woman who desired him, who would speak to him with confidence, whose eyes shone with vivacious life, who kissed with passion and fire, leaning into him as if she would make love with him standing there….

The dance brought him face-to-face with Eleanor. "I

hope you're enjoying your time in Dunkeathe," he offered.

"Yes, my lord," she answered, giving him a smile that was falsely bright, for her eyes were far too worried to suggest happiness.

"I'm honored to have you here."

"Thank you, my lord."

It was like trying to tug the words out of her. "I noticed your maidservant isn't here," he said, trying to think of some subject that would break through that wall of frightened reserve. "I trust she's not unwell."

Eleanor finally looked him directly in the eye. "She was quite well this afternoon."

"The Scots thane seems very taken with her."

If it were any other nobleman, he would have suspected the man of nefarious designs of the sort Riona had suggested. Somehow, though, it was impossible to ascribe any such motive to the jovial little Scot. Nevertheless, it *was* possible, and as host, he had a responsibility to ensure that his guests and their retainers were not mistreated or exploited. "He doesn't strike me as a man to toy with a woman's affections but—"

Eleanor stepped on the hem of her gown and nearly tripped. He reached out to steady her, and when he did, she looked up at him in a way that was akin to panic. "Fredella assures me he's behaved with nothing but the utmost respect."

Why was she so frightened? He was only expressing some concern for her maidservant. "Forgive me for upsetting you, my lady. If you are confident she's in no danger, then I will be, too," he said, smiling at her again in an attempt to erase that terrified look on her face. "I will have no women taken advantage of in my castle."

"Y-you didn't upset me, my lord," she stammered, darting a nervous glance at her cousin, who was watching her as a jailer might his prisoner.

It could be that her fear had less to do with him than Percival. "Does your cousin treat you well, my lady?"

When she didn't speak, her silence answered him. "Perhaps I should have a few words with him."

She raised panicked eyes and spoke swiftly. "No, no, my lord, that's not necessary. Please, I beg you, say nothing to him!"

He studied her as the dance forced them away from each other for several steps. When they were together again, he dropped his voice to a whisper.

"Has Percival ever laid hands on you?"

She didn't meet his gaze. "Just once, when he was drunk."

"Once is once too many," Nicholas growled, his loathing for Percival growing stronger. "Only the weakest of men hurt women. I *shall* speak to him."

"No, please, my lord," she whimpered, tears starting in her eyes. "He'll be angry with me. If you truly want to help me, smile and look as if you like me."

That lout Percival must have put pressure on her to try to win his hand. No wonder she always seemed so anxious.

Nicholas reluctantly smiled, although he felt far from happy. "So I take it your cousin is cruel when he drinks."

With an equally false smile on her face, Eleanor nodded. "Yes."

"Has he ever hurt anyone else when he was drunk?"

The dance required them to part again. As Eleanor moved away, she had the strangest expression on her face, as if she desperately wanted to tell him something, but was afraid to.

Nicholas's impatience grew until they were facing each other once more. "What has he done?"

She glanced at her cousin.

"Pay no attention to him," Nicholas quietly snapped. "I promise he'll never know how I found out."

That seemed to relieve her. "He was in the village today, at the tavern. When he was leaving to return to the castle, he met Lady Riona and he…he…"

Nicholas felt as if he'd been kicked in the stomach.

"She's not hurt," Eleanor hastened to add.

The dance came to an end—and not a moment too soon for Nicholas.

Leaving Eleanor, he headed for the door. He had to find Riona. If Percival had dared to lay a hand on her, if she'd been harmed or injured in any way, he'd wish he'd never heard of Sir Nicholas of Dunkeathe.

WONDERING WHERE Uncle Fergus could be, or what might have detained him, Riona paced the floor of her chamber. It was past time for the evening meal, but she wasn't about to go to the hall, even if Uncle Fergus might have gone there after returning from the village. Surely when he realized she wasn't there, he'd look for her here. Then she'd tell him that she wanted to go home.

She heard her uncle's familiar, and rapid, footfalls in the corridor outside the chamber. With both relief and trepidation, she hurried to the door and then stared in dismay at his enraged, florid face.

"Ah, Riona, there you are," he said as he marched into his chamber, his *feileadh* swinging with his brisk strides. "I thought you might be in the hall. I'm glad you're not."

"Weren't you?"

"No, I've been with Fredella. Something terrible has happened."

They'd seemed blissfully happy that morning. "Did you quarrel?"

"God love you, no. It's that bastard Percival. That disgusting, silly *gowk*. I ought to take my sword and lop off his head. That'd muss his fancy curls. Probably uses tongs, the popinjay."

He must have found out what had happened in the village.

"Please, uncle, don't fuss yourself," she said, hoping to make him calm, too. "As you can see, I'm quite all right. No harm was done."

Her uncle stopped pacing to look at her with furrowed brow and puzzled mien. "Has he threatened you, too?" he demanded.

Now she was as confused as he. "No, he didn't threaten me," she cautiously replied. He'd done more than threaten, but she didn't want Uncle Fergus to attack him.

Uncle Fergus ran his hand through his hair, disheveling it. "After Fredella and I got back from the village, I walked her to her lady's chamber. We found the poor girl so upset, she could hardly speak. That *gowk* Percival's told Eleanor that they're not to speak to us again. Did that *gomeral* tell you not to speak to her anymore, too?"

"No, he said nothing of that to me," Riona answered.

"That disgusting bit o' dung also told Eleanor that if she can't get Sir Nicholas to marry her, he'll pack her off to a convent in some desolate spot and leave her there—and he'd do it, too, the bloody great idiot. Can he not see the poor girl hasn't got a chance and all his threats won't make a wee bit of difference?"

Riona didn't share her uncle's opinion about Eleanor's chances. Indeed, the only woman in Dunkeathe who had no chance to marry Sir Nicholas was standing right before him. And if marrying the Norman knight got Eleanor free of her cousin, things could be worse. "Uncle, I don't think Sir Nicholas is going to choose me, but Eleanor may have a chance. If I left Dunkeathe—"

Uncle Fergus stared at her incredulously. "Poor Eleanor may be a sweet lass, but she's no competition for you, Riona. Of course he's going to pick you. He's no fool—not like that oaf Percival." Uncle Fergus shook his head. "No, no, we have to come up with a way to make Percival think twice about sending her away when Sir Nicholas doesn't pick her. Aye, and parting her from Fredella."

Clearly Uncle Fergus was determined to cling to the notion that she could win Sir Nicholas's hand in marriage. Rather than persist when he was so upset, she would set aside her own troubles until later.

"Perhaps you should go to Sir Nicholas and tell him about this," she suggested. "As a knight, he's sworn to protect women."

"Aye, that he is, but if I go to Sir Nicholas and that snake gets wind of it, I'm sure he'll take it out on Eleanor somehow once they leave Dunkeathe—and he's got the right to do what he likes with her because he's her guardian, the great daft git!"

"Then what do you think we ought to do?"

"I know what I'd like to do—get him alone in a room, just me and my *claimh mhor*," Uncle Fergus declared, swinging an imaginary sword. "I'd fix his hair for him, and more than that, too. I was all for going to the brute at once, but that only made the women cry harder. They seem to think that bastard's somebody I ought to fear." Uncle Fergus snorted with disgust. "As if any Scot in his right mind would be afraid of that dandy!"

"He's probably been well taught how to use a sword

and dagger," Riona cautioned. "And he'll be a dirty
fighter."

That gave Uncle Fergus pause—a very short one.
"Aye, he would be at that—but that's no reason I
shouldn't call the bastard out."

Riona rose and went to her uncle, putting her arm
around his shoulder. "Uncle, think how Fredella and Eleanor and I would feel if anything happened to you.
And Kenneth and everyone at home."

He cocked his head and gave her a suspicious look.
"I'm no coward, Riona. That stinking *gomeral* might
be able to frighten women, but if he thinks he can
frighten *me*—"

"Nobody doubts your bravery, Uncle, or your chiv-
alry. I know you want to help Eleanor, but you can't do
that if you're hurt. And if you should kill Percival, the
Normans might not understand and there could be a
trial and all sorts of trouble. We should think of some
other way to protect Eleanor."

Which meant she had to stay in Dunkeathe. She
couldn't leave Uncle Fergus here alone, lest a messenger come riding into Glencleith with the news that her
uncle had attacked Sir Percival and now was either
dead, or imprisoned.

Uncle Fergus sat back down on the bed and patted
the place beside him. "So, my wise and clever lass,
what do you think we should do?"

"While Eleanor is here, she's safe," Riona said,
thinking aloud as she joined him.

"Aye."

"And she'll be safe until Sir Nicholas makes his choice."

"Aye."

"So the problem becomes what to do after Sir Nicholas makes his choice."

As if she'd summoned him, the man himself suddenly strode into the chamber. Riona swiftly got to her feet while he studied her as if trying to read her mind.

"You weren't in the hall for the evening meal. Why not?"

With any other man, she might have thought he was concerned about her, but he asked the question so forcefully, he must have taken her absence as a personal insult—more evidence of his vain pride.

So she felt no need to be particularly polite as she answered. "I was here waiting for my uncle."

"You're not... You're well?" he asked less brusquely, his shoulders relaxing a very little.

"Obviously."

Sir Nicholas turned his steadfast, dark-eyed gaze onto Uncle Fergus. "And you are well?"

Riona put her hand on Uncle Fergus's arm, hoping he would let her answer. "We were otherwise engaged, my lord. A personal matter. Isn't that so, Uncle?"

Uncle Fergus looked as if he was forcibly restraining himself. "Aye, that's right."

The lord of Dunkeathe slowly crossed his arms and

raised a majestic brow. "I have reason to believe there was more to your absence than that."

What exactly had he heard?

"So, you've found out about that bloody great git, then?" Uncle Fergus demanded. "What are you going to do about him?"

"I first need to know exactly what he did."

Uncle Fergus's gaze darted from Riona to Nicholas, then his eyes brightened and he started for the door. "I'll let Riona tell you all about it and you two can figure out what's to be done."

He thought they should have a private discussion? That was the last thing she wanted. "Uncle, I don't think—" Riona cried, hurrying after him.

But Uncle Fergus had already left the chamber and closed the door behind him, leaving her alone with Sir Nicholas.

Again.

CHAPTER NINE

RIONA SLOWLY turned around, to find Sir Nicholas staring at her, a frown upon his handsome face.

"What did Sir Percival do?" he asked. "Is it because of him that you weren't in the hall?"

He thought she was afraid to face Percival? "There's only one man in this castle I wish to avoid, and he's standing before me now." She ignored the disgruntled expression that came to Sir Nicholas's face. "Sir Percival has forbidden his niece to speak to us, and her maidservant, too. My uncle is upset about that restriction. That's why he wasn't in the hall tonight."

"Does that also explain your absence?"

"Yes."

Sir Nicholas's eyes narrowed. "Lady Eleanor gave me to understand there was something more amiss between you and her cousin."

Riona colored. Clearly, Percival hadn't hesitated to tell Eleanor, at the very least.

Since Sir Nicholas knew, she couldn't deny it completely, yet because she didn't want Percival to leave and take Eleanor with him, she would make light of Percival's actions. "His advances were certainly not welcome, but his pathetic attempt to kiss me was easily countered."

Sir Nicholas started for the door. "He'll regret that, as will anyone who behaves so in my castle. He'll be gone from Dunkeathe in the morning."

Riona hurried after him and grabbed his arm to make him stop. She wouldn't mind seeing Percival in the stocks, but if he was forced to leave Dunkeathe, who could say what might happen to Eleanor? "Don't!"

Sir Nicholas regarded her with disbelief, and disapproval. "You don't want the lout punished?"

"He won't try it again."

"How can you be so sure?"

"I hurt him."

The knight's eyes flashed. "You hurt him? How?"

"With my knee, my lord. To his groin."

Sir Nicholas seemed only slightly mollified. "Fortunate for you that you knew what to do, but next time Percival might accost another who is not so well prepared."

"Then by all means, issue him a warning, my lord," she replied, "but please don't make him, and his cousin, leave Dunkeathe."

Sir Nicholas regarded her stonily. "Why should you care if they stay or go?"

"Because Eleanor's my friend."

"You've met her before?"

"No, but she's my friend all the same." Realizing she

was still holding on to him, she let go of his arm and stepped away. "Haven't you ever met someone and become fast friends in a very short time?"

Sir Nicholas's expression softened—only a little, but some. "Yes. My steward's brother, Charles. We met when we were young, and after less than a day, we were friends, until he died of a sudden fever." He thought a moment, then nodded. "Very well, my lady, they may stay—but I'll make sure Percival understands that he'd better not make any advances to women, welcome or otherwise, while he's in Dunkeathe."

"Thank you, my lord," she said, expecting him to go. Hoping he would.

Instead, he looked around her bare chamber, where there was nothing except her small wooden chest and a linen sheet and woolen blanket on the bed. "Are you planning on leaving Dunkeathe?"

"Not now."

His eyebrows rose questioningly, and she immediately regretted answering. Maybe he would think she was staying out of some bizarre hope that she could win his hand, or that she wanted to. "I don't know if you've noticed, but my uncle's developed a fondness for Lady Eleanor's maidservant—"

"I've noticed," he interrupted, coming closer.

What if he tried to kiss her again?

She'd slap his face, and more, if necessary.

"And I can appreciate why he was upset by Percival's restrictions," Sir Nicholas continued. "I'll tell Percival that if he wishes his cousin to stand a chance with me, he had best reconsider those orders."

"You'd do that?" she asked, telling herself she was relieved to hear that Eleanor was still under consideration.

"As I've told you, I have a great respect for the Scots, and any family I marry into should respect them, too." He hesitated a moment before continuing. "I also have a great deal of respect for you, my lady, and your wisdom. I did as you suggested and provided that maidservant with a small dowry to enable her to marry soon."

"You did?" she asked, surprised and pleased that he'd followed her advice.

"Yes."

He walked toward her, and the look in his eyes made her heart leap and seem to beat anew. In spite of that excitement, she backed away, ordering herself not to give in to the thrilling yearning filling her, goading her to stand still and let him catch her and sweep her into his arms.

"Percival should thank God you were able to defend yourself," he said, his voice low and intimate. "If he'd hurt you, Riona..."

His words trailed off into a silence that seemed filled with promise and anticipation.

Desperately she struggled with the emotions roiling through her. She mustn't want him. She mustn't want to be with him. She was staying to help her uncle, who wanted to help Eleanor, who needed to get away from her cousin. Eleanor required a husband who would protect her. Eleanor needed Nicholas. "I hope you won't hold Percival's behavior against Eleanor. I think any man would be blessed to have her for his wife."

"You aren't…jealous?"

"Not at all." Not really. She mustn't be. "She's a very fine young woman, my lord. Pretty and sweet."

"Too young. Too sweet. I like women of fire and spirit, women who know about hardship and struggle."

God help her!

She hit the wall. "Good for you, my lord," she said as he came inexorably closer. "I like men who leave me alone."

"Why didn't you hurt me when I kissed you, Riona?"

She swallowed hard. "Because you caught me unawares."

Liar, liar!

"Can you guess what I want to do now?" he whispered, standing but a few inches in front of her. "What I'm going to do?"

A loud cough sounded in the corridor.

Nicholas immediately stepped back.

She shouldn't be sorry. She should be glad, relieved, happy as she looked past Nicholas to the door and saw Uncle Fergus peering around the door frame, a quizzical look on his curious face. "Did she tell you everything?" he asked.

"Yes," Nicholas brusquely answered, his voice

rough, his expression cool as ever, while Riona tried to regain her missing self-control.

"Good, good!" Uncle Fergus cried, fairly bounding into the room. "What are you going to do?"

"Have a word with Sir Percival in the morning," Nicholas replied. "Since you missed the evening meal, please take some refreshment in the kitchen." He glanced at Riona. "You, too, my lady, if you so desire."

Then he walked out of the chamber.

The moment he was gone, Uncle Fergus gave Riona a wide, mischievous smile. "Came back a bit too soon, did I?"

It was all Riona could do not to groan with dismay.

WHEN NICHOLAS returned to the hall he gave no explanation for his abrupt departure, but played the genial host in spite of being anything but pleased. He wasn't just angry at Percival; he was angry with himself. He'd revealed too much when he was with Riona. Said too much. Done too much.

He had to learn to control his desire for her. There could be no honorable future for them, and he did respect her, far too much to even propose that they share his bed without benefit of marriage.

As Nicholas endured Lord Chesleigh's observations about the proper way to train horses—something he was sure the man had never actually done himself—he realized Eleanor wasn't in the hall.

Her cousin was, though, so he made his way to Percival, who was already deep in his cups. "I'd like a word with you, Percival," Nicholas said with false good cheer as he angled the man into a relatively quiet corner.

Percival gave him an ingratiating smile. "I hope Eleanor didn't offend you, my lord."

"Not at all," Nicholas replied, barely able to contain his loathing. "I'd like to speak to you privately, Percival. Will you join me in my solar tomorrow morning after mass?"

The man's eyes gleamed with delighted avarice, obviously interpreting this invitation as a good omen. "I'd be honored, my lord."

Not trusting himself to control his tongue, Nicholas merely smiled and nodded before moving off to talk to Audric, who was a blessed relief from the half-drunk Percival and the smug Lord Chesleigh.

THE NEXT MORNING, Nicholas stood at the arched solar window, hands clasped behind his back as he surveyed his courtyard, his soldiers on watch or preparing to ride out on patrol and his servants helping to load one of his guests' wagons.

"So, Lady Isabelle has decided to depart?" he asked Robert, who sat at the table checking one of his many lists.

"Yes, my lord," the steward replied. "Her guardian felt there was no need to linger here."

"What reason did he give? He may be a minor

knight, but I hope I've done nothing to give him any serious offense."

"I suspect Lady Isabelle, whatever her faults, was clever enough to deduce that she wouldn't be your choice."

In truth, Lady Isabelle hadn't impressed Nicholas as much of anything, except a woman. "No, she would not, but I'll be courtesy itself when he takes his leave. Is there anything else that needs to be discussed?"

"A messenger from your sister arrived while we were at mass," Robert answered. "She thanks you most kindly for the invitation, and she and her family will be arriving in a se'ennight."

Nicholas faced his steward. It was Marianne's opinion on his potential brides he sought, not his brother-in-law's, or that of a four-year-old boy and an infant. "I didn't invite the whole lot of them."

Robert regarded him with dismay. "Shall I send another message telling her—?"

"No. I suppose she has to bring the baby, and she doesn't want to leave Seamus or her husband."

"They *are* a very happy and contented family."

Nicholas didn't need to be reminded of that. "Anything else?"

"Until the hay is brought in, my lord, we're going to be a little short of fodder for the stables."

"Buy what we need from the neighboring estates."

Robert delicately cleared his throat. "I fear I must remind you, my lord, that we lack an abundance of móney. If we could cut back on some of the other expenses—food or drink, perhaps?"

"I don't want my guests to think I'm poor, or inhospitable."

"Of course not, my lord. Yet I must point out that we've taken quite a gamble spending so much and now—"

"I took the gamble, Robert. Not you."

"Yes, my lord."

"Anything more?"

Robert shifted and toyed with the edge of the rolled parchment he held. "Unfortunately, my lord, while no one has complained about the food or the wine, there have been some murmurings of discontent among the nobles."

"What about?" Nicholas demanded, thinking of the amount of money he was spending to keep the aristocrats housed, fed and entertained. "If it's the weather, surely they can't expect me to do anything about that."

"No, my lord, not the weather." Robert cleared his throat again and didn't meet Nicholas's steady gaze. "There are questions being asked about the Scot and his niece."

"What sort of questions?" Nicholas asked, wondering if anyone had guessed that he had feelings for Riona.

"Well, my lord, they wonder why they're still here. It's quite clear that they are not wealthy, or influential."

"Tell them what I told you—they are the only Scots

who came and I won't have other Scots claim I was too proud to entertain the notion of marrying one of their countrywomen, even if no other arrived. My guests should understand I dare not upset the Scots. They all live in fear that one day, the Saxons or the Welsh might rebel. You can also tell my noble Norman guests that Fergus Mac Gordon has some very interesting ideas about livestock that I want to hear."

"As you wish, my lord."

"Is there anything else?"

"No, my lord."

Nicholas returned to looking out the window. Sir George came reeling out of the hall. He stopped by the nearest wall and, throwing back his head, relieved himself.

"The wine," Nicholas muttered.

Robert, on the threshold, hesitated and turned back. "My lord?"

"Save what you can on the wine. Use the best only at meals. At other times, cheaper will do, especially if it's for Sir George. I don't think he'll notice, or care."

Robert smiled. "No, my lord, I don't believe he will."

Sir Percival, in a tunic of bilious green and light blue in a combination that seemed designed to dazzle the eye and boggle the mind, arrived on the threshold of the solar. The steward bowed as he passed him on the way out, while Percival sauntered into the room as if it were his own.

Nicholas wanted to strike him down on the spot. Only the knowledge that he might decide to marry the fellow's cousin kept his temper under control.

"You wanted to speak to me, my lord? About Eleanor, I hope?"

"Yes, I did."

The man's expression changed. He was trying to look as if he wasn't worried, but Nicholas had spent years among warriors of both bravery and bravado, and he didn't doubt that beneath those fine clothes, Percival was sweating.

Good. He wouldn't ask the man to sit, or offer him any wine, either.

"It has come to my attention, Percival," he said, slowly circling the well-dressed, perfumed young man, "that you have made some improper advances."

Percival colored, yet he smiled as if this was some kind of merry jest. "I fear there's been a terrible mistake."

"And you've been the one making it."

"What did she—?" Percival began, then he caught himself and tried to smile again. "What have you heard, my lord?"

"Enough."

Percival's face went from red to white as he paled. He started to stammer something, but Nicholas cut him off.

"I can appreciate that you're used to women misinterpreting your actions, Percival," he lied, hating this pathetic excuse of a man with every fiber of his being. "It must be difficult for a fellow as handsome as you to even speak to some ladies without your attention being mistaken for more than mere politeness. I can well believe you've unwittingly caused dissension in many a noble household just by your presence alone."

"Yes, yes, that's often the case," Percival eagerly concurred. "Women don't understand that I'm merely being friendly."

Friendly? Under other circumstances, Nicholas would give him *friendly*. "Since you're such a friendly sort, for the sake of good relations with the other noblemen here in Dunkeathe, I suggest you exercise more care when conversing with the ladies visiting me, both now and when we're—"

Nicholas stopped as if he'd said more than he intended, then forced himself to smile. "Should I choose your charming cousin."

That brought a wide, smug smile to the snake's face. Seeing it made Nicholas want to punch him even more.

"Naturally, my lord, I'll be happy to comply."

"Thank you." Never had it been more difficult for Nicholas to say those words. "I'd also suggest that you refrain from paying too much attention to the maidservants, too."

Percival laughed, a particularly unpleasant sound that was like a horse wheezing. "What, Sir Nicholas, would you have me act the monk?"

Again Nicholas smiled and addressed him as if they were comrades-in-arms. "The pleasures of the tavern are available."

"Ah, yes," Percival replied, as if he were making a great concession.

"There is one other matter I feel I must mention, Percival, and that's your apparent dislike of the Scots."

Percival frowned like a petulant child.

"Whatever you may think of them and for whatever reasons, I must remind you that my estate is here in Scotland, and my brother-in-law is a Scot. My bride will have to learn to live here, too, among these people. If you are still so good as to consider bestowing your cousin's hand upon me, I think she would do well to speak to Lady Riona and her uncle, to try to come to some understanding of the Scots. If she does, that may make my final choice that much easier."

Percival got an avaricious gleam in his eyes. "I was wondering if you'd be making that decision before Lammas."

Nicholas gave him a conspiratorial smile. "I must be careful, Percival. Lord Chesleigh is a powerful man, so if I'm not picking his daughter for my bride, I must at least feign finding the choice a difficult one, and that means waiting until Lammas to announce my choice."

Percival grinned, looking like the ambitious, greedy lout he was. "I understand completely."

"I thought you would," Nicholas replied.

Percival threw his arm around Nicholas's broad

shoulders, as if he was already related to him, and said, "Shall we sample the pleasures of the tavern together today?"

It was all Nicholas could do not to grab the man's arm and twist until he screamed. "You're welcome to, but I have too many demands upon my time with so many guests."

Percival dropped his arm and shrugged his narrow shoulders. "Well, that's a pity, but I suppose that's the price one must pay as host." He sauntered toward the door and breezily waved a farewell. "Until later, my lord."

"Until later," Nicholas repeated through clenched teeth as he watched him go.

CHAPTER TEN

A SE'ENNIGHT LATER, Riona sat beside Eleanor in the sunlight shining through one of the hall windows. It was a warm July day, with only a hint of rain in the air. Eleanor embroidered a band to attach to the hem of the lovely scarlet gown she owned. Riona could sew, but her skills were of a more practical sort, suitable for mending and hemming. She didn't know complicated embroidery stitches, and wouldn't have been able to afford the materials even if she did. Nevertheless, she was more than pleased to sit beside Eleanor and help her by threading needles or cutting the bits of brightly colored wool as her friend worked at her frame. They could talk quietly, and Eleanor was teaching her some of the stitches, too.

Across the hall, Joscelind, Lavinia and Priscilla were likewise together, whispering and occasionally casting their eyes about the hall. Lady Joscelind paid no heed to Riona, and Riona ignored her just as completely. The other two ladies seemed to have thrown their lot in with the beauty, and neither Eleanor nor Riona minded a whit. Audric and Lord Chesleigh were playing chess, the board set on the table on the dais. Uncle Fergus and Fredella were somewhere in the castle, and Percival had gone to the village again, along with D'Anglevoix.

Percival had been diligently avoiding Riona. What exactly their host had said to him was a mystery, but it was not one either she, Eleanor, Uncle Fergus or Fredella cared to probe too deeply. They were content that it was so, and while Riona believed Eleanor could yet be Sir Nicholas's choice, Uncle Fergus was full of plans and schemes to free her from her cousin. Unfortunately, the law was the law, and Eleanor, who could read, had seen the documents binding her to her cousin's care. It seemed there was little they could do—legally. Yesterday, Riona had spent considerable time trying to convince Uncle Fergus that an abduction would cause more trouble than it would solve. At last, thank God, he'd conceded the point. Barely.

As for the man responsible for all this scheming, Riona had no idea where Sir Nicholas was at present. He rarely lingered in the hall, except when the evening meal was over. During the day, he personally oversaw the training of his men. Sometimes he rode with patrols around his estate, looking for outlaws or others who might cause trouble. Every morning, he spent time with his steward, going over accounts and other business. He was a very busy overlord, and he certainly couldn't be called lazy.

Looking up from her embroidery, Eleanor nodded at Lavinia. "She's not fooling anyone, you know," she noted with an amused smile. "She can hardly keep her eyes off Audric."

Riona smiled, too. "He's not a bad-looking fellow, and he seems quite nice."

For a Norman, she added inwardly, because as yet, the only truly nice Norman she'd met had been Eleanor. Fredella was born and raised in Lincolnshire, so more Saxon than Norman, and more Dane than Saxon, for the Danes had held that part of England for years upon years.

"Percival thinks Audric's destined for the church," Eleanor remarked.

"Audric will never make a priest if he keeps gazing at Lavinia the way he does," Riona replied, trying not to think of another man who would not have made a good priest.

"Do you suppose Sir Nicholas has noticed their affection?"

"I don't see how he couldn't."

"Yet she's still here."

"I'm sure he has what he considers excellent political reasons for that. Perhaps he doesn't want to risk offending their families or other relatives by asking them to go. My uncle and I are still here, after all, simply to stave off the Scots' complaints."

"I don't think you're still here just because Sir Nicholas doesn't want to offend the Scots," Eleanor replied. "I think he likes you."

Riona had been dealing with Uncle Fergus's suggestions long enough that she no longer blushed to hear such talk. "He may not dislike me, but he'll never marry me—and truly, I won't be upset if he doesn't. I don't think he's the man for me."

Unless they were in bed.

She simply had to control these lustful thoughts! And she would. God help her, she would!

Priscilla giggled over something Lady Joscelind said, as she was wont to do, causing both Eleanor and Riona to instinctively cringe.

They weren't the only ones who reacted that way to Priscilla's giggles. Riona had never spoken of it to Eleanor, but she was quite sure Nicholas found that giggle aggravating. She'd seen his jaw clench too many times when Priscilla was giggling through dinner to think it was a coincidence. The night Priscilla had sat with him at the high table, Riona had wondered how he'd managed to eat.

"If Sir Nicholas doesn't want Lavinia and she doesn't want him, that's one less woman vying for him," Eleanor said as she went back to her sewing.

"Did you ever hear why Lady Mary left?"

Eleanor reached for the blue thread. "Fredella heard her maid saying that the earl wanted to go home. He couldn't stand the weather."

Riona frowned. For one thing, the July weather had been wonderful—mild, with many sunny days and enough rainy ones to ensure an excellent harvest. For another, she couldn't help feeling that any snub aimed at Dunkeathe, even to the weather, was somehow a snub of Scotland. "It's been very pleasant."

"I think that was just an excuse, too. I suppose Lady Mary thought she had no chance."

Riona couldn't disagree with that.

"It's a pity about Lady Eloise," Eleanor remarked, knotting and snipping off a sky-blue thread. "I quite liked her."

"Uncle Fergus told me Sir George didn't think she'd go through with her threat to leave without him if he didn't stay away from the wine," Riona replied as she threaded a needle with some lovely emerald thread that was to represent delicate little vines in the pattern. "He says Sir George went white as snow when he heard she'd done it."

"I was shocked, too," Eleanor said as she exchanged her needle with the small remnant of blue thread for the one Riona held out. "I daresay she's been humiliated too many times. Do you think they'll come back?"

Riona mused a moment, then shook her head as she reached for another needle. "I don't think so. It was fairly clear Sir Nicholas didn't think very highly of Sir George, and there would be little reason for him to marry Sir George's daughter when he has you and Joscelind to choose from."

Eleanor's face turned deep pink as she bent over her sewing, Riona was sorry if she'd embarrassed her friend, but that was the truth, and Eleanor, who was no fool, had to know it. It was becoming more and more obvious that the real competition was between Eleanor and Joscelind.

Not for the first time, Riona wanted to ask Eleanor how she felt about Nicholas and her chances of succeeding, but as always, she couldn't bring herself to say the words.

Instead, she was about to ask Eleanor what color thread she'd require next when Polly came hurrying in from the kitchen, looking very worried.

She spotted Riona and Eleanor and rushed over to them. "Oh, my lady!" she cried, wringing her hands.

"What is it?" Riona asked, shoving the needle in the sawdust filled cushion and setting it in Eleanor's lovely sewing box.

"It's the cook. He's been in a right foul mood since the guests come, and he's been taking it out on all the servants. He's been shouting, and cursing something fierce."

Riona immediately remembered that first night in the garden, when she heard the cook loudly chastising the servants.

"A body might get used to that, but this morning, he lit into the spit boy with a ladle and the poor lad's black-and-blue. Won't you do something?"

"Have you told Sir Nicholas?"

As upset as Riona was to think of a boy being beaten, this household wasn't her responsibility, and her interference would likely not be welcomed. Yet if Nicholas would put one of his archers in the stocks for two months for killing a dog, surely he'd not approve one of his servants, especially a lad, being beaten.

"God love you, no, my lady!" Polly exclaimed. "Why, I nearly fainted when he called me to his solar that day he give me my dowry. To be sure, he's not such an ogre as I thought. Still…" She flushed. "Beggin' your pardon," she amended before rushing on, "but Alfred said if anybody complained, he'd say they were stealing. To be accused of that before Sir Nicholas— oh, my lady!"

"Can't you tell Robert, then?"

"He's gone to the fishing village down the river. Seems Lord Chesleigh's got a hankering for eels. Besides, Alfred's good at his job and drives hard bargains with the merchants for the wine and things, so Robert won't want to lose him."

"Who else gives orders to the household?"

"Just the cook. Won't you talk to Alfred, my lady, for our sakes, please?" Polly pleaded. "He might listen to you. Fredella says your uncle says you've got a right good way with servants and you're a lady and all. Something has to be done, or Sir Nicholas is going to have a mutiny in the kitchen!"

However she felt about Sir Nicholas, and no matter what might come of this, Riona couldn't leave the boy at the mercy of a brute who'd beat him until he was black-and-blue. "I'll speak to the cook," she said, rising.

And she'd deal with Sir Nicholas if and when he complained.

"Oh, thank you, my lady!" Polly cried, relieved. "I'm sure you'll find a way to get Alfred—fat oaf that he is—to see reason! And poor Tom'll be pleased."

Riona looked down at Eleanor. "This could be unpleasant, so if you'd rather stay here, I'll understand."

Eleanor set aside her sewing and got to her feet. "I'd rather come with you."

Impressed by her resolve, glad of her company, Riona immediately started for the kitchen, followed by a silent Eleanor.

Polly, however, was the opposite of silent. "We used to have a fine cook," she said breathlessly as she trotted to keep up with Riona and Eleanor, "but Etienne went home to Normandy, and this one come in his place. He's a right villain, beggin' your pardon. He gives an order, then forgets what he said, and gets angry when that ain't done and we done something else, like we're supposed to read his mind. Three of the girls just up and left yesterday and won't come back, even after they heard what his lordship done for me. Said it wasn't worth it, as long as Alfred was here, and I don't blame 'em. I'd go, too, except that Sir Nicholas is giving me a dowry."

As they drew near the kitchen, they could hear the cook cursing and shouting orders through the door.

Riona pushed it open and found herself in an enormous room that was easily the size of her uncle's hall, manned by what seemed an army of servants. There was a huge open hearth at one end and a large wooden worktable. Ham, leeks and herbs hung from the ceiling.

In the center of the room, waving a ladle, was an enormous, and enormously irate, red-faced, middle-aged, bald man. He wore a very stained apron, and was sweating from the heat—or from the effort of berating the two women standing at the worktable, pies in front of them. The crust had come apart around the rim, and gravy had boiled over and run down the sides.

"Are you blind? Or idiots?" he screamed as other servants huddled together or watched warily as they went about their work.

"How many times did I tell you to cut the crust?" Alfred made slashing motions with his ladle. "Now they're ruined! Fit only for the pigs!" He grabbed one pie and threw it into the hearth, where it splattered against the back wall.

That's when Riona saw the boy crouched in the corner near the hearth, his thin arms thrown over his head. His thin, black-and-blue arms.

Quivering with indignant rage, she marched up to the cook and grabbed the ladle out of his chubby fingers. "Lay a hand on that boy, or any servant in this kitchen again, and you'll be sorry," she said sternly, throwing the ladle onto the floor. "And quit shouting, if you'd like to be heard. You sound like a spoiled child, or some tavern keeper, not the cook in a lord's hall."

The cook folded his fat arms over his prodigious belly and looked down his short nose at her. "And who are you, to be coming into my kitchen and telling me what to do?"

She leaned close to the cook's sweaty face, ignoring the odor of beef and gravy he gave off. "I am Lady Riona of Glencleith, and I've been in charge of my uncle's household since I was twelve years old—and never, in all that time, have I had to raise my voice and curse the servants."

"Well, Lady Riona of Whatever-you-said," he retorted, "I have been a nobleman's cook for twenty years, and I've never had any complaints from my masters."

"Not yet, anyway. I intend to tell Sir Nicholas what's been going on here."

The cook sniffed. "What will he care? He pays me well for my skill, and that's all that matters."

Riona smiled slowly, in a way that struck deserved fear into the merchants who tried to cheat her. "You think so?"

"Yes, I do!"

"We'll just have to see about that," she snapped as she turned on her heel and gestured for Eleanor. "Come. We'll go find Sir Nicholas and see who's right."

She marched out of the kitchen and into the courtyard. Then she realized she didn't know where Nicholas was, whether with his soldiers or out on patrol, or in his solar. She came to a frustrated halt, which also gave Eleanor and Polly, who'd hurried out of the kitchen after her, time to catch up.

"If you don't mind, Riona," Eleanor said anxiously, "I think I'd rather not be there when you tell Sir Nicholas about his cook."

Riona nodded her acquiescence. She was sorry Eleanor's resolution had been so short-lived, but she couldn't fault the girl for wanting to avoid any conflict within the household of the man she might marry.

As Eleanor headed for the apartments, Polly started to back away. "I should get to, um, the laundry. They always need help there," she said before she scampered off.

Riona drew in a deep breath. So, she'd have to face Nicholas alone. So be it.

She hurried up to the Saxons on guard at the gate. "Have you seen Sir Nicholas lately?"

"Yes, my lady," one respectfully replied. "He's in the inner ward with the rest of the garrison."

"Thank you."

Once on the other side of the gates, she listened for the sounds of men training. They were on the far side of the ward, away from the encampment of the soldiers who'd come with the visiting nobles.

Quickening her pace, she hurried on until she rounded a corner and discovered a troop of half-naked soldiers holding wooden swords, fighting in pairs. It was like watching a bizarre sort of dance as the men moved forward and back, swinging their weapons, attacking each other or defending themselves. The sound of wood on wood was like drumbeats, broken by the oc-

casional cry of pain when wood connected with an arm
or a leg. They must have been at it for quite some time,
for most of the men looked very tired as well as sweaty.
Perspiration dripped down their backs and chests and
soaked the waist of their breeches.

Walking among them, armed with his plain sword,
and stripped to the waist, was Nicholas. He barked out
orders, his deep voice carrying easily over the noise of
the clashing weapons, his skin glistening in the sunlight
as if it was oiled.

Lust—hot, primitive, as powerful as the priests
warned—crept into her body and enflamed her from
within. It was wrong to stand and watch when the mere
sight of him affected her so, but she simply couldn't
take her eyes off the lord of Dunkeathe as he moved.
Or when he stopped to issue a command or correction,
demonstrating how the blade should move, his muscles
rippling with his actions.

She'd never been so stirred by the sight of a half-
naked man—but then, he was like no man she'd ever
seen. He had not an ounce of fat on his lean torso. His
sinewy muscles bespoke hours of hard work, years of
training, weeks of fighting. He was no pampered,
spoiled, lazy nobleman who'd never worked for his
wealth. He was a warrior—built like a warrior, fierce
as a warrior, passionate as a warrior home from battle
seeking the pleasures of peace.

And then he saw her.

She quickly looked away as she flushed with embarrassment and fought the urge to run away. It was like catching him bathing—or as if he had caught her naked. Only the thought of the poor spit boy kept her there as Nicholas ordered his men to continue, and walked toward her.

Couldn't he at least put on some more clothes? she thought, feeling determined, but trapped, as he closed the distance between them. "Were you looking for me, my lady?" he asked evenly. "Or did you just want to watch my men at practice?"

"I was looking for you, my lord," she said, pleased that her voice was calm and steady as she replied. "I've come to talk to you about your cook, Alfred."

Nicholas frowned and crossed his arms, leaning his weight on one leg. "What about Alfred?"

She kept her gaze on his face, away from his body. "You should find another cook."

His dark brows rose. "You don't like the food?"

"It's not that, my lord. It's the way he treats the kitchen servants. He's a bully and a tyrant, and he's been beating the spit boy until he's covered in bruises. I've seen them myself."

"I see," Nicholas replied, his tone noncommittal as he turned back to his men and dismissed them. They gratefully hurried over to some buckets of water along the wall and scrambled to drink.

Not sure what he was thinking, she took a different tack. "If something isn't done to amend the situation, your servants could be driven to an act of desperation

in attempt to either make Alfred leave of his own voli-
tion, or force you to send him away. They might use
rancid meat, for instance, to sicken you and your guests,
so that he's blamed. Or engage in other kinds of sabotage. There are a whole host of ways to get revenge on
a cook, my lord."

"There will be no need for that. I won't permit the
beating of my servants, by anyone," Nicholas said.
"Such treatment inspires anger and hatred and bitter resentment, as I well know. I was beaten every day by the
man to whom I was first fostered for training."

It seemed impossible Sir Nicholas of Dunkeathe had
ever been anything but a mature man and the powerful
overlord of a castle. Yet once, he had been a mistreated
boy, and apparently with no one to help and come to
his aid.

His expression hardened, and his voice was cold
when he spoke. "Spare yourself any pity you might be
feeling for me, my lady. If I'd been taught music and
poetry instead, I wouldn't be in possession of this estate. And I paid Yves Sansouci back for every bruise,
every lash, every gash and cut." He pointed to a small
scar on his temple. "The day he gave me this, I broke
his arm and nearly crippled him. After that, my brother
and I went elsewhere, to train with a better man."

He picked up a leather jerkin that was lying on the
ground nearby.

As he tugged it over his head, she tried not to notice
that was the same jerkin he'd been wearing that first day.

The men, having had their fill, started to gather up their garments. They talked among themselves and cast glances at their commander and Riona, as they moved off toward the gates. Even as they left, however, she was well aware there were other soldiers up on the wall walk, watching them.

"The servants should have come to me," he said, apparently oblivious to the curious looks from the men.

"They didn't come to you because Alfred threatened to accuse anyone who told you with theft."

Nicholas frowned. "I require proof before I punish anyone for a crime."

"I don't think they know that, my lord." Neither had she, although once he said it, she believed him. "And you're…"

"What?" he asked when she hesitated.

Driven to it, she said, "You're very intimidating. If I were your servant, I'd think twice about coming to you with a complaint, about anything."

"I am what I am, my lady, and what my life has made me. I cannot change."

"Not even if it means your own household lives in fear of you? That isn't commanding their respect, my lord. That's tyranny and it also leads to anger and resentment."

"A castle requires discipline, my lady. Or perhaps you'd like me to tuck my soldiers into bed at night and sing them a lullaby? Maybe you'd like me to weave daisy chains for the maidservants? Or declare every second day a holiday?"

"Occasional praise can be as effective as correction."

He leaned down to grab his sword belt and scabbard that had been beneath the jerkin. "When you are in command of a castle and garrison, I'll take your advice."

Worried she'd angered him too much and that he wouldn't do anything about Alfred, she tried to lessen the tension between them. "You're right. I don't know much about commanding a garrison, especially one so large."

"A man has to protect what is his."

"I don't think there would be too many men willing to try to take Dunkeathe from you."

"Because I have such a large garrison."

"And because the king gave it to you."

Although Nicholas's eyes still burned with indignation, he didn't sound quite so annoyed. "In spite of that, I know most Scots wish me gone."

"My uncle doesn't."

"Then he's an exception," Nicholas replied as he buckled his belt about his waist. He raised an inquisitive brow. "I suppose your uncle adheres to the notion that no Scot would betray another or try to take what is his by force?"

"My uncle certainly thinks the Scots are the finest, most trustworthy people on earth, but we've heard of the betrayal of Lachlann Mac Taran, and how it nearly cost your sister her life."

"And what about you, my lady?" Nicholas asked. "Do you have a similarly high opinion of your people?"

"I think some people are greedy and ambitious and will stop at nothing to get what they want, no matter where they're born. Fortunately, my uncle's holding is too small and insignificant and rocky to be of interest to clever, scheming, ambitious men."

"Do you think *I* am a clever, scheming, ambitious man?"

She met his gaze squarely. "I believe you're ambitious, or you wouldn't have worked so hard for your success. And you aren't a fool, my lord, or again, you wouldn't be in possession of this land and this castle. As for scheming, your plan to find a bride seems rather heartless."

"If I crave wealth and power, Riona," he grimly replied, "it's because I know what it is to lack them. If my method of choosing a bride seems cold and calculated, it's because I can't marry just to satisfy my desire."

Why did he have to speak of desire?

"Sir Nicholas!" a voice bellowed, one that Riona had recently heard raised in rage and frustration.

The cook came marching toward them across the ward, his face red, his breathing heavy with the effort.

Wondering what Nicholas was going to do, Riona slid him a wary glance. His face rarely betrayed any hint of what he was thinking, but unless she was very much mistaken, Alfred was about to discover that

Nicholas of Dunkeathe had little use for men who beat defenseless boys.

The cook seemed to realize something was amiss, for before he reached them, he pointed at Riona and declared, "My lord, this Scot is filling your head with lies and false accusations. She even threatened me! Who does she think she is, anyway? She's not in charge of my kitchen."

"Neither are you," Nicholas replied, his voice cold and his tone imperious. "I am in charge of Dunkeathe, Alfred, and therefore in charge of the kitchen."

"But I am in your employ to run your kitchen, my lord," Alfred protested, his voice now more whining than defiant. "I haven't failed you in that. And my skills are without question."

"It isn't your cooking that's at issue. I understand you beat the spit boy."

After another malevolent glance at Riona, Alfred said, "He let the meat burn, my lord. Would you have me excuse him, or pat him on the head and say never mind? I had to beat him to teach him not to do it again, and by God, my lord, he won't."

"Or what? You'll kill him?"

Alfred sucked in his breath and regarded Riona as if she'd unfairly accused him of attempted murder. "I don't know what she's been saying, my lord—"

"She told me that you beat the boy. She told me that the rest of the servants aren't pleased with your governance. She told me I could have serious trouble if something isn't done."

Sweat trickled down the sides of the cook's reddening face. "What does it matter what the servants think, as long as they do their work—and by God, my lord, I see that they do!" Alfred retorted. "What sort of serious trouble is this woman—this Scot—talking about?"

"The sort of trouble I've seen many times when a commander isn't fit to lead."

"Not fit?" Alfred cried. "*I'm* not fit? I tell you, my lord, I've been cooking for noblemen since you were nothing more than a poor soldier in the pay of anybody who'd hire you and I won't be treated like this. Either she goes, or I do!"

As Riona held her breath, Nicholas's brows lowered. "Since you must be unhappy working for a man who was once nothing more than a poor soldier in the pay of anyone who'd hire him, I'm sure you'd be happier somewhere else."

The cook gulped and suddenly seemed to realize he'd said far too much, and to the wrong man. "Forgive my hasty words, my lord," he stammered. "She got me angry, that's all. You always let me have a free hand to run the kitchen as I see fit, so when she came and tried to take charge—"

"Did you try to take charge of Alfred's kitchen, my lady?" Nicholas asked as he looked at Riona, and in his dark eyes, she saw a skepticism that told her who he believed.

Her heart singing, she answered him with frank honesty. "I told him to stop beating the spit boy, my lord, and that I was going to tell you what was going on. If that's taking charge, I did—and I'd do it again."

Nicholas turned back to the cook. "Alfred, you will leave Dunkeathe immediately."

"But my lord, surely you don't mean that!"

"I assure you, I do."

"With so many noble guests and their servants? Who will supervise those lazy louts in the kitchen?"

"That will be my concern, Alfred, not yours. Collect your things and be gone before sunset. Or would you prefer to spend the next week or two in the stocks alongside Burnley?"

Alfred blanched and backed away. "All right, my lord, I'll go," he said, his whole body shaking, "and good riddance to you and your lazy servants and this damned country! I hope you all rot!"

Riona let her breath out slowly as she watched the cook run away as fast as his fat legs could take him.

As Nicholas came to stand beside her, he said, "He's right about one thing. Now I have no cook and thus no one to supervise my kitchen."

His expression speculative, he turned to her. "While I appreciate that you acted out of sympathy for the spit boy, I also recall that your uncle claims you are a wonder at the management of a household. Would it be too much to ask that you take command of my kitchen in the interim? I assure you, I'll have Robert do his utmost to hire another cook as quickly as possible."

He made that sound like a perfectly reasonable request, and there was flattery and respect in it, too. Happiness bloomed within her, at least for a moment, until certain realities intruded. "I don't know the sort of dishes Normans like."

"The servants ought to have learned something from Alfred," he countered. "All they need is someone to oversee the meals and ensure that there's enough for everyone to eat, and at the appropriate time—although given that I'm expecting my sister and her family, perhaps you could show them how to prepare a few Scots dishes."

How could she refuse to oblige him when his proposal sounded so reasonable, and she would have the chance to make something her uncle would like? "Very well, my lord."

His eyes suddenly seemed to glow, and his lips curved up in a satisfied smile. "Maybe I should even thank you, for it occurs to me that I now have a way to determine which of the ladies remaining are best able to run my household. Each of them will take it in turn, with you to start."

Riona frowned. "I didn't complain about your cook so that you could have a contest to find the most competent bride."

"Yet it gives me that opportunity just the same," he replied without so much as a hint of shame. "If you'd rather not participate, I suppose Lady Joscelind could take the first—"

"I'll do it," Riona said. "Now if you'll excuse me,

I'd best get to the kitchen and see what remains to be done for tonight's meal."

As she marched away, determined to show Nicholas, Lady Joscelind and anybody else that if she wasn't pretty or young or rich or from a powerful family, she wasn't completely useless, Nicholas went to the buckets by the wall. He found one that wasn't empty and dumped what was left of the cold water on his head.

CHAPTER ELEVEN

A SHORT TIME LATER, Robert stared at his master seated in the solar.

"Alfred has gone?" he repeated with a combination of shock, dismay and concern, "and you've asked Lady Riona to take charge of the kitchen?"

"Yes," Nicholas replied, trying to make it sound as if this was something not at all odd or out of the ordinary, although it was certainly both.

Yet what else could he do, with Alfred gone and guests still in Dunkeathe? He needed someone to supervise the kitchen, and it couldn't be him, or Robert, either. His steward had enough to do without that additional burden. Instead, he'd immediately turned to Riona, as he would ask a trusted comrade to take over command of his men in battle. Perhaps he should have taken more time to think about this decision, but he didn't regret it.

"I must point out, my lord, that Alfred's a most excellent cook. I've had many compliments on your behalf for the fine table and he keeps a tight rein on the costs and now that he knows you don't approve of his methods—"

"He beat the spit boy," Nicholas reiterated, in a tone intended to convey, once and for all, that there would be no second chances after that.

Robert flushed and shuffled his feet. "My lord, if I had known, I assure you, I would have—"

"You knew *nothing* of what was going on in the kitchen?"

Robert's blush deepened and he didn't meet Nicholas's gaze. "No, I didn't, my lord, to my shame. I should have paid more heed to the way Alfred was treating his underlings."

Nicholas nodded. "Yes, you should—and so should I. It should not have fallen to a guest to inform us of Alfred's brutality. I want you to make it clear, Robert, that from now on, I will not countenance such treatment of any servant in my household, no matter how humble he or she may be."

"Yes, my lord." Robert cleared his throat. "Unfortunately, some of the other guests might wonder about this, um, selection of Lady Riona. They'll surely think that's a mark of your favor and take it as a sign of your intention to give her that place permanently, as your wife."

"Since Lady Riona's uncle claims she has many years experience in that regard, I thought I would give her a chance to prove it. I'll also give the other ladies the same opportunity to demonstrate that they're capable of running my household."

Robert eyes widened. "As a sort of test, my lord?"

"Exactly." He rubbed his chin. "And I've asked Lady Riona to supervise the preparation of something Marianne's husband will like. He's always complaining about Norman dishes."

Robert looked shocked. "He's never said a word to me about that, my lord."

"It's nothing," Nicholas said, waving his hand dismissively. "I think Adair enjoys trying to annoy me. If it wasn't the food, it'd be something else." Nicholas gave his steward a hint of a smile. "So this time, I'll provide him with food he should enjoy and see if I'm right."

A relieved Robert grinned, then sobered. "I do hope Lady Riona's abilities haven't been overestimated by her uncle."

From what he had already seen of her relationship with the servants and even his soldiers, Nicholas didn't think they had. In some ways, she reminded him of Sir Leonard, who'd trained him after he'd left the vicious Yves's command. Sir Leonard could drink and wench and tell stories with the men he trained, yet none ever forgot who was the master, and who the student.

He'd never expected to find that quality in a woman.

As for her comments on his methods of training his men, he didn't need her advice about *that*.

Yet Sir Leonard sometimes gave out praise. Nicholas particularly remembered one rainy day, when he was cold and wet and miserable and despairing he would ever be able to wield a lance. Sir Leonard had taken him aside and told him that although he would probably never be as good as some of the others—something it had galled him to hear—he was doing better every time.

"You can't expect to be the best at everything," Sir Leonard had said. "Settle for being the best at one, and adequate at the others. Your strength is in your sword arm, not aiming a lance or swinging a mace. All you have to do is get your man to the ground, where you can use your sword." Then he'd given Nicholas one of his rare, sardonic smiles. "Just don't let your opponent kill you first."

The door to the solar burst open, and a very irate Lord Chesleigh strode into the room, followed by a scowling Sir Percival and an equally annoyed D'Anglevoix. Audric came last, although he looked less angry and more puzzled than the others.

"Is this true, my lord?" Lord Chesleigh demanded as he came to a halt, arms akimbo, utterly ignoring Robert. "Have you set that woman…that Scot…Fiona or Rianne or whatever her name is…in charge of your household?"

Nicholas rose as courtesy required, yet in a way that should have instantly told Lady Joscelind's father that his host wasn't inclined to look with favor on a man who stormed into his solar. Meanwhile, Robert sidled back into a corner.

"Lady Riona is temporarily in charge of my kitchen," Nicholas replied evenly as he came around his table.

"What, will we have to eat that stuff those Scots make out of oats?" D'Anglevoix asked in his frostiest, most patrician manner. "God, it's perfectly vile."

Lord Chesleigh shot the man a disgusted look. "It's not the food we're here to discuss," he snapped. "Am I to understand by this, my lord, that you've made your choice for your bride?"

"Yes, have you picked?" Percival seconded, looking far from pleased.

"No, I have not," Nicholas replied. "Lady Riona had a confrontation with my cook over his management of the servants, with the result that the cook has left Dunkeathe. I needed someone to take charge of my kitchen, and for now, it's going to be Lady Riona. After that, the other ladies will take their turn."

Now Audric wasn't the only one who looked puzzled.

"You see, gentlemen, I require a wife capable of running my household in a calm, efficient manner," Nicholas explained, "and this will allow me to be certain of my bride's qualifications in that respect."

Lord Chesleigh's eyes lit up, while Percival frowned. D'Anglevoix looked down his aquiline nose as if this was simply beneath his second cousin, and Audric appeared very worried indeed.

"Does anyone have any objections?" Nicholas asked. "If you do and you don't wish your relative to supervise my kitchen, you are, of course, free to take your leave." He smiled with his lips and spread his arms. "But I do hope you can understand. I'm a soldier, with little knowledge of domestic matters. My household, and all the expenses it requires, will be completely in my wife's hands. I wouldn't want to discover I'd married a woman who couldn't handle that responsibility."

"I assure you, Sir Nicholas," Lord Chesleigh declared, "that Joscelind will prove she's not only beautiful, she's very capable of managing a nobleman's household."

"Lavinia will prove herself, as well," D'Anglevoix vowed.

The silent Audric started biting his nails. Nicholas suspected he was envisioning his sister's chance to marry the lord of Dunkeathe disappearing like so much smoke in a brisk breeze.

"Well, _I_ don't think that's right or just," Percival huffed. "Your wife won't be in the kitchen cooking, will she? You'll be hiring another cook, won't you?"

"Yes, I will, but as I said, I want to know my bride is capable of ruling my household."

"If you think your cousin isn't up to it, Percival," Lord Chesleigh said, "perhaps you should cut and run before she embarrasses you with her failure."

"Eleanor won't fail," Percival replied angrily. Then he marched out of the room.

Audric bowed and followed him, still without saying a word.

Lord Chesleigh sighed and shook his head and gave

Nicholas a sympathetic smile. "Poor Percival is such a hothead," he said. "And his cousin is even less mature."

"Lady Eleanor is a pretty girl," D'Anglevoix noted, "yet prettiness can be no match for experience. Lavinia's mother was a most excellent chatelaine, and I'm sure Lavinia will be the same."

"I look forward to having that opinion borne out," Nicholas said with a polite little bow.

Lord Chesleigh gave D'Anglevoix a patronizing smile. "Yes, we'll find out how capable she is, won't we?"

Again, Nicholas had the sensation he was trying to hold off opposing armies—or that such a task would actually be easier. "Now, my lords, if no one has any objections, I have a few other matters of some importance to discuss with my steward."

"Of course," Lord Chesleigh said, turning to leave.

D'Anglevoix nodded his farewell, and strolled from the room after Lord Chesleigh.

Robert slowly let his breath out as he came forward. "That went better than I anticipated," he admitted. "I thought Lord Chesleigh might find the idea of a competition insulting."

"Not when he's sure Joscelind will win," Nicholas replied.

"Ah, my lord, here you are!" a voice proclaimed with a familiar Scots lilt. Fergus Mac Gordon came bustling into the solar, a bundle of indigo-blue wool shot through with scarlet in his hands.

"Is there something I can help you with?" Robert said, moving to intercept the jovial Scotsman.

"Not unless you're going to plan the wedding," Fergus Mac Gordon replied, laughing.

He put the bundle down on the table in front of Nicholas, gave it a pat, stepped back, crossed his arms and beamed at the Norman. "There you go. My wedding present to the groom. The finest *feileadh* and shirt in Glencleith, except my own. Although I must say, my lord, I thought you'd ask my permission first. Just a formality, of course, but I *am* her uncle."

The Scot winked as if they were sharing a great joke. "There's no point keeping it a secret."

Nicholas knew he should tell the man the truth, that Riona would never be his choice, and yet, the words didn't come. "I fear, sir, that if you or anybody else thinks I've made my decision, you're mistaken."

The little man stopped smiling. His face fell, and Nicholas nearly squirmed beneath his dismayed gaze. "Then you mean to say it's like Riona said? She's only helping for a little while? I thought she was just being modest."

"All the young ladies are going to be given the same opportunity, as a means for me to determine if they're capable of running my household."

"Ah!" the Scot cried, his happiness apparently completely restored. He rubbed his hands together like a man about to tuck into a fine meal. "A test, is it? What a clever fellow you are! But you mark my words, my lord, Riona will win. It won't even be close. You'll see. She's got a way with the servants—aye and the purse strings. She doesn't think I know just how clever with the coins she is, but she's kept us in food and drink during some rough winters." He winked at Robert. "Between your clever steward here and your wife, you'll wind up a rich and happy man."

However appalled Robert was by Mac Gordon's familiar manner, he seemed quite pleased by the compliment.

Realizing with a twinge of guilt that he'd never praised Robert's efforts, Nicholas leaned forward and pushed the bundle toward Mac Gordon. "Regardless of what happens, you should keep this until I announce my choice."

Holding up his hands as if the cloth had burst into flames, the older man shook his head and, laughing more, backed away. "There's no need. You'll see, my lord. You'll not find a better manager in all of Scotland. Or a more clever, bonnier bride. So you keep the *feileadh* and shirt for when you need them."

With another wink, he was gone.

God save him, the man was like some sort of gnome. A stubborn, amusing, sprightly gnome.

"Does he really think you'll ever wear a *feileadh?*" Robert wondered aloud.

Nicholas could hardly see himself wearing that skirted garment, either. He had gotten used to it on the Scots, but he couldn't envision himself striding around

Dunkeathe with bare knees. So he shook his head as he undid the bit of rope holding the bundle together, to reveal a white linen shirt and a long length of very fine, soft wool woven in a square pattern.

"That's a lot of cloth," Robert observed.

Nicholas did the bundle up again. "Which I'll never wear," he said as he carried it over to the chest that held all the rolls and records of the estate. He opened the lid and moved around parchments, then placed the bundle in the bottom. "There it'll stay until it's time for the man and his niece to leave."

"Then you really don't consider Lady Riona a possible bride?"

"No."

"What are these other matters you wish to discuss, my lord?" Robert inquired as Nicholas lowered the lid.

"I said that so those men would leave," Nicholas confessed without regret or embarrassment. "I've had just about my fill of Lord Chesleigh in particular."

Robert smiled. "Yes, I can see that, and I can see why," he said. "I'll go ensure that the chambers for your sister and her family are prepared."

Nicholas nodded a farewell, and when the steward was gone, he started to pace. Maybe he shouldn't have asked Riona to take over the supervision of his kitchen. He should be trying to ignore her as much as possible. Another fortnight, and he'd make his choice of bride and his financial troubles would be at an end. His hold on his estate would be secure. He would have some influence among the powerful men at court.

He couldn't risk losing that. Not for a woman who would bring nothing to the marriage except herself, no matter how competent she seemed. Or how tempting.

"WHAT DO YOU MEAN, you don't know anything about supervising kitchen servants?" Percival demanded as he stared at Eleanor with blatant disbelief. "Are you some kind of simpleton?

Eleanor cringed. "I've never had a chance to learn."

"Your mother never, ever, taught you how to manage servants?"

"I was too young to be taught much before she died, and you've never let me—"

"Damn your parents for making you a millstone around my neck!"

Eleanor could bear his criticism of her, but when Percival cursed her parents, she glared at him with all the hatred she felt. "I despise you!"

"I don't care," he retorted. "Except that it should make you that much more anxious to marry Sir Nicholas to get away from me. But now you tell me you're useless as a chatelaine."

He picked up one of her combs made of ivory, ready to throw it at her, when the sounds of a commotion in the yard stayed his hand. He marched to the window to see what was happening. "That must be Nicholas's sister and the Scot she married."

He whirled around, a gleam of malicious delight in his eyes. "The man she had to marry because they were found in her bedchamber together, in the middle of the night."

Eleanor started for the door.

He intercepted her. "Where do you think you're going? To Sir Nicholas, to tell him what a loathsome beast I am? You could, but I doubt that would inspire him to choose you, or I'd suggest it myself.

"Here's what we're going to do instead, dear cousin. You're going to seduce him. You're going to find a way to get into his bed and become his lover. Then I'll 'discover' you together and he'll have to marry you."

"That's despicable!" she cried, trying to get around him.

"So what, if it works?" Percival demanded as he grabbed her arm and held her. He ran his gaze over her face, and then her body. "You shouldn't have a great deal of trouble seducing him, Eleanor."

"I won't dishonor myself!"

"We'll have to be subtle," Percival mused aloud, ignoring her protest, her struggles, her dismay. "Give him longing looks and maybe find a way to brush against him. Seek out chances to be alone with him for a few stolen kisses."

"I won't!"

Percival's arm snaked around her and he pulled her against his slender body that smelled of wine and stale perfume. There was a hungry gleam in his eyes that she'd never seen before. "Yes, I think it would be best to go slowly at first. A few kisses of those soft lips of yours first, along with some suitable moans and sighs. Then you can claim to be overwhelmed by desire, and he'll believe it."

"I'm not going to play the harlot!"

His embrace tightened still more, so that she could scarcely breathe. "Oh yes, you will," he said, "because I promise you, my sweet cousin, that if I have to send you to that convent, you won't go there a virgin, whether Sir Nicholas has the pleasure, or I do."

His mouth crushed hers and his hand grabbed her breast. Shocked, horrified, she shoved him away with every bit of strength she had. "Don't touch me!"

He merely smiled and delicately wiped his lips with the cuff of his tunic. "Either Sir Nicholas or me, my dear," he said as he strolled to the door. "The choice is yours."

AS THEY WERE returning from the storehouse with a basket of fish for the evening meal, Polly grabbed Riona's forearm and pointed at the man who had just ridden into the courtyard. He was tall, broad-shouldered, wearing a *feileadh* and shirt and boots, and riding a very fine horse. His dark hair hung to his shoulders, with two small braids at the sides.

"That's him, Adair Mac Taran," Polly said in an enthusiastic whisper, as if she feared he would hear her even though he was several yards away. "Now, did I lie, my lady? Is he not the handsomest man you've ever seen?"

"Yes, he's very handsome."

And so he was, in a conventional sort of way. She'd always heard Adair Mac Taran described as a charmer, and she could see that, in the smile he had on his face. Not for him grim inscrutability, that stern determination, that hint of deep loneliness that made a woman want to hold him close and whisper that she would never leave him.

Riona shook her head as if to rid her mind of that ridiculous thought.

Meanwhile, a wagon rumbled into the yard behind Adair Mac Taran. Its bed was covered with a canvas and it was driven by a large, robust, brown-haired Scot likewise clad in a *feileadh* and with a *claimh mhor* slung across his back. Also seated on the wagon was the most beautiful woman Riona had ever seen, cradling a baby wrapped in a light green blanket. The woman's lovely features would make even Lady Joscelind look plain. She wore a simple, yet well-fitting gown of dark blue wool, with a fine cloak over her and she sat on that wagon seat like a queen upon her throne.

"Who's the other man?" Riona asked Polly, nodding at the fellow beside Nicholas's sister.

"That's their clansman, Roban. Their little boy must be in the back of the wagon. He's an imp, that one."

"I'm surprised that Roban's got his *claimh mhor.* That's rather a fearsome weapon for a peaceful visit. My uncle left his at home."

"Sir Nicholas gave him leave," Polly answered, "since he's such a good friend to Adair, and stood by him when his brother turned against him."

Adair Mac Taran swung down from his horse. Like Sir Nicholas, he had an athletic grace, a way of moving that seemed fluid and easy.

"Greetings, brother-in-law!" Adair cried when Nicholas came out of the hall, his jovial, bass voice echoing through the yard.

"Greetings, Adair," Nicholas replied as he reached them. "One of the grooms will show you where to stable your horse, since the usual stall is already occupied."

Then he smiled up at his sister. It was a small smile, but it softened the harsh angles of his face in a way that made Riona remember that night in the garden. "I trust the road wasn't too rough, Marianne."

The lady smiled in return. "Your men must have been working very hard indeed, for it's much improved."

"The road may be some better," Roban said as he climbed down from the wagon, "but I wish I'd had my horse beneath me and not this wooden seat."

"I'm sorry, Roban, but you would insist on driving the cart," Lady Marianne replied.

"You couldn't do it with a babe in your arms."

"Cellach would have been fine in her basket," Lady Marianne replied, and even though it was genially said, Riona heard a hint of her brother's stern resolve in her voice.

"What if Cellach got to fussing?" Adair asked as he joined his wife. "Could you see Roban carrying her in his arms on his horse?"

That made the lady laugh. "No, and I'm grateful for your help, Roban. Truly I am."

Equanimity restored, Roban chortled, his teeth visible through his dark beard.

"Where's Seamus?" Nicholas asked.

"He fell asleep," his sister answered, nodding at the back of the wagon.

"And not a minute too soon," Roban said darkly. "I thought I'd have to tie him down or he'd fall out." He rubbed his throat. "This journey's made me thirsty. I wonder if that Mairi's got more of the *uisge beatha* she makes so well?"

"I believe she has, although why you prefer that to wine, I'll never understand," Nicholas answered gravely. In spite of his serious mien, Riona could hear amusement in the lord of Dunkeathe's voice.

"Well then, if you'll excuse me," Roban replied, "I'll step over to the village, since I don't think you'll be needing me anymore today."

"No, go ahead, and have one for me," Adair said.

As Roban headed for the gates, whistling a rollicking tune, a tousled haired, towheaded little boy about four years old stuck his head out of the canvas covering of the wagon.

"Uncle Nicholas!" he cried as he climbed over the

seat. He stood up and threw out his arms. "Catch me!" he ordered—and then he launched himself at Nicholas.

With a gasp, Riona started forward, while Nicholas lunged and caught the boy in midair.

"Seamus, you're getting too big for that," Lady Marianne admonished as Riona halted and backed away, trying not to feel like a complete fool. "One of these days you're going to fall or hurt your uncle."

Man and boy both looked at Lady Marianne, the boy with skepticism and the man as if she'd called both his honor and his masculinity into question.

"Nevertheless, your mother could be right," Nicholas reluctantly admitted as he looked down at the boy, "if you keep growing the way you are."

"Oh, I can't hurt *you*," the little boy said, not a whit disturbed by his mother's admonition as he smiled up at his uncle. "You'll always catch me."

Yes, yes, he would, Riona thought. Nicholas would never fail to protect anything he loved, whether it was this castle, or his nephew, or his sister. Or his wife, whichever woman could win him.

"He does that every time," Polly noted. "Didn't I say he was an imp? God love him, though, he'll be a brave one, like his father and uncle."

Adair Mac Taran ruffled the lad's blond hair. "Now then, young rapscallion, will you go with your mother and uncle into the hall, or help me with Neas?"

"Neas!" Seamus cried, jumping up and down. "Can I ride him? Please!"

The Scot laughed, the sound like a deeper version of the boy's merriment. He scooped up his son and deposited him on the back of his horse. "Hold on tight, Seamus. Our family honor will be besmirched if you fall off."

"I won't fall," the boy declared. He looked so determined, he reminded Riona very much of his uncle, and she was quite sure he'd stay on the horse no matter what.

Lady Marianne held her baby out to her brother. "Here, take Cellach," she ordered.

"Give me your hand and I'll help you down," Nicholas answered.

"Don't be silly," Lady Marianne chided, and again, Riona heard that hint of familiar resolve. "Hold Cellach and I'll get down by myself."

With a pained look, Nicholas complied, taking the little bundle of baby awkwardly. As his sister climbed down off the cart, he gazed at the wee bairn nestled safely in his powerful arms as if she were a miracle.

He might be imposing—and he was—and he might be intimidating—and he was—but as Riona watched him, her throat tightened, and she was filled with a burning, bitter envy for the woman who would bear his child.

Once Lady Marianne was on the ground, Nicholas immediately went to give the baby back to her.

"Why don't you hold her a while longer? You seem to have a way with her," Lady Marianne said as she slipped her arm through his.

He looked as if he'd rather walk through fire. "You take her."

His sister blithely ignored him. "Now tell me all the news," she said as they started toward the hall.

Suddenly, Lady Marianne looked Riona's way. Their eyes met, and in that brief instant, the lady's curious gaze seemed as penetrating as her brother's, capable of reading the secret desires of Riona's heart.

Riona silently cursed herself for lingering in the courtyard when she had so much to do. "Come along, Polly," she said briskly, hurrying away. "We've wasted enough time already."

CHAPTER TWELVE

WITH MARIANNE STANDING to his right and Adair to his left at the high table, Nicholas waited for the priest to say the blessing for the evening meal. All the nobles were assembled here, except Lady Riona, her uncle and Roban. Riona was likely in the kitchen, ensuring all was well in hand. He had no idea where her uncle and Roban were, although he noted that Lady Eleanor's maidservant was present.

It had been interesting watching the men when they were introduced to Marianne and Adair. With Marianne, Percival had acted like the vain fool he was, D'Anglevoix had seemed to melt a little and Lord Chesleigh had been courtesy itself.

They were less sure how to react to Adair, who stood with feet planted, arms crossed and a smile on his face that seemed to dare them to think he was anything but the finest and bravest of men. Naturally, they didn't dare indicate if they were less than impressed with the warlike Scot.

The other younger nobles had reacted as expected. Lavinia had quietly said a few words, then moved away.

Priscilla had giggled, and Audric had bowed politely and said something about Scots' valor, which proved he was both wise and a gentleman. Joscelind had been impressed by Adair, and less by Marianne, although she was careful not to show much on her beautiful face.

A pale Eleanor had said little.

Nicholas's glance darted between Eleanor and Joscelind. There was no reason he couldn't be happily married to either if he tried. Whatever the flaws in her behavior, Joscelind had her beauty and her family's wealth and connections to recommend her. Eleanor was much the same, although she was also younger.

The priest started the blessing. Nicholas hurriedly and dutifully closed his eyes, and joined in thanking God for His mercy and His bounty. When Father Damon finished, the hum of the voices of the nobles, the soldiers and several servants filled the hall. In another moment, more servants started to come from the kitchen, bearing carafes of wine and baskets of bread.

"Where are the children?" Nicholas asked Marianne, thinking of his bold little nephew who leapt without looking. He was a lot like Henry that way, and Marianne.

As for Cellach, he had little experience with infants, yet she'd nestled in his arms as if she felt completely safe. It was a heady compliment, and one that gave him a powerful yearning to have a child of his own.

"Polly's with them," Marianne replied. "Cellach is sleeping soundly and I hope Seamus soon will be, too, despite his nap. It took a promise that you'll show him one of your many fighting tricks, as he calls them, to get him to stay with Polly."

"Where the devil's Roban?" Adair muttered as he scanned the hall.

"Perhaps he decided to eat at the tavern," Marianne calmly suggested.

Adair laughed. "Well then, I'll be making a jaunt into the village to fetch him later." He gave Nicholas a wry smile. "Maybe I'll have a bit to eat there myself, especially if you're serving tripe. Scots may use most of a cow, too, but I just can't get used to that."

Nicholas permitted himself a small smile of satisfaction as he prepared to reveal the culinary good news. "Roban's going to be sorry he missed this meal. We're having some Scots dishes tonight."

Adair stared at him in wide-eyed amazement.

"Alfred has left my employ, and the person currently supervising my kitchen is a Scot," Nicholas explained.

"Well, thank God and it's about time! What's his name? Maybe I know of him or his clan."

"It's a woman, and her name is Riona. She's a lady from Glencleith. Her uncle is Fergus Mac Gordon. Do you know him?"

"I don't think so, but there's something a bit familiar about the name," Adair mused aloud.

"Does this mean you've made your choice for a bride?" Marianne asked.

Adair grinned. "And she's a Scot?"

"No, it doesn't," Nicholas coolly replied. "After it became necessary for Albert to leave, I decided to allow each of the remaining ladies to take a turn in that capacity. I want to make sure my bride is capable of running a household."

Marianne's expression was not one of approval. "You mean you're giving them a *test?*"

Why did women have such a difficult time grasping the value of his plan? "I prefer to think of it as making sure they can manage my household."

One of the servants arrived with a dish of fish in some sort of batter, mercifully interrupting the discussion. Another maidservant came with wine to fill their goblets, while Marianne delicately put some of the fish onto her trencher.

"Ach, herring in oats!" Adair cried, eagerly and impatiently serving himself a large portion. "Now *this* is food!" He slapped a helping onto Nicholas's trencher. "You'll enjoy this!"

Nicholas wasn't so sure, yet he decided to give it a try. To his surprise, it wasn't bad. Not wonderful, nor the best fish he'd ever eaten, but not bad.

Judging by their expressions, Lord Chesleigh, his daughter, Percival and D'Anglevoix had decided to abstain. Well, they could starve, if that's what they preferred.

"I didn't think you'd ever consider a Scot for a bride, Nicholas," Marianne remarked, clearly enjoying the fish.

"I can't really consider Lady Riona," he replied in

French, speaking quickly so that Adair couldn't make out what he was saying. His brother-in-law knew the language, just as Nicholas had learned Gaelic, but if he spoke fast enough, he could hope Adair couldn't keep up. "Her family's too poor and have no connections at court. I'm letting her and her uncle stay until Lammas so that no Scot can claim I didn't seriously think about marrying her."

"Then your choice is a matter of money and influence?" Marianne asked.

"It's a matter of survival," Nicholas said, stabbing a piece of fish and switching to Gaelic so the Normans wouldn't be able to comprehend the conversation.

"So, brother-in-law, if it can't be the Scot, who's in the lead?" Adair asked, revealing that he'd understood Nicholas after all.

"At the moment, my preference runs to Lady Joscelind or Lady Eleanor. Both their families are rich. Lady Joscelind's father is very powerful at court, and Percival has several friends there, as well."

Marianne fixed her gaze on him. "But do you like them? Are they pleasant?"

Chewing his fish, Nicholas shrugged. "Pleasant enough."

"But Nicholas—"

Adair nudged his wife. "It's his choice, Marianne, not yours. Let the man go about it his own way, whether for good or ill." He gave his wife one of those looks he often did, the sort that suggested to Nicholas that there might indeed be such a thing as love. "You were anything but pleasant to me when we were first married and we couldn't claim to have been in love then, yet it seems to have come right after all."

Marianne smiled at her husband. "Aye, it did, *m'eudail*."

The doors to the hall burst open and two men came stumbling and staggering into the hall, their arms about one another's shoulders.

"Ooooooh," Roban and Fergus Mac Gordon sang in unison at the top of their lungs, "and that was the lass from Killamagroooooo!"

As they finished their song, Roban saluted the high table with the small wooden cask he held in his free hand. "Adair! Marianne! Look who I found—Fergus Mac Gordon!"

Like his companion, Roban was completely oblivious to the sensation they were making. Lord Chesleigh's expression was one of disgust and his daughter's delicate nose wrinkled with distaste. Sir Percival sneered, D'Anglevoix regarded them as if he'd never seen the like, and Lady Lavinia and Audric exchanged horrified looks. Lady Priscilla giggled, nervously. Lady Eleanor looked dismayed, while her maidservant's face was ashen.

Both Nicholas and Adair got to their feet as Mac Gordon staggered forward and bowed, grinning. "Greeting, chieftain of the Mac Tarans and his lovely wife!"

"Roban, you're drunk," Adair declared with amused

patience. "Go sleep it off somewhere, and I suggest your new friend retire, too."

"I'm not drunk!" the big Scot roared. "I'm well watered!"

Her face red, clearly embarrassed, Riona came rushing out of the kitchen corridor and made straight for her inebriated uncle.

"You've had a merry time, I think, Uncle," she said when she reached him, putting her arm around him. "Now I think you ought to rest."

"Rest?" he cried, throwing up his hands as if that was the most ludicrous suggestion he'd heard in years. "Who needs rest? Roban wants to hear about the time I was on the boar hunt and there was that dog, and then my boot—"

"Have you eaten, Uncle?" Riona interjected with an undercurrent of desperation in her sweet voice. "We had herring in oats tonight. I'm sure there's some left. Why don't you and Roban come with me to the kitchen?"

Nicholas got to his feet. Riona didn't deserve to be humiliated this way, for it was clear she was both embarrassed and ashamed.

"Herring in oats, did she say?" Roban cried as Nicholas started around the high table, intending to escort the two men out himself if they didn't go with her willingly. "Why didn't you say there was such food awaiting us here? I was afraid it was going to be that tripe."

Roban made a face, shuddered and said in a loud

whisper, "How those Normans stomach that stomach, I'll never know."

"We can eat later, Riona," her uncle declared. "These Normans don't know how to make music, either." He grinned at Roban. "Let's do that one about old Mac Tavish and his dog."

Prepared to drag them out of the hall if necessary, Nicholas strode toward them.

"I think you both should eat," he said when he reached them. He threw his arms around the two men and steered them toward the kitchen. "The herring was very good. I can vouch for that myself."

Her face flushed, but without so much as a glance in his direction, Riona hurried ahead of them.

"Of course it was good, boy!" Fergus bellowed. "Riona made it, didn't she? She's a wonder, isn't she?"

"Yes, she's a wonder," Nicholas replied, thinking that it had been a very, very long time since anyone had called him "boy," and wondering if Riona herself had prepared the fish.

"What did I tell ye, Roban, old son? She's all but promised to him already."

That got a reaction from Riona. She darted a look over her shoulder at her uncle that would have warned a sober man to keep quiet.

Nicholas hoped this wasn't going to ruin the relationship she had with her uncle, which was one to envy. It was probably Roban's fault they were drunk. He'd been to a tavern once or twice with Adair's friend himself, and knew how easy it was to lose track of time and how much you had to drink as Roban regaled you with stories of heroic deeds and great battles, all featuring amazing Scotsmen, of course.

Once in the kitchen, the servants, wary and curious, gave them a wide berth as he got the two men sitting on a bench beside the worktable.

"Ah, thank you, my son," Mac Gordon exclaimed. "Well, you're not my son and never will be. Nephew-in-law, though, eh?" he finished, laughing.

"I suggest you do as your niece proposes and have something to eat," he replied, ignoring Mac Gordon's comments and fighting to ignore Riona, who was dishing up some food at another table along the wall, her slender—and very tense—back to him. "I'll see you both in the morning."

"Or later in the hall," Mac Gordon declared, slapping Roban on the back and nearly knocking him over. "Roban and I will teach you how to sing."

Nicholas didn't reply as he turned to leave the kitchen. As he did, he couldn't help giving Riona one last look. When she realized he was watching her, she quickly turned away.

But not before he saw a tear upon her flushed cheek.

The sight of that single droplet stirred something deep within Nicholas—a tenderness, a longing to comfort, such as he'd never felt before.

Was this weakness?

He'd always thought so when he'd heard the minstrels singing of such a feeling.

Yet how could it be? he asked himself as he returned to his hall. Never in his life had he felt more keenly determined to protect and take care of another. He felt strong, not weak—stronger than he'd ever felt in his life, as if he could take on an army to protect Riona Mac Gordon, and see to it she never shed another tear.

AFTER RIONA had finally got Uncle Fergus and Roban fed and a little bit sober, she had to try to get them to retire, or at least persuade Uncle Fergus to go to bed.

"But my beauty, 'tis the shank o' the evening!" Uncle Fergus protested after she suggested it was getting late—again.

The servants stifled more grins and smiles.

Riona could appreciate that while this might be an amusing diversion for them, it most certainly wasn't for her. She'd rarely been so humiliated as when she'd heard Uncle Fergus singing and hurried into the hall to find him making such a scene. And then when the lord of Dunkeathe himself had felt called upon to escort him from the hall…

"Where's Fredella?" Uncle Fergus asked, looking around as if he thought she might be hiding in the corner.

"I daresay she's long abed," Riona replied, hoping this would encourage him to move.

"Who's Freerinella?" Roban asked with a sleepy grin.

"A lovely woman. Dee-lightful." Uncle Fergus winked. "And too old for you, my lad. She needs a *mature* man."

As her uncle roared with laughter at his own joke, Roban rose somewhat shakily. "Then I'm going to see what Adair's up to." He sat back down. "After I rest my eyes a wee bit," he mumbled as he folded his arms on the table and rested his head on them. In the next moment, he was snoring.

Uncle Fergus prodded him, but the man didn't move or stop snoring. "Wheest, young folks today! No stamina."

"If he's that tired, it *must* be late," Riona reasoned.

"Maybe you're right," Uncle Fergus finally conceded.

Riona sent up a quick prayer of thanks as her uncle hoisted himself up from the bench. She hurried forward to lend him her shoulder. "Let me help you, Uncle."

Mercifully he didn't protest.

"We'll go through the yard," she said. "It's faster."

Since their chambers were so far from the hall, it *was* quicker to go through the courtyard, and if that meant not having to endure the sneers and whispers of the Normans, so much the better.

"I told you about the time I went boar hunting, didn't I?" Uncle Fergus asked as they crossed the yard.

Mercifully, the sky was clear, the moon bright and the ground dry.

"And that dog got so excited?" her uncle continued

loudly. "And then there was the hole in my boot where the pup bit me? And the boar came straight at the lad—?"

"Yes, Uncle, I've heard that story. Many times," she finished under her breath, trying not so sound impatient, but in truth, she could recite that story herself. How Uncle Fergus had been visiting a clan to the north. How the weather had been perfect, until the storm rolled in. How Uncle Fergus and "the lad" had brought the most untrained, unprepared young hunting dog on the venture. How the dog had bit Uncle Fergus's foot and put a hole in his boots— "And them brand-new the day before." And then the taking off of the ruined boot and the charge of the boar, its eyes fierce, its mouth frothing, directly for the lad. And finally, how Uncle Fergus had tossed the boot aside, drawn his dirk and thrown it, killing the beast instantly.

They passed the guards at the foot of the apartments and started up the stairs. Her uncle was so unsteady on his feet, it was slow going, but eventually they reached his chamber.

"Here we are, Uncle," she said as she shoved open the door with her shoulder and helped him inside.

"Thank you, my beauty," he said as he sat heavily on the bed. "You go on to bed yourself."

He lay on his side and in the next moment was fast asleep.

Sighing wearily, she tugged off his boots and covered him with the length of his *feileadh* that normally hung over his shoulder. She kissed him good night and went out, closing the door softly behind her. At last, this long, troublesome, confusing day was nearly at an end.

"Is he all right?"

She jumped and her heart raced at the sound of the familiar deep voice behind her.

What was the lord of Dunkeathe doing there? she thought as she faced him. A torch in the wall sconce nearby flickered in the slight breeze coming in through the narrow windows, simultaneously lighting his face and putting other parts in shadow, so that it was hard to make out his expression clearly.

"He should be fine come the morning," she replied. "He doesn't usually drink so much," she added, lest he think Uncle Fergus be prone to overimbibing, like Sir George.

"Neither does Roban. I suspect they drank as much as they did because they were together. It's easy to lose track of how many you've had when you're with a fellow like Roban."

"I wouldn't know about that." She started sidling toward the stairs. She didn't want to be alone with the lord of Dunkeathe, especially standing in a corridor where anyone might see them. "I should ensure that everything that needs to be done in the kitchen has been done, and then I should retire, too. I'll have much to do tomorrow."

"The evening meal was excellent. My sister and brother-in-law were very impressed." He reached out and brushed her cheek with his knuckle, the tender action surprising her, and sending tremors of pleasure through her body. "Don't worry about what those others might think," he said softly. "I'm sure the men have all been at least as drunk as that once, if not several times. I've been that drunk myself on occasion."

Why did he have to look at her that way? Why couldn't he be arrogant and haughty, so that she could hate him? "I don't care what those Normans think."

"Yes, you do. I saw the look on your face when you came into the hall."

He sounded so sympathetic. So gentle. So tender.

He cupped his hands on her shoulders.

So strong. So welcome.

She mustn't give in to this raging yearning inside her. She should walk away and leave him.

He kissed her lightly on the forehead. "Whatever happens, I'm glad you and your uncle came to Dunkeathe."

She twisted away from him. His touch, his kiss, were just his attempt to seduce her while he chose another.

"Of course you're glad," she charged. "My presence placates the Scots, and my uncle amuses you."

His gaze full of sincerity, he shook his head. "No, Riona, not just for that. Your uncle's teaching me many things about livestock, things I've never considered." He reached out and pulled her into his arms. "And you're teaching me how much is missing from my life."

He kissed her tenderly on her cheek. Then her eye-lids. Then her nose. And then, at last, her mouth.

It was like sinking into a warm bath. Not this time the fiery passion, or fervent embrace. This time, it was languid longing, lazy yearning, as if they had all the time in the world to love.

As if she was safe and secure, and would always be protected by his strong arms. As if she was not just de-sired, but cherished and beloved.

How could she not welcome his embrace and give herself over to the feelings he inspired?

Yet it was he who stopped first. He tucked a lock of hair that had come loose from her braid behind her ear and whispered, "Riona, I wish…"

She held her breath, waiting to hear what more he would say, half afraid, half hopeful.

A guard on the wall walk outside called a greeting and another answered it.

Nicholas let go of her. "It's getting late," he said brusquely. "Good night."

Then he hurried away and down the stairs as if he was being chased.

CHAPTER THIRTEEN

NOT SURE WHETHER her uncle was awake or not, Riona gingerly pushed open the door to his chamber early the next morning.

Uncle Fergus was sitting on his bed, holding his head in his hands. For the first time since she could remember, he looked old and weary, as well as forlorn and unwell, and she immediately rushed to his side. Her own troubles, particularly her tumultuous feelings for the lord of Dunkeathe, paled beside the notion that Uncle Fergus might be sick.

"Oh, Uncle," she cried softly, sitting beside him and putting her arm around him. "Are you ill?"

He wearily raised his head. "If I'm sick, it's not from the *uisge beatha,* although that Roban must have a hollow leg, the way he drinks. Not that I'm blaming him, mind, for I could have stopped any time."

He sighed and rubbed his eyes, then rose shakily and went to the table bearing a basin and ewer. He splashed cold water over his face before he spoke again. Riona tried to be patient and control her worry, but she was going to have to ask questions if he didn't—

"Fredella's already been to see me," he said grimly as he dried his face with a square of linen. He returned to the bed and sat heavily. "I guess I made quite a spectacle of myself." He slid Riona a questioning glance. "Did I make a rare spectacle of myself?"

"You and Roban were both rather loud," she admitted. "But you don't usually drink so much."

He covered his face with his hands and moaned softly. "Yet I did yesterday—to my shame. Fredella told me she's that ashamed of me. Expected better. Thought I was a finer man. Her dead husband was a sot, you see, and she won't have anything to do with a drunkard."

"But you're not a drunkard!" Riona protested. "I could count on the fingers of one hand the times I've seen you in your cups, and I'll gladly tell her so."

"Thank you, my beauty, but this is my trouble, Riona, not yours, and so mine to mend. Leave it to me to talk to her and try to convince her I made a rare mistake."

He gave Riona a weak smile as he patted her hand. "It's like you to want to help. You're always helping. Now tell me how it's going with Sir Nicholas. He's got to be pleased about the meal last night."

"Excuse me. I'm so sorry, but may I…?"

They both turned, to see an obviously distraught Eleanor standing on the threshold, wringing her hands, her eyes red-rimmed. "Riona, please, may I speak with you a moment?"

"If it's about Fredella—" Uncle Fergus began as he got to his feet.

"No, no," Eleanor answered. "Well, she's upset, I'm sorry to say, but there's something…that is…something else has happened…."

Riona hurried to her friend. "We can speak in my chamber."

Before they left, she turned back to her uncle. "Will you be at mass?"

"Aye, I can manage that. I think I'd better manage that. It could be I'll need divine intervention. And yours, too, Eleanor."

The young woman nodded absently, and Riona realized that whatever had happened, her uncle's woes and anyone else's weren't uppermost in her mind.

Once inside Riona's chamber, and before Riona could ask her what was wrong, Eleanor started to cry—great, wrenching sobs, as if she'd been holding them inside and now they simply had to burst free.

Worried and wondering what this meant, Riona gently hugged Eleanor and stroked her hair until the girl quieted.

"What's wrong?" she asked softly as Eleanor drew back, wiping her eyes with the cuff of her fine gown.

"Oh, Riona, I don't know what else to do or who to turn to. I didn't sleep at all last night."

The dark circles under her eyes and her pale cheeks were evidence of that. "Please, tell me what's happened," Riona gently prompted.

Eleanor began to weep again. "It's so shameful. So…so disgusting. I couldn't even bring myself to tell Fredella. If only I'd been stronger. I should have stopped him somehow."

A cold shaft of fear pierced Riona. "Eleanor, has someone…?"

She hesitated, trying to think of a way to put her question so that Eleanor wouldn't feel even more ashamed if the truth was what she feared. "Has anyone…any *man*…hurt you?"

Understanding dawned in Eleanor's eyes and she shook her head. "No." Then she started to sob again, and her voice caught when she said, "Not yet."

Not yet?

"It's Percival," she said, sitting on Riona's bed. As tears slid down her cheeks, she explained, her voice halting, her anguish obvious. "He's afraid Sir Nicholas won't choose me, so he wants me to…to *seduce* him."

As Riona stared at her, aghast, she learned there was yet more.

"When I'm with him…in his bedchamber…Percival is going to find us together and *make* Sir Nicholas marry me. I tried to refuse but…" Eleanor took a deep, shuddering breath. "He said that if I don't do what he wants, he'll send me to a convent, but first he'll…he'll take…he'll *rape* me."

She broke down completely, covering her face with her hands, her shoulders shaking as more sobs racked her slender body.

Feeling sick, Riona sat beside the distraught girl and held her close, silently cursing Percival and his horrible, evil, despicable scheme, while trying to think of some way to help.

"Oh, Riona," Eleanor sobbed. "To whore myself into marriage! To trick a man that way—any man! But I can't even bear Percival's touch! I'd rather die than let him—"

"He won't," Riona said firmly, her dismay and distress overruled by her determination to protect the helpless girl who clung to her. "And Percival is a fool if he thinks Sir Nicholas could be forced into marriage, for any reason, by anyone."

Eleanor drew back, regarding Riona piteously as she sniffled. "Then what am I to do? Should I run away? I thought of that last night, but I was so afraid Percival would discover me trying to flee, or come after me and catch me and…and…"

"No, don't do that," Riona assured her. On her own, young, pretty, innocent Eleanor would surely fall prey to men as terrible as Percival. "You should go to Sir Nicholas and tell him of this terrible scheme. As a knight, he must protect you, and he will."

Eleanor's voice trembled as another tear rolled down her cheek. "If I did, Percival would surely claim I was lying, or didn't understand him properly. It would be my word against his, and even if charges could be brought against him, he's got too many powerful friends who would vouch for him. He would be free, and then he'd come after me, or anyone who tried to help me. You don't know Percival, Riona. He's vicious and vindictive. He'd never rest without punishing me, or anyone who tried to help me."

A desperate look on her face, she started to stand. "I shouldn't have come to you. If Percival finds out, he might try to hurt you, too. I should just do what Percival wants, and if Sir Nicholas won't marry me, I'll…I'll go to the convent."

Riona rose and took Eleanor firmly by the shoulders. "You mustn't even think of dishonoring yourself. Even if I'm wrong, and Nicholas could be compelled to marry you, how happy do you think you would be, knowing your marriage came about by trickery and deceit? How long before your husband came to resent you?"

She took a deep breath. Something had to be done, and by God, it would be. "The two of us will thwart Percival's plan."

Eleanor stared at her with a mixture of wonder, hope and fear. "The two of us? How?"

How indeed?

"I don't think Sir Nicholas is the sort of man to brag about his conquest, and you surely wouldn't," Riona said, thinking aloud, and going by what had already happened between herself and Nicholas, when he had…

She forced those memories away. "All we really have to do is convince Percival you're doing what he wants, that you've managed to become Sir Nicholas's lover without that actually being so."

"How can I do that?"

"You'll have to let Percival see you sneak into Nicholas's bedchamber late at night. You stay a little while, then sneak out again."

Eleanor started to visibly tremble, and her eyes were wide with fear. "What about Sir Nicholas?"

"You go to his chamber when he's already asleep."

"What if he woke up and caught me? And Percival plans to find us together. That could still happen, whether Sir Nicholas knows I'm there or not."

That was, unfortunately, true. It was too much of a risk to send Eleanor to Nicholas's chamber. "I'll go."

"*You?*" Eleanor exclaimed.

"Me," Riona confirmed. This plan had its own dangers, but not nearly so many for her, and none for Eleanor. "If I wear one of your dresses and scarves, I should be able to fool Percival. We're the same height, and both of us are slim. And he'll be expecting to see you, not me."

"But what if Sir Nicholas finds you there?"

Indeed, what then? If Nicholas couldn't be forced to marry Eleanor—and she was sure a man like him would resist any such attempt—he certainly wouldn't have any qualms about resisting a marriage to her.

Nor did she wish to marry him, either, of course.

"Even if I should be discovered, and regardless of what Sir Nicholas might say or do, Uncle Fergus would never make me marry against my will."

Studying her intently, Eleanor reached out and clasped Riona's hands in hers. "But if you're found in his chamber at night, your reputation will be tarnished forever. I can't ask you to risk that for me."

Her concern was touching, but unnecessary. "I didn't have suitors lined up at the gates of Glencleith to marry me when I was young, so it's not likely I'll be losing any now. My only worry is that dastardly cousin of yours coming into the chamber and—"

She stopped short as another idea came to her. "You should tell Percival that if he really wants to secure Sir Nicholas, you should get with child."

"With child?"

"Yes, so he shouldn't come into the chamber until you've been together several times."

Eleanor's eyes widened with understanding. "Yes, I see."

Riona believed she did, and understood the plan. "We'll let Percival think you're doing what he wants until Nicholas makes his choice and if, by chance, you're not his choice, Uncle Fergus and I will do everything we can to help you then, too, although I don't think that will be necessary. I'm sure that if Sir Nicholas wants to be happily married, he'll choose you, not Joscelind."

Eleanor didn't meet her steadfast gaze. "I'm never going to be able to thank you enough for helping me."

"You're my friend, Eleanor," Riona replied simply, and sincerely. "So tonight you should leave the hall first and wait for me in your chamber."

She thought of another possible problem. "Will you tell Fredella?"

"I don't dare," Eleanor replied. "She'd surely say something to Percival."

"As would Uncle Fergus," Riona replied. "Do you think you can convince Percival you've agreed to do as he wants?"

"I'm sure I can make him believe that I'd almost rather die than go to that convent, because I would."

"Good. Now, we had best get to mass before Percival wonders where you are."

WHEN RIONA reached Eleanor's chamber later that night after a busy day spent supervising the lord of Dunkeathe's kitchen and worrying not just about succeeding in their plan, but about Uncle Fergus's troubles with Fredella, she found an anxious Eleanor waiting.

"Fredella might be back any moment," Eleanor said quietly as Riona slipped inside the chamber illuminated by a single spluttering oil lamp hanging from the ceiling. The rest of the room was in shadows, but there was enough light for Riona to see that it was luxuriously furnished. The bed was covered with pristine linen and a silken cover. Most unexpected was the carpet on the floor, a thing so rare and fine Riona couldn't bring herself to step on it.

"She went to the chapel to pray. About your uncle, I think."

"He's upset, too," Riona said. "He doesn't usually get drunk. I tried to tell Fredella but she only hurried away."

"Every time I start to ask Fredella about him, she begins to cry." Eleanor twisted the dangling ties of her girdle in her fingers. "Riona, I've been thinking and thinking about this, and I've decided I simply can't let you do this for me. It isn't right."

"What Percival wants you to do isn't right," Riona confidently replied. "You mustn't be forced to barter your virginity for marriage at his command. There's much less risk to me sneaking into Sir Nicholas's chamber than there is for you. Don't worry, Eleanor. Everything will be well. What did Percival say when you suggested that he not interrupt?"

"I…I didn't get a chance."

Riona stared at her with dismay. That would be essential to their success.

Panic in her eyes, Eleanor suddenly held up her hand. "Somebody's coming! *Hide!*"

Riona immediately dropped down on all fours and scrambled under the bed. The stone floor was hard and cold, but she certainly didn't want to have to explain her presence there to anyone, not even Fredella.

The door opened, and Riona watched Percival's gilded red boots march into the room. She immediately prepared to scramble out from under the bed if Eleanor needed her aid.

"Wh-what are you doing here?" Eleanor stammered.

"Why did you leave the hall?" Percival slurred, and it was obvious he'd had too much wine.

Riona began to inch out of her hiding place as Eleanor backed away from him. "I—I'm tired, Percival. It's late. Most of the other nobles had retired. I saw no need to stay."

"Nicholas was still there. He's the only noble you need concern yourself with."

Riona had to move out of the way quickly as Percival sat on the bed. "Don't lie to me. And don't try to refuse to do as we agreed. Time's running out, Eleanor."

"I'm not lying to you, Percival," she said. "But please, I beg of you, don't make me do this. Don't make me sell my virtue."

"I don't give a damn about your virtue!" Percival retorted as he got to his feet and headed toward Eleanor.

Ready to attack him, Riona moved to the edge of the bed again.

He stopped. "You'll go to his chamber and you'll get in his bed and you'll let him take your maidenhead," Percival ordered, "or God help me, you'll wish you had when you're kneeling in that convent."

"I'll go, Percival," Eleanor replied, weeping. "I don't want to go to a convent. I'll do as you say. I'll go to Sir Nicholas tonight."

"Good. Don't you have something else to wear, something that shows your figure to more advantage—something like Joscelind wears?"

"There's my scarlet damask—"

"And don't wear a shift."

"Percival!"

Scorn fairly dripped from his words. "This is no time to be subtle."

"Very well, Percival," Eleanor despondently replied.

The red boots started toward the door.

"Percival?" Eleanor said, sniffling. "What if I get with child?"

"What?"

"What if I get with child?" she repeated. "People will be able to count back the days. They'll know—"

"Damn it, who cares if they can count, as long as you're married to him when the brat is born?" Percival approached her again. "Indeed, if we're to be certain of him, a child could be the very thing."

A seemingly endless moment of silence followed.

"I've changed my mind, cousin. I won't interrupt you tonight. How long until your next...?"

"A fortnight," Eleanor answered forlornly.

"Then let's pray you're fertile, for if you get with child, that will be all the more reason for him to marry you. Get him to love you more than once a night, if you can. I'm sure he's capable." Percival tapped his toe. "Perhaps I should give you some suggestions."

"Fredella could be here any moment," Eleanor noted quietly, and much to Riona's relief. The last thing she wanted to hear was Percival's suggestions.

"That old hag," Percival muttered as he again started for the door. "You'd better please Sir Nicholas, so he lets her stay here, too." He paused. "You needn't look like a martyr, my dear. I doubt you'll regret what must be done, provided he marries you, of course. Rumor has it that Nicholas of Dunkeathe is quite the lover."

"Yes, Percival."

The door opened. "I'll be watching for you," he finished as he strolled out the door.

Riona crawled out from under the bed as Eleanor started to cry again.

"I feel so filthy," she said, her breath catching with her sobs. "How can he do this to me? How can he treat my virtue as something to be so easily thrown away?"

"Because he has no honor himself," Riona said, putting her arm around her friend's shoulder. "You're very clever, letting him think not interrupting was *his* idea."

Eleanor smiled tremulously, then grew grave again as she went to the chest at the foot of the bed and opened the lid. She lifted out a gown of sumptuous scarlet silk damask, with a rounded neckline and wide gored skirt. In the moonlight, it seemed to move and shift like a living thing. Riona had never seen so beautiful a dress in all her life, let alone put one on.

"I think it should fit," Eleanor said.

Riona thought it would, too, as she took off her simple woolen gown and reached out for the scarlet dress, taking hold of it reverently.

"When this is over, you're welcome to it."

Riona shook her head. "It's too fine for me."

"I insist," Eleanor said with a spark of determination

as she helped Riona pull it over her head and down into place over her shift.

"Oh dear," Eleanor murmured.

"It fits well enough," Riona said, although it was a little tight.

"You can see your shift. It shows above the neck. If Percival sees that, he might stop you, to remind you of what he said about not wearing a shift. He'll find out it isn't me."

Riona didn't hesitate. "So I'll take off my shift," she said as she removed the gown.

While she laid it on the bed, Eleanor wordlessly, and delicately, turned away. Riona divested herself of her shift and swiftly put on the gown again. She hadn't noticed before how low the neckline was. No wonder Percival thought this would do for a seduction. It was also a snug fit, and when Eleanor tied the laces, the back of the gown wouldn't close completely. Riona could feel the air, cool on her skin.

"I don't dare bend over," she said. "I'll tear the laces."

"The veil should cover the gaps," Eleanor said, going to another chest and bringing out a long, white piece of cloth and a circlet of gold. The circlet, too, was a thing of beauty, made of entwined strips of the metal that shone in the moonlight.

Eleanor put the fabric on Riona's head, and then the circlet to hold it in place. "I think you might really be able to fool Percival," she said as she stepped back to run her gaze over Riona. "Except for those shoes. You'll have to wear a pair of my slippers."

Eleanor fetched two soft calf slippers, finely worked, and went down on one knee. "Give me your foot. I'll be your maidservant."

Riona smiled at that, and to hide her own growing nervousness. When she'd proposed this plan, it had seemed simple enough, and she'd truly believed she could sneak into Nicholas's room without being discovered.

But now, when it came to it, she wasn't so sure. What if Nicholas woke up? What if he wasn't yet in his bedchamber, and entered while she was hiding there? She could always hide under *his* bed, she supposed, until he was asleep.

"There, you're ready," Eleanor said, rising and stepping back.

When she frowned, Riona wondered what else might be amiss.

"If you don't want to go, Riona, I won't hold it against you," Eleanor said softly.

Riona gave her a comforting smile and imitated Uncle Fergus's jovial manner as she went to the door. "Don't worry, I'll be safe. Besides, when else would I have a chance to wear a gown like this?"

Once she made sure the corridor was clear, Riona crept out of the chamber and prepared to play her part.

CHAPTER FOURTEEN

A SHIVER RAN DOWN Riona's back as she quickly and quietly hurried past the door of Percival's chamber. It was open enough to allow a shaft of candlelight to waver on the floor, telling her that Percival was there and waiting. Keeping as close to the far wall as possible, she was very glad that there was no torch in a sconce nearby to light her face.

Her hand trembled as she pushed down on the latch of Nicholas's chamber door and slowly eased it open. Even more carefully, she slipped inside, then closed the door behind her.

A hand clamped over her mouth, an arm went around her like a band of iron, and she was dragged backward. Struggling, she collided with a body. A man's body.

Sir Nicholas of Dunkeathe's voice growled in her ear. "I won't be seduced into choosing a bride, Joscelind, even by someone as beautiful as you." He loosened his hold. "Now go back to your chamber," he ordered, gently pushing her away.

Whatever happened, Riona couldn't leave. Otherwise, Percival would know that his plan was a failure and Eleanor would be in jeopardy.

"I'm not Joscelind," she said as she faced him.

As he stood in the moonlight coming in through his window, he stared at her as if she were an apparition, while she regarded him with steady determination.

She must have interrupted him as he prepared for bed. He wore only an unlaced shirt that fell to midthigh, and those thighs were encased in tight-fitting woolen breeches. He had on his old, scuffed boots, which perhaps explained why she hadn't heard him creep up on her.

"I'm not here to seduce you," she declared, both for him, and for herself.

His gaze flicked down to her breasts in the tight gown and against her will, she felt her body respond— the softening of the tension, the pebbling of her nipples against the fine fabric.

"What *are* you doing here then?" he demanded, his voice low and husky. "That gown seems designed for no other purpose than seduction."

She forced herself to concentrate on the real reason for her presence there. Having been discovered, she had little choice but to tell him the truth, and hope that she could prevail upon him to help Eleanor. "It was a necessary disguise and the reason for it will become clear as I explain."

He made a sweeping gesture toward the one and only chair. "By all means, my lady, sit and explain."

She moved farther into the room, away from him, and focused her attention on her surroundings. The chamber wasn't as large as she'd expected for the lord of the castle, and was distinctly spartan, more befitting a soldier than a nobleman. The single chair had a high, plain back and no cushion. A candlestand and brazier stood together in a corner as if they were simply stored there. Other furnishings included a very battered and chipped chest and a simple wooden table with basin and ewer.

In fact, the only thing that signified she was in a lord's chamber was the bed—a very big bed, hung with thick curtains and sporting a coverlet that shimmered in the moonlight, as if it were made of silk.

"I have had my fill of sleeping on the ground, in haystacks or on cots with my feet hanging over the end," he said.

Silently cursing herself for staring as if she'd never seen a bed before—even though, in truth, she'd never seen one quite like that—she flushed and hurried to take the chair.

Nicholas sat on the end of the bed and crossed his arms. "So, my lady, why are you here?"

"For Eleanor's sake."

He coolly raised a brow. "How does coming into my bedchamber dressed as you are benefit Eleanor?"

"It's necessary for Percival to think she's been here."

Resolved to speak plainly, Riona rose to face him. "Her cousin is determined that you marry her, so much so that he's commanded her to seduce you. If she fails, Percival says he'll send her away to a convent. Being a good and honorable woman, Eleanor was rightly appalled by the idea, but she didn't know what to do, so—"

"So she came to you." It was a statement, not a question.

Did he think that wise or foolish? She couldn't tell; his features revealed nothing of his thoughts. "Yes," she admitted, continuing with her explanation. "We decided to trick Percival into thinking she was complying with his command until you make your choice."

"And what was to happen if and when I discovered you in my bedchamber?"

Riona tried to sound as calm as he, but it wasn't easy. Yet Eleanor's fate was more important than any discomfort—or anything else—she felt in the lord of Dunkeathe's presence. "I thought that wouldn't happen."

"A pity you didn't realize soldiers learn to sleep lightly and dress quickly."

She ran a swift gaze over him. "No, I hadn't anticipated that."

"And if you were found trying to get into my bedchamber, or alone with me? What then, my lady?"

Here she was on safer ground. "I knew there was no chance we could be shamed into marriage, or forced to wed. My uncle would never make me marry against my will."

"I see," he replied. His brow rose, as if they were

discussing nothing more important than a change in the weather. "I trust Lady Eleanor is suitably grateful that you're willing to risk your reputation for her sake?"

She'd had enough of trying to stay calm and composed. She'd make him appreciate that Eleanor was in serious jeopardy, and it was his fault, too. "Yes, she is— but it was a risk I was glad to take, because Percival's also told her that if she cannot persuade you to bed her, *he* will."

As she'd hoped, Nicholas ceased to look calm, but she hadn't expected to see the murderous rage that came to his face as he swiftly got to his feet. His eyes seemed to burn with it, his whole body to throb with ire. He strode to the chest and grabbed the sword and scabbard laying atop it. "By God, I'll make the man a eunuch."

Believing he would do it, she ran to block the door. "As much as I'd like to see him punished, too, he's her legal guardian. He has powerful friends, as you know, and he's vicious, which you might not. If you hurt him, he may not take it out on you, but on Eleanor."

"Then I'll just kill him."

"No!" she cried, putting her hands on his broad chest and pushing him back. It was like trying to move a stone wall, yet she persisted. "Curb your rage and think! That might only make things worse for both of you. What of your future that concerns you so much? Percival's influential friends would surely turn against you.

"Even if your explanation was accepted and you

were absolved of murder, what of Eleanor? I don't know who would become her guardian then. Do you? Can you promise me she would be any safer?"

He lowered his weapon, and she watched as he seemed to physically contain his anger. "Then what, my lady, do you suggest?"

She forced herself to answer without regard for her own selfish desire, her longing for something that could never be. "You should marry Eleanor. That way, she'll be free of Percival forever, and you'll have what you seek in a bride. She'll bring you a considerable dowry and Percival's influence."

A strange expression flickered across his face, or perhaps it was only a trick of the light. "She's young and pretty, too."

She wouldn't let him see how those words hurt her. "Yes, she is. And a better choice than any of the other ladies here."

"Really?" he inquired, his temper clearly once more under his control. "Better than Joscelind?"

"Yes, because she'll make a better wife."

"Certainly she'd be a more placid one," he agreed. "But I might offend Lord Chesleigh."

"That was the chance you took when you issued your invitation—that you might offend the ladies and relatives of those you didn't choose. You must have considered that possibility."

"Yes, I did, and I believe I'll be able to placate Lord Chesleigh if I select someone other than his daughter."

She should have expected no less. Clearly everything he did was cold and calculated, determined by ambition and his own needs.

"Are none of the other ladies remaining here to be considered?" he inquired.

"I don't believe any of the other ladies are in the race, even if they're still in Dunkeathe."

"Oh? And upon what evidence do you base that conclusion? Are you able to read minds?"

"Because you're not stupid—or is the budding romance between Audric and Lavinia something you hadn't noticed?"

"Yes, I noticed, because I am *not* stupid."

"And I'm sure you have a reason for encouraging their romance."

He inclined his head in acknowledgment.

"That leaves Lady Priscilla and her giggle. I can hardly believe you'd pick her. I've seen you when she laughs."

"As it happens, I concur." He laid his sword back on the chest. "That also leaves you, my lady."

Was he *trying* to hurt her? "I don't forget, my lord, that I'm here only to prevent the Scots from complaining."

"That was before you entered my bedchamber wearing that seductive gown," he said as he strolled toward her. "Maybe *you* thought to trick me into marriage."

"I most certainly did not," she said as she backed away, appalled by the suggestion. "I don't want to marry you."

"I'm heartbroken."

At his callous response, her anger and frustration surged forth. "Go ahead, my lord, make fun of me," she said through clenched teeth, her back straight, eyes blazing. "Treat me with the same lack of consideration you've shown to all the ladies here."

His brows rose. "I've been very considerate."

"And magnanimous, too," she sarcastically retorted. "Inviting them here to parade before you as if you're a prize bull."

"I haven't done anything except say I want a wife and offer to choose one from those willing to make the journey to Dunkeathe."

"Are you really so blind that you don't see what you've done? That you don't appreciate the trouble you've brought to Eleanor? Or the strain you've placed upon all of the ladies as they compare themselves to each other? Did you ever consider how hurt they would be when they realized that they didn't please you, or that they couldn't compete with Joscelind or Eleanor— or even, apparently, with Priscilla?"

"It was not my intent to hurt any lady's feelings. All I want is a wife." He put his hands on his hips, the action widening the gap in his shirt, exposing more of his naked chest. "If they suffer because they don't suit me, that's not my fault."

"What a convenient excuse that is."

"What else would you have me do?" he charged, a hint of pique in his deep voice.

"That's not for me to say."

"Oh, don't try playing the coy maiden with me now, my lady!" he said. "I know you better."

"Or think you do."

"As you seem to think you know me, and that I'm some sort of lascivious scoundrel who would make love with a woman just because she has the audacity to present herself in my bedchamber." He ran his gaze over her again. "Even when she arrives in a gown like that." His expression shifted. "Even if I might be sorely tempted."

As her heart started to pound, as she grew more aware of his proximity and his state of undress, she licked her dry lips and sidled toward the door. "If I believe you would do such a thing, it's because I have good cause."

"Because I kissed you."

"Aye, because you kissed me more than once—a woman you would never seriously consider for your bride."

"A woman I *can't* consider for my bride." He ran his hand through his hair and spoke with exasperation, as well as fierce pride. "Because I was born into a noble family that lost their wealth, and had to fight for everything I've got. I'm not like the other nobles here, born into wealth and privilege, a life of ease and comfort. I had to earn my money, and nearly everything I won went to pay for the care of my brother and sister. I had promised my dying mother I would take care of them, and I would die myself rather than break that oath. There were days I was soaked through from rain, and nearly starving for lack of bread, yet by the grace of God, I was able to live and succeed, to keep my family in some comfort and eventually win this land, as well as enough money to build my castle. I built the fortress I had always dreamed of, where I would be safe and secure and content. I spent nearly everything I had on it, believing I had yet enough to pay for the household and taxes for a few years yet, and if I chose to marry, I could do so at my leisure.

"But I hadn't reckoned on the Scots king deciding he needed more money for his army. Alexander's increased the taxes on my estate threefold, and I have little left. I must marry a woman with a large dowry, or I'll lose Dunkeathe. I'll be a penniless mercenary again."

His expression changed, to one searching, almost…desperate. "Can you understand why I can't let that happen, Riona? Can you appreciate that I've worked too hard to earn this reward and create this refuge to lose it now? If I did, it will be as if I've done nothing. *Am* nothing."

She heard the anguish in his voice, saw it in his dark eyes. This man, this proud warrior from a noble family, was revealing himself to her as he likely did to few, if any. His fear, his vulnerability, his loneliness and suffering, were being shown to her here, in all their humbling power.

Now she could see him as a frightened boy, beaten by a hardened soldier who tried to destroy all that was good and kind in him. She could envision him as the young knight worried about his family and desperately trying to fulfill a dying mother's promise.

She could see Nicholas as he must have been but a few months ago, when he finally thought he'd achieved everything he'd ever wanted. How pleased and satisfied, how content and proud. And then word had come from the king and he realized he might lose it all with one signature on a parchment.

He was no falsely proud, arrogant knight who had no right to respect and honor, but a man alone and lonely, vulnerable and afraid, who had kept his promise. At that realization, the feelings she'd been trying so hard to deny, to explain away, to pretend didn't exist, arose stronger than ever.

"I do understand, Nicholas," she answered softly. Sincerely. She raised her hand to caress his rough, stubbled cheek. "This estate, this castle, is your triumph and your glory, your hope and prize combined. I wish with all my heart that my dowry was enormous and my uncle the most powerful man in this kingdom, because if he was, I would do everything I could to win you and ensure that you could keep what you've worked so hard to earn."

Then, as he stared at her as if he couldn't fathom what she was saying, or doing, she brought him close and kissed him. Her passion and her longing surged forth, free and unbound. No longer would she try to rein them in. She would never be rich. Her family would never have power. But now, here, tonight, she could love him with all her woman's need and woman's heart, even if it couldn't be sanctified by marriage.

Morality, virtue, honor, scandal, shame, fear for the future—nothing mattered except him. He was all in all. No more would she deny herself the pleasure of being in his arms. She would willingly surrender.

With a low moan, Nicholas clasped her to him and his passion answered her own, fervent and strong, as he deepened the kiss. His tongue plunged into the warmth of her mouth, to swirl and twine with hers. He sidled nearer, pressing her firmly against his powerful body. His powerfully aroused body.

He was hungry for her, as she was for him. He, who surely could have any woman he wanted, wanted her.

As her lips moved hungrily over his, demanding the response that she craved, he kneaded her breast, exciting her yet more as her whole body seemed to weaken from the sensation.

He tried to slip his hand into her bodice. The gown was too tight, and the straining laces broke. She didn't care, and when the neck gaped and he plunged his warm hand inside, she welcomed his caress. His palm brushed against her flesh, lightly skimming her nipple. His hand was rough and callused—a man's hand, a warrior's hand—but never had a touch felt better, or more welcome. She moaned softly, quietly encouraging him, until he swept her into his arms and carried her to the bed. Holding her gaping bodice to her breasts, she shifted back, not taking her eyes from him. He tore off his shirt, then his boots, tossing them aside. Then he removed his breeches.

He was naked before her, magnificent in the moonlight, and hers to love, at least for tonight.

Standing, she let the gown fall, exposing her body to his hungry gaze.

"You're so beautiful," he murmured, his eyes flaring with desire, and she saw in them the confirmation that he didn't think she was too old or not pretty enough, or too much the shrew. He appreciated her just as she was. He desired her, just as she was.

Excited, aroused, she eagerly climbed onto the bed and lay down, then raised her arms to welcome him as, with slow, deliberate motions and a look that made her heartbeat race, he followed her onto the bed. He settled himself between her legs, his hips against hers, and she felt him, hard and ready. She was ready, too, and moist and anxious, as she pulled him to her, taking his mouth again with heated fervor.

Her passion soared, her longing increased. Her pulse throbbed, and nowhere more than where his erection pressed against her. She clasped her arms about him and kissed his chest, the skin salty as her lips touched and teased. When she found his nipple, she toyed with it with her tongue. He threw back his head and groaned, the sound like the growl of a lion, spurring her on.

With anxious need, her hands roved over him, feeling the shifting, bunching muscles of his back, admiring the power of his virile body. His hand slid smoothly along her ribs, and upward, to cup her breast while his lips trailed low and lower, along the beating pulse of her neck, past her collarbone, skimming her warm flesh.

Then he sucked her nipple into his mouth. Moaning, whimpering with want, she twisted with the sheer pleasure he inspired. As he did the same to the other, she arched, eagerly offering herself to him.

Keeping his weight on one hand, his palm crept up her leg, closer and closer to the place where the heat seemed hottest, the demand greatest.

Gasping, she gripped his upper arms as he reached the moist place between her thighs. He pushed slightly with the heel of his hand, the pressure increasing her pleasure and her willingness.

Leaning down closer, his chest against her breasts, he pushed again.

"More," she gasped, no other word coming to her mind.

He shifted. Moved back. She wondered—

He licked her. There.

Her eyes flew open and she raised her head. But only for a moment, because as he continued to arouse her, she fell back. She bunched the covers in her fist as his sinuous tongue took her to new realms of excitement and desire, until the building tension broke and splintered and scattered.

As she lay panting, she vaguely wondered what happened next. If that was all he intended to do. If she should speak….

He raised himself above her—the powerful, virile lord of Dunkeathe. His breath came in rough rasps as he looked down at her, his disheveled hair about his face and broad shoulders. "Riona, if you want me to stop…"

She shook her head.

"You know where this will lead?" he whispered hoarsely. "Where I want to go?"

She nodded. Her decision had been made when she kissed him in this chamber. "I want you to make love with me, Nicholas. Please."

Still he didn't move. "I make no commitment, Riona, no promises."

"I know."

"I have spent too many years—"

"I *know*," she repeated, raising herself to capture his lips with another impassioned kiss.

And she did know. She knew that she was surrendering her virtue. That there could be no regaining of the virginity she was giving him. That he wouldn't marry her. But if that was the price of a night in his arms, if that was what it would cost to share herself with this man even once, she wouldn't refuse. If she thought otherwise come the morning, she would deal with it then.

She felt him pressing against her. And then he slowly thrust inside her.

She cried out at the stab of pain.

He stilled. "I'm sorry," he murmured, his lips against her neck. "Should I—?"

"Don't stop," she said as her body grew used to him. The sensation of him within her created a new and even more undeniable urging.

With a sigh of willing submission, he thrust again, slowly. The tension—that marvelous, anxious need and what it harbinged—arose within her as he moved again, with a little more force.

And again.

Need overtook her, the fervent wish to experience that wonderful release. She gripped his shoulders as he drove himself inside her yet more forcefully. The pain became a dim memory as her own body responded. Her excitement erased everything but the silent consent to allow the passion to take her where it would.

With him.

Faster he moved, pushing deeper and harder. His breath came in hoarse rasps. She held tight to him, delighting in his potent strength, the sheer power of his body, the way he made her feel. Holding his shoulders, his arms, she arched and bucked, moving without thought or plan, guided by the insistent urging of her own flesh, until the time of exquisite release. She groaned low in her throat as the waves of pleasure poured through her body.

But that was not the end, not until the cords of his neck grew taut as harp strings and with a rough cry, he gave one more powerful thrust and joined her in ecstasy.

Panting and sated, he rested upon her as she held him close.

How long they lay together, Riona didn't know, but eventually, through the haze of sleepy, satiated pleasure, she realized that she couldn't stay. "Nicholas? My lord?"

"Hmm?" he murmured, more than half-asleep.

"I have to go."

He opened his eyes and looked at her.

"Now."

More awake, he moved away from her.

She'd known it would be so, and yet her eyes stung with tears she would not shed, not before him, as she rose from the disheveled bed. This was her choice, her decision, and she must accept the consequences.

She went to retrieve the scarlet gown. Her hair had come loose, and it fell about her naked body.

Nicholas clasped her from behind and she started at the unexpected embrace. "Are you sorry?" he whispered.

She forced away any doubt as she turned so that she was looking at him. "No. I don't regret what we did."

His smile was worth any amount of shame and regret to come. "Then I shall not. Will you come to me again, Riona?"

She could no more have refused that request than she could have murdered her uncle. "Yes."

He held her close, and as he did, he ran his hand through her long, unbound hair. "You have the most marvelous hair," he whispered. "I've often wondered how it would look loose."

"I should get dressed."

He let go of her. "I like that red gown."

"It's Eleanor's."

"Ah, yes," he said.

"For now, Percival must think Eleanor comes to your bed, not me."

"Until I make my choice."

"Yes," she replied as she went to the door.

And left him.

ELEANOR WAS anxiously waiting when Riona returned. If she noticed the knot in the lacing, or that it had been broken, she didn't speak of it.

"Was Sir Nicholas asleep?" she asked in an anxious whisper as Riona changed her clothes. "Did Percival see you? Did anyone?"

"All went well," Riona assured her. "All will be well."

As she crept back to her own chamber, she subdued any remorse or regret. If there was trouble to come, she would face it. If there were discovery and scandal and dishonor, she would accept it. She would risk all that, and more, to be held in the arms of the lord of Dunkeathe.

CHAPTER FIFTEEN

A FEW DAYS LATER, Nicholas stood by his solar window, hands clasped behind his back. Outside, the weather was fair, the fields were nearing time for harvest, and his soldiers were either on guard, or training.

He was thinking of none of those things. He was watching Riona, who was standing by the well talking with Eleanor and the soon-to-be-married Polly. Even from this distance, he could tell that Riona was smiling, her whole body alight with the vibrant joy and zeal she brought to everything she did.

Including making love. Every night he was with her was more exciting and astonishing than the last. Last night, her long, thick, marvelous hair about her naked body, she'd straddled him and bent forward so that the tips of her breasts brushed his pebbled nipples. Her weight on her hands splayed beside his head, she'd risen and lowered herself with intoxicating, maddening variety, exciting him until he thought he'd scream with both pleasure and frustration.

"My lord?"

Brought back to the present by his steward's voice,

he turned to face Robert, who lowered his eyes to study his list. "As I was saying, my lord, Lady Joscelind's requests are rather costly. Peacock and quails' eggs are but two of the items she wants to serve at the evening meal."

"Can we afford them at all, or will that leave us with nothing?"

"We can buy them, my lord, but—"

"Then do so. No one is to know that I'm running out of money."

"My lord, there's another small problem. I fear D'Anglevoix is beginning to realize that there's something between his cousin and young Audric. He's been asking me if I think Lady Lavinia's found favor with you, and by his tone, he's getting rather anxious."

"Ever since the soup was served cold and the meat was burnt when she was in charge of the kitchen, no doubt."

Robert confirmed his assumption with a nod. "And I must say, my lord, your attentions to her have not been, um, encouraging."

No, they hadn't, because he'd been distracted of late. It was all he could do to feign interest in Eleanor and Joscelind. "Is he planning to depart?"

"I believe so, my lord."

"That may be for the best. We're running out of money faster than I thought, so fewer guests will help. It's less insulting to him if he chooses to go, and less humiliating for the lady," he finished, thinking of Riona's admonitions on that point.

She was right. He had never stopped to consider how his actions might affect the ladies who came to Dunkeathe.

He expected that the parsimonious Robert would be pleased to have fewer guests to accommodate. Instead, his steward's face reddened and he shuffled his feet like a little boy facing a scolding parent. "You disagree?" Nicholas asked.

Robert raised his eyes to look at his master, and Nicholas was surprised by the near desperation written on his features. "My lord, I had guessed you wouldn't be choosing Lady Lavinia, but I must ask you…. That is, I need to know if…" He hesitated, took a deep breath and hurried on. "Do you have any interest in the Lady Priscilla?"

Was it possible? Could it be? "No, Robert," he replied. "I will not be marrying Lady Priscilla, although she did quite well when she was in charge of the kitchen. She seems a very practical young lady."

Indeed, her meal had been plain and inexpensive in the extreme, almost like soldiers' rations. "Will you be sorry to see her leave Dunkeathe when the time comes?"

Robert looked at the window, the table, the floor and then, finally, Nicholas. He took a deep breath, his chest rising and falling. "Yes!" he declared, like a man daring to defy the gods.

Nicholas stifled any hint of amusement at this sudden passionate outburst from the man who was both his steward and his friend.

Robert straightened his shoulders. "She only giggles when she's nervous. When she's with me, she's quite different."

I should hope so, Nicholas thought, but he wouldn't ever say that aloud to Robert. "I assume she likewise cares for you?"

He flushed even more. "Yes."

"What does her brother think of this?"

Robert's resolve diminished. "We haven't told Audric yet. She wanted to wait to see what happened with Lavinia. She cares a great deal for her brother. She's a very loving woman."

"If she's earned your good regard, that's all I need to hear. Does she fear Audric will not approve of a marriage between you?"

"As do I, my lord. I am but a steward."

Nicholas put his hand on Robert's shoulder. "You were born of noble blood, albeit on the wrong side of the blanket, and brother to the finest man I ever had the privilege to call my friend. You're also one of the few people I trust. If that is not enough, do you suppose some land of your own for a small estate, like those acres in the valley you've always admired, will satisfy him?"

Robert stared at Nicholas, dumbfounded. "You'd do that? You'd give me that land?"

"Gladly, although you'll owe me tithes and you'll still be my steward, I hope."

Not to mention, Robert having his own household

would mean that the giggly Priscilla would be in Dunkeathe but rarely.

"Of course I'll still be your steward!" Robert cried happily. "It's been my great honor to serve you, Nicholas, and I hope I can continue to do so for many years to come."

Pleased, Nicholas gave him a smile, which was no longer so rare a thing with him. "Why don't you go find Priscilla and tell her the news? After that, if you'd like me to speak to Audric—"

"No, that won't be necessary," Robert said as he backed toward the door, a smile on his face and joy in his eyes. "I'll do that. But I thank you for your generosity, Nicholas, from the bottom of my heart."

After he was gone, Nicholas returned to the window. Riona, Eleanor and Polly weren't at the well anymore.

He wished he could have heard the conversation between the three women. They were much together these days, and he thought he knew why. Riona was trying to teach Eleanor how to run his household.

Disturbing thought. Disturbing vision of Eleanor in his bed instead of Riona. Yet so it must be, or his years of toil and suffering would have brought him no tangible reward.

He sighed, then went to find the Duc D'Anglevoix. He might not be able to marry who he'd like, but he could think of no reason Lavinia and Audric shouldn't marry. Both had birth and property, and were of equal status.

If they were both grateful to the lord of Dunkeathe for bringing about the circumstances of their union and doing what he could to promote it, well, that was good, too.

He went first to the kitchen. After all, it was slightly possible the Norman nobleman was there.

And very possible, as he happily discovered, that Riona was, albeit looking as tense as he'd ever seen her. She was surrounded by the servants, all of them talking at once.

"What's going on here?" Nicholas demanded as he approached the group, which scattered like a flock of birds when they heard his voice.

"I fear, my lord, that there's been some, um, confusion about the evening meal," Riona said.

"Is it not the Lady Joscelind's turn to deal with such matters?" he asked, trying to sound as he usually did when faced with conflict and not betray his feelings for Riona. "Why isn't Lady Joscelind here?"

Most of the servants, abashed, stared at the ground and didn't answer. A few, like Polly, slid wary glances at Riona, then at their master.

"I understand, my lord, that she's gone to select her gown for this evening," Riona offered.

"Then somebody should go and fetch her to sort out any troubles."

Polly took a step toward him. "If you please, my lord," she said, her voice quivering but her gaze unwavering, "we don't want to take orders from Lady Joscelind."

As the other servants mumbled what sounded like approval of her sentiments, he noticed Riona sidling towards the door to the hall. Later, he'd tease her about fleeing the battle. She'd probably get that indignant fire in her lovely eyes and he'd have to kiss her annoyance away.

He forced himself to focus on the servants. "What you want is not my concern. My *orders* are that you obey her."

Polly didn't back down. "That may be, my lord, but she's given all of us about six things to do all the same time and some of it don't make sense, although it might have if she'd explained herself and didn't just stand there tellin' us we were stupid when we tried to ask a question."

The other servants nodded rapidly and murmured their agreement.

"So you decided to pester Lady Riona with your questions and complaints instead?"

Polly's face reddened and her gaze fell.

Riona hurried forward. "My lord, I believe a simple reassigning of tasks is all that's required. I'll be happy to assist, and then Lady Joscelind need not be troubled."

It was like her to help even Joscelind, for the servants' sake. But if Joscelind was responsible for the trouble, Joscelind could fix it. "I thank you for your kind and generous offer, my lady, but this is not your concern."

He addressed Polly. "Do you all have things you can do until I speak to Lady Joscelind?"

Polly's lips turned up with a hint of a grin. "Yes, my lord."

"Good." He gestured for the spit boy to come closer. "Go and tell Lady Joscelind that I wish to speak with her in my solar when she has completed her toilette, which I assume will be soon."

The lad nodded and ran off. "As for you, my lady," he said to Riona, "we shall speak of this matter later, but first, has anyone seen the Duc D'Anglevoix?"

"He's gone to the outer ward," one of the other women offered. "Leastways, that's what Rafe said."

Regretting he couldn't so much as smile at Riona in front of the servants, Nicholas nodded his thanks, then turned on his heel and headed for the tents of D'Anglevoix's soldiers, which were in the eastern part of the outer ward.

When he reached the encampment, he discovered a scene of bustling activity and raised voices, as if the men were preparing to strike their camp. Clearly, Robert was right. D'Anglevoix had finally realized his cousin would not be marrying Sir Nicholas of Dunkeathe and he was planning to depart.

It took a few questions of the Norman's soldiers, but soon enough Nicholas found the obviously disgruntled D'Anglevoix in one of the tents, barking orders at a harried-looking man. When D'Anglevoix saw Nicholas, he scowled, then ordered the man to go and see that all was made ready to leave.

"You're planning on leaving Dunkeathe, my lord?"

Nicholas inquired with feigned ignorance and disregarding the man's scowl.

"I see no reason to stay, as it's become apparent to me that you have no honorable interest in Lavinia."

He had no dishonorable interest in her, either, and for a moment, Nicholas's temper flared, until he reminded himself that although this man wasn't the power at court he had been in the past, it was never wise to make an unnecessary enemy.

"I must confess, my lord, that I've come to the same conclusion," he said, making no mention of honor. "However, I'm also quite sure she has no interest in me, either. I fear I'm too much the soldier for your well-bred cousin."

The Norman nobleman looked down his long aquiline nose at Nicholas. "Then we are agreed, and thus we shall not remain here in this…this *wilderness* any longer.

"I thank you for your hospitality, Sir Nicholas," he continued, his tone implying he would have liked to add *such as it was,* "and I wish you luck living among these savages."

Nicholas inclined his head in acknowledgment of the man's sarcastic good wishes. Then he said, "I believe Audric will be sorry to see you go."

The Norman's eyes narrowed. "Audric? What has he to do with me?"

"Perhaps not a great deal to do with you, my lord, but your charming cousin is another matter."

The Norman frowned, his face wrinkling deeply. "Lavinia?"

Nicholas refrained from inquiring who else he might be talking about. "I think Audric has conceived a great affection for Lady Lavinia. He smiles at her a good deal and while she's too modest to respond in any but the most proper, ladylike way, I believe she doesn't disapprove of his attentions. I must say, my lord, I would consider that a union to be encouraged. Audric's uncle is a most powerful and respected abbot, with close ties to Rome. The rest of his family yield some influence in political matters, and he was telling me just the other day that his other sister's husband has negotiated a trade alliance with several rich merchants in London that should make the family even more wealthy. I think Lavinia could scarcely do better for a husband, especially if they already feel some affection for one another."

D'Anglevoix seemed to be mentally counting coins as he continued to regard Nicholas. "Perhaps I should speak to Audric before we leave."

"I would if I were you, my lord. He seems a very fine young man, and if you don't secure him for Lavinia, I have no doubt some other, clever, less worthy woman might."

"Like Jos—" D'Anglevoix caught himself. "Yes, yes, as you say, I should certainly consider a marriage between my cousin and Audric. I'll speak to her at once."

"You're welcome to remain here for however long you like. A betrothal contract can take time."

Robert wasn't going to be pleased about the extended invitation, but the additional expense was worth it if it secured the allegiance of not just D'Anglevoix, but Audric, as well.

As if to prove that, D'Anglevoix smiled with the first sign of genuine pleasure Nicholas had ever seen on his face. "I had no idea you were such a wise and generous man," he admitted. "I knew you were an impressive soldier, of course, but I see you are astute and kindhearted, as well. I would have been honored to be related to you, Sir Nicholas."

"And I to you, but where a woman is concerned, it's better to give them some say where they marry, don't you think? Nothing's worse than discord between husband and wife."

"Yes, that's so," D'Anglevoix agreed, nodding his head. "I myself was blessed with an excellent wife who died much too soon. Perhaps that is how I came to forget how happy we were." He gave Nicholas a smile. "And I cannot wish any less for you."

"Thank you, my lord."

"I shall tell my men, and Lavinia, we are staying."

"And I shall return to my solar. I have a matter of household business to attend to."

WHEN NICHOLAS reached his solar, Joscelind was already waiting, looking lovely in a soft blue gown of some exotic fabric Nicholas couldn't name. Her gilded girdle set low on her slim hips, her jewelry sparkled in the sunlight coming in through the window, and her blond hair was covered by the thinnest of silken veils. Standing anxiously by the table, her hands clasped, she seemed like the perfect personification of humble, womanly beauty.

Yet whatever her outward appearance, he had seen and heard far too much to ever want her for a bride. She was haughty, imperious, spoiled and deceitful. He wouldn't have been at all surprised if she'd come into his bedchamber with nefarious designs, as he'd suspected. He'd been flabbergasted to discover Riona doing so instead.

Yet because of who Joscelind's father was and after what Riona had said about his consideration of the young ladies' feelings—or lack thereof—he was determined to treat Joscelind with courtesy and diplomacy until the time came for her to leave.

"You wanted to see me, my lord?" she asked as her smooth white brow furrowed.

"Yes. Please, sit down," he offered, gesturing at the chair.

She did, moving with the studied grace that was so different from Riona's natural easy elegance. Joscelind's actions seemed designed to show her form and figure to best advantage.

Once Joscelind was seated, she laced her fingers in her lap and raised her eyes to regard him woefully. "I fear

I've offended you, my lord, or caused you some displeasure."

"My servants are rather upset," he acknowledged, still standing by the door. "It seems there is some confusion regarding the orders you've given for the evening meal."

"Oh?" she inquired sharply. In the next instant, she was again worried and woeful. "I thought they understood me."

"Apparently they did not."

"Then they should have told me."

"I gather they tried."

Agitated, Joscelind rose, and he could see the effort she was making to control her temper. "Then I shall speak to them again."

"Yes, I believe that will be necessary. They aren't sure what to do."

Perhaps it was time he gave her some warning of her status. Riona would say that he owed her that. "Unfortunately, I cannot have a wife who causes so much conflict in the kitchen."

Angry indignation blazed in Joscelind's eyes, and her usual mask of placid composure fell away. "I've *never* had any trouble running my father's household," she declared. "My servants always do exactly *what* they're told *when* they're told, so if there's any fault here, my lord—"

She clenched her teeth, as if trying to silence herself.

He stepped into the breech and gave her an excuse.

"The servants in your father's household are no doubt used to your methods. Regrettably, mine aren't."

"Yes, I'm sure that's it," she said, quickly taking the pretext he handed her. "I'm quite certain that over time…" She lowered her head, then raised her eyes to give him a look surely intended to be beguiling. "We could come to understand each other better."

Nicholas refrained from saying that she would never have the chance to try. "Perhaps."

Raising her chin, Joscelind reached out to touch his forearm. "I would do my very best to see that it's so." Her hand slid up his arm as she continued to gaze steadily into his face. "I would do my very best to please you, my lord."

He wanted to lift her hand away, but unwilling to hurt her feelings more than he had to, he stepped back instead. "And I'm sure you'll make a most excellent wife, Joscelind."

For somebody else.

"It would be my greatest joy to see that my husband is always happy and *completely* satisfied. *Nothing* would be more important to me."

He knew exactly what she was implying and he could well believe she would use every art at her disposal to please her husband. Yet the loving would be less about intimacy and desire than vying for power and control. After the wondrous, unselfish love Riona gave him, marriage to Joscelind seemed a cold and heartless transaction.

Yet was that not what he'd sought in the beginning—
a bargain? Would his marriage to Eleanor be any less
of a trade?

Joscelind crept closer, smiling coyly. "I'm sure your
wife would always be satisfied, too, my lord. Every
woman dreams of such a strong, virile lover."

"My lady," he said not unkindly, but firmly, "I would
appreciate it if you would go to the kitchen and see to
the servants without further delay, or I fear the evening
meal will never get served."

"Oh, I'll see that it is."

He moved back. "I'm sure you will."

She came to a halt far too close to him for comfort.
"Are you really going to wait until Lammas to make
your decision?"

He nodded. He would take all the time he could, because once he married, he would not be unfaithful to
Eleanor. He honored the bonds of marriage too much
for that, and he wouldn't hurt Eleanor by taking a mistress.

And he thought, deep in his heart, that Riona would
never betray her friend by being the woman with whom
her husband committed adultery. Loving him before he
made his vow before God and swore to be faithful to
his wife was one thing; afterward was surely something else again.

"It's very difficult to wait, my lord. And I do so
worry that you'll choose another."

He didn't think she really had any doubts at all that

she would be his choice. She probably couldn't conceive that any other woman would be more appealing or worthy. "I'm sure the women I don't choose will have no trouble finding husbands. They each have much to offer."

Joscelind got a gleam in her eye that set him on his guard. "Not Lady Riona. I confess it seems a mystery to me that she's still here."

Did Joscelind suspect…? "Lady Riona and her uncle are still here because they are Scots, my lady, and I don't wish to cause any animosity among the rest of their countrymen by sending them away too soon."

"I see," Joscelind said, smiling. "They are here because of politics. I thought perhaps that little man amused you, like a sort of jester."

Nicholas tried not to clench his jaw. "He is amusing," he agreed. "And a very pleasant fellow."

"For a Scot."

"My lady, perhaps it has escaped your notice, but Dunkeathe is in Scotland. Whoever I marry will have to be respectful of the Scots."

Her soft, smooth cheeks colored. "Of course, my lord. I meant no offense."

He forced himself to smile. "I take none. I only point out that we Normans must have a care how we speak of Scots when we're in Scotland."

"Yes, my lord," she said in a small voice. "Now if you'll excuse me, I'll go to the kitchen."

CHAPTER SIXTEEN

STANDING OUTSIDE the buttery, Riona crooked her finger for Polly to join her. "In here a moment, Polly," Riona said quietly. "I want to talk to you."

Her eyes wide with curiosity, the maidservant put down her bucket and came without hesitation. "What's going on?" Polly whispered.

"It's about Lady Eleanor and her turn at running the kitchen tomorrow."

Polly shrugged. "She can't be any worse than that Lady Joscelind, or Lady Lavinia. A more scatterbrained woman I never saw. O'course, if she'd not spent half her time in here with that Audric, she might have done better."

Riona momentarily forgot what she wanted to say to Polly. "Lavinia was in the buttery with Audric?"

Polly grinned. "Yes—a lot. But it's all right, my lady. Seems they're going to be married. Lady Lavinia's maid told me, and she's that thrilled, you'd think she was the bride. Audric lives in London and Sally's always wanted—"

"I'm delighted for her," Riona said, cutting off what

was likely to be a long recitation of Sally's desires. "And that means, you realize, that Lady Lavinia won't be Sir Nicholas's bride."

"No, and God save us, not that Lady Priscilla, I hope, neither," Polly said. "Jesus, Mary and Joseph, that laugh of hers! Like a horse with the wheezes."

"So you'll agree with me, then, Lady Eleanor would be the best choice for Sir Nicholas."

"No, I don't," Polly said stoutly. "That'd be you. Lady Eleanor's a sweet girl and all, but—"

"While I appreciate your compliment, Polly, Sir Nicholas is never going to choose me. I don't have a large dowry. Lady Eleanor does, and she's pretty and gentle. I think she could even mellow Sir Nicholas a bit."

"You really think she has a better chance than you?" Polly asked, a look of dismay on her pretty face.

"Yes, I do, and you have to agree she'd be a better mistress than Lady Joscelind."

"Anybody'd be better than her. God love you, my lady, I'd rather have Alfred back than her. But I still say it ought to be you, and if it's not…well… I never took Sir Nicholas for a fool before."

"He's not a fool. He's a man who's worked hard for what he has, and must marry well in order to… Well, like any nobleman, he must marry with an eye to the future. So if you prefer Lady Eleanor for your chatelaine, you must do your best to help her tomorrow, and persuade the other servants to do likewise. I've tried to teach her as well as I can, but you and I both know that a fine meal really depends on the servants."

Polly frowned, and reluctantly nodded. "All right, since *you're* asking."

Riona smiled with genuine relief. "Good. And thank you. Eleanor will thank you, too, I'm sure. Now I'll leave you to get on with your work."

"Do you want us to ruin Lady Joscelind's meal tonight?" Polly asked as Riona started to open the door. "It'd be our pleasure and it'd serve Lady Joscelind right."

Riona shook her head. "No, no sabotage, Polly. All I ask is that you do your best for Eleanor."

Riona left the buttery and continued out in the courtyard. The air was warm, with a slight breeze that had a hint of the tang of the sea in it. Overhead, white clouds moved slowly across the sky, with darker ones on the horizon threatening rain. Lady Marianne and her husband were to leave for Lochbarr in the morning; perhaps rain would keep them in Dunkeathe another day or so.

Not sure what she ought to do, Riona strolled toward the gate. She hadn't seen Uncle Fergus since mass, but that wasn't so unusual these days. If he wasn't trying to get the recalcitrant Fredella to speak to him, he was riding about the valley helping Thomas select sheep.

"A moment if you please, Lady Riona!" a woman's voice called out in Gaelic.

She turned to find Lady Marianne hurrying across

the courtyard toward her. "How fortunate to find you! I was hoping for a chance to speak with you before we went home. I have a little time before Cellach will need me. Will you walk with me to the village?"

To refuse would be blatantly rude. "If it pleases you, my lady."

"Excellent."

Riona fell into step beside Nicholas's sister, who had the most graceful walk and perfect posture Riona had ever seen.

"The village is growing all the time," Lady Marianne noted. "I think at least five new families have come since I was here last, before Cellach was born. And there's another smithy, too, and soon another tavern, Nicholas tells me. We'll have to keep an eye on Roban next time." She slid Riona a smile. "He's quite a fellow to drink with, or so I understand."

"I think my uncle would agree."

Lady Marianne laughed softly. "So would my husband. I hope you weren't too upset with them."

"No," Riona prevaricated, wondering if she should say anything about the aftermath and her uncle. She decided against it.

They reached the gates, and the Saxon guards dutifully and respectfully came to attention as they passed by.

"I see they're still here," Lady Marianne remarked as they walked down the road that led through the inner ward toward the massive gatehouse. "Nicholas had his doubts about them at first, for they're not the smartest of men, but he claims they're good fighters."

In the ward, a group of soldiers were practicing with a quintain, a dummy mounted on a moving circular platform. It taught men to be quick to react, before they got hit with the arm of the dummy.

A familiar thrill of excitement wove its way through Riona as she tried to see if Nicholas was among them without revealing any particular interest in the activity.

"My brother still believes in training, I see," his sister remarked.

"Apparently," Riona replied, thinking some answer was called for.

"I feared he was never going to finish this castle," Lady Marianne said, gesturing at the walls. "It was only half-built when I first came here five years ago. How I hated Scotland then! It was so wet and dreary, and I knew little about the Scots. And of course, I hadn't yet met Adair."

Riona was tempted to ask about those days, for she'd heard some of the gossip about that strange courtship, but it was really none of her business.

"I must confess I didn't like Adair much at first. I thought he was quite rude. And arrogant. I believed I already knew the most arrogant man in the world— Nicholas. He can be very arrogant, don't you think?"

"Sometimes, my lady, but he deserves to be proud, after all that he's accomplished."

Lady Marianne smiled. "Indeed, he does. Just how

much he'd accomplished, I never appreciated until I came here. In fact, it wasn't until I was arguing with him over my betrothal that I found out that after my parents died, our family was left with nothing. Nicholas promised my mother that he would always look after me and he spent many a year saving all the money he could so that I could live in comfort and happiness, and Henry, too. Yet he never said a word about it, or gave any sign, or asked for our thanks—until I refused to marry the man he chose for me. He was furious and the truth came out as we quarreled. He was even more angry when I married Adair. But he came to our aid when we needed him most, and for that, I'll be forever grateful."

They passed through the second gate and continued toward the village. In the distance, Riona could make out the tavern, and the place where Percival had accosted her. At the edge of the green, the archer was being locked back in the stocks. He seemed to have accepted his fate with resignation, just as she had.

"Nicholas gave up a good deal for Henry and me, yet in spite of that, he succeeded where plenty of other men have not. His castle and his reputation are proof of that. But I don't think Nicholas feels that he's done enough, even now."

Riona knew he didn't, and why, but it was for Nicholas to voice his concerns to his sister, not her.

They came to the first few stone cottages. Lady Marianne turned down an alley that led to the river. "We can sit on the bank, if the grass is dry," she proposed.

Riona silently agreed and followed her to the stony bank.

"The grass is too wet," Marianne observed. She gestured to some large stones near the water's edge. "These rocks aren't. Not the softest seats in the world, but I can't linger long anyway."

She sat on a large one and Riona did the same.

When they were settled, Marianne gave a deep sigh. "Oh, it's lovely to have a few moments to myself."

"I know how you feel, my lady. That's one reason I came here with my uncle. I wanted to get away from my responsibilities for a little while."

How long ago it seemed since she'd had that conversation with Kenneth, and Uncle Fergus had come home with his news. How much had happened, and how her world had altered since.

"You have many responsibilities in Glencleith, I understand. Your uncle was telling me about you and all the things you do for him and your cousin and your clan."

Riona looked away. "He shouldn't boast so much. I do no more than any other woman would."

"Perhaps not, but I can appreciate what he doesn't say, because of what I've observed myself since I've been here. You may do your duty, and so might many another woman in your place, but you do it with love and cheerfulness."

"Uncle Fergus is a very lovable fellow."

Marianne laughed softly. "Aye, that he is. Quite a joy to talk to—and he loves you very much."

"Yes, he does," Riona answered. "That's why we came here even though I was sure your brother wouldn't want me. Uncle Fergus was so insistent, I didn't have the heart to disappoint him."

"You believe Nicholas won't choose you?"

Riona saw no point denying the inevitable. "Your brother has already told me that he has no intention of marrying me."

Lady Marianne frowned. "I'm very sorry to hear that."

She sounded genuinely disappointed, which made that reality a little harder to bear.

"Your brother has been very frank about why we're still here although my family has no money or power," Riona replied. "He doesn't want to risk any Scot saying he wouldn't consider a Scots bride. I am but a representative of my country."

Lady Marianne's disconcertingly intense gaze seemed to grow even more so. "Do you not care for Nicholas then?"

Riona tried to keep her face expressionless, beyond mere mild interest. "I admire and respect him for all that he's accomplished."

Lady Marianne's scrutiny was nearly as hard to endure as her brother's, although the lady's eyes were blue, not brown. "Perhaps you don't think it's any of my business, but I dearly want the brother who sacrificed so much for me to have some happiness and contentment in his life. I know what it is to love and be loved, Riona, and I want my brother to know it, too. Without love, his great castle might as well be a tomb, just a resting place for his body."

"You should speak of these things to Eleanor," Riona said, "for I believe she's going to be his choice, and she should be. She's a wonderful girl, and she'll make him a fine wife."

"That's something I never thought I'd hear—a woman praising a rival."

"We're not rivals, my lady, since your brother will never choose me. We're friends."

"If you truly are her friend, you wouldn't want her married to my brother."

Riona couldn't believe she'd heard aright.

"Oh, he's not an evil man," Lady Marianne hastened to clarify. "And I like Lady Eleanor, too. She's a lovely young woman and quite charming, in a quiet sort of way. And well connected, of course. I simply don't think she'll suit my brother at all."

Riona thought she could guess why. "To be sure, she's young and a bit ignorant of some things about running a household, but she learns quickly, and I'm sure she'll manage well, in time."

Lady Marianne's brow furrowed as she studied Riona, who desperately tried not to betray anything in her face. "Do you think she can make my brother happy?"

"Yes." *Eventually. Some day.* And then *she* would be

forgotten, or no more than a pleasant memory of a lover from days gone by.

"You mean that, don't you?"

"Yes."

Lady Marianne rose. "Then there is no more to be said, except that I'm sorry you feel that way. Now if you'll excuse me, I should get back to my children."

Riona was sorry she'd upset Lady Marianne, but there was no help for it. What good would it have done to tell her how she truly felt about Nicholas? That she would give nearly anything to be his wife? Nicholas couldn't marry her. Love would not pay taxes. Love would not protect everything Nicholas had worked and suffered for. Love meant sacrifice, as well as joy, and she would not be responsible for the loss of Dunkeathe. She wouldn't risk their affection turning to bitter resentment, perhaps even hatred. She would take what happiness she could with him, and be content.

And if she got with child…

She abruptly got to her feet and walked along the river bank, away from the castle.

A sound reached her ears from around a bend in the river shielded by a grove of willow and alder trees—a little boy's gales of merriment. A man was laughing, too. She instantly recognized that laugh, although it was rarely heard, and then softly, when they were alone.

Eager to see Nicholas, sure the little boy must be Seamus, she rounded the bend, to behold the mighty Sir Nicholas of Dunkeathe prostrate on the ground, seemingly held there by the foot of a happily triumphant four-year-old Scot waving a small wooden sword.

"I won, I won!" Seamus cried.

"I cry you mercy, valiant knight," Nicholas answered, throwing his arms out in complete surrender. "Allow me to rise before my tunic is ruined from the damp."

The little boy removed his foot. "Very well," he said with another flourish of his sword. "I give you back your life."

Nicholas rolled over and got to his feet. "Thank God," he said as he brushed bits of twig and grass from himself. Then he raised his eyes and saw Riona.

His smile of recognition made her heart sing. The glow in his eyes for her alone filled her with joy and made her quicken her pace, and his low obeisance made her feel like a queen.

"I fear I'm interrupting a tournament," she said when she reached them.

Seamus looked as if he agreed.

"We're finished, and alas, not too soon, for I was soundly beaten," Nicholas admitted. His smile disappeared as he addressed his scowling nephew. "Sir Knight, where are your manners?"

Seamus bowed. "Greetings, my lady," he muttered.

She bowed low in response. "Greetings to you, Sir Knight. I perceive you are a fine and valiant swordsman if you can triumph over your uncle. Although alas, I fear he's getting old."

When Nicholas shot her a disgruntled look, she tried to stifle her smile.

"Uncle Nicholas once beat twenty knights in a single day in a tournament," the lad said, rushing to his uncle's defense.

"I *was* much younger then," Nicholas grudgingly admitted, "and by the end of that day, my arms were so tired, I thought they'd drop off."

"You won anyway," Seamus declared, obviously not willing to allow his uncle to be criticized, even by himself.

"I was lucky," he replied. He looked at Riona with another devilish smile that played havoc with her heartbeat. "What brings you here, my lady, beyond seeing a demonstration of fine swordsmanship? Were you looking for me?"

"No. Your sister wished to speak to me."

Nicholas's grin disintegrated and his eyes narrowed a little. "What about?"

Riona wondered how much she should say to Nicholas about his sister's views. She had heard enough to know that their relationship had not always been a smooth one; it was now, and she didn't want to ruin it.

"I bet I know," Seamus piped up before Riona could answer. "Mama thinks Uncle Nicholas doesn't know how to find a wife."

Having been forewarned by her conversation with

the lady, Riona wasn't nearly as surprised as Nicholas by this observation.

"She said that to you?" Nicholas asked.

Seamus's face turned red. "Noooo," he mumbled, digging his toe into the dirt and not meeting his uncle's eye. "To Father. They didn't know I was still awake."

"I see," Nicholas said in a tone that sounded interested, not annoyed. "And how does she think I ought to go about it?"

"I didn't hear that part. They started whispering and laughing and I fell asleep."

"I'll have to ask her what I'm doing wrong."

The little boy looked up at him with a stricken countenance. "You won't tell her I said, will you?"

"Of course not. We're brothers-in-arms, sworn to be loyal forever, and such an oath means that if you wish me to keep a secret, I will until the day I die."

Seamus's eyes widened, and well they might, for there was no mistaking the firm sincerity of Nicholas's words.

"Now run along, young man," he ordered, "or your mother will be angry at me for keeping you so long."

The lad did as he was ordered, and scampered off toward the castle.

Nicholas reached out and took Riona's hand. His touch was warm and welcome, intimate and friendly. Wonderful. Achingly, heartrendingly wonderful.

They strolled toward a large willow on the riverbank, its slender branches like long, flowing hair. He parted the natural curtain and led her inside. "And now, my love," he said softly as they stood together beneath the branches, "what did Marianne really want to talk about?"

"You," Riona answered, leaning against the willow's trunk. "She wanted to be sure I knew your history and that you deserved to be happy."

She reached up to brush her fingertips across his wrinkled brow. "She was disappointed when I said you wouldn't marry me. I don't think she realizes that everything she told me only made me better understand why you can't."

He regarded her with such tenderness as he caressed her cheek, it was hard to believe he was the powerful lord of a great castle. Now, he was simply the man she loved. "Riona, perhaps I should forget marrying Eleanor."

She put her finger to his lips to silence him and shook her head. "If you lost Dunkeathe after all your efforts and suffering because of me, you might come to resent me. I won't hazard that. Let's enjoy what we have now, for the few nights we have left."

"Once I'm wed, that will be the end, Riona," he said, his voice low and mournful. "I will be faithful to the vows I make before God."

"I would expect no less. And when you announce your choice at Lammas, my uncle and I will leave."

Afterward, she would never see him again.

In spite of that, she gloried in the strength and warmth of him as they held each other, basking in his affection. Not afraid of the future, whatever it held.

And yet... "Nicholas, if I should be with child when I go home, should I send word to you or would you prefer not to know?"

Taking hold of her shoulders, he held her away from him, and in his face, she saw the answer even before he said it, and was glad. "Of course you must tell me. Girl or boy, any child of ours will be known as mine, and proudly so."

She smiled at him, loving him. Respecting him. Proud to have been his lover, come what may.

"But what of you, if that should be?" he asked, concern in his dark eyes. "How will your family treat you?"

"Uncle Fergus will be shocked, and disappointed, I'm sure. Kenneth...?" She shrugged her shoulders. "The same. But they won't abandon me or force me from Glencleith. They are too kind and generous."

"For your sake, I'm glad, but if you ever need anything, whether you bear my child or not, you mustn't hesitate to come to me."

"I will." She stroked his arms and her body warmed as she leaned closer to his. "So we won't worry about a child, but accept it as a gift, one to the other, if that should come to pass," she whispered as she wrapped her arms about him. "Now kiss me, Nicholas, and love me, while we can."

His eyes flared with exciting intensity as he took her in his arms. He kissed her fervently, while her tongue invaded the heat of his mouth, seeking that slick intimacy that foreshadowed the other.

Her upper back and shoulders against the tree, his fingertips glided over her bodice, then his palm cupped her breast. His hips pressed against hers, reminding her of what they'd done every night since she'd gone to his chamber the first time, as if she needed it. All the reminders necessary had been in his eyes when he looked at her, the smile she'd never seen him give another, the fierce passion in his kiss. And now his touch.

How she loved the strength of him, the power, the resolute will that had kept him alive for so long. She even admired the toughness he had acquired to survive.

She had to feel his naked skin, the heated flesh. Eagerly she thrust her hands under his tunic and over his flat stomach. One went higher, to brush lightly over his hardened nipple in a way that made him break the kiss to gasp, while her other hand went lower, to stroke the hardness there.

He closed his eyes and groaned as she aroused him further, delighting that she could make him feel such pleasure. Licking his neck. Kissing his jaw. Nibbling lightly on his earlobe as he stood still, powerless to move.

Until suddenly his eyes flew open—his desire-filled eyes, wild with a primitive hunger that took her breath away. "I want you now, Riona," he said, his voice husky and urgent. "Right now. Right here."

She said no word, but reached for the drawstring of his breeches and pulled the knot undone.

With a low growl that made her burn with passionate yearning, he grabbed her buttocks and lifted her. Her arms about his neck, she wrapped her legs around his waist, her skirt and shift bunching about her thighs. His breathing ragged, he moved forward so that her back was full against the tree.

Holding herself steady with one arm, she reached down and guided him into her, muffling her moan of welcome against his neck as he entered. She held tight as they loved, biting her lip to keep from crying out with the sheer pleasure of having him hard inside her, filling her anew with every thrust, his breath hot on her cheek. The tension, wondrous, delicious, seeming never ending, built and built until she could stay silent no longer.

"Faster," she begged, panting. "Harder." She had to feel that moment of shattering ecstasy. She couldn't wait. "Please…"

And then the tension snapped. Throbbing, she couldn't stifle the groan that arose deep in her throat, a primal cry of release, echoed by her lover as he, too, climaxed, there against the tree.

Afterward, he stood still, his chest rising and falling as he breathed deep while she kissed his cheek and stroked his hair.

When he eventually withdrew, she unwrapped her legs and lowered them until she was standing. He adjusted his breeches as she brushed down the skirt of her gown.

Taking a deep breath, he raised his dark eyes.

"Riona, that was…" He shook his head, and his wonderful, rare smile reappeared. "You simply astonish me. I've never met a woman like you in all my life."

"I've never met a man like you," she said, fixing her disheveled hair.

He took hold of her upper arms and kissed the tip of her nose. "You look beautiful—like a goddess of the forest."

"I think I probably look a mess, and if I don't fix my hair before I return to your castle, everyone will guess what I've been doing, if not with whom." She cocked her head and ran her gaze over his magnificent body. "If they could see you now, they'd have their suspicions about you, too."

"You think so?" he said, sidling forward and pressing her back against the tree.

Her breathing quickened. "I know so."

"You think I have the look of a man who's just made love?"

"I think you have the look of a man who's been doing something that gives him pleasure and dishevels his clothes and makes his long hair need a comb."

"Perhaps I should cut my hair."

She reached out and ran her fingers through it, marveling at its thickness. "That would be a pity, my lord."

"Then you like my hair this way, my lady?" He grinned and brushed it back over his shoulder with his hand. "I suppose I shouldn't be surprised. It's how the Scots wear it."

"I *am* a Scot," she replied, loving it when they spoke like this. Did anyone else ever hear that tender, teasing, yet incredibly arousing, tone in his voice?

Would his wife?

She pushed that thought away. "You should braid it at the sides the way Adair Mac Taran does," she suggested. "I think that would look quite fetching."

He laughed softly. "Fetching? Why the devil would I want to look *fetching?*"

"Because you are," she pertly answered as she tucked a stray lock of his hair behind his ear. "Very handsome and thus, very fetching."

"I don't care what other women think of me." He put his arms about her waist and drew her close. "Only you. What do you think of me, Riona?"

"That you're a very vain fellow who blatantly seeks compliments."

He frowned like a petulant little boy. "And here I thought you liked me."

"Sir Nicholas of Dunkeathe, if I didn't care for you a very great deal, I would not have made love with you, now or ever," she said with mock severity.

His frown dissolved to a wistful expression. "I would give nearly anything…" he began, the words trailing off.

Nearly anything was not everything, and she accepted that. "I think we had best quit dallying underneath this tree, lest we be discovered."

He nodded, becoming again the resolute, stern over-lord. "Will you return first, or should I?"

"I will," she replied. She kissed him once more lightly on the lips. "Until later, *m'eudail,*" she whispered before she hurried on her way.

ONCE RIONA reached the village, she slowed to a more leisurely pace. Although there were few people about, it not being market day, she didn't want it to appear that she was running from anything, or anybody.

She strolled toward the stall of the man with the beautiful fabric. The indigo, she noticed, was gone.

"Good day, my lady," the merchant said, nodding a greeting.

"Did my friend's cousin buy the blue fabric?" she asked.

"No, it was another lady. Very beautiful she was but…" He gestured for her to come closer to hear. "Losh, my lady, she was the haughtiest Norman you ever did see."

That had to be Joscelind.

"I've got some pretty blue ribbon, my lady. It'd be lovely on you."

She shook her head. "Not today." She turned to go and saw the archer in the stocks, head bowed. "How much longer does he have remaining in his punishment?" she paused to ask the merchant.

He thought a moment. "About a fortnight, I reckon."

"That must seem like an eternity," she noted before she walked away.

For her, time was flying by. Only three more days until Lammas, then Nicholas would announce his choice, and she'd be going back to Glencleith and what would surely be a lonely life there. Always, she would feel a loss.

"Greetings, my lady. What brings you here, I wonder—and all by yourself, too."

CHAPTER SEVENTEEN

HER MUSCLES instinctively tensing, every sense heightened and ready to fight or flee, Riona halted and looked around. It wasn't Percival she'd heard, but Lord Chesleigh, who came sauntering toward her from the direction of the tavern. He'd probably been drinking or wenching or both.

"Why not come to the village alone, eh?" he said with a smile that did nothing to relieve her wariness. "Sir Nicholas maintains law and order very well. Indeed, he's a most impressive fellow in a whole host of ways."

"Yes, he is," she agreed. She started to turn away from the Norman. "Now if you'll pardon me—"

"Are you going back to the castle? So am I," Lord Chesleigh said, falling into step beside her.

Short of breaking into a run, there was no way she could prevent him from walking with her, although why he would want to, she couldn't guess.

Until he told her.

"I was hoping to have some private conversation with you, my dear. To warn you."

She stopped and stared at him incredulously, making no secret of her surprise and suspicion. "Warn me? About what?"

"Your uncle's in grave danger."

"Who would want to hurt my uncle?" she demanded. Her eyes narrowed. "And why would *you* seek to warn me?"

"If you love your uncle, you should listen to me." They were beside an alley that led to a small storage building behind the baker's. "What I have to say requires privacy. This way."

He ordered her as if she were his servant—and did he really think she'd go anywhere with him? "You can talk to me right here."

His face hardened. "Don't be a fool. What I have to say is important, and not for anyone who happens to be walking by to hear. If you want to help your uncle, you'll do as I say."

She could defend herself. She'd done so before with Percival—as she would remind Lord Chesleigh. "Very well, but I can protect myself, if you have any intention of—"

"You're hardly the sort of woman to attract such attention from me," he replied with a sneer.

That was probably true. No doubt he would consider a Scot utterly unworthy of him.

"Good," she snapped as she marched down the alley and around the storehouse. She noted a woodpile with several large branches near the corner—potential weapons, should she require one.

"Now then," she said sternly when Lord Chesleigh joined her, "who's threatening my uncle? And how do you know about it?"

"I know because the person you both should fear is me."

Her hands balled into fists and her blood rose, hot and fierce.

"Come, come, there's no need for temper," he said, "although I suppose Nicholas may like that sort of thing—a contrast to his coldness."

"What does he have to do with this?"

"He has everything to do with this." Lord Chesleigh tucked his thumbs into his wide belt and for the first time, she noticed the small dagger tucked in it. "Unfortunately for us both, my dear, it hasn't escaped my notice that our host seems to have a most unaccountable affection for you."

"That's not true," she retorted, willing him to believe her, wondering if someone had seen her sneaking into Nicholas's chamber at night and realized who she was.

Lord Chesleigh shook his head. "Others may not have perceived it, but I certainly have. I am a very perceptive man."

"Or a very imaginative one," she replied. "Do you have any evidence to support this outrageous accusation, my lord?"

He continued to smile that terrible smile. "There's no need to act indignant, my lady. I don't care if you're bedding him or not. Indeed, you may bed him all you like, or as often as he'll have you, and it's nothing to me." He ran his gaze over her. "When you're angry, I begin to see your appeal myself."

Before she could speak, his face turned as hard and cold as a block of ice. "What I *do* care about is who he marries. My daughter is to marry Nicholas, and it will be dangerous for anyone to try to thwart that plan. Therefore, my dear, you may be the man's mistress, but not his wife—or your beloved uncle could meet with a most unfortunate end."

Oh, God. He would do it, too. She saw it in his face, heard it in his voice. He was ruthless and without mercy.

"If what you say is true, *I* am the impediment to your plans, not my uncle. Why aren't you threatening *my* life?"

"Because, my dear, you might be willing to risk your own safety by going to Nicholas and telling him what I've said here today, but you'll never put your uncle's life in danger."

"If anything happened to him, I would accuse you of his murder."

"Why, who said anything about murder?" Lord Chesleigh's eyes gleamed with malicious intent. "I think an accusation of treason much more entertaining. A few years rotting in a prison, followed by drawing and quartering…that's more what I had in mind."

She fought the sudden wave of nausea as she envisioned her uncle suffering that terrible fate and summoned her courage. "He's no traitor and you'd never be able to prove otherwise."

"You underestimate me, my dear. I can prove anything I care to, in a court of law or elsewhere. Alas for you, King Henry lives in dread of treason, as all monarchs must. It might take but a whisper to persuade him to have your uncle charged."

She realized something he seemed to have forgotten. "We aren't Henry's subjects. We're Scots."

"Alexander has no desire to rouse conflict with the English court, at least not for now and least of all for a man like your uncle. He's nobody."

Riona stared at Lord Chesleigh in horror. She could believe he would accuse her uncle, and it would unfold as he predicted. But she wasn't willing to surrender yet. "I could tell Sir Nicholas of your plans, and anyone else who would charge my uncle with such a crime."

"Oh, my dear," the nobleman said with a patronizing laugh. "You really are naive. I have many friends at court who will confirm anything I say, regardless of its veracity, and other men who will be only too happy to provide sufficient evidence in the form of letters and secret pledges."

"You mean they'd fabricate lies?"

"Now you're beginning to catch on." Lord Chesleigh's lips curved up into a heartless smile. "But surely there's no need for animosity. You may enjoy Sir Nicholas any way you like, except as his wife. You may even continue to do so after he marries Joscelind, if Nicholas still wants you. I understand that such men have their needs and one woman may not meet them."

"What of your daughter?" Riona demanded, disgusted with the man and appalled at his callous ambition that would pay so little heed to his own daughter's happiness.

"She's well aware that a wife has the most power and influence, not a mistress. As to…other matters, I'm sure a man like Nicholas can satisfy you both."

"What about Eleanor? What if Nicholas chooses her? Will you threaten her? Or her cousin?"

Lord Chesleigh laughed. "If Nicholas actually chooses that slip of a green girl, Percival can be easily persuaded to change his mind about a betrothal. He's no more worry to me than a nit in my groom's hair."

He backed Riona up against the wall of the storehouse. "So, my dear, you are free to bed the man, but not to wed him—or your uncle's life will be forfeit."

The blood throbbed through Riona's veins, the blood of warriors, the proud blood of her people. But for the sake of her uncle, she could do nothing. Lord Chesleigh had found the chink in her armor. "Yes, my lord, I understand."

"Excellent." His gaze flicked over her body. "Should Sir Nicholas ever tire of you—"

Riona shoved him away with all her might. "I'd rather die!"

The Norman merely chuckled. "We'll see who does the dying, my dear. Never forget who is powerful, and who is not. Be sure that I will do exactly as I say I will if you or anyone else gets in my way."

"SO HERE YOU ARE, my beauty!"

Riona turned away from the window, where she'd been watching the sun set over the hills in a glory of orange, pink and purple, to find a beaming Uncle Fergus on the threshold of her chamber.

His smile faded. "You're not sick?"

"No, no," she hastened to answer. "I thought that I should stay out of the hall while Joscelind's in charge."

"Ah, a wise notion," he replied, coming into her chamber. "I should likely stay out of there myself. Not that she could do anything any better than you."

"You seem cheerful, Uncle," Riona noted, doing her best to sound so herself.

He grinned again, and expansively held out his arms. "Congratulate me, my beauty. Fredella's forgiven me at last!"

With that, he bounded toward her and engulfed Riona in a hearty embrace. She clung to him tightly, loving him. Grateful to him for all that he'd done for her. For treating her like his own daughter. For thinking she was worthy of a man like Nicholas. For bringing her to Dunkeathe.

"So, all is well between you and Fredella, then?" she asked when they moved apart.

"Better than well," he replied. "She's agreed to marry me."

Riona clasped her hands together and tears came to her eyes. Happy tears, she told herself, refusing to let any selfish concern for her own sorrows mar this joyful news. "Oh, that's wonderful. You deserve every happiness."

"Of course, we have to wait until Eleanor's safe. Fredella won't leave her under that lout Percival's thumb."

"I think it's very possible that Sir Nicholas will choose her if she does well supervising the kitchen, and I don't think she'll fail."

"Sir Nicholas?" Uncle Fergus replied, looking at Riona as if she'd suddenly denounced the pope.

"Well, yes. Who else were you thinking—?"

"Not Nicholas, that's for certain, since he's going to marry you. No, no, I've got another plan entirely." He sat on the bed and pulled her down beside him. "Fredella and me agree that all Percival cares about is getting his cousin married off to some rich nobleman he can brag about, so once Sir Nicholas makes his announcement and Percival realizes she's not the man's choice, I'll ask him if Eleanor can come visit Glencleith for a bit. A man like that must be more than ready to get back to his tailor, as well as his friends, such as they are."

Riona regarded her excited uncle warily. Percival might indeed welcome the chance to get back to London, or even York. On the other hand… "He'll never agree to let her go. If he wants to get Eleanor married, he's more likely to insist she go with him, so he can show her off to prospective grooms. Or he'll send her to a convent, just as he threatened."

Uncle Fergus's eyes continued to gleam with unbridled satisfaction. "That's why I'll tell him a rich, unmarried thane related to Alexander himself is also coming to visit Glencleith."

Riona frowned. "What rich, unmarried thane are you talking about?"

Uncle Fergus's grin widened, so that he looked like a mischievous sprite. "Have you not heard of my kinsman, Duncan Mac Dougal?"

"Of course." Everybody had. He was as famous a warrior as Nicholas of Dunkeathe, or Adair Mac Taran, and just as handsome, or so people said. "But he's never come to Glencleith before. Why would he now?"

Uncle Fergus chortled. "Well, he might not, but Percival wouldn't know that, would he? I can invite the man just the same, and if he doesn't come, it doesn't matter, as long as Eleanor is safe in Glencleith with Fredella and me. I promise you, my beauty, once we've got her with us, Percival will need an army to get her back."

Knowing that he meant it, and that he'd protect Eleanor with his life, yet certain his plan would prove unnecessary because Eleanor would surely be Nicholas's bride, Riona embraced him and kissed his cheek. "I love you, Uncle," she said, her breath catching.

"Come, come, my beauty," Uncle Fergus said softly as he stroked her hair. "There's no need for tears. Eleanor's going to be safe, I'm going to marry Fredella and you'll have a fine husband yourself. The more time I spend with Sir Nicholas, the better I like him."

"Me, too," Riona whispered.

NICHOLAS STUCK his head into Marianne's chamber, intent on having a private conversation with her before she left for Lochbarr tomorrow.

His sister sat in a beam of late afternoon sunlight, her hair unbound, rocking the slumbering Cellach's cradle with her foot. She had a distaff topped with raw wool under her left arm, and on her right side dangled a drop spindle, the yarn stretching out as it twisted. As she worked and watched her baby, she crooned a lullaby.

She looked so calm, so peaceful, so contented and happy—so different from the Marianne who'd once stood in this very chamber begging him to reconsider the plans he'd made for her.

Perhaps, given that he'd refused to listen, he shouldn't expect to spend the rest of his life as happily married as she.

Marianne glanced up and gave him a welcoming smile, reminding him to silently thank God anew that she'd forgiven him for what he tried to do.

"I thought Seamus was going to keep you busy all day," she said quietly as he ventured farther into the room.

"It seems I'm less entertaining than some kittens in the stable," he replied as he approached the cradle. He'd checked where his nephew was and what he was doing the moment he'd returned to Dunkeathe. "Where's Adair?"

"Making sure all is in readiness for our departure in the morning."

"You're welcome to stay until Lammas."

Marianne shook her head. "Thank you, Nicholas, but Adair prefers to celebrate the harvest at home. He likes to go to his father's grave on the anniversary of his death."

Nicholas silently nodded and looked down at the child slumbering in the cradle. Cellach's lashes fanned across her soft cheeks, and her little mouth puckered up in a bow. She was like a slumbering cherub, and he hoped he would one day be looking down on such a heavenly, sleeping child of his own.

If Riona had his child, he hoped it would look like her, that it would have her eyes, her hair, her fire, her spirit. Her bold bravery. Her charm.

One thing above all was certain: if they should have a child together, he would indeed acknowledge it, and be proud to do so.

Marianne gestured at a second chair close to the window. "Apparently in my son's eyes, I'm much less entertaining than you, so I know exactly how you feel."

"You're his mother and he loves you very much," Nicholas replied as he sat.

"While you're his brave, amazing uncle who's won so many tournaments," she countered as she set aside her spinning. She got a gleam of mischief in her blue eyes that were so like their late mother's. "His brave, amazing uncle who has come to ask something of his sister?"

Nicholas felt himself blush. Now that the time had come to ask her opinion of the women vying for his hand, he felt remarkably foolish and very, very young, even though he was a full ten years older than she. "I wanted to ask your opinion of the remaining ladies."

"Then it's true there were more?"

"There were ten originally."

Marianne's eyes widened. "Ten? I'm impressed. Not that I doubt you're considered a fine prize—"

He rose abruptly and strode to the window.

"What's the matter, Nicholas? Are you upset I called you a 'prize'?"

"That's a little disconcerting, yes," he admitted as he watched Polly stroll across the yard toward the kitchen, a basket of greens in her arms. It seemed she was in no great rush to complete her task.

"And now you know a little of how I felt when you betrothed me to Hamish Mac Glogan."

Nicholas faced his sister and apologized again. "I'm sorry. I should have listened to you and paid heed to your wishes."

He returned to his chair, determined to sit still if it killed him and not display any hint of emotional disturbance or worry. "I'll gladly listen to you now, if you'll tell me what you think of the ladies who've come to be my bride."

Marianne rocked the cradle with her foot a few more times before she answered. "Lady Joscelind is very beautiful and her father is important at Henry's court, I hear."

He nodded. "Very important, or so our brother says, and she seems most keen to have me. The idea of having Lord Chesleigh for a father-in-law isn't a welcome one, but the man does have influence at court, and the dowry should be considerable."

"Henry would know about Lord Chesleigh's power at court," Marianne confirmed. She slid Nicholas a questioning glance. "I thought Henry might still be here. It must have been urgent business that called him away so soon after he arrived."

Nicholas didn't answer. His relationship with his brother had never been an easy one, and Marianne knew that better than anyone.

She sighed wearily. "One of these days, Nicholas, you're going to have to treat Henry with more respect. He's a grown man, and well regarded in England."

"When he treats me with the respect I deserve, I'll consider it."

"I should never try to play the peacemaker," Marianne replied as she rocked the cradle again, the corners of her mouth turned down in a frown. "You never listen to me."

"I may not listen when the subject is Henry, but I really do want to hear your opinion of my potential brides."

She tilted her head to study his face. "That sounds sincere."

"It is. You know I've little experience with women—ladies," he amended. "I've spent most of my time training or fighting in battles and tournaments."

"So you require a woman's opinion. I understand."

A woman who isn't Riona, he silently added.

Marianne folded her hands in her lap. "Lady Lavinia appears to be a nice, quiet young woman."

"Yes, she is."

"But I fear she has her eye elsewhere."

Nicholas nodded. "Audric."

"I gather from your tone that you're not jealous?"

"Not a bit. I wish them well."

"If you are as aware of that little romance as I am, why is Lady Lavinia still here?"

"Because it pleases me to let their romance blossom here."

"I never realized you could be so generous," Marianne said gravely, although her eyes were amused.

"Generous?" Nicholas replied, folding his arms over his chest. "I call it practical. I don't want her, so why shouldn't Audric have his chance? And they'll both think of me with goodwill in the future."

"Her cousin may not."

"D'Anglevoix became quite agreeable when I reminded him that Audric's uncle is an important leader in the church and their family are noted for excellent trading alliances that have made them very wealthy."

"So encouraging their romance is simply politics?"

Nicholas shrugged. "Call it a political romance, if that pleases you more."

"Are you looking for a political romance, Nicholas?" Marianne asked, regarding him in a way that made him shift uncomfortably.

"I'm looking for a wife who must bring certain things to the marriage—wealth and family influence are the most important to a man in my position. I'm a Norman overlord in Scotland, which means I require the money to hire soldiers to keep my estate safe, as well as influence to ensure it remains in my hands."

"Don't you want to be happy, too?"

"First I have to be sure Dunkeathe is securely mine and that I don't have to worry about money."

Marianne's anxious gaze searched his face. "Are you in financial difficulties, Nicholas?"

"No," he snapped. Then, because it was Marianne, he added, "At least not yet, and if I marry well, not at all."

"If you're in trouble, you can always come to Adair and me for aid, as we came to you."

Nicholas frowned. "I don't want to go begging my sister for money."

"So you'll marry for it?"

"Money is only one consideration," he replied.

"Well, thank heavens for that," Marianne said with a sarcasm that cut him like a knife. "And here I was thinking you were being *completely* mercenary. Tell me, Nicholas, what is your wife to get out of this marriage?"

"Security, a large household to rule, children. *Me*. Or perhaps you think your brother isn't worthy of any of these women?"

Instead of quarreling more, as he'd expected since this was Marianne, his sister only shook her head and sighed sadly. "I thought Adair and I had shown you how wonderful marriage can be when you're in love with your spouse."

"I do hope to love my wife—eventually," Nicholas replied. "I likewise hope she will come to love me."

"There is no lady here you love already?"

He hesitated for the briefest of moments. "No."

Cellach started to fuss and Marianne again rocked the cradle. "I hope you're right, Nicholas, and that love will come. But I have to tell you that whatever financial difficulties you have, or any other troubles, I'm sure you can overcome them without a mercenary marriage, as you've already overcome so much. Marriage is for the rest of your life."

"Yes, I have overcome many troubles—because I was a mercenary," he replied. "If I marry a poor woman, with no dowry and no way to ensure that I have powerful friends among the nobility, I will not be safe, and I cannot then be happy."

"I see."

Nicholas didn't believe she did, but he couldn't expect her to. Her life had been vastly different from his, thanks to his efforts. "So what do you think of Lady Eleanor?" he asked, still determined to get her opinion.

After all, he'd paid for Marianne to stay ten years with the good sisters in that convent; she herself once said she'd learned a lot about women during that time.

Mercifully, Marianne answered without questioning or criticizing him. "She seems a sweet young thing. A bit too young, perhaps, given the size of the household she'll have to command. And her cousin…" She shrugged. "I cannot like him. I fear he's a very vain, selfish young man."

"I don't like him, either, but it wouldn't be him I'd be marrying."

"Yet you'd be related to him."

"Yes, and he has many friends at court, which is where I expect he'll be spending his time once he's got Eleanor off his hands."

"Eleanor seems very young to be chatelaine of Dunkeathe."

"She's seventeen."

"A very sheltered seventeen, I think."

"You weren't much older when you married Adair."

"Lochbarr is not Dunkeathe, and you're not Adair."

"What's that supposed to mean?"

Marianne rose and went to him, resting her hand on his shoulder and looking at him with obvious affection and concern. "It means, dear brother, that your castle is much different from Adair's home, and you're a very different sort of man. You should choose a bride who isn't afraid of you."

A woman who would confront him face-to-face, boldly, eyes blazing, chin raised.

"Eleanor's not afraid of me," he protested.

Marianne put her finger to her lips and nodded at the cradle. "Shh. You'll wake Cellach."

"I don't think Eleanor's afraid of me," he repeated in a softer voice.

"Very well, Nicholas, she's not. But she's not happy, either. I've barely seen her smile the whole time I've been here, even when she's talking to you. What do her eyes tell you?"

Nicholas strode to the window again. "They don't talk," he replied. Not *her* eyes, anyway. Not to him.

"If she was happy, I think you'd be able to see that in her eyes."

The way he could see the affection and desire unfurl in Riona's when they were alone. He had seen nothing like that in Eleanor's timid, wary expression, and she often seemed to avoid looking directly at him at all.

"If she doesn't want me for a husband, she has only to say so," he muttered. "I won't have an unwilling bride." He looked at his sister. "You made me see the folly of trying to force a woman into a marriage she doesn't want. If Eleanor doesn't wish to marry me, that will be the end of it."

Marianne glanced down at the cradle as Cellach sighed and shifted, then raised her eyes. "Should I assume that Eleanor is your first choice?"

"Either her or Joscelind."

"What of the Lady Riona?"

Nicholas went to the chair and picked up the distaff Marianne had left lying there. He fingered the fleece, absently noting its softness and wondering how it compared to that of the sheep Fergus Mac Gordon thought so highly of.

He also wondered if he should tell Marianne that he knew that she'd talked to Riona about him, but decided against it. He didn't want to reveal that he'd been alone with Riona at all. "I could never seriously consider her. Her family is too poor and unimportant."

"That may be, but she's a fine young woman—very competent and quite pleasant. The servants seem to adore her, and I've noticed that even the guards at the gate treat her with deference and respect. You'll excuse me for saying so, brother, but given their usual attitude to Scots, that's quite an achievement."

"I cannot marry a poor woman."

"You would rather marry a proud and haughty woman who will make your household a battleground, or a young, frightened girl who's too afraid to even look at you?"

"I can't afford to marry any but a rich woman." Frustrated, he started to pace. "And I'm *tired*, Marianne. Tired of fighting. Tired of scrimping and saving every ha'penny. Tired of worrying.

"When I have money to pay my taxes and my garrison, when I have friends at court to look out for my interests, then I can rest and be content. If I can also come to love my wife, I'll count that as a blessing. But if not, I'll enjoy the ease I've won by taking her for my bride, and treat her well regardless."

"I only want you to be happy, brother," Marianne said softly, her eyes full of a sorrow that it pained him to see.

"I will be, Marianne," he vowed. "You'll see."

"Who are you trying to convince, Nicholas? Me—or you?"

"This is useless," he declared, heading for the door. "Until you've worked and suffered and strove as I have, you can't possibly understand."

NICHOLAS strode into his solar and closed the door. Hands splayed, head bowed, he leaned on the table and, sighing, closed his eyes.

Like a man utterly exhausted, or bending under a burden he no longer wished to carry.

CHAPTER EIGHTEEN

THAT NIGHT, Riona had barely closed the door to Nicholas's chamber before he swept her into his arms. Her toes brushed the stone floor as she clung to him passionately, returning his fervent kiss.

He let her down slowly, her breasts brushing against his chest, his face visible in the small flame from the oil lamp on the table. "I've missed you," he said in a low whisper that made her heart beat with delicious anticipation.

He took off the scarf she still wore to fool Percival, and tossed it onto the chest nearby. She noticed a familiar-looking bundle sitting there, but she forgot it as he trailed his finger from her lips to her chin and then slowly down her neck to the valley between her breasts. She had on the scarlet gown again. She wore it as often as she could because it was his favorite.

"I've missed you, too," she admitted, her body warming as it always did when he touched her. "What's that on your chest?"

He looked down at his tunic. "Where?"

She laughed softly, and for a moment, her mood

lightened. "Not there." She pointed at the bundle on the wooden chest. "There."

"Oh, that," he replied.

He went and got it, and as he did, his serious expression filled her with trepidation and dismay. "Your uncle gave me this, but of course I can't keep it. Will you take it back to him?"

"What is it?" she asked, although deep in her heart, she suspected she knew.

"A *feileadh* and shirt—my wedding present for when I married you."

She briefly closed her eyes. It was a dagger to the heart, although she knew her uncle had meant well. "He didn't tell me he'd done that."

"He didn't give me a chance to refuse."

Riona took the bundle and set it down on the bed. "He still can't conceive that you won't be marrying me."

Nicholas took her shoulders in his powerful warrior's hands and regarded her steadily, his gaze full of a yearning that devastated her, because she knew that there could be no future for them. "I would choose you, Riona, if I could. If I were rich and influential, I would send all those others packing tomorrow and carry you to the chapel in my arms to make you mine."

"But you can't," she said, her heart aching, her voice steady. "And you must beware Lord Chesleigh when you choose Eleanor. He's ambitious and dishonest, and he'll stop at nothing to get what he wants."

She couldn't tell Nicholas directly about Lord Chesleigh's threat to her uncle's life, but she would do what she could.

"Percival's influence should counter anything Lord Chesleigh can do," he replied.

"I'm not so sure. You must be prepared to fight Chesleigh, whether in court or in battle, after you marry."

Nicholas nodded, and she knew he would heed her words.

"Enough of such grim talk," she said with false cheer. "I don't want to ruin our last few nights with worries about villainous Normans. I'd rather talk about you."

Nicholas seemed anxious to shake off the weight of heavier matters, too, as he smiled. "Oh? Perhaps I'd rather talk about *you*, and what I'm going to do with you when I carry you to my bed."

She backed away from him. They had so little time left, she would enhance her store of memories while she could. "Not yet. First, my lord of Dunkeathe, I have a boon to beg."

He frowned, and she regretted worrying him. "I'd like to see you in a *feileadh* before I leave Dunkeathe, that's all. Would you put it on for me now?"

His smile held relief at her simple request. "You'd like to make a Scot of me?"

Trying to maintain this lighter mood between them, she returned his smile. "A *feileadh's* very comfortable, or so Uncle Fergus says."

"A bit breezy, though, don't you think?"

"I wouldn't know. I've never worn one. Will you put it on for me, Nicholas? Just for a little while?"

"Your wish is my command, my lady, except that I don't know how to wrap the plaid properly," he replied. "Adair tried to explain it to me once, but I confess I didn't really listen."

"I'll help you." She ran her gaze over him. "The shirt first?"

"Very well, my lady. The shirt first."

He undid his belt and tossed it onto the table. After pulling off his tunic, he set that beside the belt, so that he was wearing only his breeches and boots.

Her mind strayed to thoughts of making love until they were both satisfied and exhausted, and she had to leave to return to her own chamber.

He drew on the white shirt, which smelled faintly of lavender, then discovered that he couldn't get his arms into the sleeves. "It doesn't fit," he said, his words muffled by fabric as he struggled to get it on.

"Your shoulders are too broad," she replied, hurrying to help him.

She didn't resist the urge to blatantly caress him while she did.

"Are you trying to make this more difficult?" he asked as he continued to struggle with the garment.

"Not particularly," she replied, caressing him again.

When he succeeded in getting the shirt off and tossed it onto the chest, she tilted her head to admire him. "Let's not bother with a shirt."

"Wanton wench—and if you keep looking at me like that, I'm going to pick you up and carry you to the bed right now."

"Then I won't look at you," she pertly replied. "Or you can keep your breeches on until I've got the fabric around you."

He started to undo the tie of his breeches. "If I'm to wear that plaid, I think I should wear it as the Scots do, and that means naked underneath—or so Adair's informed me. Don't you think I should?"

Her cheeks warmed with a blush, and the memory of his naked body. "If you wish."

He shook his head as he got one boot off. "If *you* wish."

"I won't stop you."

"When you look at me like that, it makes me want to kiss you." He got the other boot off and kicked it into the corner. "Of course, there seems to be very little these days that doesn't make me want to kiss you."

She put the fabric on the floor and started to unroll it. "What are you doing" he asked.

"I've got to spread this out."

"What, on the floor?"

"It's too long for the bed."

"Ah, the bed."

His deep, husky voice alone could make her moist and ready for him. But although she would gladly make love with him now, she did want to see him in a *feileadh*—another recollection to take with her when she went home.

By the time he had his breeches off, she had laid the fabric out so that it was flat on the floor, stretching from the window nearly to the door.

"Is this going to take a long time?" he asked as he stood wearing nothing but a smile, and shamelessly displaying the extent of his eagerness to make love with her.

She raised a brow. "Can you not control that, my lord?"

"I'm naked and I'm with you, so no, I can't."

"Peacocks have their tail feathers and you have that. I suppose both are impressive displays of manhood."

"Suppose?"

"I've never seen a naked man aroused, except for you," she confessed as she crouched and made a series of folds in the center of the fabric.

After she finished, she pushed the center together, so that it was narrower there, and slipped his belt underneath the narrow portion.

"Now, if you'll just lie down here where the belt is, I'll wrap the fabric around you," she ordered, pointing to the center.

He didn't immediately do as she said. "That floor's going to be damn cold." He raised a brow. "Or is this a clever scheme to cool my ardor?"

Considering how long he could love her before he climaxed, she doubted that would happen. "I'm sure that takes more than a cold floor."

"You may be right," he said as he lay down on the

fabric. When he was flat on his back, she stood at his feet. "If somebody were to come in now, you'd present an interesting spectacle," she noted.

"Are you going to stand there and make fun of me now that you have me completely at your mercy and looking ridiculous, or are you going to show me how to wear this?"

"Much as I'd love to stand here and admire you all night, I don't want you to catch a chill. Please raise your arms."

He did, and she knelt and pulled the right side of the fabric across his torso. She also lightly—and quite deliberately—brushed his penis with the back of her hand as she did.

"Brazen hussy."

"If your little soldier is going to stand at attention and get in my way, that's not my fault."

"*Little* soldier?"

"Big soldier," she amended as she drew the left side over the right, surreptitiously caressing him again. "Now you may fasten your belt and stand up."

"My *big* belt," he muttered as he obeyed. "On my *big* feet."

"I don't think your feet are particularly enormous. As for the other parts of you, I'll just have to take your word that they're impressive."

"In that case, I assure you, my lady, I'm *very* impressive. Bards are going to sing songs about me someday," he said as he rose.

The *feileadh* looked like two overlapping skirts, held in place by the belt. He frowned as he looked down. "Are you sure this is right?"

"You have to adjust the part hanging over your belt, that's all."

"How do I do that?"

"I'll show you." She took hold of one side of the overhanging fabric, and arranged it so that the extra fabric wound from his waist across his back, to drape over his left shoulder. "There."

She stepped back to admire her handiwork. And him.

He looked even more magnificent and handsome in the *feileadh* than she'd imagined.

"Do I meet with your approval?" he asked as she stood staring at him. "Do I look like a Scot?"

She didn't answer with words. She launched herself at him and took his mouth with a heated kiss, grinding her hips against him in blatant, brazen invitation.

He instantly responded with equal fervor, clasping her to him.

"I want you to make love with me, Nicholas. Now!" she ordered, panting as if she'd run for miles to be in his arms.

"Gladly," he growled.

He kissed her passionately and thrust his tongue between her lips. His hands stroked and caressed her body, gliding over the fabric until, with a low growl of pure animal hunger, he picked her up and took her to his bed. Watching her, his eyes full of heated need, he hurried to take off his belt.

"No!" she gasped, half sitting. "Like that."

She reached up and grabbed his belt to pull him down on top of her. Her eager hands attacked him, stroking his back, his chest, his nipples. With soft moans and anxious whimpers, she bent her legs, so that her skirt fell about her hips, exposing her nakedness to him. As he raised himself on his hands, she grabbed his buttocks and pushed him closer. The *feileadh* bunched between them, but not enough to keep him from thrusting eagerly inside her warm, moist, ready body.

She came nearly at once, arching and bucking and breathing hard through clenched teeth, her hands gripping his arms until her knuckles were white. She called out his name as wave after wave of pleasure ripped though her while he continued to thrust until, with a cry of ecstasy, he climaxed.

Sated and spent, he fell against her. "By the saints…" he murmured, gasping for air.

Her breathing was ragged, too. "I thought the *feileadh* would suit you, but I had no idea…"

He raised himself and looked down at her flushed face. "Was it just the *feileadh?*"

She smiled like one drugged, or drunk, blissfully replete with the euphoria of making love. "Not just the *feileadh*. Your body. Your legs. Your knees." She lazily caressed his cheek. "You've got very handsome knees,

Nicholas of Dunkeathe. I'd suggest you wear a *feileadh* all the time, but your maidservants would surely be too distracted."

"And you?" he said, lightly kissing her nose. "Wouldn't you be distracted?"

Her happiness diminished. "If I were still here, yes, I'd be distracted."

"I'm sorry, Riona," he said, and there was sorrow and remorse in his dark eyes.

"I'm not sorry," she said sincerely as she brushed a lock of hair from his face. "And I don't—I *won't*—regret the time I've spent with you."

He tenderly stroked her cheek. "You truly are an amazing and generous woman, Riona Mac Gordon. How I wish I could marry for love."

She had longed to hear him say that he loved her, yet hearing it now gave her nothing but pain, and the certain knowledge that her heart would break when she left Dunkeathe, and him. "Whatever we've shared, it's enough," she lied.

He drew her closer. "Stay the night with me, Riona."

"You know I can't."

"A while longer then," he implored. "Just be with me for a bit longer."

She couldn't bring herself to refuse his request. "Very well—but you'd better take off that *feileadh,* or I'm going to want to make love with you again."

"Are you trying to tempt me?"

"I think you're the one tempting me, my lord."

He didn't take off the *feileadh* until later.

Much later.

NICHOLAS AWOKE when a beam of early-morning light fell across his eyes. As he opened them, squinting, he thought of Riona, as he had every morning since the first time they'd made love, and even before then.

Last night she'd been trying so hard to keep things happy and carefree between them, as if she could make him forget the inevitable. More poignant than tears would have been, her efforts had brought pain along with happiness, sorrow with the pleasure.

He'd tried to respond in kind, to sound merry and happy in spite of what must be. She deserved no less, and so he hadn't refused her request to don the *feileadh*, even though he was sure he'd look ridiculous.

Clearly, to her, he hadn't.

He smiled to himself as he recalled her passionate attack. What a lover. What a woman! And how he would miss her when she was gone.

Dreading the day she must go home, he'd asked her to stay with him longer. No, he'd *begged* her, and while he would rather die than beg of any man, he didn't regret beseeching her to remain with him.

They'd talked and laughed and whispered like children as she told him stories of Glencleith and he told her some of the pleasant things that had happened in his life, until passion had kindled again. He began to caress her, and she him. Then they'd kissed, soft and gentle, warm and tender. They made love again, as if time meant nothing.

Once again he'd been tempted to ask her to be his wife. To live with him and run his household and bear his children. To make him happy and joyful in a way he'd never imagined, and to let him try to make her happy, too.

Yet as always, the memory of the worst days of his youth, when he was beaten and starving, cold and wet, completely at the mercy of men bigger and stronger than he, arose.

And silenced him.

He couldn't lose Dunkeathe and all it represented.

Yet what if Marianne was right, and he came to regret losing Riona even more?

Dunkeathe was a fortress, a pile of stone. Riona was light and joy, happiness and bliss. She was loving and generous, shrewd and resolute. Dunkeathe would be empty once she was gone.

He would be empty, and more lonely than he'd ever been before, in his great fortress of cold, hard stone. What if he discovered that he'd given up the greater prize for a castle and the capricious favor of kings?

He rolled onto his back—and instantly realized he wasn't alone.

Then he saw the long blond hair.

CHAPTER NINETEEN

"Shite!"

The earthy curse exploded from Nicholas as he scrambled out of the bed.

Her hair loose and unkempt, Joscelind emitted a little shriek as she sat up, holding the sheets to her bare breasts.

"Get out of my bed," Nicholas ordered, quite oblivious to the fact that he, too, was naked.

"But my lord—"

"Now!" he roared, the word reverberating around the room.

"You don't want me? Even though I'm willing to give myself to you before our marriage?"

"No!"

More enraged and outraged than he'd ever been in his life, Nicholas grabbed his discarded breeches and tugged them on. He spotted the *feileadh*—the garment he'd worn last night, the one his beloved Riona had shown him how to wear—neatly folded on the chest. Riona must have put it there before she left, before this other woman had come into his chamber and crawled into his bed.

As he yanked on his boots, Joscelind covered her face with her hands and started to weep—or sound as if she were.

"Stop that," he snapped. "I'll not be swayed by false tears. Get up and get dressed and get out of my bedchamber. If you're discovered here—"

"If I'm discovered here, you'll have to marry me, if you're an honorable man."

He reached for his shirt and tugged it on. "Then woe to you, my lady, for I'm not *that* honorable."

Joscelind slowly and deliberately climbed from his bed, his sheet wrapped about her. "Who do you think you are?" she demanded as if she were the one sinned against. "You're nothing but an upstart mercenary who managed to persuade some fool of a king to give you an estate. You should be grateful I'd lower myself to sleep with you before marriage."

Fists pounded on the door, and a Saxon voice called out, "My lord? Is anything amiss, my lord?"

Damn her! And damn *him* for shouting. "No," he called out. "All is well. A bad dream."

"Will you marry me?" Joscelind asked without lowering her voice.

He swiveled on his heel and glared at her. "Even before this little trick of yours, you would *never* have been my choice. As for lowering yourself, I'm sorry being in my bed is so demeaning. You should have saved yourself the trouble."

Shooting him an enraged look, she ran to the door

and threw it open. "Guards!" she called out before he could stop her. "Come back!"

Nicholas grabbed hold of the door to close it. "Don't bring scandal and shame on yourself. Your trick didn't work. Your gamble didn't pay off. Accept that and go, before your reputation is ruined."

Her lip curled as she regarded him with wrathful contempt. "My reputation won't be ruined, because you're going to marry me. You can act as if you're pleased you've successfully seduced me, or you can look like a lascivious cad forced to do the honorable thing, but either way, you *will* marry me. My father will insist. Need I remind you he's a rich and powerful man?"

The Saxon guards returned, breathless from running back up the stairs. They came to a stunned halt at the sight of Joscelind wearing only a sheet, on the threshold of Nicholas's bedchamber—as well they might.

"Joscelind," he warned through clenched teeth.

She ignored him. "Fetch my father," she commanded imperiously. "At once!"

The guards looked to Nicholas for confirmation.

There was nothing else to be done. Joscelind had forced his hand. "Go."

As they left, he went back into the room and threw himself into his chair to await Lord Chesleigh. "Get dressed, Joscelind."

She slammed the door and marched up to him. Then she raised her hand and slapped him hard across the face. "I am not some whore you can use and discard."

He didn't so much as flinch when she struck him. He had Yves Sansouci to thank for that. He'd endured harder blows than that many a time. "You came to my bed and now you demand to be paid. What does that make you, if not a harlot?"

She raised her hand to strike him again, but he caught her wrist and held it only tight enough to still.

It was then he saw the bruises on her arm.

His rage changed to anger of a different sort. He knew wounds too well not to realize that these could be no accident. They came from a man's harsh grip.

"Who did that?" he asked as he released her and got to his feet.

"If you don't marry me," she replied, her eyes gleaming, her lips thinned, "I'll say *you* did."

Appalled and disgusted that she would even suggest making that accusation, he said, "I have never hurt a woman in my life, and no one can say otherwise."

She stuck out her noble chin. "I'll say you enticed me to your bedchamber and when I refused to make love with you, you forced me. That mark is proof of how you held me."

God help him, she would, too. "I've never taken a woman against her will. It was your father, wasn't it?"

Her face flushed, but she pressed her lips tight and didn't answer.

"Why did he do it? Or does he require no excuse to hurt you?"

A tear rolled down her cheek, but still she didn't speak.

He thought of what Riona had said about the pressure being brought to bear on the women here because of him, and cursed the day he'd thought of his plan to find a wife—except for one thing. It had brought him Riona.

"My lady," he said, his tone less angry and more reasonable, "if Lord Chesleigh were a loving father and you told him that I raped you, he would demand that I be tried and executed—or he'd challenge me himself. No loving father would insist you wed the man who forced himself upon you." He thought of Percival's scheme. "Or did he send you here?"

Before she could answer—if she were willing to answer—Lord Chesleigh rushed into the room. He took one look at his sheet-clad, disheveled daughter, then he strode across the room and struck her with a fierce, backhanded blow. "Whore!"

Nicholas grabbed Lord Chesleigh's arm and yanked him back so hard, he nearly pulled the man off his feet. "Strike her again and you'll have me to deal with," he growled before he cast the man off.

Lord Chesleigh straightened and ran a haughty, disdainful gaze over Nicholas, his shirt unlaced, his hair uncombed. "I'll have you to deal with regardless, *son-in-law*," he declared as Joscelind had put her hand to her red cheek and started to weep. "I don't know what honeyed words you used to seduce my daughter, but honor demands that you marry her. I won't have my family name besmirched, especially by an upstart like you."

"At least now I know what you really think of me, my lord," Nicholas said with undisguised loathing.

Percival appeared in the door. "Why the noise? What's going—?" He looked from Nicholas to Joscelind, then glared at Nicholas. "What kind of lustful, lascivious scoundrel are you?" he demanded. "Eleanor's not enough to slake—?"

"Eleanor?" Joscelind shrieked, turning on Nicholas. "You've been with her, too? What have you been doing, using us as some sort of harem?"

"I haven't made love with you, or Eleanor," Nicholas replied, his rage now under the same iron control that had stood him in good stead on many a battlefield.

Percival's face was so red, it was nearly purple. "Rogue!" he cried. "How dare you deny it! Eleanor's been your lover for days."

As Lord Chesleigh and his daughter glowered at Nicholas, he serenely met Percival's heated stare. "You have proof of this accusation, this stain upon your cousin's reputation?"

Percival blinked, then flushed. "I've seen her enter your chamber at night."

"If that were true, why didn't you stop her? Why didn't you ask her what she was doing?"

Beads of sweat dampened Percival's forehead.

"Perhaps you didn't ask these questions because she didn't come to my chamber at night, or any other time."

"Eleanor will confirm what I say!" Percival fiercely averred.

"Are you sure?"

Fear, doubt, dismay—all appeared in Percival's face. "Of course she will," he stammered. Then he straightened his narrow shoulders. "You know it's true. If you're an honorable man, you'll marry Eleanor."

"He can't," Joscelind declared. "I'm the one everyone *knows* has been in his bed. He *has* to marry me. My family's honor—"

"Perhaps you should have considered our family *honor* before you acted like a harlot," her father snarled. "But you *will* be married to this knight."

Joscelind pointed at Nicholas. "He seduced me! He told me he'd marry me. That I was his choice. Why wait until Lammas, he said."

"That's not true," Nicholas countered. "I made no attempt to seduce your daughter, my lord, and she would *never* have been my choice even if I had."

Percival suddenly looked less upset. "Because you're going to marry Eleanor, aren't you?" he asked with more than a trace of desperation.

"The hell he is!" Lord Chesleigh declared. He marched up to Nicholas until they were nearly nose-to-nose. "Whether you've taken my daughter's maidenhood or not, you *will* marry her. Otherwise, I'll see to it that you lose this fine castle you've built and everything that goes with it—wealth, influence, the soldiers you command. I'll have you reduced to nothing more than a common soldier again—and you know I have the power to do it."

"He *can't* marry Joscelind," Percival protested. "He's got to marry Eleanor. She might be with child."

Silence fell and everybody stared at Percival as if he'd turned green.

Nicholas wasn't sure if he should believe Percival or not—yet it if *was* true, whose child was it?

Looking at the vain man standing before him, mindful of the man's threats, he feared he knew. "Eleanor has never been my lover," he repeated coldly. "If the child resembles its father, won't it look like you?"

"I've never laid a hand on her!"

"No?"

"No! I thought she was the woman sleeping with you. But if she wasn't…" His eyes widened and his mouth fell open. "It was that Scot—that Riona!"

"Did somebody mention my niece?" Fergus Mac Gordon asked, peering around the door frame.

As he took in the sight of the irate Lord Chesleigh, an equally upset Sir Percival, a very undressed Lady Joscelind and Nicholas's state, his brow furrowed. Then his expression changed, to one of shock, dismay and disappointment.

Nicholas suddenly felt like the scoundrel these other men claimed he was, but for a different reason. However lonely and unhappy he'd been, and however happy Riona had made him, he'd sinned a great sin against the jovial little man and his niece. He'd treated Riona as if she were his whore, worthy of only a few fleeting nights of pleasure in his bed. She deserved more. Much more.

Sick with remorse, he cursed himself for his stupid, greedy, ambitious plan. His vanity. His arrogance. All the trouble he'd caused. And the trouble to come.

"I think we should leave this chamber and allow the lady to dress," he said, grabbing his sword belt as he headed for the door. "We'll assemble in the hall, where we shall settle this matter once and for all. I will decide today—now—who will be my bride."

RIONA HURRIED to her chamber door in answer to a flurry of knocks to find Uncle Fergus standing there, although standing was not precisely accurate. He was fairly jumping from foot to foot as if he were on hot coals.

"What is it? What's wrong?" she asked, fearing that there was some new trouble with Fredella.

"You didn't hear all that noise from Sir Nicholas's chamber?"

"I was asleep." Because she'd been exhausted after last night.

Then she gasped. "Has he been hurt?" she cried, trying to push past her uncle.

He barred the way. "No, he's not hurt. He's going to choose his bride this morning."

She stopped struggling and stared at her uncle in stunned disbelief. "Now?"

She backed away as Uncle Fergus entered the chamber. He closed the door, and when he turned to her, he was as serious as she'd ever seen him.

"My beauty," Uncle Fergus said sorrowfully, "something's happened…something I didn't expect from an honorable man. It seems, Riona, that he's not waited until Lammas to bed the woman he wants."

He couldn't be thinking of her, or he wouldn't be speaking in that way. Percival must have lost his patience and demanded that Nicholas wed Eleanor without waiting until Lammas, and told everyone why.

Uncle Fergus rubbed his chin. "Wheest, I wouldn't believe it myself, except that I saw her, wrapped in a sheet in his bedchamber."

"He took Eleanor to his bed?" she whispered in dismay. Was it possible Eleanor wasn't the naive girl she seemed? Yet what of Nicholas? How could he…after they had…after she…?

"Eleanor?" Uncle Fergus repeated incredulously. "Of course not Eleanor. How could you even think it was that sweet child? It was that Joscelind."

Joscelind?

Everything changed, and Riona knew without doubt that Nicholas was innocent. This was a trick, a scheme like Percival's, to force Nicholas to marry.

Energy flooded through her body, as well as determination, and love. "Uncle, I'm sure Nicholas didn't seduce her. I'm sure she came to his chamber without his knowledge or consent, as a ploy to make him marry her. He was probably already asleep when she slipped under the sheets like an adder to make it look like they were lovers."

Uncle Fergus regarded Riona with neither relief, nor disbelief, but with a searching, steady gravitas. "Why do you say that, Riona? Are you so sure Nicholas wouldn't bed a willing and beautiful woman whether they were married or not?"

Seeing her beloved and trusting uncle's grave demeanor, shame trickled through her. She had deceived him, and she became achingly, keenly aware of the disappointment she would bring to the man who loved her like a father when he learned the truth.

Yet the time had come to be honest, for Nicholas's sake, and Eleanor's.

She sat and patted the bed beside her. His expression puzzled and worried, her uncle joined her. She took his hands in hers and looked into his questioning eyes.

When she was with Nicholas it was so easy to have no regrets. When their love was a secret between them, it was easy to believe it would always be so. But that could not be.

"Uncle, I know she's not his lover. I am."

"You?" he gasped with disbelief. "You're his lover?"

She nodded. "Aye."

"Then…he's going to marry you? That's what he's going to say in the hall now?"

It tore her heart, but it had to be said. "No. He's going to marry Eleanor."

She waited for him to look at her with disgust, with shame, with revulsion, hoping those feelings would fade and he would be kind to her, even if she'd lost his good opinion forever.

Instead, an ire such as she'd never seen arose in Uncle Fergus's eyes. "*Eleanor?* He makes love with you but he'll marry another?"

She held his hands tighter, willing him to listen and understand, a little. "He *must* marry her. He needs her dowry and her cousin's influence, or he could lose Dunkeathe, and she needs Nicholas to get away from Percival. I knew that before I went to his bed, Uncle. I've never expected him to change his mind, and I still don't."

"Well, *I* do!" Uncle Fergus cried, jumping to his feet. "That bastard! He never even handfasted with you, did he? That I could understand. He'd have a year and a day to make up his mind and share your bed. But this? Do these Normans think our women are theirs for the using?"

"Uncle, he didn't use me," she protested, trying to hold him to make him stay. "I gave—"

"He *took!*" Uncle Fergus bellowed. "He took you and he took your honor and he took my *feileadh!* I'll show him what we do to men like that!"

He charged out the door.

Gathering up her skirts, Riona ran after him and begged God to help her stop him before blood was shed.

"LET ME THROUGH, you bloody Norman bastards!" Uncle Fergus shouted in Gaelic as he shoved his way through the crowd gathered in the hall. He stormed toward Nicholas standing on the dais, feet planted, arms crossed, looking every inch the commanding master of this castle. As Riona hurried after her uncle, she didn't see the tender, teasing lover of their nights together, but the stern, unyielding lord of Dunkeathe. The lover was gone forever; whatever happened next, their time together was over.

"Draw your sword, you Norman dog!" Uncle Fergus cried as several soldiers surrounded him. "What are you, a coward as well as a liar?"

Nicholas answered him in Gaelic. "When have I ever lied to you?"

"You said you were going to marry Riona!"

"I said no such thing."

"The devil you did! You took the *feileadh*."

"You gave me no chance to refuse your gift. It will be returned to you, if that is what you wish."

"Of course it's what I wish, you bloody Norman lout not fit to stand on Scots soil!"

By now, Riona, breathlessly panting, had pushed her way to the front of the crowd. She joined Eleanor, who was looking pale and frightened; Percival, who recoiled when he saw her; Joscelind, dressed but with her hair uncovered and barely combed, as if she were determined to show to all that she'd spent the night doing something other than rest; and Lord Chesleigh, arms akimbo, furiously indignant. Nearby and to one side was Priscilla, not giggling for once as she held tight to

Robert's arm. Her brother beside her whispered to Lavinia, who in turn whispered to D'Anglevoix, who stared at Nicholas as if he wasn't sure whether he should admire or despise him. Lady Marianne, her husband and Roban, who should have been leaving, stood near the dais, watching soberly. Riona had passed Fredella and Polly among the servants by the door.

Filling the hall were more soldiers and servants, as if everyone not immediately involved in a task were there.

She didn't look at her uncle. She watched Nicholas, willing him to meet her gaze, to see that she was prepared for what was coming.

He did look at her, and she saw his resolve. Knew what he was going to do. What he *must* do. Despite her uncle's angry protests and Joscelind's act, in spite of the feelings he had for her, he would announce that Eleanor would be his bride.

"My lords and ladies," he began, ignoring Uncle Fergus, who was being held by the guards. "Circumstances have forced me to announce the choice of my bride today, instead of at Lammas, as I'd planned."

Riona clasped her sweating hands together, took a deep breath and readied herself for the impending blow.

"I wish to marry…"

Oh, God give her strength!

Nicholas's gaze flew to her like an arrow shot from Cupid's bow. "Lady Riona."

A cacophony erupted.

"You damned well better marry my beauty!" her uncle shouted.

Lord Chesleigh and Percival tried to drown each other out as they protested. The servants and soldiers clapped and cheered.

Eleanor fell to her knees. "Oh, thank God, thank God!" she cried, smiling through her tears.

As an equally overcome Fredella joined her, Lady Marianne jumped up and down and threw her arms around her husband, while Roban stamped his feet and bellowed his congratulations to the clan of the Mac Gordons.

Riona saw and heard none of it. All she was aware of was Nicholas as he left the dais and came straight toward her, his eyes shining with loving devotion and a glorious smile on his handsome face.

But no matter how her heart leapt and how thrilled she was, this couldn't be. He would lose everything if he married her. All he'd worked for. Suffered for.

And Uncle Fergus might die.

When he reached her, his gaze searched her face, her soul, and when he spoke, his voice was low and husky, warm and tender. "Riona, will you marry me?"

She was afraid to say yes, afraid that if she did, her dream would turn into a nightmare. "You could lose Dunkeathe if you marry me."

He took her hands in his. "I would rather lose it, and anything else I own, than you."

"But you might come to resent me—"

"Never," he said firmly, his voice strong, his gaze resolute. "I could *never* resent you, Riona. Even if you broke my heart, I could never resent you." He went down on one knee. "If you will marry me, I will gain much more than Dunkeathe. I will gain such joy as I've never known, and I'll find all the contentment I seek in your arms. Please say you will do me this great honor, Riona."

How could she say no? She couldn't, nor could she say yes, as tears of joy filled her eyes and a sob choked her.

He didn't need the word. Rising, he swept her into his arms and kissed her. Thoroughly. Passionately. Fervently. Regardless of everyone and everything around them, as if they were alone.

Holding him tight, returning his kiss, she knew absolutely that whatever happened, whatever challenges they faced, they would be together, because Nicholas loved her more than his reward.

Finally she let herself feel the great happiness that she'd been trying to hold in check and gave in to the pure blissful joy of being loved by him, and loving him in return.

"By God, if you don't wed my daughter, you'll rue the day you were born!" Lord Chesleigh declared. "I'll see you stripped of everything you possess."

"You can't do this to me," Joscelind cried as she grabbed Nicholas's arm and pulled him away. "You can't treat me this way."

Nicholas looked at them as if they were vermin. The tender lover disappeared, and he was once more the stern, determined warrior, winner of tournaments, champion of the king. "I am well aware of what you can do, my lord, but know you this. I would rather live in a hovel with Riona by my side than marry your daughter and have you for a relative."

Never in her life had Riona felt so happy, and so humbled.

And proud—prouder, even, than being a Scot.

Uncle Fergus, Adair and Roban stepped forward, their expressions ones that should have made Lord Chesleigh reconsider his threats. Audric and D'Anglevoix likewise came to stand with Uncle Fergus and Adair Mac Taran, opposed to Lord Chesleigh.

"And I must ask myself, my lord," Nicholas continued, "why you are so determined to see me married to your daughter if I am so unworthy to be allied to your great and noble family. Perhaps you have a reason I have yet to fathom—but I will, in time."

Lord Chesleigh scowled. "I *thought* you were a better man."

"I will be a better man, if Riona will be my wife."

Confident now in Nicholas's love, Riona said, "Lord Chesleigh threatened to have Uncle Fergus imprisoned for treason if you chose me."

"Oh, he did, did he?" Nicholas reached out and grabbed the man by his tunic, hauling him close. "If you ever try to harm Riona or her uncle, Chesleigh, you die. Try to harm *anyone* in her family, and you die."

When Nicholas released him, Lord Chesleigh stumbled back. "You can't threaten me!" he cried. "You're *nothing* compared to me! You're no one!"

"I am the lord of Dunkeathe, and regardless of your threats, or anything you do, Riona will be my lady. Woe betide the man who tries to stop us."

"Don't fuss yourself over the man, Nicholas," Uncle Fergus said, no longer angry, but gleefully delighted. "His threats against you are useless in Scotland. Alexander will ne'er take away the estate of my nephew-in-law. He owes me a great debt that he has yet to repay."

This was the first Riona had heard of such a debt. She didn't think her uncle would lie about such a thing, but perhaps, with his love for her and his belief that she should marry Nicholas—

"I saved the king's life when he was a lad," Uncle Fergus continued. "We were hunting and he was charged by a wild boar. I killed it."

Riona gasped. "*Alexander* was the lad?"

"*That's* what I heard about Fergus Mac Gordon!" Adair Mac Taran cried triumphantly.

"Aye," Uncle Fergus said with a grin, "so it was, and Alexander told me that day that if ever I require his aid, I have but to ask."

"But…but that was years ago," Riona said doubtfully, fearing that time and distance would have eroded such a vow.

"Aye, it was, but I send reminders from time to time." Uncle Fergus crossed his arms and rocked back on his heels, clearly pleased by the effect of his announcement. "I'm not the best hand with money, but I'm not completely hopeless when it comes to kings and courtiers. I have my friends, too. It was the toss of the dirk that was the best part of the story anyway."

Fredella appeared as if out of nowhere and threw her arms around Uncle Fergus and hugged him tightly. "Wheest, girl, let me breathe," he said, laughing.

Nicholas again addressed Lord Chesleigh, who was not laughing. "So much for your threats, my lord."

"What about Eleanor?" Percival demanded, dragging her forward by the arm. "Her dowry will be better than Joscelind's. You'll have no need to call on anyone's favors for your prosperity. Nor did she try to entrap you—"

"She didn't, but *you* did," Nicholas charged, glaring at him with revulsion. "I know all about your plan to force Eleanor into my bed, and then make us marry."

Nicholas reached out and took hold of Percival's wrist. His expression grim, he tightened his grip until Percival cried out and released his cousin. She ran to Uncle Fergus, who put his arm protectively around her. His other arm was around Fredella.

"You are free to remain here, my lady, if that is what you wish," Nicholas said to her. "I'll protect you even if we don't marry. But you never wanted to marry me, did you?"

"No, my lord, I've *never* wanted to marry you."

Her denial was so strong, so absolute, so firmly spoken, Riona could hardly believe it was the same young woman speaking.

"There you have it, Percival," Nicholas said evenly. "She doesn't want me, and even if my choice wasn't already made, I'll not have an unwilling bride."

"I'm her legal guardian, not you!" Percival exclaimed. "She has to do what I say, and go where I take her. You have no rights where she's concerned."

"Then go to the courts," Eleanor cried, her hands balled into fists, her whole body trembling with rage. "And while you're in London trying to get the means to make me do what you want, I'll be here. Away from *you!*"

"Come, Joscelind. We're going," Lord Chesleigh announced. "Let's leave this man with the barbarians."

Before Joscelind moved, Nicholas stepped forward. "If he's the one who hurt you, you're welcome to stay here, too."

Riona could easily believe Lord Chesleigh was a violent man. And it was no wonder to her that Nicholas would generously offer Joscelind refuge, despite what she had done.

Joscelind's eyes narrowed, as if she feared a trick. "You'd do that for me? After...everything?"

"Yes."

Still skeptical, Joscelind addressed Riona. "What about you? Surely you don't want me to stay."

Riona went to Nicholas and took his hand. Holding it, secure in his love, she said, "Whatever has happened between us is in the past, and if you wish to stay, I have no objections."

"Joscelind, come with me, or I'll cast you off as I would an old shoe," her father commanded.

She turned to go with him.

"Joscelind, please, reconsider," Riona said.

Joscelind raised her chin and fierce pride shone in her eyes. "And what? Lose my family and my dowry? Be grateful for your mercy? Watch the two of you be married? I would rather endure whatever punishment my father decrees for my shameful behavior than be dependent on your charity."

"Then I wish you well, my lady, and whatever happiness you can find."

More regal and dignified than ever, Joscelind nodded, turned and followed her father.

But before Lord Chesleigh and his daughter reached the door, a man Riona had never seen before strode into the hall. His boots and breeches were splattered with mud and his hair windblown as if he'd ridden hard and come a long distance in a short time. "Nicholas!" he cried. "And Lord Chesleigh. How fortunate."

"Who the devil are you?" Lord Chesleigh demanded.

Still holding Riona's hand, Nicholas hurried forward. "This is Henry, my brother."

Lord Chesleigh sniffed. "Whoever he is, he should let my daughter and me pass."

"You're leaving, my lord?" Henry politely inquired.

"Yes. At once."

"Excellent. You'll be pleased to hear I've brought you an escort, for it seems several very powerful people in London are very anxious to talk to you about some of your associates and their activities. I gather they've already prepared a place for you in the Tower."

Lord Chesleigh blanched. And then he went for his sword.

He was too slow. Nicholas had let go of Riona, pulled out his sword, and set the tip on the man's neck before Lord Chesleigh had even gotten his weapon out of its sheath.

"I don't think that would be wise, my lord," Nicholas warned as Riona let out her breath slowly.

"You've got a dungeon hereabouts, don't you, Nicholas?" his brother asked.

"Yes, I do."

"Wonderful! The men and our horses are too fatigued from our journey to start back to London today." Henry gestured to two of Nicholas's soldiers. "Take his lordship to the dungeon."

The soldiers hurried to obey, grabbing the Norman and frog-marching him out of the hall.

"Joscelind!" her father cried out desperately. "Joscelind!"

"Don't worry, Father," she said coldly as she followed them. "I won't desert you. And I'll do all I can to prove your innocence. Otherwise, *I'll* be left with nothing."

When they were gone, it was as if everyone in the hall exhaled at the same time.

"Who was she?" Henry asked his brother.

"Lord Chesleigh's daughter. Are there accusations against her, as well?"

"No, and I must say, I'm glad. It would be a great pity to have such a beauty imprisoned in the Tower."

Riona was glad, too. She didn't like Joscelind, but she wouldn't wish disgrace and poverty on her, either.

Henry suddenly started and pointed. "Percival!"

Near the kitchen entrance, Percival stopped and stared as if he'd been shot by an arrow and pinned to the wall.

"What? What do you want?" he demanded as he inched toward the door.

Henry strolled toward him. "So this is where you've got to," he said with a smile. "I hear your tailor is very upset with you—a small matter of a few hundred marks owing, I believe. And your jeweler is unhappy, too. Indeed, I believe you're in debt to most of the merchants and half the usurers in London."

"You're lying!"

"I could be wrong, of course," Henry replied. "But I certainly wouldn't let my brother marry any relative of yours until he had the dowry in his hands."

"Is that true?" Eleanor demanded of her cousin. "What about *my* money?"

Like a trapped rat, Percival's gaze darted from the main door far away to the kitchen doors nearby blocked by Polly and the rest of servants. He broke for the kitchen, shoving Polly and the others roughly out of the way. Several of the soldiers nearby immediately gave chase.

"Shall I go after him, too?" Henry asked his brother.

Nicholas shook his head. "He won't get far. My men are well trained. They can run for miles if they must, and I'm sure he can't."

Riona put a comforting arm around the distraught Eleanor, who might have nothing now except her title. "Perhaps you exaggerated a bit about the debts?" she asked Henry hopefully.

Nicholas's brother shook his head. "I wish I could say I had, but I fear it's all too true."

"Never mind, my girl!" Uncle Fergus exclaimed. "You'll always have a home with Fredella and me."

"She can always stay with us," Marianne offered.

"Or Nicholas and I," Riona added.

As Eleanor smiled tremulously, and all seemed resolved at last, the servants began to whisper and murmur among themselves, clearly excited and pleased, while the remaining Norman nobles hurried to speak to Riona and Nicholas, as did Marianne, Adair and Roban.

After a little time had passed, Henry managed to draw his brother aside. "So, what did I interrupt?"

CHAPTER TWENTY

"WHAT THE DEVIL are you wearing?"

Facing his brother a month later on his wedding day, Nicholas glanced down at his garments. "You should know by now it's called a *feileadh*. Fergus Mac Gordon gave it to me for a wedding gift."

"Since when have you taken to dressing like a Scot?"

"Since I thought it would please Riona and her uncle, and most of my tenants who are, I point out, Scots. Adair gave me the brooch."

"You're looking damn smug."

"I'm damn happy."

"Where's Adair got to?"

"He went to help Marianne with the children."

"I suppose next time I see you, you'll have a child or two yourself."

"That depends how long you stay away this time, but yes, I hope to have children," Nicholas replied, pretending to adjust the fabric at his shoulder.

In reality, he didn't want Henry to see how the idea of being a father thrilled him, lest he be mocked about that, too. Yet he couldn't imagine anything that would make him happier, or more blissfully content, than having a child with Riona—except the attempt to get the children.

He tried to stifle any such thoughts for the time being. His current ensemble didn't do much to hide the effect on his body.

Henry sat on the end of Nicholas's bed. "That skirt looks uncomfortable."

"It's very comfortable, and it's not a skirt. It's one long piece of fabric. Ask Adair how comfortable it is if you don't believe me. No chafing, for one thing."

Henry's eyes narrowed. "What are you wearing underneath? Adair once told me—"

"Since I'm not a Scot," Nicholas interrupted, "I'm wearing something." He couldn't resist wiping the smirk off Henry's face. "But there's a great deal to be said for wearing it as the Scots do, especially when you're in love with a very desirable and passionate woman."

Henry's smirk disappeared and his eyes widened. "Good God, you haven't…" He frowned. "Have you?"

"My dear brother, surely you don't expect me to reveal such intimate details?"

Henry gave him a skeptical frown.

Nicholas decided to change the subject. "You're determined to leave in a fortnight?"

Henry nodded.

Nicholas shook his head. "I despair of you ever settling down, Henry, I truly do."

"Now you're sounding like Marianne. But not all of us are such mighty warriors that kings give us estates."

Nicholas heard the frustration and tinge of bitterness in his brother's voice. He didn't want any old arguments or rivalries to ruin his wedding day, so he clapped his brother on the shoulder instead. "Since *I* am settled down, come and see me happily wed."

To his surprise, Henry's expression was gravely serious. "You're sure about this then, Nicholas? You really want to marry this Scot?"

Nicholas nodded, equally serious, and sincere. "I really want to marry her, Henry. I love her."

"First Marianne, now you…I'm beginning to think there might be something to this love business."

"There is. I highly recommend it," Nicholas replied as he steered his brother to the door.

The sooner he was married, the sooner he could return to this chamber with his lovely, loving bride.

POLLY REGARDED the woman who was soon to be the chatelaine of Dunkeathe with awe and admiration as they stood together in the bride's chamber.

This would be the last time Riona would dress here. After today, and for the rest of her life, she would share Nicholas's chamber, and his bed—a thought that filled her with pure and perfect joy and contentment.

"Oh, my lady, you look beautiful," Polly murmured, her hands clasped in front of her bodice.

"I'm sure it's only the gown. Or my happiness,"

Riona said as she looked down at the scarlet dress that Eleanor had given her. She had no finer gown, and after what had happened the first time she'd worn it, she couldn't resist wearing it today. Eleanor had helped her add some new fabric to the bodice, though, so that the gown wasn't so tight or the neckline so low. Eleanor had also cleverly made it seem as if the embroidered panels had always been a part of the dress, not later additions.

Nicholas didn't know that she was wearing the scarlet gown. She'd sworn Eleanor, Polly and Fredella to secrecy and they'd worked on it only in this chamber. She was looking forward to seeing the expression on his face—not quite as much as she was looking forward to being his bride, but it was something that made her smile every time she thought of it.

"I think you *do* look beautiful," Polly insisted, "and so will Sir Nicholas." She studied Riona some more. "Aren't you going to braid your hair or put it up?"

Riona shook her head. Nicholas loved her hair, and she would wear it this way for him.

"Is there anything else you need me for, my lady?" Polly's eyes sparkled mischievously. "Need any advice from an old married lady?"

"I hardly think a week of marriage allows one to be considered 'an old married lady,'" Riona observed, "although it would depend on the husband, I suppose."

"That's true, I daresay," Polly said with a merry laugh. "In that case, I expect to be a bride forever."

"So do I," Riona said, sharing a companionable smile. "Thank you, Polly. All I need do now is wait for Uncle Fergus. You go on. I'll see you in the chapel."

"And Thomas, too. Mind, I never thought Sir Nicholas would invite us to sit in the hall, and above the salt. I'll hardly know how to act! Sara and Lilah will be thinking I'm getting above myself, but I swear I'm humble as can be, my lady, except for being proud to be Thomas's wife."

"I know exactly how you feel," Riona said.

The cheerful Polly—maidservant no longer, but busy farmer's wife except on this special day—hurried away, leaving Riona alone to wait for Uncle Fergus, who was to escort her to the chapel, and Nicholas.

There was a rap at the door and Riona turned, expecting to see her uncle.

Kenneth stood there, dressed in his finest *feileadh* and shirt and boots, looking shy and awkward as if he wasn't sure he belonged there.

Riona squealed with delight and rushed to embrace him. "Oh, Kenneth, you're here! I'm so glad!"

He hugged her, too. "Of course I am. I couldn't miss this. But you could have knocked me down with a breath when I heard you were marrying the Norman." He pulled back and examined her smiling face. "It's true, then? This isn't some rumor spread by the Normans for reasons I'm too dim to fathom?"

"It's true," she said, her smile growing. "And I couldn't be happier. Nicholas is a wonderful man. You'll see."

"So Father was right about him after all? My God, I'll never hear the end of it."

"No, I expect you won't," she said, laughing and already imagining Uncle Fergus's version of what had happened here in Dunkeathe.

"And Father getting married, too! Is it something in the well water here, or what?"

"I don't think so," Riona replied, "but perhaps you'd better be careful what you drink."

"Aye, or who knows what might happen?" he said in a boyishly offhand manner as he wandered farther into her chamber.

She knew him too well to be fooled by his attempted nonchalance.

"How's Aigneas?"

"Well, and very happy. She's handfasted with a fellow from the next valley."

"Oh, I see. Have you met any of the young ladies here? Lavinia and Priscilla and Eleanor?"

"Aye. They were all flitting about the hall and made a great fuss over me when they found out who I was."

"I'm sure they did, and you being such a braw, bonny fellow, too. It's a pity Lavinia and Priscilla are already spoken for, isn't it?"

Kenneth ran his hand along the window sill as if checking that the mason had done a proper job. "Aye, they were all bonny lasses. That's a nice gown you've got on, Riona."

He was trying to change the subject, but she wasn't

going to let him. "It was Eleanor's. She's a sweet and generous girl. Did your father tell you she's going to go back to Glencleith with you after the wedding?"

Kenneth glanced at her sharply. "She is?"

"Aye."

He resumed his former study of the window frame. "How long's she going to stay?"

Riona stifled a smile. "I don't know, but it could be for some time." She frowned as if gravely concerned. "She's my very good friend, so I must insist that you treat her kindly and courteously, even if she's a Norman."

He shrugged. "Of course I'll be polite."

"Good. And you must see that she's not too lonely, all by herself among the Scots."

"I have other things to do than play nursemaid to a Norman."

"Surely you can spare a little time for her? Otherwise, it might be better if she stayed here in Dunkeathe with—"

"No need for that. She'll have Father and Fredella in Glencleith, too. And there's plenty of girls her age there."

It was getting very difficult to keep a straight face. "Well, if it does get to be too much of a chore, you may bring her back here. Nicholas and I will be happy to have her."

"I'll remember that."

"Here you *both* are!" Uncle Fergus declared from

the doorway. Like Kenneth, he was attired in a fine white linen shirt and *feileadh*. "I was wondering where you'd got to, Kenneth, my lad."

He ran his approving gaze over Riona. "Riona, my beauty, you look as lovely as your sainted mother." His smile grew wistful. "I'm going to miss you so much, I'm thinking it would have been better if we'd stayed at home."

Riona hurried to him and took his arm, giving him a loving squeeze. "I'll miss you, too, Uncle. Unfortunately, it's too late to change what's happened. I've fallen in love with the lord of Dunkeathe."

Her uncle regarded her tenderly. "Really and truly?"

"Really and truly, and he with me—just like you predicted."

Uncle Fergus cleared his throat. "I suppose, then," he said gruffly, "we'd best get you married."

He patted her hand and addressed his son. "Come on, Kenneth. The pipers are waiting. We're going to show these Normans how to do a proper wedding."

SEVERAL HOURS LATER—although not nearly soon enough for Nicholas—he was at the threshold of his bedchamber, his bride in his arms.

"I could have walked up the stairs at least," she said, laughing.

"I don't want you fatigued," he replied, his voice soft and low as he carried her over the threshold.

The candlestand had been moved out of the corner,

and now six fine beeswax candles illuminated the room, as well as his beautiful, bonny bride.

Bonny. It was what her uncle called her, and it suited her to perfection. Bonny and happy and lovely and his. "It's going to be a very long night."

"If that's supposed to scare me, or intimidate me, you've failed miserably," she replied, nuzzling his neck.

"I never could intimidate you. But now I must set you down. My arms are not as strong as they once were."

"When you defeated twenty knights in a single day?" she inquired pertly as she slipped down out of his arms, brushing against him in a way that made his body instantly respond.

He encircled her waist. "Weak arms or not, have I told you today how much I love you?"

"I don't think your arms are at all weak," she chided as she squeezed his forearms. "They certainly feel strong to me, like the rest of you. But you may tell me again how much you love me."

He kissed the tip of her nose. "I love you with all my heart—all the heart I didn't even know I had."

"As I love you," she said as she took his face between her hands and gently brought him down to kiss.

As always when they kissed, passion flared and flamed. With slow languor, because they had all night, he deepened the kiss. He ran his fingers through the miracle of her thick, long and unbound hair, while her hand slid across his hip to boldly caress him through his clothing.

"You *are* a wanton wench," he murmured as his lips left hers to trail across her cheek toward her shell-like ear.

"Since you think me so wanton and seem to disapprove, perhaps you'd like me to stop?" she whispered as she continued to stroke him.

He closed his eyes. "No."

She leaned closer and caressed with more pressure, as she kissed his neck. "Good. Because it so happens, my husband, that I don't want to."

His hands were on a meandering journey of their own, up her back, then down and around. "Your uncle told me you were stubborn."

"Alas for you, he's quite right."

"Alas for you, I've been dreaming of this night for a month. It was all I could do to keep my distance."

"I thought it would be for the best, after everything," she replied as she began to undo the brooch holding his plaid over his shoulder. "It wasn't easy for me, either. More than once, I was very tempted to sneak into your chamber again."

She freed the broach. As the fabric fell from his shoulder, she stepped away, turning to set the brooch down on the table.

"I was very tempted to invite you to meet me under that willow tree," he replied softly, coming up behind her and grabbing her around the waist, the memory of that memorable coupling returning.

"Undo my laces for me?" she asked, her breathing

fast and shallow as she held back her hair, exposing the knot at her neck.

"Gladly," he said, pressing his lips there. Who would ever guess a nape could be so enticing?

She sighed rapturously as he worked to undo the knot while continuing to kiss her neck. Then he started to pull out the laces.

She cast a pert look at him over her shoulder. "I'm thinking that's taking much too long."

"I'm finding this very…interesting."

She turned and, with quicker motions, started to undo the lacing at the neck of his shirt. "I'm not that patient."

"You would strip me naked here and now?"

She looked up into his face, and in her eyes, he saw the answer. The very exciting answer.

Although it seemed a sort of titillating torture, he let her. The first to go was his shirt. With a movement like another caress, she put her hands beneath it and lifted it from him. She picked up the end of the fabric that had fallen from his shoulder and, laying it over her arm, went to work on his belt. In the next moment, that, too, was gone. She gathered the fabric into her arms, then stopped to stare at what he was wearing beneath the *feileadh*.

"What's that?" she demanded, her brows furrowed.

"The Saxons call them *braies*. A Scot I am not, and it's a breezy day. What if the wind had been stronger?"

She turned away and started to fold the fabric.

He tugged off his boots, then removed the *braies*.
After a few moments, when she still hadn't said anything, or even looked his way again, he said, "I've got
them off now."

She didn't answer.

He crept up behind her and slid his arms around her
waist as she put the fabric on the chest. "Surely you're
not angry with me?"

To both his relief and chagrin, she burst out laughing. She continued to laugh so hard, she could hardly
stand up. She staggered over to the bed and collapsed
upon it.

"I'm sorry," she said, wiping her eyes. "You
looked...that is, those...those *things*... I've never seen
anything like them, except on a baby...."

"I am *not* a baby."

"I didn't mean to offend you." She ran her gaze over
his naked body. "You look much better as you are now."
Her eyes darkened with desire, and glistened with the
hunger he'd also missed as she inched back farther on
the bed. "*Much* better."

He moved closer. "Then I'm not offended. But
you're still dressed."

"I am, aren't I?"

"We can't have that on our wedding night." He got
on the bed and started to crawl toward her, like a stalking cat.

Her breathing quickened, exciting him more. "I suppose I should take off my gown then."

"I like that gown," he said softly, sitting back on his haunches between her legs.

"I know. That's why I wore it."

"I like it best without a shift under it." He ran his hand up her leg, so that her garments bunched around her hips. "What have we here?" he asked with seeming seriousness when he reached her buttocks.

She bent her knees and lifted her hips so that he could push her clothes under her. Then she sat up and lifted her arms. "Will you assist me?"

"With pleasure," he murmured as he pulled first the gown, then her white shift over her head.

Now she, too, was naked, her hair flowing about her shoulders and breasts.

She was his to cherish, to honor, to protect for the rest of his life—a finer, better reward than any he had ever thought to dream of, or hope for. "I love you, Riona."

Her smile was the light that brightened the darkness of his world. That proved there was goodness and generosity and gentleness and affection, even for him. That told him that as long as she was with him, he would never be lonely again.

"I love you, Nicholas," she whispered, holding out her arms. "My husband."

He moved forward into her embrace and gave himself over to the pleasure of kissing her. And touching her. Letting his fingers glide over her warm, soft skin. Brushing her flesh with his lips. Licking and teasing with his tongue until she squirmed with readiness and begged him to take her.

And oh, how willingly he complied! Yet he tried to control himself, to be slow and patient, to enjoy this time when they had so much time. No need for her to rise and flee his bed tonight, or ever again. No fears of discovery, or taint of shame and scandal.

Yet in spite of his determination, the sensation of her moist warmth was too much. He discovered he couldn't be patient after a month without her in his bed.

So when she urged him to be faster, to push harder, he lost all pretext of restraint. With wild passion, burning need and unbridled urgency, he loved her. She arched and wrapped her legs about him, pulling him closer still. She raised herself and licked his nipple, then sucked it into her mouth.

He felt the onward rush, the anticipation of release, and then, the sweet, swift ecstasy of climax. She fell back and grabbed the coverlet in her hands, her head turning from side to side as she, too, felt the explosive, throbbing finish.

Groaning, spent, he kissed her, then collapsed against her sweat-slicked body. Panting, he lay there, until he felt her slowly stroking his hair.

"Did it feel different?"

He half opened his eyes to look at her. "Different?"

"Now that we are husband and wife? Did making love feel any different?"

He thought about it a moment, then smiled. "Every

time I make love with you is better than the last." He toyed with a lock of her marvelous hair. "What about you? Was it different for you?"

"Oh, yes."

"How so?"

"No guilt, no shame."

"Ah." It must have been so difficult for her before, and he was ashamed to think how easy it had been for him.

"I've upset you."

"I was just realizing what a selfish lout I was. I should have sent you away that first night."

"I'm glad you didn't. Otherwise, I wouldn't be here now."

He moved away, and only then realized they'd made love on top of the covers. "I suppose I could have let you get under the sheets first," he said.

"I was too preoccupied to notice," she said, smiling and slipping under the linen.

He joined her and put his arm about her, so that her head rested on his chest. "I'm so happy, Riona, and so blessed. Yet it could have ended so badly, for you and for me. You might have been disgraced and shamed, and I could have wound up married to somebody else."

"Let's thank God it didn't turn out that way." She sat up and regarded him gravely. "I've been keeping a secret from you, Nicholas. I was going to tell you later, after we'd been married a few more days, but I think I should tell you tonight."

Worried, confused, wondering if there was something else he'd overlooked or ignored, he anxiously waited for her to continue.

She smiled gloriously. "I'm with child."

He was afraid he hadn't heard right, that his conversation with Henry had put thoughts into this head. "What did you say?"

She kissed him on the mouth, then smiled. "I'm with child, Nicholas. You're going to be a father."

Delighted, thrilled, excited in a whole new way, he grabbed her and held her close. "Riona, Riona," he cried softly. "A child!"

"Our child," she said, looking up into his face. "Our *first*, I hope."

Riona had never seen Nicholas smile as he did then. All the cares and worries, all the duties and responsibilities, the sternly commanding mien, completely disappeared, and he was a young man happy and in love.

"Whatever more God brings us, or whatever else lies ahead, I can only thank Him for all that I've already received," he whispered tenderly. He caressed her cheek, and used the Scots endearment that his sister had taught him as he bent to kiss her again. *"M'eudail."*

My love.

If you enjoyed what you just read,
then we've got an offer you can't resist!

Take 2 bestselling novels FREE!
Plus get a FREE surprise gift!

MARGARET MOORE

77003 BRIDE OF LOCHBARR   ___ $6.50 U.S. ___ $7.99 CAN.

(limited quantities available)

TOTAL AMOUNT	$ _____
POSTAGE & HANDLING	$ _____
($1.00 FOR 1 BOOK, 50¢ for each additional)	
APPLICABLE TAXES*	$ _____
TOTAL PAYABLE	$ _____

(check or money order—please do not send cash)

To order, complete this form and send it, along with a check or money order for the total above, payable to HQN Books, to: **In the U.S.:** 3010 Walden Avenue, P.O. Box 9077, Buffalo, NY 14269-9077; **In Canada:** P.O. Box 636, Fort Erie, Ontario, L2A 5X3.

Name: _____
Address: _____ City: _____
State/Prov.: _____ Zip/Postal Code: _____
Account Number (if applicable): _____

075 CSAS

*New York residents remit applicable sales taxes.
*Canadian residents remit applicable GST and provincial taxes.

HQN™

We *are* romance™

www.HQNBooks.com

PHMM0205BL